A row

JEANNIE JOHNSON

ORION

An Orion paperback

First published in Great Britain in 2003
by Orion
This paperback edition published in 2003
by Orion Books Ltd,
Orion House, 5 Upper St Martin's Lane,
London WC2H 9EA

A CIP catalogue record for this book is available from the British Library.

Typeset at The Spartan Press Ltd,
Lymington, Hants
Printed and bound in Great Britain by
Clays Ltd, St Ives plc

To my husband Dennis, a great supporter of the arts – namely me. To the great team at Orion Publishing, and last, but by no means least, to Jan Rozek, who fought the Nazis, fled the Communists, and became a miner in South Wales.

One

Janet saw Henry waving from his two-seater sports car outside the Odeon Cinema and knew she'd be going home alone.

'He can't resist me,' said a gleeful Dorothea, squeezing her arm before galloping off down the steps on four-inch heels.

Feeling less than happy, Janet followed. Yet again Dorothea's fiancé had turned up when least expected, his hair slick, his chin shiny – and his hands everywhere.

'Like a scene from an X-rated film,' Janet muttered to herself then called, 'Goodnight, sweethearts,' and headed up Union Street.

'You don't have to go,' Dorothea shouted after her.

Janet glanced over her shoulder. Her friend had not disengaged herself from Henry's lascivious embrace. Of course she had to go. Playing gooseberry was not her idea of fun.

'It's a fine night and I fancy a walk,' she lied although the sky was turning leaden and a cold breeze was sending discarded ice-lolly papers dancing in a circle on the pavement.

'Are you sure?'

'Of course I am.'

'Sorry about this . . .'

'Rubbish,' Janet muttered. 'Flattery will get Henry everything he wants.'

Right on cue, she heard him say, 'Darling, you look just like Doris Day. I could eat you.'

She almost ran up Union Street in case they heard her laughing. An article in *Moviegoer* had remarked that Doris

Day was as wholesome as apple pie. Dorothea was something else entirely, and Henry knew it, damn him! This was not the first time he'd turned up to collect Dorothea after a girls' night out for some late night groping in Leigh Woods or Durdham Down.

Her laughter had died by the time she turned into the Castle Street area, a desolate stretch of bombed out ruins where the city shopping centre used to be.

'Once I Had a Secret Love', 'The Deadwood Stage' and 'Take Me Back to the Black Hills' were still in her head. Doris Day had been Calamity Jane, singing heroine of the last frontier, not exactly to her taste, but Dorothea loved musicals and Doris Day in particular. She was putty in Henry's hands.

The desolation that used to be Castle Street lacked buildings, pavements and streetlights, but wasn't completely dark. Lights suspended from temporary cables threw pools of ice blue. Makeshift walkways bridging deep cellars once hidden beneath pre-war buildings and now exposed to the sky echoed to her footsteps. Almost as though I'm being followed, she thought.

The past was beneath her feet. The future fluttered above her head. Masses of red, white and blue bunting shimmied on rough rope strung between the few streetlights and a huge banner proclaiming,

BRISTOL WELCOMES A NEW ELIZABETHAN AGE

The banner cracked stiffly in the evening breeze. With the bunting it seemed incongruously brazen, optimistically garish against the forest of weeds growing from crumbling walls and mountains of rubble.

Typically for June, it began to drizzle, not enough to warrant an umbrella, but certainly enough to dampen a woman's sugar-stiff hairdo or send globules of Brylcreem down masculine necks. Dark shadows in ruined doorways came to life as courting couples left to search for buses and taxicabs.

Janet quickened her step. Why linger? It was hardly worth admiring the view and the smell of greenery was tempered with that of ancient dust and recent rubbish.

Some way ahead the streetlights ended, the well-lit ground sharply defined like a cliff edge falling away into an ink black sea.

She barely noticed the moving shadow or the smell of a burning cigarette, its glow as the smoker flung it to the ground at her approach. With contempt born of familiarity, she walked into the darkness – and sorely wished she hadn't.

'Do not scream!'

He was strong, smelled of sweat, dirt and dust.

She sucked in her breath, instantly limp, instantly afraid.

He held her arm behind her back in a vice-like grip. His free hand pressed tightly against her windpipe.

'Do not scream,' he said again.

Despite her predicament, her senses remained sharp. She heard a church clock strike the half hour, strained her ears for the sound of footsteps.

More quietly this time, 'Do not scream', soft and moist against her ear. He said the words so precisely, so purposefully, as though he had only lately learned how to roll them over his tongue.

It was so very dark, midnight black, and, strangely enough, she was glad. She could not see the face of her attacker. She could smell him, hear him, feel the brute force of his body grinding her onto the bruising stones and scratching weeds, but she could not distinguish his features.

Clumsy, quick fingers groped beneath her sweater then between her legs. His breath surged against her ear like the hot waves of an urgent tide, rising, falling and rising again in time with his thrusting body and the pain he inflicted on her.

Best to close her eyes. Best not to allow even the tiniest chance of seeing his features. She didn't want to remember his face. The feel of his body and the heat of his breath would stay with her for a very long time. Putting a face to such a dreadful occasion could well haunt her for the rest of her life. She would not allow it.

A grey donkey with bright yellow spots, a battleship and a model aeroplane were among the toys keeping the youngsters happy as the adults munched ham sandwiches and swigged back glasses of beer, lemonade or a sickly sweet punch made from dubious ingredients.

'This is a time of celebration! Let's give a toast to the new Queen.'

The workers of C. W. Smith Toys and their families raised their glasses in response to their employer, Colin Smith, founder and chairman of the company. His cheeks were red. His eyes were merry and he stood rigidly straight, as a man with tin legs is wont to do.

The words went up as one voice, loud enough to lift the raftered roof of the toy factory in which they were having the firm's celebration in the week before the Coronation itself.

'To the new Queen.'

'And God bless her,' Colin added, steadying himself with one hand while raising his glass high above his head.

After the toast, Charlotte Hennessey-White sat back down at the table she was sharing with Colin's wife, Edna. Polly Hills, whose husband had provided the tins of ham marked 'Ministry of Food' at a knockdown price, was sitting with them, her feet tapping in time to the tinny music from a wind-up record player. It was struggling to be heard above the din of chatting adults and shouting children.

Charlotte leaned close to Edna. 'Your husband is thoroughly enjoying this, my dear.'

Polly, her face more flushed than Colin's, overheard the remark, and gave Edna a nudge in the ribs. 'Like the King 'imself. Whoops. I mean Queen. Gotta get used to that, ain't we?'

Edna sighed and nostalgia misted her eyes. 'I was a schoolgirl when her father was crowned. Where has the time gone?

It doesn't seem that long ago all three of us were on Temple Meads Station waiting for the men to come home after the war. Thank God they did.'

Polly swigged back the last of her drink then sighed heavily. 'Trust mine to get himself killed. Bloody fool!'

Edna coloured up. 'Sorry, Polly.'

Polly, her bleached blonde hair set off sharply by her black and white Prince of Wales check dress, shrugged her shoulders. 'Some lived. Some died. Gavin died, or at least I presume he did. Either that or he didn't want the responsibility of a wife and kid. But never mind. I ended up marrying Billy Hills. It ain't so bad.' She pouted her bright red lips and rested her chin on her hand. 'Still. Would 'ave been nice to live in Canada. All that space, all them mountains.'

Charlotte looked surprised. 'My dear! I didn't know Carol's father was Canadian. I had always assumed him to be American.'

Polly eyed her warily. Was she being sarcastic? What else could you think with a voice like that? It was just too Celia Johnson. Why couldn't she adopt a more rounded accent like Greer Garson? Couldn't say that though, could she? Well, not exactly, but she had to say something. 'Does Greer Garson have auburn hair?'

Charlotte didn't bat an eyelid. 'I do believe so. Why do you ask?'

'Same as yours. You don't sound like 'er though, do yow?' She purposely laid on the Bristol accent as only a girl from the Dings could. If Charlotte noticed she didn't let it show.

'I don't suppose I do. Would you like me to sound like her?'

Polly rose to her feet, swayed when she got there and had to rest her hands on the table to steady herself. 'No offence, Charlotte *old thing*, but why can't you be a bit more like us? Why didn't you mess about a bit during the war like we did? I mean, ole David was away and a woman does 'ave needs, just like a bloke, don't she?'

Charlotte's face gave nothing away. 'Yes. A woman does have needs.' She knew Polly well. Being saucily provocative was a form of entertainment to her. Charlotte maintained her surveillance of those attending the party and stayed silent.

Realizing that Charlotte wasn't going to bite, Polly sniffed disdainfully and wiggled her empty glass. 'I'm off to get another of these and to see where my darlin' ole man's got to. Anyone else want one?' Her voice was loud and her movements were as voluptuous as her figure.

Charlotte and Edna declined.

'Please yourselves.' Polly staggered into something resembling a dance and accompanied herself with a song. 'A little of what you fancy does you good . . .' She tottered a few steps forwards, staggered, and tottered almost as many back.

'Gracie Fields used to sing that, didn't she?' she trilled over her shoulder. 'She was common. Just like me.'

She giggled, then burst into song as she wound her way to where the dark red punch was lined up in half a dozen large enamel jugs.

'I think she was being cheeky about the way you speak,' Edna said, looking and feeling more embarrassed than Charlotte.

'I know.'

Edna looked genuinely concerned. 'Why didn't you say something?'

Charlotte smiled in the way of one who is almost smug about such things. 'One thing I have learned about Polly is that she's a rough diamond on the surface but a chocolate éclair underneath. In short, she deals with her insecurities by insulting other people. You can't hold it against her. Opportunities seem to have passed her by and at times she's quite bitter about it.'

'You mean like Carol's father not coming back?'

'That and Billy not sticking with Colin. Things seem to have gone downhill ever since.'

Edna looked proudly to where Colin was standing, talking

loudly and surrounded by the people who worked for him. In the war years he'd made toys from bits of discarded wood while serving in the Pacific Ocean. Somehow he'd got them sent home and sold at a time when toys were impossible to get hold of. On coming back from the war minus his legs, he'd started it up as a full-time business.

'Making toys here at home when imports were banned was an outstanding idea,' said Charlotte.

Edna nodded. 'And Billy was partly responsible for it being successful. Colin did try to get him to stay, but . . . you know what Billy's like.'

'He has a definite inclination for less legal ways of making money.'

Edna agreed. 'A waste of time and effort seeing as it never seems to go quite right. He doesn't even have the old van any more, just a bicycle pulling an orange box on wheels behind it. Goodness knows what would have happened if they'd had children.'

Charlotte flicked a well-manicured fingernail at a crumb that had stuck to her lipstick. 'At least he regards Carol as his own. Not many men are magnanimous enough to accept the child of a previous liaison.'

Edna flinched, her half-finished drink pausing on the journey from table to mouth.

Charlotte saw the look and instantly regretted her comment. 'Edna! I'm sorry! I didn't mean to resurrect old ghosts . . .'

Edna pushed a lock of plain brown hair away from her forehead and blinked nervously. She wasn't always brave and never found it easy to express *exactly* how she felt, but she did so now.

'There are times when I wish I'd been braver back then and stood up to my mother. But there – it's all water under the bridge.' She paused, suddenly aware of how tightly she was holding her glass.

'And you're happy?' asked Charlotte, her grey eyes steadily

scrutinizing Edna's moon-shaped face and thinking how gentle she looked, how brave she really was.

Edna didn't get a chance to answer. Colin chose that moment to come over and pat his wife on the head. Polly was right behind him, a glass of punch in each hand. She burst out laughing.

'What you doin', Colin? Just 'cos she got big brown eyes, don't mean to say she's a bloody pet spaniel, you know.' Her speech was slurred.

Edna looked embarrassed for Colin as much as for herself. Charlotte looked amused but trusted to Colin taking care of himself.

'My legs were casualties in the war.'

Polly was drunkenly adamant. 'So?'

Some of Colin's workforce chose that moment to crowd around him. 'Sing one of them sea shanties,' they shouted, 'the one that's as blue as the sea!'

Polly looked miffed. She did when she thought she was being sidelined and instantly targeted Charlotte. 'Well?'

Charlotte lowered her voice. 'It's not easy to bend down and kiss one's wife if one's legs will not bend.'

'Oh! I forgot.'

And that is Polly all over, thought Charlotte. She doesn't think before she speaks.

Despite being pink-cheeked and unsteady on her feet, Polly downed both her drinks, then raised the empty glasses. 'Anyone else for another?'

Again Edna and Charlotte declined. Before Polly had gone a few yards she was lost in the crowd that thronged around Colin and his rip-roaring voice.

'Yes,' Edna said suddenly. 'Regarding your question, yes, I am happy. I have regrets, but they're bearable. I can forgive myself, but I don't think I will ever forgive my mother.'

'Oh darling,' said Charlotte. She patted Edna's hand. 'Don't you think you should? After all, she is your mother.'

'No. In fact, sometimes I hate her,' she said quickly as

though wanting to get the fact and the words out of her system. 'What about you?' she said suddenly. 'Do you have any regrets?'

Charlotte had a serene way of smiling that masked her thoughts. She rarely gave much away, but on this occasion Edna had caught her unawares. She saw something flicker in Charlotte's eyes as if a sad memory had swiftly crossed her mind.

Charlotte sighed and said, 'Yes. I have regrets. But I'll live with them.'

Edna opened her mouth to ask what they were, but Charlotte cut her short. 'What a jolly crowd.' She got up from the table as she said it, her gaze fixed on Colin and his workforce as if they were the most exotic people she'd ever seen. 'Do you think we should join them?' She had a fixed smile on her face, but overall, her expression was slightly stiff, like a crisp sugar coating hiding something softer, more vulnerable beneath.

Ask nothing, thought Edna, as she watched an oddly self-conscious Charlotte trying to look at ease as she joined Colin's employees on their pre-Coronation booze-up. Whatever regrets Charlotte had, she most certainly did not want to talk about them.

Two

Just as the grandfather clock in the hallway struck eight, Charlotte shut the study door behind her. She'd got up early to work on some reports regarding yet another batch of refugees from Poland, Hungary and Czechoslovakia. Just because the war was long over didn't mean that everyone had gone home and picked up their lives where they'd left off. Europe still had problems.

Everything was filled out in triplicate, stapled into files, and photographs attached to forms. Charlotte was still helping people just as she always had, only now she worked for the Bureau for Displaced Persons, a busy branch of the Home Office.

The clattering of crockery and the slamming of the broom cupboard came from the kitchen, evidence enough that Mrs Grey had arrived and would prefer everyone to be out of her way before she started cleaning.

Charlotte caught a quick glimpse of herself in the hallway mirror. Just enough make-up to make her look sophisticated rather than dramatic, and just enough grey among the chestnut to look distinguished rather than old.

She was about to grab her handbag and leave before Mrs Grey found something to complain about, then wondered if her daughter, Janet, might want a lift to the hospital where she worked as a secretary.

She peered towards the kitchen area. The coast was clear. Quietly, she began to climb the stairs then suddenly thought how absurd it was. *Mrs Grey works for you*! *You don't have to creep around your own house.* Taking a deep breath, in an act of sheer bravado, she purposely avoided the Persian rugs on the landing and walked on the lino. You'll regret this, she told herself. She knocked on Janet's door. There was no response.

'Janet?'

Silence. She tried the handle. The door opened.

A draught of chill air hit her face. She could see that the bottom half of the bedroom window was open, the curtains billowing in a stiff breeze. Beyond the window came a strange cry not normally heard in Royal York Crescent at such an early hour. Pulling the curtains to one side, she poked her head out. A hunched figure pushed a handcart laden with rags, old fire irons and a small, galvanized boiler streaked with the dried soap of a thousand washdays. His cry of 'Ole rags an' ole ferrule' was almost lost on the breeze. Ferrule, she knew, meant ferrous metal. His usual haul would be iron bedsteads, brass curtain rails with rings the size of saucers, and iron ranges torn from their moorings and replaced with gas stoves in a pleasant shade of cream.

The sound of footsteps made her turn round. Mrs Grey had discovered her and looked very put out. 'I'm very vexed with Miss Janet, ma'am. Very vexed indeed.'

Inwardly Charlotte sighed. Outwardly she smiled and said cheerfully, 'I didn't hear her leave this morning. Did she have any breakfast?'

Mrs Grey's chin seemed to curl upwards with indignation. 'She crept out. She said she wasn't creeping, but I know creeping when I see it. She was creeping.'

Charlotte did a quick mental calculation as a means of taking a broad perspective of the situation. Mrs Grey had used the same verb a number of times, four in fact, but had not answered Charlotte's question so she repeated it. 'And no breakfast?'

'None! Not even a slice of toast with a scraping of butter! But that's not why I'm vexed,' she said. 'Creeping out so no one could hear, I can cope with. Giving away good clothes to the rag and bone man is quite another matter.'

Charlotte attempted to help her strip the bedclothes, but got a disapproving glare for her effort. Mrs Grey liked to do things herself. Instead she asked, 'Were they old clothes?'

'Well, no, but that's not the point . . .'

'Did you want them for yourself? I mean, if you did I shall certainly ask Janet—'

'Certainly not!'

Charlotte stood helplessly, waiting to be enlightened. Whatever it was, Mrs Grey looked more agitated than years back when she'd found out two rashers of bacon equalled one-ounce ration allowance for the week. She'd been devastated then and didn't look much better now.

'They weren't ever so best, but good enough to wear out weeknights or shopping or to the pictures – that sort of thing.'

Charlotte went back to the window and glanced out again. The rag and bone man was leaving the crescent, his handcart loaded.

'Pictures?' she said casually.

'Yes,' hissed Mrs Grey.

Charlotte got the gist of where this was going. For Mrs Grey, to be occupied in polishing, making beds and cooking, was akin to being divine. Pleasure, as opposed to work, was almost wicked.

Her voice dropped as low as when she went to confession up at St Patrick's just off Dowry Square. 'She wore them the other night when she went to the pictures.'

'Goodness,' said Charlotte wondering how best to make her escape.

Gripping the window sash with both hands, she slammed it shut. Mrs Grey nearly jumped out of her skin.

'Perhaps they'd gone out of fashion,' Charlotte suggested.

Mrs Grey looked extremely affronted. 'Fashion is no reason for giving away good clothes.'

'Never mind. I expect the rag and bone man will sell them cheaply to someone who really needs them,' said Charlotte. 'There are so many people out there with no clothes and not much of anything, Mrs Grey. And I have to get to my office and see what I can do for a small proportion of them.'

There wasn't time to fuss. She left Mrs Grey in Janet's bedroom where she appeared to be taking her annoyance out on the feather-filled pillows and the unyielding mattress.

The fact that Janet had given some old clothes away did not trouble her unduly. Perhaps she'd ripped them or perhaps they didn't fit her any more. Her daughter must have had good reasons and she had no intention of questioning her motives.

The clock in the hall struck quarter past. Neatly attired in a smart green suit and black suede court shoes, she was ready to leave.

With the aid of the mirror in the hall, she fixed a trilby style hat on her head then headed for the front door. On reaching it, she called over her shoulder, 'I must be off now, Mrs Grey. Would you take some tea into the doctor before he goes to surgery?'

Mrs Grey appeared at the top of the stairs with an armful of sheets destined for the laundry. 'S'pose I will,' she sniffed, then marched off along the landing.

Bridewell, the central police station, was not far from the Odeon Cinema and close to the Broadmead Shopping Centre, which was still being built.

A crime had been committed. It was only right that it should be reported. It didn't occur to Janet as odd that she countenanced telling the police about it, but could not bring herself to tell her own mother. This *thing* had happened to her. It was an intimate thing, an invasion of her privacy, of her body. Telling her mother would intensify the effect of the violation. Reporting it to the police as a crime *against* her person was somehow different. They would go out, catch him and put him in prison and that would be the end of it. He would be locked away, just as the incident itself would be locked away in her mind.

Before leaving home, she had dressed in a brown checked suit matched with a pale orange silk blouse and low, sensible shoes. After surveying herself in the mirror, she changed her mind. Dark hair, dark eyes, dark suit. Dowdy, she thought, he's making you dress dowdy.

No! She would not have that. Even now, just forty-eight hours after the event when despair had fought tooth and nail with determination, she would not let herself be intimidated by him. The brown suit came off. A red dress with a black patent belt and matching patent sandals made her feel much better. She found black button earrings and red lipstick too.

When she entered the police station, she willed her legs not to shake as she took her place in the queue behind two other people. Stiffening her calves and gritting her teeth, she forced herself to concentrate on those in front of her. Their problems might take your mind off yours, she told herself determinedly.

The first in line was a man in a tan overcoat that smelt of mothballs. The collar and shoulders were liberally speckled with dandruff and, despite the muggy weather, his belt was tightly fastened giving him the look of a badly packaged parcel. He was reporting the loss of his dog.

'Black and white. Part collie. Part terrier. About this high.' He bent down and indicated height from the floor with a flattened palm.

She saw the raised eyebrows of the uniformed policeman behind the desk as he twiddled his pencil and said with a hint of mockery, 'We'll circulate the details, sir. What did you say his name was?'

'Gloria!'

The policeman, who she now saw from the stripes on his sleeve, was a sergeant, raised his eyes to heaven as if to ask relief from such suffering.

'*Her*! Gloria!'

As the man left and the woman in front of her shuffled forward, Janet felt a great urge to use the lavatory – or take flight.

Feeling cold despite the full skirt and long sleeves of her dress, she wrapped her arms around herself, tilted her head back and looked at the ceiling. She didn't want to be here. She wished with all her might that she could change things. If only she'd caught the bus instead of walking.

In her head she rehearsed the words she would say to the desk sergeant. He would probably get her tea and offer his sympathy. They might have a policewoman on duty. There were a few of them around nowadays. It might be easier talking to a woman, one who wouldn't insist on telling her father, talking it through, analysing and dissecting every little detail until everything lay out on the table as opposed to being locked away in her mind. That's what her mother would do: go over it again and again until it was all wrung from her like water from a dripping wet dress.

The waiting room was dull, nothing to look at except an ancient clock and a few wanted posters with curling corners. Yes, she was doing the right thing. It would be best for the police to break the news to her mother. She could imagine it now, her mother serenely sitting in her armchair with a pink and green chintz cover.

'Madam, we are sorry to report . . .' Who else would they tell? What about the newspapers?

Oh no, she couldn't stand being front-page news in the *Bristol Evening Post.* For the first time since arriving at Bridewell, her courage began to fail her. What should she do?

The woman in front of her was taking her time, relating in

a very deep voice – the sort only acquired by smoking forty a day – of how some man had taken her purse when she'd set it down on a Woolworths counter in order to purchase a doll for her granddaughter.

Janet looked down at the floor and caught a glimpse of the woman's feet. She was wearing men's black dancing pumps. They looked too small, the aged black leather digging into the woman's thick-set ankles.

The minute hand on the wall clock jerked forward. Janet gave herself a deadline. One more minute. If the woman went on for just one more minute . . . Two, then three went by. So much for setting herself a limit.

'Next!'

At last she was face to face with a representative of the local constabulary. His bulk filled the square opening above the desk. The opening was set in glass partitioning, a film of old dirt and the curling posters she'd observed earlier, obliterating clear observation of the room beyond the counter. Janet opened her mouth to speak, but her tongue seemed to shrivel up in her mouth.

'Well, me dear?'

Watery blue eyes fixed on hers. She glanced over her shoulder. How many more were in the queue and likely to listen to what she had to say? There was no one. She swallowed hard. 'A man attacked me.'

He immediately swapped his pencil for a pen. 'Name?'

'I don't know his name.'

The policeman sighed impatiently. '*Your* name, young lady!'

She fiddled nervously with her handbag. It was black patent like her belt and sandals. The sweat from her hands had left moist patterns of palm and fingers all over it.

She cleared her throat. 'Janet Hennessey-White.'

After dipping the pen into an inkwell and shaking off the residue he began to scratch her name in his ledger.

'Is that your full name?'

'Well no, it's actually Janet Abigail Hennessey-White, and this man—'

'How do you spell that?'

She told him. The tip of his tongue wavered at the side of his mouth as he wrote her name. She couldn't believe it. Was he really more interested in getting her name right than finding her attacker?

'Address?'

A draught of air came into the waiting room as the door to the street opened behind her. Nervously Janet glanced over her shoulder again.

A uniformed constable smiled and nodded at her then opened another door and disappeared.

Thank you.

The sergeant scratched her address line by line. Janet bit her bottom lip as her eyes followed the slow progress of the pen to inkwell and back to the ledger. Her nerve was slipping and if someone did come in, she might lose it completely. She had to hurry him up.

'My telephone number is—'

His response was immediate, like a bird of prey suddenly spotting an easy meal. We don't need that. Not everyone has got a telephone, you know. Only them that can afford it.'

Janet hugged her handbag. 'I only thought—'

He stretched to his full height – far too tall for the opening through which he was speaking. He appeared cut off at the neck. 'You don't need to think, miss. That's what we're here for. You've lost something or had something stolen, and we know how to go about looking for it. Now!' he said, sliding his wooden handled pen into a groove in the counter, 'Let me guess. You've lost something, though not your handbag I see.' He pointed to the black patent bag that was looking positively dull with perspiration.

'I've already told you. A man attacked me.'

'Oh yes.' He sounded unconvinced and eyed her cautiously.

Janet was disappointed. Somehow she had expected him to spring into action, take quick notes and order a bevy of police constables to scour the streets – and that before she had given a description of either the man or what had happened. The rest of her words came tumbling out.

She squeezed her eyes tightly shut.

Please, don't let anyone come in. Please don't let anyone hear this.

At last she found her voice. 'A man dragged me onto the waste land and then he . . .' She fought to say the word, half-hoping that he would say it for her. He did not. He was unsmiling.

She managed to blurt it out. 'He raped me!'

Sounds from the world outside, traffic, footsteps and the cry of '*Evening World* and *Evening Post*' came in with new arrivals. She was vaguely aware of a brightly coloured dress, a man smelling of pipe tobacco and stale sweat. They took their place in the queue behind her. The door opened again. Someone else joined the queue, then another, and another. The place was filling up.

The sergeant glanced at the door each time it opened before turning his attention back to her. 'So where and when did this *alleged* offence happen?' He stressed the word 'alleged', so it sounded almost criminal.

'On Friday night when I left the Odeon. I decided to cut up through—'

'What time was this?'

Having caught the gist of the sergeant's questioning, the newly arrived were silent. She could feel them watching her and passing instant judgement based on what the policeman was saying.

She couldn't stop her voice from shaking. 'After ten – about ten thirty.'

The sergeant let out a heavy, knowing sigh. 'Right! It was after ten, getting dark and you had decided to walk home alone and a man forced his attentions on you in a sexual manner. Don't you think you were asking for it?'

He had not lowered his voice. Janet felt the colour racing up her neck and onto her cheeks. She could feel the gazes of those behind her piercing into her back.

'No!'

'An old boyfriend, was it?'

'No! Of course it wasn't!'

Her face was on fire. She wanted to scream. She wanted to cry, but most of all she wanted to get out of here, away from his accusations and those of the people standing in the queue.

His expression smug, he leaned on the counter, brawny hands clasped before him. He eyed her up and down as though wearing red and being attractive was a far bigger crime than the one she was reporting.

'Girls like you ruin a lot of blokes' lives, so before you go making accusations I suggest you consider your own actions very carefully indeed. You were walking home in the dark all alone. What were you hoping for?'

She couldn't believe what he was insinuating. 'I'm not a tart!' Angry tears filled her eyes. If she didn't get out of here they'd soon be running down her cheeks. She mustn't let it happen.

A pin could have dropped and sounded like an atomic bomb in that dingy room. Ears were straining, eyes watching with avid interest. The Bristol Old Vic would be hard pushed to present something as dramatic as this.

The sergeant smiled, as much in response to the avid attention of his audience as for her benefit. 'Perhaps not, but no respectable woman should be out alone after ten o'clock at night. Now go home, forget what happened and be a good girl in future.'

Her patience snapped and she stamped her foot. 'How dare you! I'll have you know that my parents have influence in very high places.'

The sergeant, his features leaden, slammed his ledger shut. 'I don't care who they are or where you're from. High class you may be, but there's an old saying . . . the colonel's lady and Rosie O'Grady are sisters under the skin . . .'

Janet was speechless. She turned and fled.

Outside, fresh wet air slapped against her hot face. An overcast sky had burst with rain and water dripped from her hair, down her face, from her nose and trickled down her neck. Pavements empty of pedestrians shone with water. Such was her anger that she never thought to question where everyone was. She simply ran through the downpour, oblivious to the headscarves and umbrellas barricading shop doorways.

Her headlong flight might have continued except that a small figure bounced out of the entrance to the Arcade, an enclosed avenue of semi-derelict shops that connected one street with another. It provided a little shelter even though most of its roof was missing.

The figure bumped into her and blocked her path. 'Boo!'

She spun, holding the small shoulders of the interceptor until they both came to a standstill. Rain and tears blurred her vision, but the smiling face was familiar.

'Janet! Janet! We've been to see the Coronation Clock. It's got lots of colours and wooden people walking around when it strikes the time.'

Susan, one of Edna's children, beamed up at her. 'Come on. We've saved a place for you.'

Janet allowed herself to be dragged towards the crowd of sheltering shoppers. She saw Edna waving. 'Over here,' she shouted.

Edna's face was shiny with rain, her cheeks were pink, and her eyes sparkled. There was not a trace of make-up. 'What a downpour!'

She wore a silk headscarf which Janet recognized as being a present from her mother many Christmases ago. Goodness, but Edna really knew how to make things do. Typical of that generation; the war had made people more careful.

'I'm pretty wet already,' Janet said almost apologetically.

'Pretty wet? Is that what you call it? Yer own mother wouldn't recognize you.' Polly had been hard to spot, sandwiched as she was between the pushchair in which reposed Edna's youngest and a lady with large bosoms wearing a man's raincoat and a checked cap. As usual Polly was dressed in black and white. It was an odd thought at an odd time, but Janet found herself presuming her underwear to be white. Black wasn't so much decadent as almost unavailable and Polly never wore any other colours than black and white.

'Stand in a bit. You're still getting wet,' said Edna pulling her close just as if she were one of her children. 'Goodness, I can feel you shivering. How about a coffee or a cup of tea in Carwardines once it's dried up?'

Under the circumstances, Janet wasn't sure that she wanted company. 'I don't really—'

Polly cut her short. 'Good idea.'

'Can I have a cocoa?' asked Susan who was proudly hanging onto Janet's hand as if she were a treasured find.

Edna said she could and asked her son, Peter, if he too wanted cocoa or lemonade. He slapped his side as he thought about it. At the same time he stamped his feet, not angrily, but as though he was getting ready to run.

'You can bring Trigger,' Edna added with a brief pat of his shoulder, 'but he has to be quiet. Carwardines only let in well-behaved horses.'

She gave Janet a wink. Strange how it made Janet feel that little bit better, as though anything could be got over if you really tried. Look at Edna's husband: no legs, but still he coped.

Despite the dreadfulness of her day, Janet felt less ashamed, less indignant. Normal people living normal lives who knew nothing of what she had been through surrounded her. She was still Janet as they'd always known her.

Suddenly the crowd began to disperse and Susan began to dance. 'It's stopped raining! It's stopped raining!' She tugged Janet out of the Arcade entrance. At the same time Peter spurred on his invisible mount and let out a loud neigh of appreciation.

'High spirits,' said Edna with a mix of pride and embarrassment, and when Janet didn't respond she touched her arm. 'Are you all right?'

There was genuine concern in her face and, for a solitary second, Janet had a strong urge to tell her what had happened on Friday night and where she'd been today.

Just when the urge was at its strongest, Susan piped up, 'We've left Aunty Polly behind.'

Everyone gathered in a huddle and looked around.

'Window shopping, I expect,' said Edna.

Janet stretched her neck and studied a spot in front of a window that had been hidden by the crowd sheltering from the rain. 'There,' she said pointing.

'Not that again,' Edna muttered.

Janet didn't question to what she was referring. Her own problems pressed too heavily so she only glanced very briefly in Polly's direction.

Sharply attractive in her black and white flowered dress, Polly was standing quite still, her attention fixed on a poster that seemed mostly to consist of blue sky and an arched iron bridge crossing an equally blue bay.

Edna called out to her. 'Polly?'

Polly seemed oblivious to everything except the poster.

Edna called again. This time Polly seemed to hear. It was as if someone had turned a large key to get her going again. Despite her age – mid-thirties – Polly maintained a girlish exuberance, especially now with her hair tangled to curls by the rain.

She seemed to bounce rather than walk towards them and

her smile stretched from ear to ear. 'Did you know it's only ten pounds to go to Australia?'

'Yes, I did know that,' snapped Edna and turned away abruptly. 'Let's get to Carwardines.' She began to push her way through the crowds, Janet following right behind, pulled along by Susan.

'You didn't tell me!' Polly grumbled as she trailed along behind.

'Why should I?'

Polly sounded almost angry. 'Why should you? You know damn well why! You know I've been wanting to leave this country for years.'

Although she wasn't quite sure of the significance of the conversation, Janet said, 'There are times when I'd like to fly away and never come back.'

'Your mother wouldn't like it,' said Edna, her knuckles white with the force of her grip on the pushchair.

Janet's laugh was like a wooden spoon banging around the inside of a saucepan. 'I doubt whether she'd notice. She leads a busy life helping other people. We've got nothing in common.'

Edna turned sharply to her, a shocked expression on her face. 'That's not true. Your mother is the most caring person I know and I can't believe that you're not as good-hearted as she is. Susan wouldn't have run out to fetch you if you weren't. Children are very knowing.'

Janet said nothing, but unclamped a splat of wet hair from her cheek and brushed it back.

'Aunty Polly's gone again,' said a serious Susan in a matter of fact voice.

Edna had exasperation written all over her face. 'She's gone back to look at that poster. This could be serious.'

Janet considered asking why Edna looked worried, but changed her mind. Polly was old enough to look after herself. And anyway, she had her own problems, and, as if on cue, she was reminded of them.

A middle-aged couple just two feet away had stopped and were eyeing her with curious discernment. 'It's her!' Their voices were full of contempt.

Her? Did they mean her? Had she seen them somewhere before? Their clothes at least looked vaguely familiar. The woman wore a flowered dress with a dull white collar. The man wore an old-fashioned pinstripe suit with baggy trousers.

'Hussy!' said the woman, her thin lips pursed above a pointed chin.

'Out at all hours, leading decent men astray,' hissed the man through a grey moustache and yellow teeth.

Janet felt the colour draining from her face. It was like remembering a bad dream. These people were standing behind her in the police station. They had heard everything. But she wasn't going to let them treat her like this.

'You stupid, stupid people!' she shouted. 'You don't know what you're talking about.'

Passing shoppers stopped and stared. Even the man selling newspapers from a stand paused and looked in her direction, perhaps considering her a potential threat to his own pitch.

Edna grabbed her arm. 'Janet! What is it?'

'They're calling me names.' Janet couldn't stop shaking. Her voice dropped to a whisper. 'It's not true! I didn't encourage him. I told the policeman that. I didn't even know him.'

The couple melted into the crowd.

Edna's voice was soft and soothing. 'Oh, Janet!' She placed her arm around Janet's shoulders.

Janet felt strangely comforted. Edna wasn't asking her what had happened. The look in her eyes said it all. There was no need for details. There was only comfort. No wonder she was so good with children.

'It was dark. I think he was foreign,' she said in a small voice and looked round to see where Polly was.

Realizing her reason for doing so, Edna said. 'Relax. She's still looking at that poster about Australia.'

Janet nodded appreciatively. She didn't want Polly, Dorothea or her mother to hear her secret. It was all too painful.

Edna squeezed her shoulder. Her voice was gentle. 'You need to talk to someone. I suppose you don't want to talk to your mother?'

Janet shook her head.

Edna pressed a clean handkerchief into her hand. 'I could never talk to mine – though I have to say that Charlotte is a lot easier to get on with than my mother ever was.'

'I just want someone to listen, not to tell me what to do.'

'I understand. Dry your tears. I also take it you don't want Polly to know.'

'I'd rather she didn't.'

'Then she won't.'

Polly chose that exact moment to get back. 'What's up with her?' she said, indicating Janet with a jutting of her chin.

'Just a headache,' said Edna.

'Right,' said Polly and didn't really seem to care whether it was the truth or not.

Her gaze kept wandering back to the window and the poster of Sydney Harbour.

Edna was worried. Marriage to Billy had never quite suited Polly. Perish the thought, but she'd actually enjoyed the war and although at first it had seemed that Billy could provide her with the life she craved, it had never quite come off. Australia might very well suit Polly, thought Edna – but what would Billy think?

Carwardines ground their own coffee on the premises in large rotating grinders. When Polly was out of earshot, Edna suggested to Janet that they meet somewhere private where people they knew weren't likely to go.

'Will you give me time to collect myself?' said Janet.

'Take all the time in the world.'

'I'll phone you from work if I can. I'll wait until everyone is out of the office. I don't want anyone to hear.' A rumble of thunder sounded overhead. 'More rain,' Janet said with a weak smile.

Edna only nodded. Like today, life could be very sunny for a while then things could change without warning. Sometimes you saw the clouds and sometimes you didn't. You just took shelter where you could.

Three

'There's too many cars on the road,' Charlotte muttered to herself as she finally arrived at the Bureau of Displaced Persons.

'The master wants you in his dungeon,' said one of her grinning colleagues as she made her way to the office she shared with several men, all doing the same work as she.

Charlotte merely raised her eyebrows in acknowledgement and made her way to the office of Nathaniel Brookman, Officer in Charge. She fully expected an enquiry as to why she was late and had rehearsed in her mind an apology that was cheerful rather than servile.

'Here I am,' she said brightly as she pushed open the door.

'Good morning,' said Brookman, but didn't look up. 'Do sit down.'

Charlotte eyed him thoughtfully as he scrawled away at the forms and files in front of him. Not an attractive man by any means, with a round head, a scrawny neck and a walrus moustache. Wire-rimmed spectacles sat precariously above the hook in his nose.

His office reflected his personality – or rather lack of it. A battalion of metal filing cabinets stood against dark green walls, which were completely bereft of pictures, posters or even a calendar. There were no untidy piles awaiting attention or filing. Every useable surface was bare of anything except what was currently in use. Nathaniel Brookman was a man of meticulous and old-fashioned habits. He also suffered from rheumatism, thus while the rest of the building smelt of old plaster and beeswax, his office smelt of wintergreen ointment.

'I have something for you,' he said.

Expecting to be briefed on a new influx of Polish refugees within the privacy of his office was not unusual. Neither was handing her a letter, but what he said next surprised her.

'This has come from Germany addressed to you. Please read it.'

Leaving her to read on, his attention went back to the paperwork stacked neatly before him.

Already apprehensive, Charlotte unfolded the letter and felt a tightening in her chest, her heart racing as her eyes tripped over the words.

Afterwards, hands shaking, she refolded the stiff paper, unsure what to say, unsure what was expected of her. Eight years since the end of the war. Lives had been rebuilt, past liaisons and indiscretions laid to rest. And now this.

Without looking up Brookman said, 'I take it the information is correct – she is a friend of yours?'

'Yes.' She said it softly as though she didn't really want to admit to it. As the shock of the letter's contents sank in, her gaze drifted to the window behind Brookman's head. Through it she could see the city's church spires, islands amid remaining war ruins and reconstruction.

'Is the information correct?' he repeated, eyeing her over his glasses.

'I'm sorry,' she said, realizing he hadn't heard her the first time. 'Yes. She is a friend of mine.'

He put his pen down, straightened in his chair and folded his hands in front of him. 'Of course this sort of thing is really nothing to do with us. Not that I am condemning the actions of women – *some* women during the war. The Americans were very generous and our rations were very meagre. But reuniting *any* of the parties involved or resulting from such liaisons is really nothing to do with the

Home Office or the Bureau for Displaced Persons. Priority as you know, is to aid the resettlement of refugees from a Europe that is still in turmoil despite the success of the Marshall Plan. Herr Josef Schumann is one of our most valued contacts dealing with the resettlement of war orphans in tandem with the Pestalozzi Children's Trust. Obviously he thought it best to be discreet. American liaisons are not always viewed with toleration. He seems certain you knew the woman concerned.'

'Yes.'

The contents of the letter had already sent Charlotte's heart racing. At the mention of Josef's name, it beat even faster.

Nathaniel Brookman took off his glasses and looked at her meaningfully. 'Is this woman married?'

'Yes. Very happily so.'

He rubbed thoughtfully at the bridge of his nose where his glasses had left an angry red mark. 'Then I will leave it to your own judgement whether you show her the letter. Personally I'd be loath to cause any trouble between husband and wife. The war is over. In my opinion you should let sleeping dogs lie and write to Herr Schumann accordingly. Some things are best forgotten. I suggest you tell him she's dead.'

Such a cruel comment yet Charlotte knew it wasn't meant that way. It would be unrealistic to dismiss it out of hand. But she needed time to think.

'I'll do what I think is best.' She placed the letter in the zipped purse formed within the silk lining of her handbag and clipped it tightly shut.

Again Brookman slid his glasses off his nose and rubbed at the raw line making it even redder than it was before. 'I can't understand why he didn't send the letter direct to you. He knows your address, I take it?'

'Yes. But Herr Schumann is very professional. He would prefer to use official channels.'

Brookman sniffed in an approving manner. 'That's one thing you can say for the Huns – they are very efficient. Very efficient indeed!'

It was around eleven o'clock when she eventually left the office and its dusty odours behind.

Outside it was a warm June day, but with the promise of rain that everyone hoped would stay away until after the Coronation of the new Queen Bess. Bunting flapped from lampposts, buildings sported banners that spanned their entire frontage. Even on building sites where reinforced concrete grew skywards from bombed out rubble Union Jacks fluttered from scaffolding.

Charlotte was in turmoil. Josef! She'd never thought to hear that name again, certainly not to hear *from* him.

The sound of concrete mixers and the clanging of metal girders raised by a clanking crane sounded to one side. The city was full of the noise of reconstruction.

Today she took a short cut between two neighbouring sites where new shops and offices were being built. Noise, machines, dust, men shouting orders, a cacophony of sound, smells and textures tumbled out onto the pavement. Nothing unusual in any of them, until angry voices erupted from among the bricks, bags of cement and piles of wood to her right. Then a full-scale fight broke out onto the pot-holed path in front of her.

Shouts, cries and words muffled by struggle rumbled between the scuffles. Clouds of dust whirled around her feet as two shabbily dressed men fell onto the cracked pavement and fought on the ground, their feet encased in Wellington boots, which scratched and scuffed against the cracked kerbs and loose gravel.

She stopped in her tracks, raised her hands in horror and shouted for them to stop. 'Stop it! Stop it!' she yelled again and again. Of course they ignored her. I sound feeble, she thought and looked around for help. Two men with brawny arms and hard expressions ran towards them from the site. A smarter man in a double-breasted suit followed. The men with brawny arms wore frayed shirts, sleeves rolled up to the elbows. Thick leather belts circled their waists. Tatty braces held up their trousers.

At first she was relieved. These men were going to do something. Relief turned to horror as steel toe-capped boots sliced into soft bellies.

'Stop it! Stop it!' she cried again.

They paid her no heed. Fists as big as shovels grabbed the fighting men's collars and hauled them to their feet. The man in the suit was grim-faced, but looked as though he might be in charge.

She directed her question at him. 'Are they all right?'

He glanced at her briefly then turned away without answering. The two bullies with rolled up sleeves man-handled the men back towards the site where a concrete building threw dark shadows over the dusty earth. From within those shadows the man in the suit now stood, watching her. Despite the bright sunshine she felt suddenly cold. For a moment her eyes met his before he moved swiftly away and was gone.

In that split instant she had the distinct impression that she'd seen him somewhere before. She shook her head and told herself she was probably imagining things. There was nothing she could do and she had quite enough problems to think about without enquiring further, though something about the fighting men stayed with her.

That evening before dinner she kissed David on the head. He did not respond. He never did. *You're both middle-aged, a time of mellow fruitfulness. Physical affection is best left to the young.*

She remembered the letter from Josef and felt an instant pang of regret for past moments that had been short, but very sweet. Pull yourself together, she said to herself, then swallowed hard and adopted her cheeriest smile.

'Has Janet gone out?' she asked, noticing that only two places had been set on the green and white tablecloth.

David put down the medical journal he was reading. 'She told Mrs Grey she had a headache.'

'Again?' Charlotte frowned. 'She's had a headache for three or four days. I've hardly seen her.'

'You've been busy.'

'Oh dear. Yes, I have. Do you think she's very ill? Something more than a headache?'

'I don't know. She won't let me examine her, but I understand she hasn't been to the office for three days according to John Hooper, one of the surgeons she works for.'

Charlotte recalled the empty room and the rag and bone man to whom Janet had given some of her clothes. She decided not to mention it to David. After all, it wasn't very important and she had his ill health to consider. Instead she said, 'That's not like her. I'll just go up and see if she's all right.'

David called after her, 'Tell her that whether she likes it or not I'm coming up in the morning to give her a thorough medical examination. That should sort out whether she's ill or not.'

The bedroom door was locked. Charlotte tapped at it softly. 'Janet? Do you want any dinner?'

'No!'

'Have you had an aspirin, darling?'

'No . . . I mean . . . yes . . .'

Charlotte sighed with exasperation. Children not eating – even when they are adults – are still a cause of concern. 'I'll get Mrs Grey to make you some sandwiches.'

'No!'

'Chocolate cake?'

Chocolate was the ultimate temptation, a luxury made wickedly tempting by years of deprivation.

'No! I don't want anything! Go away.'

Charlotte bit her lip. Kindness deserved a positive response and she was annoyed at not getting it. After taking a deep breath, she adopted a firm voice. 'I think you need a doctor, Janet. Your father's going to examine you in the morning. We are concerned, darling.'

'There's no need! I'm feeling much better.'

'That's good. I expect they're missing you at the hospital. Good medical secretaries are hard to come by. Your father will tell you that.'

Charlotte listened, her ear close to the door. Not a sound. She sighed. Defeat was difficult to take.

'Goodnight, dear. Have a good night's sleep.'

On the other side of the bedroom door Janet was staring out of the window. Twinkling lights festooned the wedge of city she could see between the cliffs towering on either side of the Avon Gorge. Trees rose dark and thick on both sides of the river. Straggly growths stuck out of fissures in the towering cliffs.

Why me?

Again and again . . . *Why me . . .*

If only . . . if I hadn't gone . . . if I hadn't walked . . .

Don't scream . . .

A carousel of words whirled in her head. She couldn't turn the clock back. The damage was done. Would people be able to tell what had happened to her? Was 'Damaged Goods' printed across her forehead?

He'd smelt of dust, just like the ruined buildings and the concrete blowing from the building sites.

Don't scream.

She could still feel his breath against her ear and those two words again and again and again.

She shuddered at the thought of him, the way he'd smelt, the way he'd said those words.

He'd had a foreign accent. Not Welsh. Not Scottish. Nothing like that. More like . . .

She closed her eyes and willed herself to hear the voice again. More like . . . European. Similar to the accents of the people her mother was helping to settle in this country. She'd met some of them. They'd stared at her as one might a rare butterfly. She'd stared back like a cocksure crow at a band of redundant scarecrows. People from Poland, Czechoslovakia, Yugoslavia, places in Eastern Europe she knew little about. They were pouring in, so she'd heard, and not everyone was happy about it.

We don't want them here . . . bloody foreigners . . . coming over here taking our jobs . . . taking our houses . . . raping our women . . .

Earlier that evening Mrs Grey had knocked at the bedroom door to say that Dorothea had called. 'She wants to know whether you're still going to the Coronation Ball at the Grand Spa,' explained Mrs Grey, her voice muffled by the door.

Janet had sat on the edge of the bed, gripping the bedding and gritting her jaw. 'I'll let her know.'

She stared out at the night. God, it was partly Dorothea's fault that she'd got raped anyway. It was *her* who'd wanted to see the damned stupid film, *her* that had got picked up by that cretin of a boyfriend.

Janet wasn't so ungenerous that she'd lay the blame at anyone's door. Her resolve to rise above the incident and get on with her life was still strong. At least she didn't feel quite so alone. She had told someone and Edna had offered to listen. Janet instinctively knew it was the right thing to do.

The next morning Charlotte took the letter from her bag meaning to rip it into shreds. Was it wise to tell a happily married woman that the past had come back into her life?

Tell him she's dead.

She paused and sighed. God, but it seemed so brusque, so final. Best to leave it for a while. The rolltop desk grated open to reveal a leather surface, a host of small drawers with mother-of-pearl handles and brass keyholes. She opened one of the drawers, put the letter in and locked it.

Wait and see, she decided. But not for too long. Someone was desperate for a response.

Four

As the lights of the Broadway Picture House went out, Polly Hills paused, looked up and down the street, and stopped dead when she spotted Billy's checked cap bobbing out of the window of a scruffy black van. Balancing on three-inch heels, she tottered down the steps and along the pavement.

'Where'd you get this?' she said accusingly, eyeing the vehicle with a suspicion born of experience.

Billy's grin never wavered. 'It's a mate's. I'm doin' a bit of work for 'im so I thought you might like a ride 'ome in a high-class vehicle complete with yer own chauffeur!'

He looked her straight in the eye as he said it. Amazing, she thought! It might even be the truth.

'Well, mustn't grumble I suppose,' she said tartly, 'It certainly beats the Raleigh and the bicycle clips!'

Billy winked and tapped a finger yellow with nicotine against the side of his nose. 'Just you watch, darlin', we're gonna be goin' places!'

Unconvinced, Polly folded her arms and said, 'Oh yeah. You said that to me when I was still living in York Street and look where I ended up. A bleedin' council 'ouse in Knowle West. Call that going places?'

Billy's engagingly confident expression never faltered. 'I know fings didn't go right in the past, but you wait and see . . .'

Polly didn't want to hear it. She had her own plans. Ten pounds to Australia; it seemed too good to be true. She'd made an appointment to find out more and, when the time was right, she'd tell Billy all about it.

Billy got the message that his promises were falling on deaf ears and offered a diversion.

'Want some chips?'

'OK.'

Stomach rumbling and her taste buds twitching in anticipation, she headed for the chip shop.

'Hey!' Billy shouted out after her.

She turned round knowing full well what he was going to say. She'd heard it all before.

'It will get better, Poll,' he said and winked again, as if that one little action held all the promise in the world – which it did. It was just that Billy had trouble keeping promises.

First he'd quit working with Colin making and selling toys, then the ramshackle properties left to him by his father had been demolished. The bit of money he'd got for them went into slightly suspect schemes that all went west, hence the move to Knowle West.

The council had built the estate in the thirties. The houses were squarely constructed of red brick and had metal-framed windows that poured with condensation no matter the time of year. The garden of each house was segregated from the road and from its neighbours by a privet hedge. Empty bags of Smith's Crisp wrappers and Fry's Five Boys nestled against the roots of hedges along with discarded Tizer bottles of thick glass and wire-fixed corks, the quarry of streetwise kids bent on getting back the penny deposit. Some hedges were neat. Some were overgrown due to the fact that no one owned a pair of shears or had the inclination to cut them.

Sunshine, a house by the beach, wide open spaces, mooned Polly as the heat from the chip shop fryers hit her full in the face. Appreciatively, she rubbed her hands together. Nice and warm them fryers, but no substitute for a warmer climate.

'Put in a bit of cracklin', darlin',' grated a familiar voice at the head of the queue. Polly recognized Muriel Harolds, one of the usherettes who used to be on the buses before she'd got a job at the Broadway.

Mouth like the bloody Avon Gorge, thought Polly. Muriel had probably needed one in the days when she was a clippie, shouting her mouth off as she told them to move down the bus so she could get more on. And she'd certainly had a few on in 'er time, mused Polly, and not just on the buses!

Their eyes met just as Muriel was about to leave, half a crown's worth of supper for her and her old man tucked under her fleshy arm.

''Night, Poll.' There was a surly contempt in the way she said it.

Polly adopted the same tone in response. ''Night, Muriel,' she muttered, adding 'You old cow' under her breath.

They eyed each other warily, as they had from the moment they'd met. Muriel thought she was better qualified to have Polly's job – and Polly knew it.

'Good riddance,' she murmured once Muriel had left, taking her fish and chips and her hostile glare with her.

Her relief didn't last. Muriel's face, pink from the heat of the chip shop, poked back through the door. 'I see your old man's got a van. Where'd 'e nick that, then?'

Polly glared and tapped at her nose. 'Mind yer own bleedin' business! And if you must know, it ain't nicked, it belongs to a mate. My Billy knows a lot of likely blokes.'

'Not as many as you've known in yer time,' sneered Muriel.

'Oh yeah! It's a well-known fact, Muriel Harolds, that you've had more on top than a double-decker bus!'

'Common cow!'

'Slag!'

'Slut!'

'Takes one to know one!'

The rest of the queue, relishing a bit of entertainment

while waiting for their cod lots, pressed forward and began to egg them on.

'Go on! Bash 'er one!'

'Rip 'er bloody eyes out.'

'Look at 'er! Mutton dressed as lamb!'

Muriel dashed off before Polly could make a move. If it hadn't been late and she wasn't waiting to be served, Polly would have gone after her. They'd never got on. Polly considered Muriel a right old tart who needed her mouth washed out with soap and water. The fact that she herself let a few choice words slip now and again was neither here nor there. Polly considered herself better than Muriel. It didn't occur to her to question the crowd as to who they considered was mutton dressed as lamb. It had to be Muriel.

It didn't take long to get served after that. Hamblins, the fish and chip shop owners, didn't like dealing with trouble-makers that late at night and the police weren't keen on coming out either.

Fish and chips wrapped in newspaper and hugged to her chest, Polly installed herself in the passenger seat of the van, her right knee raised higher than her left by virtue of the sacks on the floor. 'What's that?' she said indicating them with her foot.

Billy started the engine. 'Money in the bank!'

'Oh ah!' Polly knew better than to query further. Instead she concentrated on gaining the best position possible on the ripped leather seat. An exposed spring squealed in protest. 'So how long 'ave you got this?'

'Could buy it if I want to.'

Polly continued to wriggle. 'It ain't exactly first-class, is it? Look at these seats! They're all ripped. It ain't aff scratching my bum. And this stuff you've got packed in 'ere – there's 'ardly room to bloody breathe!'

'I can get the seats fixed. And the stuff'll be going.' He smirked, his mouth tilting to one side like a wickedly naughty adolescent. 'Got to get rid of it before it burns a hole in the floor.'

Polly sighed. 'Don't tell me any more! It's 'otter than these bloody fish and chips I've got in me lap.'

The van was old, the controls none too smooth. As Billy pulled away the vehicle jerked violently forward then stopped dead. The engine had stalled. A hoard of boxes in the rear fell into the back of Polly's head and her forehead bumped onto the dashboard. 'Oh for Chrissakes!'

The parcel of chips caught on something sharp and was ripped open. Vinegar, grease and a fillet of cod fell out of the paper and onto her lap. The chips showered the floor and the dusty sack at her feet.

Polly was livid. 'Billy Hills, this van is a death trap!'

'Stop moaning, Poll. A second-class ride's better than a first-class walk, ain't it?'

'You've got to be bloody kidding! Look at my uniform!'

'It'll wash, won't it?' he said in easy, amiable tones as he concentrated on pushing the boxes back behind the seats.

'The vinegar's gone through to my knickers!'

She held her clothes away from her legs. 'I smell like two penn'orth of cod! I'll have all the bloody cats following me now!'

'Lovely smell! Better than the best French perfume.'

'Well, I know which I'd prefer!'

'Right! Soon be home. I expect yer Aunty Meg's done us a bit of supper anyway. I don't mind a bit of bread and cheese.'

Polly closed her eyes and shook her head in exasperation. There was grease on her lap, dusty chips and squashed cod round her feet. What a waste!

It was at times like these that she really wished that things had turned out differently. Most of the time Billy made enough to survive, but the flow of money wasn't regular and he tended to shift from one dodgy venture to another in a constant search for instant wealth.

Sometimes when Polly looked in the mirror after another application of peroxide to her greying hair she wondered where the old Polly had gone, the one who had danced the jitterbug and canoodled in a darkened picture house with Canadian or American servicemen. If Carol's father had come back from the war, she would never have married Billy, would never have been working at the Broadway and would not be living in a council house. It had all been a pipedream. The glamorous life she'd dreamed of having in a country barely touched by war never happened.

As they drove along Billy prattled on about his latest scam for making money. It was something to do with gambling. Polly shut her ears. She had other plans. Was this the time to mention Australia? Perhaps not. Not just yet.

She began to hum and look distractedly out of the window, her thoughts filled with the vision of a sun-filled home and a beach at the end of the garden.

Billy misinterpreted her reason for appearing uninterested. 'OK! I'll shut up.'

Polly hummed 'One Day My Prince Will Come', her daughter Carol's favourite song from the film *Snow White and the Seven Dwarfs.*

'What's that tune yer singing?'

'"Some Day My Prince Will Come".'

Keeping his eyes on the road he leaned closer and whispered, 'Yer prince is right 'ere, sweet'eart.'

Polly eyed him disdainfully. 'Where? All I can see is a bloody frog!'

The light from the streetlamp next to the garden gate filtered through the curtains and hit Colin's metal legs, which Edna had placed in the corner of the bedroom after helping him out of them.

'They look like the bottom half of a medieval knight waiting for his top half to arrive before going into action,'

Edna laughed. 'Do they have to stand there in *that* particular corner every night?'

'You'd give a pet dog its own special place. So why not my legs? Aren't they worth more than a dog?' Colin joked.

Catching his mood she flippantly asked, 'Should we get them their own bed?'

Colin laughed. 'Come here,' he said and patted the space in the bed beside him. She got in and helped him turn towards her. There was no embarrassment between them about this. Most people, Edna realized, were uncomfortable with disability. Colin had no problem with the fact that his legs had been blasted out from under him and she'd got used to it. He was one of the lucky ones – he'd come home.

'I love you, Edna.' He stroked her hair. His breath was soft and warm. They kissed and embraced just like any other married couple, except perhaps that there was a little more sensitivity when it came to making love. Colin's strong shoulders and overdeveloped biceps compensated for his lack of legs. Sometimes he forgot that his legs were truncated at the knees and that his body wasn't quite so easily manoeuvred as it used to be. Sometimes there was just pain, his phantom legs kicking in the night, kidding his brain into thinking they were still there, strips of flesh clinging tenuously to shattered bones.

They lay on their sides facing each other, his palm warm on her breast, his lips moist on her throat.

She ran her hands over the firmness of his shoulders and chest. Colin made her feel secure, more safe and loved than she'd ever felt in her life. There was great pleasure in touching him, helping him move towards her, clasping his pelvis tightly against her own, until the moment they were ready to join together when Colin rolled onto his back and Edna moved on top of him.

'I'm going to Charlotte's tomorrow,' Edna said after they'd made love and kissed affectionately in its warm aftermath.

'On a Saturday?'

'I thought I'd take the children to the zoo afterwards.'

'Do you want me to come?'

Edna sensed his disinclination. 'Only if you really want to.'

'Hmm. If it was just the zoo I would. Old Charlotte's a good sort, but I know what it'll be like once you and her get together – non-stop women's talk.'

'And you think she's bossy,' she said with a laugh and a tap on his chin.

'Right, so I'll give it a miss – if you don't mind.'

'I don't mind.'

It was exactly what she'd thought he'd say which is why she'd lied. She was going to see Janet, not Charlotte. The zoo was a busy place and the animals would keep the children occupied whilst she talked to Janet and found out exactly what had happened to her and how she could help. They would meet at three o'clock. There was just one thing worrying her. Edna propped herself up on one elbow. 'I want to ask you something.'

He kept his eyes tightly closed and pretended not to notice. 'I'm so sleepy,' he said in the sort of voice one of the children might use.

Edna smiled to herself. Colin *was* a child at times.

Just as she expected, he opened one eye. 'What is it?'

She traced circles across his chest with her finger. 'What do you think about secrets?'

'You should keep them,' he said with a yawn. His eyes snapped open. 'What have you done?'

Edna laughed. 'Nothing. It's not me.' She tried to think of the best way to put it. 'If something happened to a member of a friend's family and they wanted you to keep it secret, even though you thought that friend could help that person, would you still keep the secret?'

'Yes,' said Colin. Then he yawned again and closed his eyes.

Edna lay back on the pillow and did the same. Sleep would

be a long time coming, she thought, and opened them again. Keeping Janet's secret from Charlotte had been worrying her for days. But a secret was a secret. As far as Edna knew, she was the only person Janet had confided in. For Charlotte's as well as Janet's sake, she resolved to give her full support.

In no time at all Colin was snoring. Edna nudged him in the ribs.

'Sorry,' he said sleepily, reached out and gripped the side of the mattress. Edna obliged, got one hand into his shoulder, one under his hip and moved him onto his side. Despite having overdeveloped arm muscles, turning over wasn't easy.

She lay awake for what seemed like hours then finally gave up trying. Being careful not to disturb Colin, she pushed back the bedclothes, swung her legs out of bed and tucked her feet into her slippers.

Light fell through the round window at the top of the stairs and lay in a distorted oval like a maladjusted mat.

She stepped into the girls' room first. Susan was sound asleep, pink lips intermittently sucking on an equally pink thumb. Pamela was in her cot. She too was sucking on her thumb and had kicked her bedclothes down to her ankles.

Edna pulled the bedding up over her warm little body. If anyone had ever told her she'd have such adorable children she'd never have believed it. And three of them! And another on the way – hopefully. So far she'd told no one – not even Colin. She wanted to be sure.

On entering Peter's room she found that he too had kicked off his bedclothes.

She lingered after covering him up and gently pushed his sandy hair back from his forehead. Being brought up with two girls wasn't always easy for him. He'd asked her if she could buy him a brother. 'Not a baby one,' he'd ordered. 'I'd like one that's big enough to play football.'

Remembering what he'd said brought a lump to her

throat. How could she tell him that he already had a brother who was older than him and might very well play football?

She hugged herself and stifled a sob. Even though he had a good home, well-off adoptive parents and a better life in Brazil than she could have offered in Bristol, it had never been easy to forget Sherman, her firstborn, illegitimate and given up for adoption during the war. At times like these she imagined her brown-skinned, brown-eyed little boy waking, having breakfast, going to school and saying goodbye to the people who had raised him.

Never mind, she told herself as she brushed away a tear, it's all in the past. There's a new age dawning and a bright future to look forward to, new houses, new jobs, new outlooks. A young queen is about to be crowned. The past is dead.

Five

The tea lady was pushing her trolley around the office and duly arrived at Charlotte's desk.

'With or without?' she asked, as the piping hot liquid poured from the urn.

Charlotte was halfway through the details of a man called Lech Rostok from Danzig when something about the two men fighting suddenly hit her. She sat bolt upright. The papers she'd been reading fell from her hand.

'Polish! They were speaking in Polish!'

Eyes that had been lowered over files in the office she shared with six others turned in her direction.

'Just thinking aloud,' she explained with a casual smile and a shake of her head.

'I do that,' said the tea lady, her hair a busy frizz around her dumpling face. 'Now is that with or without sugar?' she asked again. Charlotte declined. 'I knew a Pole during the war,' said the tea lady, a far away look in her eyes as she hugged her oversized teapot close to her chest. 'Drunken swine!'

'Oh dear!'

The tea lady moved on and Charlotte's thoughts went back to the building site, the two men fighting, two others brutalizing them, and the other man wearing a double-breasted suit. The latter had watched, done nothing and said nothing, but he'd struck a cord. Where had she seen him before?

She stared at the dull cream walls as if the crazed pattern of cracking plaster was a map by which she could obtain answers to her questions. Much as she stared, it told her nothing.

The canteen at Bristol Royal Infirmary always smelt of cottage pie even when it wasn't on the menu.

'It's rissoles,' Dorothea said to Janet as she poked her fork into one of the two crisp-coated items that sat on her plate.

Janet swallowed a mouthful of cheese sandwich. 'Of course it is. It's Friday.'

Dorothea gobbled away, eyed the greyish bread of Janet's sandwich, and gulped before saying, 'That doesn't look very appetizing.'

'The bread tastes like cardboard and the cheese tastes like soap.'

'So why didn't you have the rissoles?' asked Dorothea as she began on her second.

'I don't like snakes.'

Dorothea stopped chewing and looked puzzled. 'Snakes?'

Janet kept a straight face. 'Mrs Grey's sister works in the kitchen and she reckons that with things still in short supply, they put any old rubbish into things like rissoles and pies.'

'Oh my God!' Cutlery clattered onto the plate, chair legs scraped swiftly across the floor as Dorothea sprang to her feet. Janet caught a glimpse of her face, just enough to see that she was whitewash pale, before she scooted off towards the corridor, the lavatory, and a heaving of recently bolted lunch into the china bowl.

Janet smiled to herself and murmured, 'That'll teach you to leave me to walk home on my own.'

A while ago, Dorothea had made the mistake of disclosing her hatred of snakes. Never tell people your secrets, thought Janet as she pushed the sandwich and tea away and got up from the table. So far she had only told two people what had happened on the night she'd walked home alone from the Odeon. One was the unsympathetic policeman, a mistake she bitterly regretted. The other was Edna. Janet trusted her not to tell anyone else.

On Saturday, at three in the afternoon, Janet entered the zoo and made her way to the monkey temple.

Complete with domed roof and pillared exterior, it hinted at the Far East and dark jungles. It actually stood in the centre of a concrete compound viewed from steps round its perimeter and its occupants squatted in small groups over its roof, swung from its pillars or looked up the high walls with pleading eyes to the spectators looking back at them.

Janet looked at her watch. Edna was late, understandable having three children to deal with.

She looked towards the wide lawns where Rosie the Indian elephant was being led up and down by her keeper, a bevy of people sitting on a swaying howdah suspended over her back.

'Aunty Janet!'

She turned at the sound of her name and spotted Susan running towards her, closely followed by her brother Peter who, bearing in mind the proximity of the elephant, seemed to have adopted a suitably regal canter on Trigger.

Wearing a dress of sunshine yellow that complemented her brown eyes and hair, Edna brought up the rear, with Pamela in the pushchair.

'Sorry we're late. We had to see Alfred first,' said Edna breathlessly. 'He's a gorilla,' she added in response to Janet's puzzled expression. 'Hold on a minute until I get these ice creams sorted out.'

Three Lyons Maid vanilla ice creams were unwrapped and popped into three sets of wafers. The two eldest children were given whole ones; the youngest made do with half, Edna keeping the remainder for herself.

Susan was first to get her ice cream and placed herself next to Janet. 'What's that monkey doing?' she asked.

'Eating fleas,' said Janet.

'Well, I prefer ice cream,' said Susan and followed it with a lingering lick, almost as if she were trying to make the monkeys jealous.

Satisfied that the children were occupied watching the monkey colony and out of earshot, Edna looked at Janet, said nothing but merely waited for her to begin.

'I'd been to the pictures,' Janet began. The words came easier than she'd expected and the story poured out. Edna remained silent.

At last Janet finished all she had to say and felt better for it. Having someone listen but not comment made her realize how much she'd needed to talk about it, to get the experience out into the open.

'Who else have you told?' asked Edna.

'I went to the police station.' Janet stared at a pair of monkeys who were presently squabbling over orange peel. 'They made me feel cheap, as though I wanted it to happen, so I ran from there. That was on the day I bumped into you.'

Edna's expression was deadly serious. 'The law is run by men and is biased. They'd say it was your word against his – if they should ever catch him. Would you recognize him?'

Polly shook her head. 'Perhaps his accent, but then . . .' She couldn't be sure. Everything seemed so unfair. There seemed so little she could do.

Edna eyed the monkeys, her hands clasped and resting on the barrier. 'You have to put it behind you.'

'It's not easy. I feel so second-rate.'

Edna laughed.

Janet frowned. 'What's so funny?'

Edna's expression turned serious. 'You're such a good-looking girl. How could you possibly be second-rate?'

'You know how it is. I'd hoped to meet the right man and have a white wedding just like any other girl.'

'You can still do that.'

Janet's face and voice contorted with despair. 'How can I? You have to be a virgin to have a white wedding.'

Something in Edna's look made her feel terribly young, terribly naive.

'It's not that important.'

'It is to me! I made myself a promise a very long time ago that I would be a virgin on my wedding day.'

'Goodness! What an odd thing to say. I was beginning to think that idea had had its day. Obviously I was wrong.'

Janet gazed at something in the distance that was there but wasn't, a memory from when she was younger and had come home to find . . . She shook the experience from her mind.

'I suppose so,' she said softly. 'But I had my reasons for wanting that. It doesn't matter now. Anyway, it was different for your generation.'

Edna waited for her to continue but, realizing that she wasn't going to explain herself took her courage in both hands and said, 'Not everyone is a virgin when they marry. I wasn't.'

Janet stopped eyeing one particular monkey who was holding his hands out to the watching crowds, like a beggar asking for alms. 'You? I can't believe it! I mean, you've got Colin and three kids . . .' Janet's voice trailed away.

Edna shrugged, gave a tiny smile and shook her head so that her brown curls fell forward from the pink slides she was wearing to pin it back. 'No one is perfect, Janet. Not even me. Not even your mother.'

Janet prickled at the last remark. No, her mother was not quite the respectable woman she pretended to be. But that too was a secret. 'I'm not like my mother at all. That's why I can't tell her anything. We're so different.'

Edna laughed.

Janet looked offended. 'But I'm not like her.'

'You don't know that just yet, and believe me, I should know. I'm not like my mother, thank goodness, in fact I'm probably more like my father. But I *am* a mother myself so I know a good one when I see one. I think I see the best of Charlotte in you. Isn't it true you enjoy working at the hospital? You obviously do care for other people just as she does.'

Janet studied her hands as if seeing them for the first time and not being too sure why she had fingers. 'I love my job. I think I love my mother although at times she seems indifferent, at others surprising – even shocking.'

Edna accepted that Charlotte's serenity could be misconstrued as indifference so did not challenge the comment. Shocking was not quite such an easily accepted description, but she chose not to react. Janet was feeling fragile. It was best to take things slowly.

She said, 'We all experience sad and terrible times in our lives. There's no guarantee given out at the beginning that it's going to be perfect right until the end. I've certainly had my share, that's for sure.'

'Ah yes, Colin.'

'Not just Colin.'

Edna studied her children. She rarely talked about her firstborn, but she thought about him a lot. Would his absence help to heal Janet's hurt? It had to be worth using it.

'I had a child before I married Colin. I had to give him up.'

Janet stared at her dumbstruck. 'I didn't know . . . I mean . . . I know you two fell out just before that Christmas you came to stay with us.' The details were vague. She'd been at an age when her own problems had seemed far more important than those of grown-ups.

'It wasn't Colin's. I had a romance, a brief affair while he was away. But I was still the same person I was before and I am now, though older of course. And Colin loved me still. It was just one of those things that happened. I have to live with it, but it changes nothing. I'm still the same and so are you. People love us for what we are, not what we've done or had done to us.'

Janet blinked. Edna was no longer the person she'd thought she was. It was difficult to say anything.

The silence lingered. Both women pretended to watch the

children who, in turn, watched the monkeys as they dashed over the green dome of the mock Indian temple, screeching, scrabbling and fighting amongst themselves for the scattered peanuts and orange peel.

Edna remained tight-lipped until she judged the moment was right to speak. 'You've had a horrible experience, Janet, but you cannot allow it to ruin your life. You have to go on. People depend on you.'

Janet swallowed at the dryness in her throat. 'I'll never forget that voice.'

Edna stroked Janet's hair back from her face and tucked it behind her ear. Janet didn't move, didn't look at her. Her voice was soft. 'You'll do it. You're strong, just like your mother.'

Janet shook her head away from Edna's soothing fingers. 'I am *not* like my mother!'

At first Edna looked taken aback, but rallied quickly. She shrugged. 'Hopefully I'm not like mine.'

Perhaps because her feelings were in turmoil, Janet did not *want* to be soothed. She suddenly snapped, 'I'm not a child. Please don't treat me like one.' She untangled herself from Edna's sympathy and walked away.

Edna watched, aching because she knew how it was to feel confused, to bear disappointment and to wonder what to do next. Things would get better. She knew they would.

'She'll be all right,' she said softly to herself.

There was no time to dwell on Janet's plight. Pamela began to squall so loudly that all the monkeys retreated to the very top of their carved concrete home.

That was uncalled for, Janet said to herself. Edna's been good to you. She stopped beneath a weeping willow. Feathery leaves threw delicate shadows across her face.

Edna had surprised her, and not just with her confession about having had a child before marriage. On the surface she appeared almost mousy, yet it occurred to Janet that she understood the vagaries of life and dealt with them better than most people.

*

The next day was Coronation Eve. It was also Pamela's birthday and she was to have a party at the semi-detached where they now lived.

Colin had suggested that everyone wear their Coronation fancy dress seeing as the little girl's birthday was so close to the enthronement of a new monarch and that they were all going to different places on the great day itself.

Colin's parents were dressed as John Bull and Rule Britannia – the latter costume consisted of some suitably draped bed-sheets and a cardboard helmet coloured in with child's crayons.

The room was a riot of noise. Children and adults were getting into the swing of things, talking, singing and helping small hands handle big spoons and wobbly red jelly.

Polly's daughter, Carol, was dressed in a Bo-Peep costume. At nine she was the eldest child there, and had her mother's looks and the cheek to match.

Edna overheard Colin's mother ask Charlotte how her children were getting on.

'Geoffrey's enjoying university very much. And Janet loves her job at the hospital.'

'I always thought your Geoffrey wanted to be a soldier,' Polly said as she took Charlotte's empty teacup.

'I didn't want him to be. Neither did David. He wanted him to be a doctor.'

'How's Janet?' asked Edna from behind a tray of tea, bread and butter plus a pot of strawberry jam.

'Fine,' said Charlotte.

'Good,' said Edna, smiled and wished she didn't know that Janet was far from fine.

'Who's for jelly?' Polly in her Pearly King costume, an obvious choice for someone who favoured wearing black and white, had a large glass bowl jammed under her arm and close to her bosom. Rows of podgy little hands shot into the air.

'Not if yer gonna dip yer titty in it,' said Carol, her hands on her hips and a perky tilt to her chin. The comment earned her a clipped ear.

The house in Kingscott Avenue was blessed with a garage and an inside toilet and bathroom located at the top of the stairs. A television sat like a small cupboard in one corner of the room and was drawing plenty of admiring glances and perhaps a little envy from some quarters.

'Puts me in mind of a bloody gert eye watching me,' said Polly between ladling out jelly and readjusting the bowl beneath her generous breast.

'I can't wait to see the Coronation,' said Edna, her face as bright as any child's and her eyes gleaming. 'Fancy being able to see the Queen and Westminster Abbey in my own living room. It's a miracle, it really is. I've invited some of the neighbours.'

'Ain't they got radios?' asked Polly.

Edna ignored the sarcasm and tried again. 'It'll be quite a little party. You can come yourself if you like.'

'Don't need to, do I? I'll be seeing the Coronation on the big screen up the Broadway. That's the great thing about working in a picture 'ouse. They'll be showing it for days after and I'll get to know every single detail.'

Edna persisted. 'But it's better on the day. In fact it'll be quite a party.'

'You just said that.'

Edna blushed. 'I'm sorry, I just thought—'

'Don't bother. We're 'avin' a street party on the night. I got a lot of stuff to get ready. Anyway I prefer a bigger screen. Like I said, I can see it all at the pictures.'

Charlotte, who had heard the conversation, made a big thing of wiping Pamela's face. It wasn't really that bad, but she had to hide her smile. She knew her friends so well. Edna was being generous, longing to share her enthusiasm for the television set with anyone. But Polly was proud. She had no intention of appearing hard done by.

Polly's daughter Carol chose that moment to push between Edna and her mother. 'Got any more of that fruit cake?'

Polly slammed a piece on her daughter's plate. 'There you are.'

Carol inspected it, turning it this way and that. 'It ain't got no cherry.'

'No,' sniggered Polly and whispered close to Charlotte's ear, 'an' neither have I.'

Edna heard her and looked shocked. 'Polly!'

Charlotte pretended she hadn't heard. Polly liked to shock people. It was part of her armoury. Instead she turned to Edna's parents who were sitting in the armchairs, tea plates balanced on knees, tea grimly raised to unsmiling lips. They were strangely quiet, Edna's father glancing nervously at his wife as though waiting for her to stand up and put a stop to the merriment. At one time she might very well have done. Her sharp eyes never missed a thing.

If something odd was going on between the old pair, all those gathered took little notice. This was the children's time.

Charlotte asked them if they'd like more tea. Edna's father held out his cup. Edna's mother looked at her as though she was speaking a foreign language.

'There you are.' Charlotte handed Mr Burbage a piece of cake and tried again with Edna's mother. 'What about you, Mrs Burbage?'

'I think she'd like a piece,' said Edna's father, his eyes darting nervously from one woman to the other.

Up at the table, Polly's Aunty Meg, who had just come in from washing dishes, raised the lid on the teapot. 'We need a fresh brew, I think.'

Edna's mother pushed past Charlotte and snatched the teapot from beneath Meg's nose. 'That's my job!'

Taken aback, Meg asked 'Are you sure?'

Mrs Burbage was adamant. 'It's my turn to make tea now. Mother did it this morning. Now it's my turn.'

Meg frowned and muttered, 'Mother? Your mother's been dead for years.' She raised her eyebrows in Edna's direction. Edna purposely ignored her. Meg shrugged her shoulders. Who could blame her? Ethel Burbage had always been a cow.

'Silly old bat,' said Polly, who was refilling the empty dish of a little lad with a very large appetite.

Looking anxious, Edna's father got to his feet. Aunty Meg placed a hand on his shoulder and pushed him gently back into his chair. 'You sit there. I'll go out an' give 'er a hand.' She turned to Edna. 'Your gran died ten years ago, didn't she?'

'Yes.'

'I thought so.'

Meg made her way to what she still called a scullery where a pale green kitchen cabinet stood to the right of the draining board. Ethel Burbage was bent over the sink ladling tea into a dark brown teapot. 'One for Mum, one for Dad, one for Uncle Stan and one for the pot.'

As Meg watched she became aware that Charlotte had joined her. They stood silently as Edna's mother tipped the slops into the pot and promptly filled the whole thing up with cold water from the tap.

Meg whispered against Charlotte's ear. 'I think she's going doolally.'

'She would choose today' Edna said angrily as she came out into the kitchen for a fresh tray of cake.

Meg took the brown pot gently but firmly out of the other woman's grasp and said, 'Ethel! What the bloody 'ell are you thinking of? This pot's cold. P'raps the gas is gone. We'd better make another then, ain't we?'

Edna turned her back on the scene and went back into the living room. She swallowed her anger and exchanged a brief look with her father. His anxious expression aroused her sympathy though did nothing for the simmering resentment she'd felt for her mother all these years.

'Aunty Meg's giving her a hand,' she said matter of factly. She just couldn't bring herself to talk about her mother in soft, gentle tones. Selfish and spiteful suited much better. Turn away, she told herself, dish out some more cake.

Polly gave her a hand. 'Not right, is she?' she said, making no effort to be tactful.

'It's been going on a while,' said Edna and described the first time she'd realized that her mother was not her old self. 'She told us that her granny was making her a grey scarf for Christmas and that they would match the gloves she was wearing. She seemed oblivious to the fact that the temperature was in the eighties and climbing.'

Edna had hoped it would be explanation enough. Polly persisted. 'What are you going to do about it?'

'Nothing. There's nothing I can do. I have three children and a husband to think about.'

Edna pushed the problem to the back of her mind. This was Pamela's birthday. The child was strapped into her high chair as Edna spooned jelly into her open mouth while pondering past disappointments rather than any pity she might feel for her mother.

A spoon hammering against the side of the chair interrupted her concentration. A freckled face framed by sandy hair looked up at her. 'Where's Daddy?' asked Peter.

'Getting dressed, of course,' said Susan. The eldest at seven, she looked more like her mother although she had also inherited her father's amiable confidence and his unruly thatch of gingery fair hair.

Peter frowned and, looking slightly worried, whispered, 'Is he going to wear a dress like yours, Mum?'

Susan interjected in her usual knowledgeable manner. 'He's going to put on fancy dress, you silly boy. It's going to be a very special dress.'

Polly nudged Edna in the ribs. 'Not dressed as Widow Twanky, is he?'

Edna laughed. 'Of course not. He won't be wearing a dress.' She beamed at the small faces around the table. 'He'll look bright and merry – just like us!'

All the children were wearing different outfits, most made from crêpe paper in the appropriate colours of red, white and blue. Edna was dressed in a gingham dress with puff sleeves. She wore her hair in pigtails ending in big white bows, which made her feel very girlish even though she was in her early thirties and a mother. Today was magical. Tomorrow would be even better because everyone would be dressing up, partying and toasting the new queen with anything drinkable.

Charlotte was dressed in something long, made of mauve lamé and possibly dating from before the First World War. Her hair was covered by a beaded cap and when she wasn't dishing out jelly she was carrying an ebony cigarette holder.

'And before you ask I'm supposed to be Mata Hari,' she informed Polly.

'I see.' Polly turned to Edna. 'Obviously you're Alice in Wonderland.'

'No, I'm not,' said Edna, embarrassed because she'd considered her outfit so obvious and badly wanted both today and tomorrow to be a great success.

Polly looked surprised, but also took wicked pleasure from Edna's discomfort. 'Go on then. Tell me who you're supposed to be.'

Before Edna could explain a loud clattering and clanking sound came down the stairs and along the hall. The door suddenly burst open and half a dozen small voices squealed with delight.

All eyes turned to where Colin Smith filled the frame. They gasped in amazement. Colin's body and arms were covered in cardboard that had been painted battleship grey to resemble metal. The colander on his head – used mostly for straining dried peas that turned to a mush when they were cooked – was made of real metal. So, unfortunately, were the shiny legs sticking out of what remained of his Royal Navy shorts (tropical-issue). They'd once been white, but were now grey and toned with the rest of his outfit. A host of metal kitchen utensils dangled and jangled from his waist.

Polly sighed knowingly. 'Ah! The Tin Man!' She grinned at Edna. 'And Dorothy!'

'I'm the Tin Man and I'm going to take you all to find the Wizard of Oz,' Colin exclaimed loudly.

Even Edna's father smiled as the children, including Polly's daughter Carol, abandoned quivering jellies and bright pink blancmange. Like a wave of noisy gulls they fell off their chairs and surrounded him. A flock of small voices squealed with delight.

Colin's parents locked hands, their eyes moist.

Meg chose that moment to come in with the teapot. Ethel breezed in behind her carrying a tray of cups. She looked a lot calmer, but it didn't last long. Instead of placing them on the table she stopped in her tracks and stared at Colin. Suddenly she screamed, lifted the tray and let it fly.

'Get out! Get out!'

Cups flew everywhere. The tray hit Colin in the chest and for a moment he wobbled before he managed to grab the door surround.

Edna ran to his side, catching him as he toppled.

The rest of the room was pandemonium, children crying and adults trying to calm things down. Ethel Burbage crouched between two chairs, fingers in her ears and eyes tightly closed.

Charlotte leaned over her. 'It's all right, Mrs Burbage. It's only Colin in his costume.'

Meg bent down beside her. 'Now there's a bloody awful way to carry on, Ethel. It's only yer son-in-law dressed up for the kiddies' party. Who did you think it was, aye? Boris bloody Karloff?'

'Storks have got long legs. He's got long legs and I don't want to have a baby. I don't know how it got there. Besides, I've changed my mind!'

'What's she on about?' asked Polly.

Charlotte touched her arm. 'She thinks Colin is a stork.'

Polly looked dumbstruck.

'His legs,' mouthed Charlotte. 'She thinks she's about to have a baby. Am I right, Meg?'

'Blimey,' said Meg. 'Now you are going back a bit.'

Charlotte went on. 'She thinks she's about to give birth and she's frightened because no one's told her anything about it and she's not sure how it got there.'

'It wasn't considered nice to discuss things like that in our day,' said Meg.

'Still isn't for some,' Polly added.

Meg sighed. 'We was told the stork brought it or it came from out our belly button. It was a bloody big shock when you found out the truth, I can tell you. For some it was even more of a shock when they found out how it got in! Leave her to me,' she added to Charlotte. 'I've seen this before.' Her face was grave.

For once Charlotte was grateful not to take charge of a situation. She stood up and smoothed her dress down over her hips.

'She'll be all right.' She patted Edna's arm.

Edna shrugged and said bitterly. 'I don't care whether she is or isn't! I wanted today to be perfect. My mother's spoilt it, just as she's spoilt everything in my life.'

Six

On the morning of Coronation Day Polly fixed a paper crown onto her daughter's golden curls with the help of Aunty Meg's spikiest hairpins. Carol made faces, wincing each time a pin was used.

Polly gave her a good shake. 'Stop wriggling, you little mare!'

Carol pouted and folded her arms. 'Why've I got to wear this bloody thing anyway? I wore it yesterday.'

Polly turned her round to face her. 'Because you've got to be the best.' Impatiently she smoothed the child's wild curls into some sort of order. 'And you won't be if you swear like that. I don't know where the bl—' She stopped herself from using the same word and made a mental note to mend her own ways, which she'd promised to do a thousand times before. 'Yesterday doesn't count,' she went on. 'Today does. This street's going to win the prize for 'avin' the best Coronation costumes of all – an' the best decorations.'

And it can do with all the help it can bloody get, she thought. Truth was, she didn't think they had a cat in hell's chance. Red-brick council houses, front doors the same green as the buses and metal-framed windows running with condensation, were the devil's own work to make jolly. She vaguely wondered how the celebrations for the Coronation were going in Australia. That sunny poster viewed on a damp day in England shone brightly in her mind. A new country for ten pounds each. Once Billy was in the mood . . .

'Can I go swimming on Saturday?'

'No!'

'Not another Coronation!'

'No, not another Coronation. You gets things from swimming baths like bad legs and bad arms – and worse.'

'Like Geraldine Harvey?' Carol bobbed away and went round the room dragging one leg behind her as she hopped forward. 'She walks like this 'cos she's got irons up 'er legs.'

'That's why yer not goin' swimming.' The paper hat fell over her eyes. 'Damn!' Polly grabbed her arm as she loped past and straightened the hat with the aid of a few more hairgrips.

'Ow!'

'Keep still.'

Carol brightened. 'Is Aunty Meg coming to the party?'

Polly nodded. 'You know she is. She's upstairs putting on her costume.' Meg was going to be wearing her Pearly Queen outfit from yesterday. Polly would again be her male escort only today she'd added a moustache by virtue of a line of black lead scrolled along her top lip.

'Is Dad coming to the party?'

Polly gritted her teeth and looked at the clock. 'He'd bloody well better be.'

Charlotte was getting ready to help judge the best street party in the whole of Bristol. A local newspaper was sponsoring the event and she felt very proud that they'd asked her to help adjudicate.

She wore a new dress of royal blue with a cinched-in waist and a slimline skirt with a kick-pleat at the back that reached to mid-calf. Charlotte prided herself that, despite having just had her forty-seventh birthday, her figure had not yet gone to seed. In an effort to add a touch of patriotic fervour, she pinned a bunch of bright red cherries to her lapel then finished the outfit with white gloves and a matching handbag. Her shoes were navy blue. She twirled in front of the mirror.

David gave her a quick peck on the cheek. 'You look wonderful, darling.'

'You could come with me,' she said brightly.

David stopped by the door, a copy of *The Times* tucked beneath his arm. He looked tense. 'I thought you had enough judges? And I do have to collect Geoffrey from Temple Meads.'

'You could pick him up from the station and then keep me company,' she said as she fixed the red straw hat to her head, its shape similar to an upside down dinner plate.

David checked his watch. 'I thought Janet was going with you.'

'She has a headache again. Do you think there's anything seriously wrong with her?'

'How can I tell? The headache disappears the moment I mention examining her.'

'Still, she might be better by now.'

Charlotte had arranged to meet the other judges at eleven o'clock at the Mansion House. The Lord Mayor would be attending along with the High Sheriff of Bristol and other notable dignitaries including the editor of the local newspaper group. Speeches would be read, tea and cakes would be on offer and there might – depending on the generosity of Harveys, the famous wine merchants – even be a little sweet sherry with which to toast the incoming monarch.

Charlotte glanced at her watch as she went up the stairs. Ten thirty. The breakfast tray Mrs Grey had taken up to Janet's room earlier that morning was still outside the door.

Charlotte knocked. 'Janet? Are you up to keeping me company, darling or will you go with your father to fetch Geoffrey?'

There was a moment of silence before Janet answered. 'I'd rather stay here.'

Janet's voice seemed a little terse and although her daughter's recurring headaches worried her, Charlotte took her duties to the city very seriously.

'I'll see you later, darling. Hope you feel better.'

On the other side of the door Janet looked at herself in the mirror and thought of her conversation with Edna. A bastard child! She could hardly believe it. Funny how you could look at people and assume from their present demeanour, their unassuming ordinariness, that they'd never done anything outrageous in their life. Yet Edna had got pregnant by a man who wasn't her husband. She had got on with her life – just as she would have to.

Just look at it, thought Geoffrey as the train pulled into Temple Meads Station. He scowled contemptuously at the stupid little triangular flags fluttering above the platform. If he'd had his way he would not have come home to join in the celebrations for something he didn't believe in. But he could hardly tell his parents that university had caused his views on things to change. Their world – both past and present – was very different to the world he lived in.

As he turned the handle on the carriage door, he saw his father waving to him from where he stood at the side of the newspaper stand. Just before pushing the door open he remembered the badge gleaming a dull red in the lapel of his coat. In all probability his parents would not have a clue what it actually represented. But he couldn't take that chance. He unpinned it from the front of the lapel and re-pinned it on the reverse, then patted it flat. No one would know he was wearing it.

He adopted a happy smile and stepped out onto the platform. Hopefully these few weeks would pass with as little unpleasantness as possible. After that he would rejoin his friends, people with enquiring minds who did not accept that the old ways were still the best.

Dusk in Camborne Road found Polly and her neighbours full of food and slightly tipsy.

A beaming policeman stood on the corner against a privet

hedge that someone had tried to clip into the shape of a crown, but which actually resembled a doughnut. The policeman swayed from the knees up and looked as though he might tip over. He was tall and thin but his heavy boots anchored him to the spot.

Music blared out from a wind-up record player that sat on a fold-up card table next to a lamppost. Rows of trestle tables groaned with Spam sandwiches, cheese rolls, jellies, blancmanges and thick slices of homemade fruit cake that stuck to the teeth and lay heavy in the belly.

'You'd think 'e'ed join the party,' said Aunty Meg, eyeing the young policeman. There again, 'e don't look old enough to be out.'

Polly was unconvinced. 'He's a copper. He's always on duty.'

Being married to Billy had taught Polly a lot. Many's the time he'd been out selling nylons, chocolate or clockwork toys from Hong Kong on the wooden cart he pulled along behind his bicycle. Just as he was getting an interested little crowd around him, the local bobby would appear.

'Round the corner,' the copper would say. And Billy would go round the corner, knowing what the next question would be.

'Got a licence?'

Of course he didn't. So a ten shilling note would change hands – more if he wasn't selling anything but doing a book on Ascot or the Gold Cup. Street bookies were becoming an endangered species.

Aunty Meg slipped a crochet needle out from the pocket of her manly jacket and used it to scratch at her hair, which she wore in 'earphones' – plaits coiled around her ears, dated now but Meg reckoned she was too old to change. 'Where's Billy?' she asked Polly.

'As far away from 'ere as possible.' She grimaced. 'I hope.'

Unfortunately that wasn't the case. At that very moment

Billy entered the opposite end of the street in the borrowed black van.

Polly swallowed hard. Pound to a penny there would still be boxes in the back that hadn't so much fallen off the back of a lorry as flown swiftly from one vehicle to the other.

Polly glanced at the young constable hoping to God he'd seen nothing. Luckily he was eyeing up a threesome of giggling girls so hadn't noticed Billy's arrival. The girls were all around seventeen years old, giddy with the minimum of ruby wine and dry cider and showing a good six inches of bare thigh above steel-clasped stocking tops as they kicked their legs into the air.

Reasoning the copper was a soft touch and easily distracted, the Pearly King cap was flung to one side, the tie was loosened and shirt buttons were undone enough to show her cleavage. She checked the effect. *Not bad, considering you're no spring chicken.*

Swinging her hips and thrusting her bust forward, she swept to the side of the unsuspecting policeman and rested her hand on his shoulder. A Mae West type of voice would do the job.

'Joining the party, honey?'

He looked terrified. My God but Mae West had a lot to answer for, thought Polly and stifled a giggle. The policeman's helmet wobbled as he swallowed.

'No, madam! I'm on duty.'

A faint blush crept over his face. Polly was pleased because it meant she wasn't past it by a long chalk. She couldn't resist laying it on a bit thicker.

'Oh come on, darling. Nice young man like you. Wouldn't hurt to join in the fun, would it?' She pressed her body against his chest, one leg looped provocatively around his.

Looking terrified, he took a backward step, Polly still clinging on. 'I've got a beat to pound,' he said, his voice trembling. Polly sniffed. He smelt of bubble-gum, a smell she associated with children and young people – but he *was* young! God, she thought, I must be gettin' bloody old!

He did his best to disentangle himself.

'I can think of better things to do,' Polly went on, provocatively sliding her hands over her breasts then leaning against his arm, looking doe-eyed up into his face. 'Want to help me do 'em?' He looked petrified.

Polly kept going. 'Aw, come on, sweetheart. I know you're fancying a bit really. I saw you looking at them young pieces kicking their legs in the air and showing their knickers. They'll do you no good, darlin'. Too young. No experience. But me . . . well . . . I knows what I'm doin', don't I?'

Perhaps stiff with passion before her arrival, he now stiffened with duty. 'Now go along, madam. There's a good girl.' His voice creaked with fear rather than authority.

Polly pretended to take umbrage. 'Good girl! You cheeky bugger! I'm a married woman and you with no more than bum fluff on yer face!'

He edged away, walking backwards then turning to attain more speed in the direction of the main road. Polly would have said good riddance, the job was done. But he'd riled her.

She made as if to run after him. 'Aw, come on! Don't leave a girl wanting!'

His strides quickened and turned into a run, his boots clomping like an elephant all along the pavement. Once he was on the main road he broke into an ungainly canter. Polly stopped and bent double with laughter. She'd had a few good laughs today and doing for a bobby had been the greatest one.

Meg was the first to greet her when she got back.

'Poor bugger! He'll probably pee the bed tonight with you going after 'im like that.'

Polly just grinned. Tonight was turning out to be more fun than she'd expected. She almost felt young again. She told Billy what she'd just done but was careful to button her shirt up first.

Billy cocked his head to one side. 'Poor bloke. You must 'ave frightened 'im to death running after 'im like that and looking the way you do.'

Polly punched his arm. 'Cheeky sod. I understood gentlemen prefer blondes.'

Billy grinned and swiped his finger along her upper lip. 'They do but not if they got moustaches!'

Polly's mouth dropped open. She'd forgotten the blacked on moustache. But she laughed and thumped him in the chest. Billy gasped and bent double. 'Blimey! Ever thought about doin' a round with Joe Louis?'

She'd have given him another whack, but someone passed him a bottle of brown ale and there was no sense in spilling good beer.

'I could do with that,' he said after a good swig. 'My chest's as dry as Wes'on sands.'

'Make the most of it. The beer's nearly gone. You should have come earlier.' Polly was annoyed. She eyed him suspiciously.

'I've been working. Did you win the best party prize?'

Polly shook her head and eyed contemptuously the streets of red-brick houses. 'Mansfield Street down in Bemmie won it.' She spat the slang word for Bedminster, an area of Victorian back to backs and tobacco factories. The same tone continued. 'Still, what do you expect living somewhere like this?' Another minute alone with him and she'd have mentioned Australia, but Billy's mind was firmly fixed on business.

'Oi!' Billy shouted to the assembled neighbours and waved his arms. 'Never mind not winning. I've got prizes for everyone.'

A loud cheer went up. A host of adults and children followed him to the back of the van. Geraldine Harvey brought up the rear dragging her callipered leg behind her.

Aunty Meg nudged Polly. 'D'you think you should let our Carol play with 'er? It might still be catching.'

Both women watched the nine-year-old Geraldine hop as quickly as she could behind the rest of the bunch, her eyes as bright with excitement as any child there.

'You could be right. I've stopped 'er going swimming, but you never know, do you? I'll ask David Hennessey-White, the doctor I know up in Clifton. I'll be having tea with 'is wife next week.' The last two sentences were spoken loudly.

She winced as Meg elbowed her ribs. 'Show off!'

Polly looked smug and unrepentant. She liked her neighbours to know that she was on first name terms with a doctor and counted his wife as one of her friends. It gave her status – which was more than Billy did. There were times when she almost regretted the path she'd taken. Billy was well-known for trading in items that were scarce and not so scarce – at knock down prices. He was always promising her the earth, but so far it hadn't arrived on the doorstep.

Still dressed in her Bo-Peep party frock of red, white and blue, torn and dirty now, Carol pushed her way to the front. 'Dad! Me first!'

A beaming Billy spread his arms wide. 'As always, my princess!'

Aunty Meg leaned close and spoke low out the side of her mouth. 'One of these days that husband of yours is going to touch.'

Polly shrugged. 'What can I do?'

She knew what Meg meant. Billy was getting involved with bigger fish, the blokes that ran the street bookies and a few other professions that were far from being legal.

'God save the Queen, and she saved these for you lot,' Billy shouted, bringing out a box from the rear of the van. 'Now don't push, there's plenty for all.'

Bars of chocolate were passed into eagerly stretched out hands.

Once the crowd had diminished and were happily munching on nicked Five Boys, Turkish Delight and Fry's Chocolate Cream, Polly grabbed Billy's arm. 'All right, Wee Willie

Winkie, where did you get it? And don't tell me it really was the Queen. She's probably gone to bed with a headache after wearing that crown all day.'

Billy's eyes twinkled and a sly grin lifted one side of his mouth making it seem crooked. 'I just knew someone who wanted to get rid of it. Had too many and wanted them with none to have some. A bit like Robin Hood – you know?'

Polly folded her arms and eyed him accusingly. 'Oh yes, Billy Hills! I knows all right! And one of these days the Sheriff of Nottingham is going to come into Sherwood Forest, take you away and lock you in his dungeon!'

Seven

By the time Janet got out of the bath her skin was codfish white and wrinkled, but she felt cleaner than she had for ages. Dorothea rang just afterwards.

'And where have you been hiding? Haven't found a lover that I didn't get to first, have you?'

Janet gritted her teeth. 'I haven't got a boyfriend.'

'I didn't say a boyfriend, darling. I said a lover. The former is a regular indulgence, the latter is a more infrequent and deliciously wicked liaison.'

Janet wondered just how much Henry knew about Dorothea's morals. Did he really think he was the only man in her life?

'My mother would say you're a vamp.'

Taking it as a compliment, Dorothea laughed. 'The boys say I'm a red hot momma!'

There are other words to describe you, thought Janet, but held her tongue. Instead she said, 'I'll see you tonight at about eight?'

'The ball, the ball! The Coronation Ball!' Dorothea trilled. 'You can tell me then all that's been happening. I've hardly seen you at work. We have so little time to chat when you keep having days off. What's wrong with you?'

'A very bad headache, perhaps a touch of flu. It comes and goes. So I come into work when it goes and stay home when it comes back.'

'Reee . . . ally?' Dorothea stretched the word questioningly. 'Sure you're not . . . you know . . . Have Stephen and you been naughty?'

Janet baulked at the thought. Stephen was a friend of Henry's and was wheeled out on a regular basis as her partner for the evening when they went out in a foursome. Dorothea, Stephen too, read more into the relationship than she did.

'No! Don't be so stupid!'

Dorothea feigned hurt feelings. 'All right, darling. No need to snap.'

Janet self-consciously ran her hand over her stomach. She gripped the telephone receiver hard as she replaced it in its cradle. Oh God. Not that! It didn't happen on the first occasion, did it? Pray, she thought as she did a quick mental check of her monthly diary. One week, she calculated, until she would know.

Dorothea was waiting outside the Grand Spa, her arm looped through that of Henry. Janet's date, Stephen, was with them, his hair astoundingly neat, his jaw strong, his blue eyes shining with interest the moment he saw her.

'You look nice,' he said and tried to take her hand. She withdrew it swiftly and saw the injured look on his face. 'No need to be prickly.'

'Time of the month!' laughed Henry.

Dorothea laughed with him.

Janet wished it was the time of the month. But she wouldn't let either that or them spoil the evening. 'I'm going to enjoy myself,' she stated and marched off ahead of them into the ballroom.

'Wait for me, Janet, darling,' called Stephen waving the invitation as his gangly frame set out behind her. He offered her his arm. 'They won't let you in without a ticket,' he said in the sort of accent beloved of the best BBC announcer.

'Why?' asked Janet tersely as she slid her arm in his.

Stephen laughed. 'Golly, I know it's the dawning of a new age and all that, but really, we still have certain standards, don't we? The rich man in his castle, the poor man at his gate . . . Do you know what I mean?'

'Yes!' snapped Janet, seeing him for the snob he was and letting go his arm.

Red, white and blue bunting hung from the ballroom ceiling. Union Jacks fluttered from walls, crêpe paper of the same colours was strung between the sparkling chandeliers. Everyone was smiling and laughing. Those that didn't usually drink were getting very drunk; those that didn't usually dance were cavorting around the floor not caring that their feet were treading on those of their partners, or that their sense of rhythm was at variance with that of the band.

Stephen bought her a glass of overpriced champagne, which he seemed to think entitled him to more than he deserved.

'Just a kiss?' he said, puckering his lips and closing his eyes.

'Just a dance,' she replied.

She didn't really want him that close, and she tensed as he put his arms around her. The first time, she thought . . . the first time since that night . . . She had to get used to men again, and Stephen was as good as any to aid that process. Rape was something like falling off a horse. You had to get back on in case you lost your nerve. All the same, she was glad when the dance ended. But Henry, Dorothea's intended, was in a party mood. He grabbed her hand before she had a chance to put her bottom down on a chair.

'Dance with me.' He swung her out at arm's length towards the crowded dance floor.

Janet spun herself back towards her chair. 'No!'

'He won't eat you, darling,' cried Dorothea.

Janet gave in. The dance floor was crowded. A press of massed bodies all foxtrotting to something by Mantovani necessitated him holding her tightly to his body. The noise, the heat, the close proximity of him and the dancers made her want to run, but the dance floor was too tightly packed. She'd have to wait for the right moment.

Henry whispered something close to her ear, which she didn't quite catch. There was just too much noise. She said 'Yes' anyway and hoped it was the right answer.

'Do you mean that?'

She left her thoughts and looked up into his face. 'What?'

'I asked if you would let me feel whether you're wearing a corset or a roll-on.' He sounded as though he might have been joking, but there was no mistaking the look in his eyes. Janet stiffened as his fingers traced circles on her bare back.

Disgusted and angry, she spun quickly away. He followed her as she nudged her way through the dancing couples, whose faces were red from too much alcohol, their bodies sticky with sweat. The smell of perspiration, drink and perfume mixed with that of dusty flags and warm nylon.

A man sporting a Union Jack dicky bow and a girl with a sash of red and blue against a white dress bumped against them. Janet stopped dead. Henry bumped up behind her, his body tight against hers.

'Don't touch me!'

Perhaps he didn't hear. His hands were on her hips and his breath was moist on the nape of her neck. His voice was low. 'I already know what Dorothea wears. In fact she's peeled her rubber garment off while I've been putting mine in place – if you know what I mean.' His tongue flicked at her ear.

Of course she knew what he meant! 'What a surprise,' she said with heavy sarcasm. 'And there was I thinking Dorothea was the next Virgin Mary!'

As they left the dance floor, his right hand closed over her arm. His left caressed her bare shoulder. 'But I'd still like to see yours,' he said in that confident, crystal cut voice of his.

Janet turned, her eyes blazing with fury. 'You're a cad, Henry Claude Pollet. Nothing but a cad!'

He looked fit to burst into laughter. 'A cad! Why! My dear! How sweetly old-fashioned you are.'

'I'd call you something else if we weren't in public,' hissed Janet as she tried to think of the worse words she'd ever heard. Her mother's friend Polly came to mind. Now there was a lady who knew a few choice insults.

Back at the table she drank warm champagne while Dorothea prattled on about how she and Henry would get married in June next year, or perhaps the year after that. 'Coronation Year will certainly be a year to remember,' she trilled tipsily, her head gradually sinking onto Henry's shoulder, her eyes looking up into his as her hand slid beneath the table.

Face pink with embarrassment, Janet looked swiftly away.

Coronation Year would most certainly be a time to remember as far as she was concerned too and everything about it seemed to concern sex. But somehow little of what was said or done by her companions was very important. In an odd way what had happened made her feel outside their circle, outside of herself. She was in company yet alone.

Stephen, now almost as bubbly as the many glasses of champagne he'd consumed, suddenly grabbed her hand and held it to his lips. 'I think I love you, Janet. How about us getting married? We could make it a double wedding, my darling. What do you say?'

Janet looked at Dorothea who was still looking up at Henry and smiling in a secretive, stupid way. Henry himself appeared to be viewing the gathering through half-lowered lids, his mouth slightly open and his breathing interspersed with short, high pitched gasps of delight.

The sight of them and what they were doing was offensive enough. Mention of a double white wedding with friends who seemed suddenly like strangers was even worse.

'Stephen, you're drunk.'

'Ah!' he said wagging his finger. 'Ah! But I may be drunk now, but tomorrow I will be again the sort of chap you've always known me to be. To use that old-fashioned term—'

'A pompous ass! Seems I'm good at using old-fashioned terms,' she said angrily, rising from the table just as Henry sighed heavily in a loud and climactic manner.

She couldn't look at him and didn't bother to say another word. The ladies' lavatories offered sanctuary, if only for a few minutes.

Bunching her skirts up around her, she sat in a cubicle, closed her eyes, and thought about what she should do next. The whole country was celebrating the Coronation, but she was feeling wretched and confused. Why couldn't it have been Dorothea who'd got accosted on her way home from the pictures? She probably wouldn't have minded too much. No, that was unfair. Behind closed lids she remembered how childishly provocative she'd been with the American boys during the war. If she'd been older her virginity would have gone then. When had she made the decision to wait until she was married? The answer to that brought back a memory from just after the war: a darkened bedroom, two bodies locked in sexual intercourse . . . Her mother was to blame and didn't even know it.

Once she had regained some self-control she went back out into the heaving throng of people some of whom were singing 'Land of Hope and Glory' in direct opposition to another faction who preferred to render 'There'll Always Be An England'.

Ball gowns, mostly in white, the one patriotic colour the majority of women possessed, whirled around the dance floor. Military uniforms were as numerous as evening suits, some still smelling of mothballs after a few years sitting in the wardrobe.

Loud voices discussed the pros and cons of the new age, principally with regard to the spawning of hundreds of television sets at pretty reasonable prices.

'Did you see it? Did you see it on television?'

'Yes! Wasn't it marvellous!'

'I heard it on radio . . .'

Someone grabbed her arm. 'Come and dance!'

'No!' she shook him off, skirted the dance floor and headed for the bar where the crowd seemed less concentrated.

Through the throng of people, clouded by the smoke of hundreds of cigarettes and cigars, she saw one man standing alone. Nice face, she thought. He smiled at her. She found herself smiling back and stopped it immediately. What if he thought she was fast? She looked away. He'd lose interest. She looked back at him. His eyes were still on her. It was a steadfast look, almost as if he'd been expecting her to look at him again.

She didn't particularly want a drink and did think about leaving.

You'd be a coward, said a small voice in her head.

The voice was right. She wondered whose voice it was: hers or Edna's.

Summoning all the willpower she possessed, she approached the bar. She would buy a drink. If she felt really brave she would enquire what such a handsome man was doing all alone on Coronation Night.

Head high and a frozen smile on her face she walked over to him.

His gaze never left her. Ex-military, she thought judging by the laid-back shoulders and his unyielding gaze. He moved aside so she had a place at the bar.

'Good evening, miss. Can I get you anything?'

She looked him up and down. Was he being fresh? Well, she was having none of that! She forced herself to sound imperious. 'I beg your pardon, young man?'

He slid a silver tray from off the bar, tucked it under his arm and bowed his head in a stiff, slightly continental manner.

Janet realized her mistake immediately. He was a waiter.

'At your service, miss.'

She regained her composure although she felt like an idiot. 'Gin and tonic please.'

What a fool! Fancy thinking he was a guest at the ball! But she mustn't let it show. Besides it was hardly an unreasonable mistake. The chap wore a black suit, white shirt and bow tie –

not really such a difference from the men who had bought tickets to attend and looked stiffer than he did with their tailor-made suits. He was good-looking, but his accent unnerved her.

Her drink was placed in front of her. 'One shilling and sixpence please, miss.'

It was only a few words more than he'd said before, but enough to let her know that he was foreign. She rummaged hurriedly in her purse, wanting to hand him the money as quickly as possible so he would go away and she wouldn't hear him speak again. She pulled out a pound note. 'It's all the change I have.'

He took it, reached into the till behind him, then turned back to her. 'I am sorry, miss. I have no change.'

'I'll see if one of my friends has some.' She looked for Dorothea, saw Henry on his way to the gents, but chose not to call to him.

'Can I help?'

A man standing beside her, obviously the worse for wear, wound his arm around her, his fingers purposely grazing the edge of her left bosom.

'I'll do you a deal, little lady. You give me a kiss and I'll buy you a drink. How's that?' His mouth expelled a cloud of alcoholic fumes into her face.

Grimacing, she turned her head and tried to shrug his arm away and unpeel his groping fingers with her own. It didn't work.

He leaned closer, his weight heavy upon her right shoulder. 'Now come on, little lady – just a kiss. That's not too much to give away, is it?'

He was laughing in her face. A gold tooth flashed at the back of his mouth. His breath was pure malt whisky and his neck smelled of eau de cologne.

'Leave me alone!' She was vaguely aware that the waiter was doing something with money overflowing from a saucer on the back bar. She tried again to push the drunk away before realizing that the waiter had hold of one of the man's arms.

'Sir. The lady's drink has been paid for and she does not require your attentions.' His voice was as steady as his gaze.

The man's drunken lust turned to anger. His bloodshot eyes flickered blearily as he faced the waiter. 'Get your hands off me, you foreign bastard! What are you doing over here anyway? Taking our jobs! Raping our women! Is this what we fought a war for?'

The drunk's expression was ugly.

Sensing violence, Janet stepped back.

The waiter grabbed the man by both lapels, his eyes dark with anger, his words shooting like bullets. 'Freedom! That's what we fought for! But some of us didn't get it. We were betrayed. It was the likes of you that sold my country to Stalin!'

Wide-eyed and scared, Janet looked around for help. Thankfully the prospect of a scuffle was swiftly terminated. The foxtrot had ended. A deluge of dancers flowed from the floor and descended on the bar.

Regardless of a full glass and the fact that she'd handed over a pound note and received no change, Janet fled. She wanted to go home. She wanted to be safe.

Dorothea caught her just as she collected her stole from the cloakroom. 'You're not going, are you?' She had a tight expression on her face and her cheeks were flushed.

'I am indeed.'

'Oh goodness. We do look miserable, don't we?'

'Yes, we do.' Why did she have to speak to her as if she were a pet parrot?

Dorothea wriggled and rubbed at her hips. 'I've got a good excuse. My girdle's killing me. I'd take it off, but my stockings would fall down.'

Janet wasn't interested. 'I'm going.' Tonight she *chose* to go home alone.

She made to push past. She didn't want to hear about

Dorothea's foundation garments and she didn't want to look into her face and remember what she'd been doing with Henry in a public place. The fact that her hand had been beneath the table was beside the point.

Dorothea was persistent. 'Janet! How could you! Poor Stephen! He's terribly upset, you know.'

'How dreadful.'

Dorothea talked into her beaded evening bag as she poked around at the contents with one long finger. 'What a shame! You seemed so well suited. Everyone thought so.'

She lit a cigarette after fixing it into her tortoiseshell holder. She offered one to Janet, who shook her head. Smoke curled from between Dorothea's bright red lips. She waved the cigarette holder like the conductor of the London Philharmonic and brought one of Charlotte's favourite sayings to mind. *Smoking is a social prop. It's a weakness. I am not weak.*

Dorothea was saying, 'He's not a bad catch, you know.'

'Then you marry him.'

Dorothea sniggered like some comedian in an end of the pier show. 'I would if I could. But Henry and Stephen? They call that bigamy, don't they? Mind you,' she dug her elbow into Janet's arm, 'two men in one bed! That would be fun.'

Janet managed a strained smile as she flung her stole around her shoulders, anxious to be as far away from both Henry and Stephen as possible. There was only one problem. 'I'm going home now. Have you got any money for the taxi? I gave the pound note I had reserved to the waiter.'

Dorothea's eyebrows soared skywards. 'You drank that much!'

She explained things in the sort of tone her mother would have used. 'I had one drink. He didn't have any change. Then I dropped my purse. It must have fallen out.'

The excuse was accepted and two half crowns were handed over. Dorothea shook her head forlornly. 'Well, fancy going home this early on Coronation Night. You may never see such a colourful spectacle again, darling.'

Janet dropped the money into her purse. 'Never mind. There's always Rodgers and Hammerstein.' She didn't mention Doris Day and the film they'd seen, one she was never likely to forget.

But Dorothea was adamant.

'Oh, come on.' She grabbed Janet's arm and almost frog-marched her back into the cloakroom. She wriggled provocatively. 'You can at least give me a hand with this girdle. It's got to come off.'

Janet brushed her arm away. Her voice was cutting. 'Get Henry to give you a hand. I hear he's had plenty of experience!'

'Janet! Don't go!'

She made for the exit. People were milling around in the reception hall, a richly decorated place of wood panelling and brass handrails. She pushed her way to the front doors, stepped on someone's foot and glanced back over her shoulder to offer an apology. As she did so she espied the waiter who had interceded between her and the drunk.

'Miss! Miss!'

He was waving his hand high in the air. Did he want her gratitude? Well, he'd be out of luck. A long line of taxis waited outside and she got into the first one and slammed the door behind her.

'Excuse me, but I think I was here first.'

She was speechless. What an idiot! She'd been in such a hurry to escape the crowd and, more specifically, the waiter and his foreign accent, that she hadn't noticed the taxi was already occupied.

'I have to have this cab,' she blurted and threw a nervous glance out of the cab's back window. The waiter was standing on the edge of the pavement, a confused, crestfallen expression on his face. A piece of paper fluttered from his raised hand. He was waving her pound note in the air.

The other occupant of the cab followed her gaze and did an immediate appraisal of the situation whilst the cab driver regarded them over his shoulder, patient amusement flickering over his face.

'Obviously I have acquired a lady in distress. Drive on, cabbie.'

'Where to, chum?'

'Just drive. I'll let you know where Miss . . .' He paused expectantly.

Janet was nervous. She was in a cab with a strange man. After reminding herself that the cab driver was a witness to any difficult situation that might arise, she found her voice. 'Hennessey-White. Janet Hennessey-White.'

The cab pulled away. The man sitting beside her settled himself more comfortably, crossing one leg casually over the other. She felt his eyes upon her, but chose not to look at him.

'Your father wouldn't be David Hennessey-White, would he?'

She stopped staring out of the window and looked at him instead.

He was dark-haired, dark-eyed and his smile seemed to span the bottom half of his face. He introduced himself. 'Jonathan Driver.' His face was familiar. 'We met when you were with him at a hospital charity benefit. He introduced us.'

It was as if a spell had been broken. 'Oh yes!' She *knew* him and so did her father. Suddenly she felt safe.

'Wasn't the party to your liking?' he asked.

She shook her head. 'Not really. Too much noise. Too many drunks.'

'And that was just the women?' His smile broadened.

Janet saw the joke and suddenly found it easy to laugh. 'Ladies on the loose. Snooty about street parties, but better at behaving badly than any factory girl.'

'A wise observation that I have to agree with.'

Janet felt herself wanting to continue the conversation. 'So why did you leave?'

He shrugged. 'I found myself sober and alone. How can you celebrate anything by yourself?'

The taxi driver chose that moment to interrupt. 'Excuse me, chum. We're on Queens Road. Where do you wanna go now?'

'Well?' said Janet's fellow passenger. 'Shall we have our own party? I know a coffee bar on the corner of Penn Street that keeps very odd hours and it has a jukebox. Do you like modern music?'

'Like Doris Day?' Janet said grimly.

He laughed loudly, throwing back his head and showing a mouthful of perfectly white teeth.

'Certainly not Doris Day. In my opinion she's just too sugary for words. I like this new stuff from Bill Haley and Jerry Lee Lewis. Have you heard of them?'

'Yes.'

She had. Bill Haley sang 'Rock Around the Clock'. Jerry Lee Lewis sang . . . she couldn't remember, but oh boy, was she interested. Different music, a different kind of person. He was taking her to a place that was ushering in a different era.

Jonathan directed the cab driver to the coffee bar and paid the fare when they got there. It occurred to her to offer to pay her half. She didn't want him getting any ideas. Then she remembered that Dorothea had only given her enough money to get home. From the coffee bar to Clifton wasn't that far, but enough to take care of the money she had.

Frothy coffee was served in cups the size of soup dishes on trendy metal tables with red Formica tops that were slotted into booths between red vinyl bench seats. The air steamed as much as the chrome-plated coffee machine that hissed like a railway engine each time a fresh cup of coffee was drawn off. Pat Boone was crooning 'Love Letters in the Sand' when they first sat down. A few minutes later and the Wurlitzer, a splendid affair of multicoloured plastic, sparkling chrome and pink neon, flipped onto Nat King Cole and 'The Twelfth of Never'.

What a fool she felt sitting there in a full-length skirt with enough net to curtain a small house. Curious eyes had scrutinized them on entering, but turned away once they'd attained the privacy of the booth, though Janet still looked at them, fascinated by their make-up, their clothes, their hair-styles.

'I like ponytails, and those skirts and sweaters,' she said wistfully, then suddenly realized she must sound silly, even weak. She didn't want him to think that. 'But I'm not frivolous, you understand!'

He had a look on his face that she couldn't quite interpret, initial surprise swiftly turning to interest. 'You're a doctor's daughter. You couldn't possibly be frivolous.'

It was the right thing to say. She became less defensive. 'So we met at a charity event. I take it you're a doctor.' She turned in her top lip in order to suck away a residue of milky froth.

He sat straight and said proudly, 'Absolutely! I work at the sanatorium at Pucklechurch.'

Janet controlled a shudder. 'Contagious disease?'

'Polio actually, though years ago it was used for TB sufferers. And you work in paediatrics, I believe?'

She nodded. 'But only as a secretary.'

'You sound as if you're apologizing for not following in your father's footsteps.'

'My brother Geoffrey is expected to do that, though I'm not sure it's ever likely to happen.'

'Shame. It's a great profession. I don't think there is any other that is quite so satisfying.' His sincerity was palpable. He seemed to glow as if she had pressed a button that sent a wave of electricity through his body.

'So what made you become a doctor?'

He told her how he'd left his family on their Suffolk farm. 'My mother had polio,' he said and lowered his eyes to his coffee. As if to overcome his deep felt hurt, he took a hefty swig before continuing. 'She got it about the same time as

Franklin D. Roosevelt. I felt I had to do something about it once I was old enough.' He shrugged. 'In my own small way of course, not on the grand scale like some who are trying to perfect a vaccine. I've done a lot of research on the subject and feel I have a lot to offer, but you know how it is. The old guard of the medical profession are not always appreciative of progress.'

His frankness surprised and delighted her. He was talking to her as if she were an equal and not merely someone who typed up the notes after the preliminary examinations. She asked him, 'Is your mother dead?'

'No.'

'I'm sorry, it's just that I thought . . .' Her voice petered out. She hated making mistakes like that and possibly upsetting people.

Jonathan seemed unconcerned. It was as though he'd been waiting for someone who would understand what he was talking about and not just on a medical level. He said, 'That's why I went to work at the sanatorium under Professor Pritchard. My mother thinks it's wonderful. She's a brave lady. Life goes on, she said to me. You can't just lie back and die when things happen to your body that you have no control over. You have to go forward. Don't you think so?'

'Yes. Yes. Of course.'

He smiled broadly as though he'd broken through some sort of barrier. 'I knew you'd agree. We're alike, you and me.'

She grinned ruefully. 'We must be. We both hated the Coronation Ball.'

He laughed at her flippancy then surprised her by taking both her hands in his. Her first inclination was to draw back, but his expression had turned deadly serious. This was not an attempt at seduction. He spoke profoundly.

'Never let anyone force you into doing something or being anything other than what you are.'

'I don't intend to.'

His smile returned. He let go her hands. 'I'm glad. Really glad.'

Both in the coffee bar and on the way home he talked incessantly about his job. He became increasingly animated as he expounded theories on how patients might better be served.

'At present they have this crazy idea that even when the contagious period is over, parents should be kept at arm's length from their children. To the outside world they appear insensitive, but in their learned opinion they really feel that emotional upset – parents visiting, children getting upset when they leave – is detrimental to recovery. I think otherwise.'

No doctor, not even her father, had ever spoken to her like this. His openness gave her confidence.

'I know little about polio except how debilitating it can be. I've seen people – children even – with irons up their legs or withered arms. I understand it attacks the nervous system to varying degrees.'

He nodded vigorously. 'It does indeed. And every summer is the same – a batch of cases, mostly children. Incubation of the disease is approximately from three to thirty-five days. In some cases it attacks the respiratory system. These are the patients that need the help of an iron lung for a while.'

They hardly noticed the taxi coming to a standstill.

'Are you both getting out,' said the cab driver, half-turning in his seat. If he was hoping to see them in an intimate clinch, he was disappointed.

'We're there?' Janet peered out at her home in Royal York Crescent in disbelief. The journey home had gone so quickly. And she was so calm! She could hardly believe it. This was the first time since the attack that she'd been alone with a man. Medicine, and principally polio, had been their main topic of conversation.

'Are you in the telephone directory?' he asked as she pushed the door open.

The question caught her unawares. What he really meant was could he ring her, perhaps see her again?

She paused, fully prepared to tell him not to bother, but their conversation burned in her brain. He'd made her feel more worthy than she had felt for a long while.

Her smile was hesitant, but she managed to say, 'Yes. You'll find it under my father's name.'

She turned away from the taxi and told herself that he would not telephone and, even if he did, she would not go out with him. Before she got to the front door, she found herself trying to remember what he looked like, her immediate impression of him.

It came to her quickly. Bedside manner. He had the perfect bedside manner. When he talked his expression was completely in tune with what he was saying. Even the most crotchety of patients couldn't help but be impressed.

Charlotte was coming out of the study when Janet entered the hallway of the tall Regency town house with its high ceilings and tall windows. She wore a dressing gown of soft green wool that highlighted the gleam of her hair and the greyness of her eyes. She smiled warmly, though her eyes looked tired.

'Did you have a nice time, dear?'

Janet kissed her mother's cheek. 'It didn't start too well, but it got much better as the evening went on.'

'Good,' said Charlotte.

Janet felt her eyes watching her as she made her way up the stairs to bed. Deep down she knew that her mother wanted to know more about her evening, just as any mother would. But Janet had never been inclined to talk openly with her mother, not since that incident from her youth, which she remembered, but had never spoken about.

Eight

Nathanial Brookman wore an old-fashioned shirt collar, the wings of which met tightly at the front, threatening to cut off his oxygen supply and forcing him to hold his head high. This made him seem to be constantly looking down his nose.

Charlotte judged him to be around her own age, though his clothes and attitude placed him firmly in the last century. She was sitting across from him on the other side of his very large, very dark and very solid oak desk. Excited by what she had remembered about the men on the building site, she presumed that he would be too.

'There were two men fighting, right there at my feet. They came tumbling out, arguing angrily. What they said didn't quite register at first, then the other day I realized why I couldn't get them out of my mind. They were shouting at each other—'

My dear lady,' said Brookman, hardly raising his eyes from the papers in front of him, please do not worry yourself about what they were saying. I think it advisable that their words *were* incoherent. Gentlemen,' he said condescendingly, 'do not always act like gentlemen or use words suitable for a lady's ears.'

Charlotte took a deep breath and counted to ten. Brookman wouldn't understand that his comment was insulting and he would look at her aghast if she mentioned having intuitive suspicions about the building site and the men employed there. But she had to get through to him, so she pressed on determinedly.

'They weren't swearing,' she began, but stopped when she realized her words were falling on deaf ears. Brookman was already re-engrossed in his files, his head held stiffly over the page.

The rudeness of the man!

At times like these she wished she could belt out a few well-chosen, Anglo-Saxon expletives. Polly would have done so. But Charlotte wasn't Polly. Instead she adopted her most superior expression and said loudly and clearly, 'I do not think I was mistaken. They were speaking Polish. If no one here is brave enough to enquire further, then all I can say is if you want a man to do a difficult job, get a *woman!*'

Too angry even to say goodbye, she slammed the door behind her. Damn him! Hopefully the slamming of the door was enough to cause a big enough draught to blow his papers all over the floor.

Curiosity fuelled her determination to snoop a little. Who were the men she'd seen and, most important of all, were alien workers being employed on a building site? So far refugees from Europe had only been allotted the most menial jobs, certainly not the more highly paid ones in construction. Neither she nor any of her colleagues had placed these men on the site. So where had they come from? Today was as good a time as any other to start nosing around.

Outside the sunshine was very bright, bouncing off parked cars and the plate glass of new shop windows. It was in marked contrast to the office she had just left and she was obliged to don a pair of yellow-framed sunglasses.

The building site was a short walk from the offices of the ministry that protected the rights of alien workers, a most definite incongruity if her suspicions were correct.

Concrete mixers filled the air with a sound like grinding teeth chomping through meals of dust, sand, cement and chippings. Armies of men in dusty clothes with red faces and brawny arms tended them. As some tipped the finished product out and wheeled it away to form floors, walls and load bearing pillars, others refilled the machines with fresh fodder.

A few men stopped work and stared after her. I'm not surprised, she thought. It can't be usual to see a woman smartly dressed and wearing shoes completely unsuitable for walking in *their* territory. All the same the more mature doffed their caps or touched their forelocks.

I wonder what they'd have done if I'd been younger? she thought. A wolf whistle perhaps? She smiled to herself. Respect and some answers to her questions would be better appreciated.

After picking her way carefully over the rutted, dusty ground she reached a green painted shed that seemed to be disguising itself as an office. Moss clung to the wooden steps leading up to it and a wooden handrail, long dried in the sun and an obvious source of splinters, ran up one side.

The door opened just as she was about to knock. The young man who came out looked surprised.

'Madam!' He held the door wide open and inclined his head in a stiffly formal bow. 'Good morning.'

She noticed he spoke the words very precisely, almost as if he'd been rehearsing them for the arrival of someone important. Obviously she was not expected so it couldn't be for her.

'Thank you.' She noted the almond-shaped eyes, the wide cheekbones and crisp curly hair, possibly Slavic.

No pre-judgements, she told herself. And keep smiling. It pays to keep smiling.

The man behind the desk sprang to his feet, stared at her as if about to speak then immediately thought better of it and addressed the young man who still stood at the door.

'You're not paid to stand and stare. Get that mixer going.'

The young man started to shut the door. The older man

grabbed it and heaved it open. 'The lady's not staying. I think she maybe lost her way.'

Charlotte did a quick appraisal of the man in front of her. Skin the colour of uncooked dough, pale blue eyes, broad-shouldered, but weak-chinned and with a hairline that was gradually waving goodbye to his forehead. Hostile eyes glared at her from beneath a beetled brow. She was certain that if she'd been a man he would have manhandled her off of the site immediately.

His tone was brusque. 'Building sites are no place for a lady!'

He grabbed a battered brown trilby from a four-inch nail, stuck it on his head, then picked up rolls of crisp blueprints and tucked them under his arm.

A line from the Bible that was also very well advertised on the side of a tin of Lyle's treacle, skipped unbidden into Charlotte's head. *Out of the strong came forth sweetness.*

She smiled her most sugary smile and leaned towards him as though he was a film star and she was his greatest fan. Her voice was pure treacle. 'I do apologize, but I thought I might enquire how the two men are, the ones that were fighting the other day.'

He flashed her a sharp look before gathering up more bits of paper and rolls of drawings. Obviously he was preparing to leave the office and get her off the site.

'You weren't the man who broke them apart, were you?' she asked with an air of genuine concern.

'No. I was not.' He glared at her with open hostility. Charlotte continued to smile although her jaw ached. Her handbag was looped over one arm. Her white-gloved fists were tightly clenched. She had a strong urge to punch him on the nose.

'So how are those poor men?'

He came round from behind the desk, grabbed her elbow in a pincer-like grip and propelled her to the door. 'They're

OK. Just two men fighting. Happens all the time. Now, if you don't mind, I've got work to do.'

Charlotte kept talking. 'Were they foreign? I couldn't help thinking they were. It was their voices, you see. They sounded so different.'

She fancied his grip loosened and a wary anger simmered in his eyes.

'Lady,' he said, poking a finger at his sweat-stained trilby so it sat further back on his head, 'I wouldn't like to say. You wouldn't believe the kind of language the men use on this site. And quite frankly, I don't think you should stay around to hear it.'

She stumbled slightly as he guided her out of the door and down the three rough steps. Once firm ground was reached she started to fumble in her handbag.

'If any men on your site do get hurt, perhaps you could get in touch. My husband is a doctor.' She passed him a neat little black and white card she'd had printed which stated, ***Dr and Mrs D.L.E. Hennessey-White.*** The cards were mainly for handing out at social gatherings, far better than rummaging in a handbag or pocket for pen and note-paper.

He took it but continued to guide her physically and forcibly towards the entrance, the pavement and the crowds of shoppers walking and laughing in the warm summer sun.

'Well, goodbye, Mr . . . ?' she said, once her feet were on less pitted ground. 'Goodbye!'

He turned smartly away, his broad shoulders rolling and his stride lengthening like some down-market John Wayne. Her dismissal was absolute.

She studied him thoughtfully as he went back up the steps and into the office. His surly behaviour made her even more suspicious than she had been. She made herself an instant promise. As soon as she had the time she would satisfy her curiosity. Life was too busy at the moment, what with sorting out work and accommodation for the people in her care, plus finding time for David, who was never well nowadays. Thank goodness Geoffrey was away studying in Cambridge and that Janet had a good job and *seemed* happy enough, though she did worry at times that she was seeing less and less of her.

Between refugee, community and hospital work, she would approach Brookman again, ask his opinion and see if there was any way he could investigate matters.

It seemed a satisfactory way forward. As she walked into the crowds she chanced to glance back. A shiny black car had pulled into the kerb. Curious, though she couldn't quite say why, she stood and watched as the driver got out, went round to the passenger side and opened the door. A tall, well-made man got out. He paused, eyed the entrance with a look of serious intent, then fixed his hat firmly on his head.

Charlotte's heart beat like a drum. The man in the double-breasted suit again! Some memory from the past attempted to resurface, but didn't quite make it. The feeling that she knew him from somewhere would not go away. Much as she racked her brain, his name and the place she'd first seen him refused to come to mind.

The foreman on the building site flicked the card she'd given him between his fingers. The man who had just arrived listened attentively to him, his driver standing close to his shoulder.

'A snooper,' he said. 'Doctor's wife according to this card.'

'And she saw us break up the fight between Stanislav and Kubenchski?'

'Yes, Mr O'Hara.'

The man called Mr O'Hara took a deep breath. At first he looked as though he would throw the card away, but suddenly seemed to change his mind.

'I know her from somewhere.'

'Is that right?' said the foreman. His eyes fixed expectantly on O'Hara's face in the belief he was about to get an explanation.

O'Hara was explaining nothing. Hell, he thought, eyeing the neatly printed name and address. I *do* know that dame. He smiled as he slid the card into his trouser pocket. 'Let me know if the lady comes sniffing round again.'

'Do you want me to warn her off?'

O'Hara eyed the foreman as though he had more chance of becoming Miss Weston-super-Mare than taking care of Mrs Hennessey-White.

'No. That's my department.'

After the business was done and money – a lot of money – had changed hands, he got back in his car. As his chauffeur drove, O'Hara looked out of the car window, his lips drawn in a laconic smile. My, he thought, but there was a lot of rebuilding going on in Europe. It was so easy to make money if you didn't do it by the book. And wasn't it great being a big fish in a little pond? That's what Bristol was compared to Chicago or New York. He'd known the latter cities well before the war. His business had been less than legal there too. The war had intervened and, along with a lot of other city boys, he'd been shipped to Europe and managed to spend most of the war in England.

Under normal circumstances he should had gone back home once the war had ended. New York and Chicago were cities where men like him could make money just by ensuring the right union was paying the right dues to the right people. New York had become rich on wartime business. Labour had been at a premium and had continued into the post-war period. But he couldn't go home, and although he sometimes felt bitter about it, he consoled himself with the fact that he was doing pretty well in England.

He was a respectable businessman, though respectability was not an issue for Mickey O'Hara. He'd paid good money for a fake passport, ration and identity papers, and best of all he had paid for the fact that Mickey O'Hara had never committed a crime.

*

Charlotte needed Colin's help but, as always, she didn't want to ask him for it outright. She also thought she might snatch a moment with Edna, perhaps test the water before deciding to hand over the letter.

'I'm going to take you on a trip and then for tea and buns,' she said, having bumped into Edna in Whiteladies Road where she was shopping for new shoes for her energetic and shoe-destroying son. 'I'll pick you up at ten o'clock on Saturday morning and I won't take no for an answer.'

So here they were standing beneath the ceremonial crown that stood in the middle of the Centre. The crown's four sturdy legs were decorated with flags and paper flowers and straddled the wide path that formed a cross between walled flowerbeds where blooms of red, white and blue danced in the breeze.

'Ships used to tie up here,' Colin explained to the children.

'There's no water,' Peter wailed.

'No,' Colin remarked sardonically. 'Them that planned this preferred concrete and their own glory to water. Shame! They took no account at all of Bristol's maritime history.'

'A bit like ripping out its heart,' said Edna sadly.

Colin smiled at her equally sadly and stroked her hair.

'I'm inclined to agree with you,' Charlotte remarked. She kept her gaze fixed on the crown, feeling a little uncomfortable at their public show of affection. It was not something she and David indulged in – even in private. She went on, 'Perhaps one day a more enlightened corporation might reinstate the water and have the boats mooring again as far as Colston Avenue.'

Colin's pale complexion turned pink as he burst out laughing. 'Have you ever come across an enlightened corporation in your career as a professional busybody?'

Edna sucked in her breath. 'Colin!'

Charlotte waved the remark aside. Colin liked goading her. 'You're probably right, Colin. At some time in the future they'll probably replace it with an even worse concrete construction – despite busybodies like me.'

'I hope I won't be around to see it,' said Colin. 'Bloody corporation!'

Charlotte shook her head and smiled. She enjoyed Colin and Edna's company and admired their resilience in the face of Colin's disablement. Normally, she'd be exuberant, talking louder, running around the flowerbeds with the children, but the existence of the letter lay heavy. What if she disclosed its existence and their marriage broke up as a result? Anything could happen. She shivered.

'It's much larger than I expected,' Colin exclaimed, breaking into her thoughts, his head tilted back, face turned upwards to study the underside of the elaborate construction. 'Good job the Queen, bless her, didn't wear anything this big on her head.'

'She could live in it,' said Edna, gazing up at it from underneath.

'Is it a house?' asked Susan.

'No. It's a crown,' Edna explained.

Charlotte and Edna stood on either side of Colin looking up intermittently and ready to catch him should he lose his balance though he was using the handle of Pamela's pushchair to keep him steady. Edna held the hands of the older children.

'So there you are,' said Charlotte in the same sort of voice she used when giving a talk to the Townswomen's Guild, 'A wonderful tribute to our new Queen. I promised to walk underneath it with you and I have.'

Colin eyed her speculatively, a hint of a smile playing around his mouth. 'But I have seen it before, Charlotte. Me and Edna do have a car now, you know. So come on, what's on yer mind?'

A blushing Edna tapped his arm in admonishment. Charlotte saw the gesture and almost blushed herself. Of course she had an ulterior motive and rebuked herself for underestimating Colin's astute nature. The blush retreated in the face of her usual self-control and she laughed. 'How clever of you. You've found me out. How did you guess?'

Colin grinned, winked and tapped both his tin legs. 'I've got built-in radar.'

'Colin!' Edna's blush inched over her jaw and down her neck.

'It's all right, Edna.'

It never failed to amuse Charlotte that Edna thought her vulnerable to Colin's challenging sense of humour, as though people from Clifton with plummy voices never laughed or told rude jokes. She asked, 'Can I buy you tea? The Civic Restaurant's open.'

They made their way to one of the wartime facilities that had not as yet faded away with the last of the rationing. Civic restaurants had been around almost since war was first declared and seemed likely to linger – perhaps as long as the prefabricated houses. The latter were fast approaching their ten-year dismantlement date. Charlotte thought it a shame. For the first time a lot of people had inside bathrooms, a big improvement on an outside lavatory and a tin bath hanging on the back wall.

'I thought you could help,' Charlotte began as they drank tea served in thick china cups and bit into hot teacakes smothered in precious butter and real raspberry jam. 'As you know, I am doing work for the Bureau of Displaced Persons. These people are unable to return to their own countries. Most would be killed if they did. A large number of them came over during the last decade when things were in turmoil after the war. Since the Iron Curtain came down we're seeing more and more people applying to live in this country. Our aim is to find them adequate accommodation and jobs. At present they are being restricted to the most labour intensive and menial of jobs – mining, steel-making, road-digging. But there are those of us who think this unfair. Some of these people are highly qualified and deserve better than that. We are going to put it to our superiors that there are more skilled jobs needing to be done. I thought you, Colin, might be able to help with this.'

Colin eyed her intently, a knowing smile playing on his lips. Colin was clever at seeing through people and turning comments on their heads. She didn't want him to do too much of that today. She wanted him to be serious.

Where are they from?' asked Edna, her face clouded.

Charlotte answered, 'Some are Ukranians, Lithuanians, Yugoslavs – even a few Germans among them. The majority are Polish.'

'Are they skilled?' Colin asked.

Charlotte sighed regretfully as if having a skill or profession was some kind of drawback. 'Yes. That's why we feel they're being wasted, but' – she shrugged and shook her head – 'I'm afraid that if they wish to settle in this country they are only allowed to take certain jobs. We're getting enough accusations that they're taking jobs from our own people. Everyone wants to forget the war, but the problems it left us with won't go away just like that.' She shrugged again. 'I wish it were otherwise.'

Colin met the steady gaze she gave him over the top of her teacup. He grinned and lifted one of his legs with both hands to get it into a more comfortable position. 'And you'd like me to help you break the mould.'

Her spirits rose. She knew that look, but pretended she hadn't noticed, sipped her tea and looked round at the place they were in as if it had lately acquired a certain ostentation rather than being pretty basic and smelling of fat fried many times over and still sitting in the pans.

'So,' said Colin, 'if I agree to take some of these people on, you then have to persuade your bureau—'

'Actually the Home Office,' Charlotte corrected.

' . . . The Home Office,' Colin went on, 'that the jobs I am offering are very menial.'

Charlotte nodded. 'Yes. At least, to start with.'

They all fell silent as they picked the last crumbs left on their plates. It was all too thought-provoking for words.

'Funny old world,' said Colin at last, his eyes following his wife's gentle movements as she adjusted her daughter's pillow to accommodate her sleepy head. 'What do you think then, Edna?'

'I'm sure we can help,' said Edna, her eyes bright as her hand covered that of her husband.

Charlotte was suddenly reminded of the old saying that behind every successful man was a very strong woman. Edna's gentle exterior was deceptive. Charlotte sighed with satisfaction.

Colin agreed to look at the particulars of any people she referred to him.

After that their conversation turned to family matters.

Edna started talking about how well Pamela was walking compared with Susan and her brother at that age. Recognizing that he wasn't likely to get a word in on this subject, Colin struggled to his feet. 'Excuse me, ladies.'

He made his way to the lavatory making a loud clanking noise each time one of his legs hit against the metal leg of a table.

Exuberant that Colin had agreed to help, Charlotte didn't think too carefully about what she was saying. 'You sometimes get the youngest outperforming the oldest though it isn't really fair to compare. I mean, are you comparing the right ones?'

Edna looked startled.

Charlotte could have bitten off her tongue. She had sounded as if she were talking about Edna's children, and in particular the son she'd given up for adoption. She made an effort to make amends. 'I meant a child of two and one of seven.'

Edna collected herself. Her smile was as soft and gentle as her large brown eyes. Her gaze settled on the child sleeping in the pushchair of tubular metal, a little chipped nowadays seeing as she'd used it for all three of her children.

'It's all right, Charlotte. It hurts to remember, but don't think that I don't. It's just that I try not to mention my wicked past and my firstborn child when Colin's around.'

'Wicked? I'd hardly call it that.'

Edna grimaced. 'You haven't heard my mother. Despite her mind being weak nowadays her views on my eternal shame have got worse rather than better.'

'I thought she might have mellowed with the years.'

'Oh no! Not her. I close my ears to her as much as possible. Sherman *was* a part of my life, just as his father was part of my life. I don't advertise the fact that I have an illegitimate child – people being the way they are. But I don't forget it either.'

Charlotte sipped her tea and thought of the letter locked in her bureau. She felt compelled to ask the obvious question. 'What would you do if something from your past suddenly caught up with you?'

Edna looked at her questioningly. 'What are you getting at?'

Charlotte gathered her thoughts. She purposely inverted the situation. 'Let's say Sherman's father wrote to you and wanted to meet you again?'

'I don't think that's ever likely to happen.'

'But what if he did. What would you do?'

Edna looked towards the restaurant door. It rattled as though it were about to fall off its hinges every time a bus went by. The whole place was beyond its best. Before very long it would be no more than a pile of dust and jagged wood.

She waited for the buses to go by and the door to stop rattling before she answered.

'Sometimes at night I imagine how it would be, how I'd tell him about Sherman and then about Colin and me. And then I think of Colin.' She turned to face Charlotte. 'And then I feel scared. I couldn't be sure that someone wouldn't get hurt.'

Nine

Janet stared through the office window over the rooftops to the misted skyline of the city centre. There were plenty of reports, letters and patients' notes to be typed, taken for signature, and the filing was brimming from the tiered wire trays sitting on her desk. She hated office work. Its only redeeming feature was the fact that she was fascinated by medicine and the hospital. Sometimes when she was out of the office she wandered along the hospital corridors chatting to medical staff, but mostly to patients. It felt good to talk to them about their ailments, to calm their fears, even to try to explain a surgical procedure or a course of medication. The more she did it, the more she wanted to do it. Paperwork, especially typing, was another matter entirely.

The office which she shared with Dorothea and two other secretaries was plain but not dark. On the contrary, the fact that they were on the fifth floor meant the office was bathed in light from a sky that seemed almost touchable. Because they looked down at it from St Michael's Hill, the city seemed like a counterpane left rumpled by a recent sleeper into hillocks of varying shape and size.

Her reverie was disturbed as the door swung open. Dorothea entered and twirled into her chair, slapping a pile of papers and a shorthand notepad onto her desk.

'One of these days Doctor Bailey is going to ask me to take down more than shorthand – mark my words,' she said with a ribald giggle.

Why wasn't it Dorothea that got raped? Janet gazed out of

the window, no longer seeing the panoramic view but a kind of map, a table of possibilities and probabilities. She answered her own question: availability. She'd been in the wrong place at the wrong time. Dorothea had been elsewhere, willingly surrendering to Henry's sexual advances.

'Are you listening to me?' Dorothea asked from over the top of an Imperial typewriter, a squat object of black metal and brass-edged keys.

Janet eyed Dorothea's round face and the permanently parted red lips. Her permed hair bounced in curly bangs as she rested her chin on her hand and her elbow on her typewriter. She had a willing look about her, of course she did. Dorothea had the reputation of being a jolly sort who had a way with even the most crotchety of the senior surgeons. She was a coquette, a girl who promised and quite often delivered.

'Of course I am. Why do you ask?'

'It's ten forty-five,' said Dorothea.

Janet looked at her blankly.

Dorothea jerked her chin at the untouched cup of tea still sitting on Janet's desk.

Janet shrugged. 'I didn't feel like it.'

Dorothea grinned wickedly. 'I always feel like it – and I don't mean tea.'

Janet raised her eyes to heaven and got up from her desk, cup and saucer in hand. Just as she got to the door, Grace Argyle, Secretary to the Chief Medical Officer and self-appointed Mother Superior to the secretaries and the typing pool, entered. She was a grey person, though not in the light, fluid way that the sky is grey. Iron-grey hair cropped close to her head, steel grey eyes, and lip colour resembling unpolished tin made her seem solid and unyielding, which she was. She was also built like a battleship.

The keys of Dorothea's typewriter immediately clattered into life.

Janet stood to one side of the door to let her pass, hoping

that once she was through she could slip out quickly herself without too many questions. Grace Argyle stopped and looked her up and down. 'Where are you going?'

'To empty my cup,' said Janet raising it slightly and half-wishing she had the courage to throw it over her.

'Don't be long!'

Once outside, Janet took a deep breath. The antiseptic smell of the hospital corridor was preferable to Miss Argyle's mix of musty tweed and lavender water.

Maude, the other secretary with whom she shared the office, was coming along the corridor, shrugging a short box jacket from off her shoulders having just returned from the dentist. On seeing Janet, she glanced at her watch. 'Is the old bat on the warpath yet?' she asked with rushed nervousness.

Janet smiled wanly. 'Don't worry. You've got a legitimate excuse.'

'Don't be long emptying that teacup,' Maude called after her.

Janet opened her mouth, meaning to say that it didn't take very long to empty a teacup. But she was out of the office and, although Miss Argyle had verbally warned her not to do it, she couldn't help herself. The hospital was full of patients who appeared to appreciate her presence.

'I'm going to visit a friend of my mother's in Logan Ward,' she lied.

'Watch out,' Maude shouted after her, the sleeves of her jacket dragging on the floor as she rushed towards the office door.

I'll be careful,' Janet shouted back. For the first time in days she smiled at someone other than a child. Grace Argyle was a Harpy who liked to be in control of her 'girls'. Janet had already been warned by her not to go wandering around the hospital.

'Once more,' Miss Argyle had said, 'and your employment could very well be terminated.'

It was a dire warning, but Jonathan's words rang in her

ears. 'Do what you think is right.' Well, that was exactly what she was going to do. Visiting the 'proper' hospital, getting away from the offices, was the best part of working here.

No one questioned her as she wandered around. Few of the nursing staff knew the secretaries, so she could pretend to be a visitor, one who had travelled miles, but could not, because of distance, visit at the normal visiting hour of seven p.m. to eight p.m.

The corridor adjacent to the geriatric ward was empty except for what appeared to be a bundle of laundry buried inside a fawn and brown dressing gown. She thought she heard groaning. On further examination she noticed the wisps of hair and was instantly reminded of 'old man's beard', the cotton soft growth that clings to September hedgerows.

The thin skin of the hand hanging over the chair arm was peppered with liver spots. His fingers flicked convulsively as she approached and he lifted his head, his face contorted into a pain-filled grimace.

Concerned, she dropped to his side so that her face was level with his. 'Are you all right?'

Blinking as if trying to focus, he screwed up his face so that his eyes were no more than glistening dots among wrinkly folds. 'I don't like it here. I like flowers. I like fresh air. Can you take me to the garden? Can you? Can you?' He was like a wilful child, repeating until someone gave in to him.

Janet patted his hand and smiled up into the half-hidden eyes. 'I can't. I'm sorry.'

'Fresh air? Can I have fresh air? Please?' he whined.

There was no point in explaining that there was no garden, but she couldn't help but pity him. She could understand him wanting fresh air. The wards were stuffy.

'I can't promise you a garden, but I think I know where we can have some fresh air,' she said finally.

After getting to her feet, she released the footbrake on the wheelchair and pushed him off along the corridor. They stopped at a place where it widened, glass windows in thin metal frames forming an enclosed balcony with casements that opened. Like the window frames, the handles had been painted recently and were difficult to open.

The old man muttered loudly behind her, 'I grew marigolds, gladioli, tulips, cabbages, kidney beans, Brussels sprouts . . .' The litany of flowers and vegetables went on and on. It was as if his achievements in the garden were being used as encouragement for her to use greater strength to satisfy his needs.

'There!' she exclaimed as the dried paint finally flaked away and the window swung open. A stiff breeze blew across the roofs of the city. The old man squinted against it, his hair floating like mist around his head.

Janet bent over him. 'Is that better?'

He closed his eyes. If he were taking deep breaths it was hardly noticeable. The whole man seemed little more than dressing gown and pyjamas. Only skin and sinew held his bones together. Lines curved from the sides of his closed eyes, creased his cheeks, drooped like muddied ruts from the sides of his mouth and formed a criss-cross pattern, like a small chessboard, over his chin. An old man now, concerned only about his garden, but what had he looked like during his youth, she wondered? Had his garden been as important to him way back then as it was now? And what sort of life had he planned as a young man? Had everything gone according to plan? Had unforeseen events occurred just as it had in her life?

She hadn't noticed that he'd stopped breathing. Perhaps she'd been too wrapped up in her own thoughts, but something in his face had definitely changed. Was it her imagination or was he paler than he had been? Had his lips turned blue? Had his eyes closed for ever?

Gently she shook his arm. 'Sir?' She had forgotten to ask his name, but wished she had. People responded more easily to their names than they did to formal address. 'Sir?

Can you hear me?' She shook him again. His eyes remained shut. His mouth dropped open and a sound like the cackle of a strangled cockerel erupted from his throat. 'Wake up! Wake up!'

Someone in uniform pushed her aside. 'Mr Sharples! I've been looking for you.'

A ward sister, trimly pristine in royal blue dress and diaphanous white veil, bent over the man. 'Mr Sharples! Mr Sharples!'

Janet stood helplessly as the man's limp wrist was checked for a pulse. Even before the ward sister told her it was so, she knew he was dead.

The ward sister straightened. 'How did he get here?'

Janet could only tell the truth. 'I pushed him. He wanted some fresh air.'

Dark brows frowned at her. 'I know you, don't I?'

Janet nodded. 'I work in the secretarial unit.'

'Oh dear. This could cause problems. You know I have to make a report, don't you? I'll have to mention that I couldn't find him and that you'd wheeled him off. You shouldn't have done that.'

'Wasn't he dying anyway?'

The ward sister sighed apologetically and shrugged her shoulders. 'That's not the point. I wasn't there when it happened and you were. I'm sorry.'

Judging by her voice and her regrets at having to report the matter, this was a woman who cared for her charges. Janet couldn't possibly be mad at her.

'I had to do it,' Janet explained. 'He was missing his garden. I think that when the fresh air hit him he imagined he was back there again. I was just trying to help.'

'I know. Mr Sharples loved his garden. But that's not the point.'

Miss Argyle stood behind the huge cherrywood desk in the office of the Chief Medical Officer. He had gone to play golf that afternoon, but not before discussing a suitable reprimand for Janet's misdemeanour.

Grace Argyle's backside amply filled the big leather chair. She indicated that Janet be seated in the small chair purposely placed by her in front of the desk. It was modern, low and had thin metal legs and no arms. Janet found herself looking up at Grace Argyle and felt intimidated – which was exactly how Miss Argyle wanted her to feel.

First, her 'crime' was read out in full.

At last Grace Argyle looked with ungracious disapproval down her long nose and sniffed so forcibly that her nostrils momentarily disappeared. She stated, 'We expect an apology.'

We! It was almost as though she were part of the hospital board, some kind of medical royalty. What a nerve! All the same, this was no time for her resentment to show. She had to apologize.

'I'm sorry,' sighed Janet, her gaze fixed on the floor. 'I didn't think, and Mr Sharples so wanted . . .'

'Mr Sharples? Who, might I ask, is Mr Sharples?'

Surprised, Janet looked up at her. 'The old man . . . the man who died.'

'Oh!' Grace Argyle shuffled her papers, studied where necessary, and then readjusted her spectacles. 'Ah yes. Indeed that was his name.'

Good grief! This woman had worked at the hospital for thirty years yet Janet doubted whether she actually regarded the names on the medical records and reports as people. Her own attitude was very different. Every day she noted the names, ages and ailments of people, even checked if they'd got better and gone home. It was none of her concern really, but she just couldn't help it.

'It is not for you to interfere or interact in any way with hospital patients. There are nurses and doctors aplenty for that. Take note, Miss Hennessey-White, you are a secretary and are here purely to carry out the day-to-day tasks that the position calls for. Your father may be a doctor, but you, young woman, are not!'

'I'm sorry,' Janet said again, longing for the ordeal to be over before she choked on the amount of humble pie Miss Argyle expected her to swallow.

'So you should be. However,' she went on, 'this is not the first time you have violated hospital regulations. Therefore, in order to remove temptation – or rather – to remove *you* from temptation, it has been decided that you are transferred to the Housekeeping and Catering Department.'

Janet couldn't believe her ears. 'Housekeeping and Catering?' Surely she'd heard wrong.

'Housekeeping and Catering,' Miss Argyle repeated along with another powerful sniff up her supercilious nostrils.

Janet went limp in her chair.

'In future you will be dealing with the day-to-day support tasks of the hospital – clothing, bedding – that sort of thing. Seamstresses and kitchen assistants make up most of the staff in that department.'

The most menial of staff. That she could cope with. But it was not a medical department. Janet was numb. Taking an interest in patient welfare had always helped lessen the routine boredom of the job.

'Please,' she implored getting to her feet and leaning over the desk, 'please, Grace, don't send me down there. I promise I won't—'

Grace Argyle sprang to her feet. '*Miss* Argyle to you, *Miss* Hennessey-White!'

The matter was settled. Dorothea helped her move her things, the tip-tapping of her high-heeled shoes running alongside Janet as she marched close-lipped to her new domain, her eyes staring straight ahead.

'We'll still see each other at tea break and lunchtime,' Dorothea was saying. 'Nothing's going to alter that much.'

Through clenched teeth Janet said, 'It is for me!'

'It's just another office,' Dorothea went on in as optimistic a tone as she could muster, desperate to make Janet feel better. 'One office is very like another,' she said brightly.

The Head Housekeeper pointed to the door of Janet's new office. 'Just there,' she said then scurried off as if she had far better to do than instruct a new typist where the laundry lists and invoices were typed.

Janet came to a standstill in the doorway of her new office. Her heart sank as she took in the grim surroundings. Crestfallen, she looked at Dorothea. 'What were you saying about one office being much like another?'

'Oh dear.'

The pair of them stood silently staring into a room with brown-varnished walls. The window was as large as the one through which Janet had frequently admired the view. Unfortunately it looked out on a place of boxes and bins where delivery vehicles unloaded kitchen supplies and sluice room appliances. Surely something better must happen?

A few days later a message came to her from Jonathan via the message pad on the hall table. It asked her to meet him on the following Tuesday night at the Rockabilly Coffee Bar in Regents Street, Clifton. He did not leave a return telephone number. Refusing was obviously not an option. Feeling down in the mouth, but disinclined to say no, she pulled a new pale blue sweater over her head, slid into a pair of blue gingham matador pants and poked her toes into a pair of high-heeled mules. To complete the picture, she tied a chiffon scarf around her neck and tied her hair back into a rudimentary ponytail. After a quick look in the mirror, the ponytail was discarded. Her hair was too short. 'More like a bob-tailed nag,' she muttered and headed down the stairs.

Jonathan was already there when she arrived. He greeted her with a smile and told her they were giving free Lincoln biscuits with each cup of coffee.

'Two biscuits for each customer,' said the waitress with a bright smile and a swish of her ponytail as she put the order on the table. 'You get more if you come in on a Saturday night. How about it?' She ignored Janet and directed her question at Jonathan. One hand resting on her hip, she swayed seductively as she waited for him to answer. The jukebox dropped another record onto the turntable, 'Young at Heart' by Frank Sinatra.

'Oh my dear! It's a great shame, but I'm busy most Saturdays. Perhaps some other time?'

Janet smiled down into her coffee. Jonathan looked and sounded as though he really meant it. Yes, she decided. A *very* good bedside manner.

The waitress sighed. 'Perhaps,' she said regretfully and went off to serve someone else.

He smiled at Janet. 'Pressure of work. You know how it is. I managed to get Professor Pritchard to implement nightshifts for doctors. He wasn't keen at first, but once I'd persuaded him that as the senior physician, he didn't have to be part of the rota he readily agreed. Of course, that means that I have to do the lion's share of nightshifts, but there is method in my madness. I'm after his job. He knows it, and so does the Board of Management. It's all a matter of time.'

Janet listened, but made no comment. Her thoughts were elsewhere. The tabletop was a dire shade of green, peppered with black spots, which she traced from one to the other as if she were joining them up with a pencil, like a game in a colouring book. She was comparing the green with the grimness of the office she now worked in. Anything was preferable to that. To think she'd swapped such a wonderful view of the city for a collection of dustbins and delivery vans. Opening the window on a particularly warm day was obviously out of the question when the dustbins were full.

'Janet?' His voice jerked her from her thoughts. 'Am I that boring?' He grinned as he said it and made her feel guilty. 'I know I do go on a bit about what I do. I apologize. I can't seem to help it. You see, I'm just not the sort to talk about fashions, films or music – at least not for too long. I suppose it's because of my mother being crippled by polio that's made me the way I am. But there . . .' He shrugged. 'It can't be helped.'

'I *adore* you going on about your job. I'm as interested in medicine as you are, it's just that something's happened . . .' She hung her head. 'It's my own fault really.' Sighing, she slumped back in her chair and told him about wheeling Mr Sharples away from outside his ward, him dying and Miss Argyle having her demoted to a job and an office she hated.

He leaned across the table and kissed her cheek. 'That's for being a wonderful person,' he said. 'I wish everyone cared for the patients as much as you do.'

She sensed he really meant it. 'Thank you.'

For a while they sat there, silently thoughtful, at ease with each other like old friends who know that continuous conversation does not prove appreciation of mutual companionship.

'Why don't you think about being a nurse?' Jonathan said at last.

Janet shrugged. 'I suppose I should think about doing something like that. I certainly don't want to stay where I am.' Thoughts of the grim office, the boring job suddenly seemed to flood over and make her angry. 'Damn Grace Argyle! Spinsters like her should get a man in their life, then perhaps she wouldn't be so rotten to anyone who happens to be younger—'

'And prettier,' Jonathan interrupted.

'And . . .' She faltered, suddenly realizing what he'd said.

He was looking at her over the top of his coffee cup. It was an intense look, almost as if he were a little apprehensive as to what her reaction might be. 'You see? I talk about my job a lot, but it doesn't mean that I don't notice things. My mother tells me I'm a very sensitive, observant and caring person. Mothers can't be wrong, can they?'

No man she knew mentioned his mother as much as Jonathan did, but Janet was too absorbed in her own problems to worry about such trivia. She spooned the froth on the coffee to the right side of the cup, then slowly spooned it all back again.

'I think I might have to look for another job. I hate typing out laundry lists and I feel as though I'm working in the Black Hole of Calcutta.'

Jonathan's grin diminished, but still fluttered around his mouth. 'Then maybe it is the time to think about leaving.'

His thoughtfulness seemed to deepen, his grin disappearing altogether. It was almost, thought Janet, a scheming look and she wondered what was on his mind.

'So what will you next ask of the indomitable Professor Pritchard?' she asked him after putting her irritation about the new job behind her and taking a sip of her coffee, now cold in her cup.

He winked mischievously. 'Who knows, but whatever it is I promise to tell you all about it.'

Janet agreed to meet Dorothea for lunch on Saturday at the Queens Road branch of Carwardines. Dorothea, her hair restrained with a tartan Alice band that matched her trews and was teamed with a green, short-sleeved sweater, asked, 'So how's the new boyfriend?'

Janet pretended to be more interested in buttering her teacake. 'He's fine, though he isn't necessarily a boyfriend.'

Dorothea licked the butter off her nose and chewed on the large portion of teacake she'd just bitten off. 'So if he isn't a boyfriend, what is he?'

'Just a friend,' Janet replied with cool self-assurance, pleased that Jonathan talked to her about medicine, not about her being desirable, an obvious prelude to sexual advances.

Dorothea's heavily made up eyes opened wide. 'You mean he hasn't tried anything?'

'No. He's a gentleman.'

Dorothea sputtered breadcrumbs into her coffee. 'I don't

believe *that*! Believe me, it's just a matter of time before his hands wander and he tries to get you into bed.'

Janet was instantly defensive. 'He isn't like that.'

'All men are like that.'

'Not Jonathan.'

Dorothea looked at her sidelong. 'Are you sure?'

Janet self-consciously smoothed her skirt over her knees. She didn't want to think about Jonathan in a sexual way. He was a friend and she wanted him to remain so. 'Can we change the subject?'

Dorothea made a face before continuing. 'So when do you see your doctor friend again?'

'Tuesday, perhaps Wednesday.'

'Not tonight?'

It was the question Janet dreaded Dorothea asking. Jonathan was conscientious.

'He has to work this evening.'

'My, my! What a terribly committed young man! But you don't want to stay at home, darling. Henry's away, but I'm sure I can find a replacement for him. I've got quite a few numbers in my little black book.' Dorothea prattled on. 'I can always fix you up with Stephen. You know he's got a crush on you. You could do worse, you know, and you probably will if you run off from dances before the witching hour. Stephen was *very* disappointed. I mean, it was the Coronation Ball.'

'He'll manage without me, I'm sure.'

'Of course he will, darling! If it isn't you, it'll be someone else. Are you sure your doctor friend really is working this evening? After all, no man can do without a woman. It's a bit like smoking, it's something you just have to have.'

Janet eyed her friend accusingly. 'And you should know,' she said tartly.

'Of course I do,' said Dorothea as she slowly and seductively slid a cigarette into its holder.

Janet eyed the lips that pouted around the ebony black

stem. They were bright red. Dorothea's eyebrows, already dark, were heavily pencilled, more like Elizabeth Taylor than Doris Day.

'I'm just cautious.'

'I'm not. I do what comes naturally.'

Janet lowered her voice. 'Yes, but you do it too often and with too many different people.'

Dorothea sucked on her cigarette holder and stuck her nose in the air. 'Better that than being frigid. That's what you are, Janet Hennessy-White. You're frigid!'

The comment seemed to ricochet around the chocolate brown walls and over the heads of the other customers.

Janet blushed crimson. People were turning in their direction. Some expressions were full of interest, others of condemnation. 'Dorothea, will you please lower your voice. You're causing a scene and anyway, that's a ridiculous statement.'

Dorothea leaned so low across the table that one breast dipped into the sugar bowl. 'When was the last time you let a man put his hand up your skirt?'

Janet flushed. 'Never!'

'Or on your bosom?'

'Never!'

'And you're really telling me you're not frigid?'

'No! I mean – yes. I'm not frigid.'

They were talking far too loudly in a very public place. Her face felt as if a firework had gone off next to her cheeks.

'So if you're not going out with your doctor, where are you going tonight? It is Saturday after all.'

'Out! Out with a friend.' She was disappointed that Jonathan was not available, but she was damned sure she wasn't going to show it.

Luckily a cousin and an aunt of Dorothea's arrived unexpectedly and brought the showdown to a halt. Janet left, her feet seeming to take on a mind of their own and leading her to Durdham Down where big ladies with small dogs were taking the air, and courting couples strolled hand in hand, oblivious to the shouts of playing children and screaming seagulls.

Although the day was warm, a light breeze blowing up from the Avon Gorge cooled her warm face and her anger. Of course she wasn't frigid and in time she'd prove it, but she wouldn't be rushed.

A man stood on the bandstand belting out 'Take me Back to the Black Hills', yet another Doris Day number from *Calamity Jane.* Janet kicked at the grass. God, but Doris Day had a lot to answer for. She was just about to turn for home when a jubilant and childlike voice interrupted her thoughts.

'Aunty Janet! We're having a picnic and we've got fruit cake,' boasted Susan, her podgy fingers already around Janet's hand.

Peter came galloping up behind his sister, both hands slapping his right thigh. 'Whoa, Trigger,' he said, pulling on pretend reins. Accompanying his action with a loud neigh, he came to a halt.

A dark grey blanket formed a backdrop for a green checked tablecloth on which were sandwiches of thickly sliced bread; wedges of butter-gold fruit cake oozing with moist sultanas, currants and scarlet cherries; fairy cakes topped with pink and white icing; and an apple pie, its crust golden and glistening with brown Demerara.

Edna sat at one corner of the blanket, her legs folded beneath her. 'I thought it was you,' she said. Her brown hair was restrained by a pale blue Alice band, which matched the stripes on her dress. Janet thought how girlish she looked.

'I've been to lunch with my friend Dorothea,' Janet explained.

'And had nothing more than a coffee, I bet,' said Edna thrusting a plate at her.

'Trigger's hungry,' said Peter and flopped near his mother.

Once everyone was munching on something – except Pamela who'd dozed off – Edna's attention focused on Janet.

'So how are you?'

Janet took a slice of offered fruitcake. 'Better. I'm sorry for running off at the zoo. The things you said meant a lot to me.'

Edna waved one hand as though shooing away a fly. 'What I meant was . . .' She paused, leaned closer and murmured, 'Are you all right?' She jerked her chin and cast a glance at Janet's midriff.

Janet nodded. 'I have to say I hate periods, but I was very glad to see it this time.'

'There!' Edna exclaimed matter of factly, her face cheerful again, and touched with a youthful innocence that belied her actual maturity. 'So now you can get on with your life.'

It all seemed so easy on the outside, but what about inside? The memory was still there, festering every so often, ready to jump out and mar the present. 'I suppose so.'

'You'll find a good man. Just like I did.'

'It's early days,' said Janet, then went on to tell her about Jonathan. 'He's just a friend.'

Edna laughed and looked like a girl again. 'Best friends are best loved.'

'You won't tell my mother?'

'Not if you don't want me to, though I can't think why—'

Susan interrupted, her 'Princess Anne' curls dancing around her face in coppery profusion. 'Would you like a fairy cake, Aunty Janet?'

'How can I refuse?' She took yet another cake then turned to Edna. 'You've got lovely children.'

Edna smiled proudly. 'I think so. Do you like children?'

'I like yours. If ever you want someone to take them off your hands for a day out, I'm quite willing to oblige.'

Edna looked surprised. 'And I'm quite willing to let you do that, or at least Peter and Susan. Pamela's a bit too young for you to handle. But I could do with the help.' She suddenly looked very sheepish. 'Normally I wouldn't complain, but there's another on the way.'

'That's wonderful! I'm only too pleased to help out.'

'Can we go to the park, Aunty Janet?' asked Susan who, in the absence of daisies, had made a chain of buttercups, which she was presently wearing around her neck.

'Weston-super-Mare!' shouted Peter who was galloping around in a circle and making clip-clopping sounds. 'I want to ride on the donkeys. Whoooaaa!'

The sun was warm, the trees were green, and Janet had found herself something to do on Saturdays. Rather the children than accompany Dorothea on weekends as well as during the week, and it would help her forget what she couldn't change.

Janet became aware that Edna was studying her thoughtfully. 'You don't need to do it,' she said.

'Yes, I do, Edna. I appreciate you sparing the time to listen to my woes. It's only fair that I do something for you.'

Perhaps her fairy godmother had been sitting in the sycamores, listening earlier that day because the moment Janet stepped into the hall of the house in Royal York Crescent the phone was ringing and Jonathan was on the end of it.

'I managed to get away. Are you free tonight?'

Of course she was!

'Can you get to the Palm d'Or? Do you know it?'

Of course she did.

She told her mother that she was off out. 'We're out too. The Red Cross are holding a charity ball at the Francis Hotel in Bath. Your father's booked us a room.' She said all this without looking up from the letter she was frowning over.

Tonight was the first time for a while that Janet hummed to herself as she chose what to wear. She'd bought a tight skirt in pale blue, a matching, short-sleeved sweater and white 'flatties'. With her dark hair and eyes, she looked and felt like a ballet dancer.

The taxi came at eight. She almost collided with Geoffrey on the pavement outside the front gate. Home for the weekend, he was going out too and was wearing his bicycle clips and a thick duffle coat despite the night being mild.

'Give my regards to Dorothea,' he said.

She looked him up and down, not entirely surprised at the 'beatnik' look he'd adopted. Scruffiness had always sat comfortably with him.

'I didn't say I was going out with Dorothea. Anyway, I didn't know you were that close.'

Geoffrey grinned. 'Come on, Jan. Everyone in trousers has got close – very close – to your friend Dorothea at some time or another. The moment I was out of short trousers and into long ones, they were off!'

Still grinning he closed the door of the taxi behind her and whistled as he got astride his bicycle. Goodness, she thought smiling to herself, Dorothea was too wicked to be believed. What would her mother say?

A pink neon sign outside the Palm D'Or flashed the statement that cocktails were being served. She craned her neck as she handed the taxi driver the fare and waved the change away.

He was there, the colour of the light contorting the colours of his face, the outline of his body.

Over cocktails they talked work. Between mouthfuls of food he talked more of work and she smiled to herself. Dorothea would consider his conversation boring. She found it fascinating.

He tapped at her nose. 'Penny for them?'

'My thoughts?' She smiled and ran one finger around the rim of the wine glass. 'My mother always wanted to be a doctor, you know. My brother's supposed to follow in my father's footsteps, but he's not that keen.'

'Not keen?' Jonathan sounded and looked shocked to his shoes. He poured more red wine into their glasses. 'Why ever not? What job could be more rewarding? What job could be more glamorous?'

They clinked glasses.

'To doctors,' said Janet, the wine, the evening and Jonathan all contributing to repair her confidence and boost her ego.

'To the perfect profession,' he added.

He told her about the newest physiotherapy techniques being used in the treatment of poliomyelitis, infantile paralysis. 'The original exercises were introduced by an Australian nurse, a Sister Kenny. Of course things are moving on, but slowly. Then there's the heat treatment. We put hot cloths on the affected areas in an effort to get them responding, perhaps even repairing themselves.'

'Does it work?'

'It seems to, though the ultimate cure for the disease will be inoculation. It's coming, but . . .' He shrugged helplessly and she read impatience in his expression. 'These things have to be tested. They take time. Too late for my mother,' he added ruefully.

'She must be very proud of you.'

He nodded. 'She is, just as I am of her. We're both very determined to kill this disease dead.'

'What does your father feel about it?'

'Oh, he's not very interested. Mother leaves him to get on and run the farm and he leaves us to do as we please.'

Janet got the distinct impression that his father was shut out from this relationship. Jonathan and his mother seemed extraordinarily close, too close perhaps. She had imagined her sitting weak and fragile in a wheelchair. Apparently weakness didn't come into it.

'You sound completely absorbed by your profession,' she said. 'Will there ever be room in your life for anything or anyone else?' She hadn't wanted it to sound as though she were prying as to his intentions towards her – it just seemed to come out that way.

The swift blink, the tight smile conveyed to her that he'd been half-expecting the question. She was instantly entranced with the way one side of his mouth seemed to curl up higher than the other side, as if both the question and the answer couldn't help but amuse. She also thought of how much he looked like Superman, the Clark Kent version but without the horn-rimmed spectacles.

'I'm just a man. But my work comes first. A woman in my life – any woman – has to take second place.' His smile broke suddenly. 'With one exception of course – my mother. As I've already told you, my choice of career was due to her in the first place. I couldn't get involved with anyone without her approval.'

It was not at all the explanation Janet had expected. His mother had a say in more than his career. It went some way to explaining why he had never tried to seduce her.

He smiled a little wryly and went on. 'I'm afraid I sound a little cold, a little odd perhaps. But believe me, I'm not. It's just that relationships have to be on my terms. I do hope you understand.'

'Of course.' She smiled as if she did, but what exactly did he mean, 'on his terms'?

They talked further about her predicament at the hospital and the possibility of getting another job. 'I can't promise anything,' he said slowly, 'but I will keep my ears open.'

Janet sighed. 'Anything rather than the Catering and Housekeeping Department.'

He insisted on sharing a taxi with her. 'I can't let you go home alone.'

At least he's considerate, she thought to herself as she gathered up her angora cardigan and prepared to leave.

All that Dorothea had said earlier that day seemed to stick in her brain, like melted toffee. But I'm not frigid, she said to herself and suddenly wanted to prove that she wasn't. She made a quick decision. If he tries to kiss me, I'll let him.

It didn't seem likely to happen. At first they sat apart, her hand on the seat, his close by. Lightly at first, his fingers covered hers, then gripped her hand, then ran up her arm, around her neck. He pulled her face to his and gently kissed her lips.

It wasn't exactly passion, but she didn't want passion, at least, not yet. His gentleness and, what she interpreted as sensitivity, was all she needed.

She wanted to say something, wanted to do something, but she wasn't quite sure what. The one thing she didn't want to do was run away. He wasn't threatening like Henry or insipid like Stephen. She didn't feel she wanted to throw herself at him. He was attractive but safe, just like a doctor should be.

The streetlights were out when the taxi pulled up in Royal York Crescent. A small porch lantern had been left on which threw enough light for her to see the pavement, the drive and the steps to the door.

He held her hand and said, 'How about Tuesday? I wish I could do better, but you know how it is in this profession . . .'

'You're a very busy man. Name me a doctor who isn't!'

One more kiss before leaving him in the cab. Pressing her door key against her smile she ran to the front door, the gravel crunching underfoot.

The cab lingered. Jonathan was being considerate, making sure she got to the front door safely. The caring professional, she thought as her feet tapped sharply against the marble steps before she raised her arm to put the key in the door . . . which suddenly sprang open.

Dorothea flew out, her hair in disarray, her lipstick kissed away and a very self-satisfied smile on her face. 'Darling,' she whispered. 'A taxi! How convenient!'

Janet stood transfixed, her jaw dropping as Dorothea waved one hand, her handbag swinging over her elbow as her other hand grappled with the buttons of her suit.

She was amazed to see Jonathan get out of the taxi, open the door and let her in. He shrugged and shot Janet a helpless look, got into the taxi, and closed the door behind him.

With mixed feelings, she watched as it pulled away. What had Dorothea been up to? What would she be up to next?

Some sound registered in the hall behind her where only one table lamp cast a sphere of light over the scattered Turkish and Persian rugs. A pair of feet appeared on the stairs and as they descended swiftly grew into Geoffrey's bare and hairy legs.

'Is she gone?'

Dorothea's dishevelled appearance and her brother's bare legs said it all. Janet stepped into the hall and closed the door behind her.

'What have you two been up to?' she asked, although she already knew the answer. Her parents were staying overnight in Bath. Geoffrey and Dorothea had obviously taken full advantage of the situation.

Geoffrey remained halfway down the stairs, his hair flopped over his eyes. He made no attempt whatsoever to hide his nudity.

Janet shook her head at him. 'How could you?'

He raised his eyebrows just as he used to do as a boy when he'd flushed tadpoles down the lavatory then denied ever having had any. 'What?'

'You and Dorothea. You've been to bed with her.' Sombrely, Janet pointed at the glistening sheath that drooped like a dewdrop at the end of his penis.

'Oh!' he grinned. 'Umm . . . do excuse me. Must go to the lavatory.'

Both hands covering his crotch and the drooping johnny, he bounded noiselessly back up the stairs.

Janet maintained her serious expression until he was gone. Then she rocked with laughter and leaned against the wall for support in case she fell over.

She felt better than she had for a long time even though Dorothea had left in a taxi with Jonathan, a man who had brought something better to her life. Perhaps Dorothea would flutter her eyelashes at him, but she trusted it would make no impression. Jonathan had his own rules about relationships and she trusted him to keep to them.

Later, as she snuggled down beneath the shiny satin of a pale mauve eiderdown and her eyes closed in sleep, it was Jonathan she heard in her head. The foreign voice, the one who had told her not to scream, had melted away – at least for now.

Ten

Charlotte wrenched open the bottom half of the study window. The morning air was humid and she found herself praying for rain. In gathering the files she needed, her gaze lingered on the small drawer in which she'd placed the letter from Josef. Such a lovely man . . .

'You look pensive.'

David's voice made her start. The desk lid rattled as she rolled it firmly shut. 'I've got a bit of a headache.'

David raised his eyebrows in mock surprise. 'At least Janet's got over hers, or I presume she has. She seems a lot brighter this last week, don't you think?'

Charlotte agreed though felt guilty that David had noticed and she hadn't. Damn the letter, she thought, and made a vow to rip it up the moment she got back.

On reaching the office she headed straight for Brookman's door, knocked and entered without waiting for his invitation.

'Do not say a word, dear lady,' he said before she had a chance to open her mouth. 'I have something . . .' he began and reached for the post in his tray.

More Home Office documentation, she decided, in triplicate and couched in the most convoluted English ever invented. She waved it aside. 'I went back to the building site I told you about. The men I suspected of being Polish were gone, whisked away in case I asked any more difficult questions. But I've got a suspicion that they are being employed illegally and are being paid the most meagre of wages. I would think it unlikely that they're paying any taxes on their earnings either.'

He was less than congenial. 'You have no proof!'

'If I get proof, will you investigate? I'll ask the people concerned – I mean the Poles. Not the employers.'

Brookman sighed and flung down his pen. '*If* you can get them to talk. Just remember that if they are being paid the going rate English will suddenly be a completely unknown language to them.'

His attitude annoyed her. These men were *not* being paid the going rate for their labour. Something about their appearance convinced her of it. Now, what was it? Suddenly it came to her. Wellingtons! Wearing cheap Wellington boots on a sunny day was not the norm for men earning good wages.

'I'll find someone to talk. I know I will.'

'Before you go . . .'

Brookman took a large brown envelope from the tray he'd been fussing with earlier and handed it to her. 'It's from our German friend.'

'Oh!' It was all she could say. The envelope felt fairly bulky. She took it into the other office to read. The covering letter was from Josef. The other was from Sherman's adoptive grandmother.

My dear Charlotte,

Signora Carlotti is most concerned that nothing has been resolved following the death of his parents with regard to the future of the little boy who she knows as Carlos. Because she is so far away and is concerned for the boy's welfare, she has asked me to trace the father of the child with a view to the boy going to live with him in the United States of America. She found a letter from one of the clothing parcels that her father used to send over. The orphanage gave it to her when Carlos was adopted along with the name given him at birth and his mother's name.

Matron had broken the rules, but in this case we are glad she did. The father had signed his name on the letter. Using my contacts in both the Red Cross and the US Military, I have indeed traced the boy's father. As you will see from the enclosed letter, Signora Carlotti has written to him and is presently awaiting a response. I have asked her to let me know as soon as she receives this. As you know the child is still in our care here in Germany. We look after him well and keep him occupied on one of our projects, trades and skills with which to build his own future, but nothing can replace a proper family life with people who love him. If his mother does not want him, perhaps you will let me know.

I know you will do your best. The warmth of your humanity has stayed with me over the years and I thank you for letting me into your life.

With warmest regards,

Josef

Warmest regards. Was that all he could say? Had she expected too much?

Feeling slightly wounded by what she could only regard as the sort of signing off one would receive from a close friend, she ripped open the letter from Signora Carlotti. She read it quickly. The Signora was getting concerned. The boy was with strangers in a foreign land. He should be with someone who loved him.

I'll deal with it later, she told herself as she left the building. She also promised herself she'd make enquiries regarding the men on the building site regardless of what Brookman might think. Eventually that is, once she'd coped with the business of the day.

Feeling single-minded rather than curious, she pushed her way through the early morning crowds on their way to shops, banks and offices.

'Yoohoo! Mrs White! Mrs White!'

Charlotte turned round. Mrs Grey was the only person she knew who didn't use her full surname. And there she was, her face pink with effort, she rushed up, her hat tipping to one side and a shopping basket rattling with tins of Spam, beans and corned beef over one arm. She clapped her hand to her mouth before speaking, her eyes two chips of bright blue above her blotchy cheeks.

'I forgot you were out this morning. Polly don't have a key! She won't be able to get in.'

Charlotte glanced at her watch then unlocked her car. 'Never mind. I can dash up and let her in. I've got time.'

The traffic was light and although a bus had broken down on Park Street, Charlotte made good time. As she pulled up Polly was walking through the front gate.

'I've got the key,' Charlotte shouted and rushed breathlessly through the gate too. 'Mrs Grey forgot,' she explained. 'I'll let you in, but I've got to go out again. Can you manage?'

Polly stood saucily, hands on hips. 'No! Them dusters are a bit awkward to use and that whistle on the tea kettle gives me the willies.'

'Sorry!'

'You look all in. Fancy a quick cuppa?'

Charlotte's watch told her she had enough time.

Polly began to tell her how busy they'd been at the pictures the night before. 'They 'ad *Brief Encounter* on last night. God knows, but it's been on enough times. But there you are. Good film, though. Married woman carrying on with married man – at least – I think he was married. Real naughty. Lovely, though. Made me think of the first time I went to see it after the war. Remember who I was supposed to be seeing it with too.'

Polly's reference to adultery infiltrated Charlotte's thoughts and the letters from Germany came into her mind. She asked, 'Would you ever want to turn the clock back – or have the clock catch up with you?'

Polly frowned. 'How do you mean?'

'Well . . .' Charlotte paused. What was the best way to put this? The same way she'd put it to Edna? 'What if something or someone from your past came back?'

'To haunt me?'

'No. I mean *actually* came back and wanted to see you. Your American, for instance.'

'Canadian.'

'Sorry.'

'I don't know.' Polly shook her head. Normally her blonde hair would flop over her eyes. Today it was tucked up in a turban and although there were more lines on her face than there used to be, she wasn't bad for her age.

Charlotte sighed. 'Not an easy question, is it? Old loves. Old indiscretions.' She looked down into her tea and clicked her neatly trimmed nails against the rim of the cup. What would she do? The funny thing was she ached for Josef to be here, but perhaps she was only feeling that way because it could not be so. The unobtainable was bewitching.

'If Carol's dad came back I'd have to let him see her,' said Polly.

'What about Billy?'

'I'd talk to him first.'

Polly tilted her head to one side, her eyes fixed on Charlotte's face. 'Got yer own skeleton in the cupboard then, Charlotte? Some bloke you 'ad a bit of a fling with come back to claim you for 'is own?'

Charlotte almost blushed, but she was used to Polly trying to make her embarrassed. 'No! Nothing quite like that.'

And the strange thing was she was telling the truth. It wasn't like that. The letter sitting in her bureau and the ones that had arrived this morning covered a very specific subject. But she couldn't possibly pass it on until she had gleaned some idea of its likely effect. Edna and Polly had answered in a similar vein. She'd think upon their answers for now and make a decision when the time was right – whenever that was.

'I must be off now,' she said and headed quickly for the door before Polly could ask her anything else she didn't want to answer. She needn't have worried. Polly threw her a perfunctory wave and turned on the vacuum cleaner.

After cutting through Ashley Down and onto the Gloucester Road, she took a left and entered the St Paul's district of Bristol, a place of once superior merchants' houses built in the late eighteenth and nineteenth centuries.

Number 191 Little City Road was a four- or five-storey building with steps leading up to the front door and flanked by an ostentatious though crumbling portico. Another flight led down to a basement through a gap in a row of railings that leaned dangerously outwards, their iron spikes a hazard to passers-by.

Charlotte peered up at it through the car windscreen. The area had gone downhill somewhat since its heyday, but this house looked worse than most. Raw brick showed where flaking stucco had finally fallen off. Net curtains dimmed from white to dog's tooth yellow hung behind windows of scum-covered glass. Charlotte hazarded a guess as to what it was like on the inside and made a mental note to have it inspected.

The three Polish men she was to take to new lodgings and jobs at Pensford, a mining village to the south of Bristol, greeted her with politely shy smiles as they piled into her car.

'Nice to meet you,' she said, and smiled back, barely managing to suppress the urge to wrinkle her nose. The stench of male sweat and mouldy clothes filled the car. Unthinking, she reached for the window handle then paused. What was she thinking of? She couldn't possibly upset their sensibilities. It was her job to be friendly but efficient, to make them feel at home.

She pushed in the clutch and pulled away from the kerb.

Perhaps it might be an idea to run a class on personal hygiene. A vision sprang suddenly to mind. *This is soap. This is a flannel.* Upturned faces, both foreign and British men and women being told that if you didn't bathe regularly you didn't smell too sweet.

Her attention was brought back to reality as the man sitting beside her dealt with the immediate problem.

'We open window?'

Charlotte breathed a sign of relief. 'Yes. It is a little warm, isn't it?'

'No. We stink. The woman in there is dirty.'

'Her house is dirty. So we are not clean,' said a second man who had broad shoulders and a crumpled face that looked as though it had been slept in and refused to flatten out.

'And she won't use bath – won't let us use it,' said the one who had opened the window.

At moments like these, Charlotte was ashamed to be British. Some landladies were pretty fair. Some, like this one by the sound of it, were less so, but beggars couldn't be choosers. Notices were appearing in many boarding house windows saying 'No Pets. No Poles. No Children' and just lately 'No Blacks'. Unlike the Eastern Europeans at least the latter had British passports. They didn't have to carry a document around with '*Alien*' stamped on it.

Blasted woman! Well it would have to be dealt with. It took a right Tartar to deal with a Tartar in this profession – and she was it!

'You must insist on using it,' Charlotte proclaimed stridently as if her word alone was enough to break down the bathroom door. 'A man is entitled to a bath after work. Either she complies or she won't be getting her rent money. There cannot be any logical reason for her denying you a bath. Water is no longer rationed.'

'That is so,' said the first man who had spoken, 'but coal is.'

Charlotte frowned. 'I don't understand.'

'Her coal house is full for the winter so she keeps more coal in the bath,' he explained nonchalantly.

Charlotte noticed how he used his hands to add emphasis to what he was saying as his eyes took in the passing scene. He looked to be in his late twenties and had chiselled features. In the Hitler years, his looks would have been termed Aryan.

'And in the kitchen, and in the cupboard in my room,' echoed the man with the crumpled face.

The third man, who had sunken dark eyes and prominent cheekbones, said something in Polish. The man who had explained about the coal grinned as he interpreted what he'd said. 'He wants to know when he can have a proper home with a bath like he used to have. He will not worry about servants.'

Charlotte's eyebrows rose in surprise. 'No landlady will supply servants!'

The blond man explained. 'You do not understand. He used to have servants.'

'Oh!' Charlotte concentrated on the road ahead. She was learning things about these people all the time. She was also learning more about her own people, and some of it was not very attractive.

'Have you all had breakfast?' she asked as she made off towards Bedminster and the Bridgwater Road that would take them out to the village of Pensford, one of the many mining villages fringing the south and east of the city.

'Oh yes.' It was the first one again. 'Bread and jam.'

'Is that all?' This was terrible.

They all nodded and told her it was so. Her anger at Mrs Halifax, the landlady, plummeted to new depths. Working men needed a decent send-off first thing in the morning. Perhaps the woman had compensated by giving them a packed lunch and it was hidden away in their pockets. But she wouldn't ask just yet. She had to deal with the landlady at the new boarding house. It wouldn't be fair to take her annoyance out on her and Charlotte prided herself on always being fair. She also had to deal with the foreman at the mine.

A woman! A woman! She could see his face now, his mouth twitching as he fought to control the urge to spit or swear. He would hate having to deal with a woman, as if they were of a specific breed incapable of filling in a host of Government forms.

You'll be fine, she told herself, and immediately assumed the confident air of someone who knows how to handle people.

Brent View Cottage was down a narrow lane, which left the main road on the right-hand side after entering the village and crossing over the river just past the Miners' Institute.

Charlotte checked the particulars filled in on the official form. The landlady's name was Mrs Stanley. Hopefully she'd be an improvement on Mrs Halifax, though you couldn't always tell on first sight of either the landlady or the lodgings.

The large cottage was not chocolate box pretty like those set in the rolling hills of Devon or Dorset. This was a mining area, the tail end of the Welsh coal seams. Its no-nonsense construction reflected a hard industry where men still crawled on their bellies in the narrower parts of the seam and clawed the coal from the earth by physical force with a short-handled pickaxe.

The cottage was heavily built of local pennant stone, its roof shading a fretwork weatherboard and set back windows. Scarlet geraniums glared through glass panes and bustled against the trelliswork that formed a porch around the door. It seemed well looked after.

Charlotte breathed a sigh of relief though reserved judgement. But she was hopeful. Despite its austere construction, the place had a far sunnier aspect than the lodging house in St Paul's. As if to confirm first impressions, the sun obliged by peering out from behind a cloud at the same time as Charlotte lifted the brass knocker and tapped on the door.

A pair of bright, deep-set eyes set in a round, friendly face appeared. 'Come in, me dears.' The door was flung wide. Mrs Stanley was a woman of round body and ruddy complexion. Red veins ran together and glowed on each cheek, reminding Charlotte of the wooden Dutch dolls from many years ago, their facial features formed entirely by the vivid application of red and black paint. Red polka dots patterned the old-fashioned apron she wore, the same red as the geraniums, both brightly contrasting with her grey hair, which was gripped firmly by half a dozen steel pincers from the brow backwards on each side of her head. Flappers used the same contraptions back in the twenties to produce Marcel waves. Mrs Stanley was most definitely of that generation, but her head presently resembled an armour-plated porcupine.

They stepped straight from the road into the sitting room where a brass fender glowed against an old-fashioned coal black range. Even though it was summer, a copper kettle puffed away merrily on a hot, black hob. Porcelain cups with gilt borders sat around a red-checked tea cosy in the centre of the table. Tea had brewed.

Charlotte introduced the three men and Mrs Stanley wrote down their names phonetically, exactly as Charlotte pronounced them.

'Jan, Ivan and Paul,' Mrs Stanley stated after failing in her attempts to remember how to pronounce their surnames. Their first names were easier to remember.

As they all made themselves comfortable in Mrs Stanley's front parlour, Charlotte took the opportunity to ask the men if they'd been given a packed lunch. It turned out they hadn't. She gave Mrs Stanley a pleading look and the woman nodded knowingly.

'They'll have a good packed lunch when they go down,' she said emphatically. 'Men 'ave got to be fed right doin' a 'ard job like that.'

Charlotte could have kissed her.

They drank tea and ate digestives while waiting for Mrs Stanley to make up some food to take with them. Charlotte took the opportunity to study closely the place where the men would be staying.

Mrs Stanley, she decided, didn't fall into the same category as Mrs Halifax. The sitting room was furnished with old but solid mahogany furniture dating from the end of the last century. The walls were covered in green and brown Victorian wallpaper and there were thickly patterned rugs on the floor that had a vaguely oriental look about them. Despite the dark decor the room felt warm and the fresh smell of beeswax was evidence to its cleanliness.

Photographs in ebony and plain wooden frames sat on the sideboard and hung from the wall above it on long chains that were hooked to a picture rail. Charlotte got up from her chair and studied a sepia print of a man in dark clothes standing on the deck of a ship.

'My Ernest,' Mrs Stanley explained bustling back into the room with the same sunny disposition as the geraniums sitting on the window ledge. 'Merchant navy. Got torpedoed in the Mediterranean. 'Course, he was only young in that photo.'

'I'm sorry,' Charlotte said assuming he was dead.

Mrs Stanley burst into laughter. 'Oh no! You've got the wrong idea. He ain't dead, me dear. Some Italians in a fishing boat rescued him and, as luck would 'ave it, an old maid with some money owned it. Took a fancy to 'im, she did. And what with that hot sun and warm sea, well, you can guess the rest. He had what he wanted out there and decided not to come home. But I keep his photo 'ere and use 'im as an excuse – just in case any bloke wants to move in on me. And I'm quite comfortable, you see. Ernest said I could keep the cottage though it's been in his family for generations. But I do like meeting people. And I do like male company,' she added with a salacious smirk. 'That's why I take in lodgers.'

Charlotte was still smiling on the drive to the mine. Mrs Stanley had almost made her forget that she still had to face the foreman.

'Nice lady,' said Ivan who had again taken the seat beside her in the car.

'Yes,' said Charlotte. 'I think so too.'

Just as she had expected, the foreman at the mine was surprised at having to deal with a woman. Eyebrows thick as caterpillars beetled over his nose and, although she would stand her ground and make sure things were done properly, he made her feel guilty at being there. Perhaps, she thought, the Poles would be better received if a man had brought them and couldn't help feeling a little regretful on their behalf. But you insisted, she said to herself. You insisted you could manage and Mr Brookman had been fair enough to accept that. He was one of the few who didn't mind whether it was a man or a woman sorting things out – as long as the job was done.

The formalities were completed. Each man produced his identification, a book the size of a passport with the word 'Alien' stamped across the front. The foreman studied each one carefully before handing her 'Authorisation to Employ' slips for each one.

Charlotte started to relax. Perhaps everything was going to run smoothly and she'd be away and back home more quickly than she'd expected. But then she saw the look on Ivan's face. He was staring at something in the vicinity of the foreman's tie and his face was white with anger.

He grabbed the thin, grey book from Charlotte's hand. 'I am not staying here.' His mouth was fixed in a firm, straight line. He spun on his heel and started to walk away.

Charlotte was taken completely by surprise. 'Why? What's wrong?'

Running after him on high but fairly sensible heels, she grabbed his arm before he got clean away and tried to reason with him. 'This man has to look at your identification details before employing you. After that I have to take your book to the police station for stamping because you've changed both your address and your job. Do you understand that?'

'Of course I do.'

Ivan's features were hard as stone. He explained something in Polish to the others, his eyes never leaving the face of the foreman.

Sensing he was being criticized, the foreman's face turned angry. 'They can stop talkin' in that foreign chatter round 'ere. I'm not 'aving it. Tell them that.'

Charlotte spun on him. Her manner was clipped. 'I'll tell them no such thing. This is a free country and they're quite entitled to use whatever language they like.'

'Not 'ere they ain't!'

'Be careful what you are saying, Mr Pratley or you won't be getting any cheap labour from us at all.' Her tone was frosty.

'We pay them well!'

Charlotte put on her most superior manner, sniffed and turned away. 'That's not what I hear. However, we cannot dispute your claim that they have to go through a training period first.'

'Of course they do!' Pratley shouted. 'They get full pay once they've done that.'

'Then I hope it won't be too long,' Charlotte responded, her eyes blazing. 'I'm not here to argue. They want work. You want labour. That's all that matters.'

'I am not working for him!' growled Ivan.

The others looked from one to another, exchanged excited comments in Polish, then looked to Ivan and said something.

'I am not staying,' he said. 'The others are not so sure. They do not wish to upset anyone.'

The foreman waved one brawny arm, an aggressive gesture that failed to impress because anyone watching could see there was fear in his eyes. 'Tell them they can either start now or get out!'

Ivan flung his arm up dismissively, spat on the ground and walked away. Charlotte, not understanding quite what was going on, ran after him. She found him leaning on her car breathing deeply and frowning savagely.

Now it was her turn to be angry. 'What do you think you are playing at? Have you no gratitude for what we are trying to do for you?'

He faced her quickly, his eyes narrowing. 'To you personally, yes! As a country, no!'

Charlotte took a deep breath. She did not understand, but had no intention of failing in her efforts to see these men settled. 'Look! Stay here and calm down. I'll go back and see what the others want to do.'

'They will stay and work. They are new to this country. It is their first job.'

She went back to find out anyway. Sure enough, Ivan was right.

'We stay,' said the one with the crumpled face who had taken his cap from his head and was twisting it nervously, his eyes darting from her to the gross features and piggy eyes of the foreman. The man who couldn't speak English merely nodded. He too had taken his cap off.

The foreman took a watch from his waistcoat pocket, flicked it open and studied the time. 'Well, I can't bloody wait around for your other bloke. He's your responsibility. I've got work to do.'

Charlotte thought about the watch. Surely Ivan wasn't adverse to such a British show of ostentation? The foreman held one side of his coat open as he slid the watch back in its rightful place. Something shone in his lapel. Charlotte narrowed her eyes. It was a badge, nothing more than a red star. She thought she knew what it signified, but couldn't be sure.

Once she'd sorted out bus times with the two men who'd decided to stay she said her goodbyes. They were on their own now – except of course that regular reports would be sent to the Home Office on their behaviour and they had to carry their Alien Book around at all times.

When she got outside Ivan was still leaning over the car,

hands clenched tightly together, his gaze fixed on the horizon.

Outwardly businesslike, but inwardly apprehensive, she opened the driver's side door. She would most certainly be getting to the bottom of this.

'Get in!'

Ivan did as ordered.

He was waiting for her to say something and she was certainly aching to do so. It finally burst out when her grip on the wheel could get no tighter.

'You have to have a job!'

'I know.' He didn't even blink. His voice was steady.

Charlotte moderated her tone. She refused to be angry. 'You cannot stay in this country if you do not get one.'

'I know that too.'

He sounded as though his anger was being reined in but, like a wilful horse, fighting it all the way. If she was ever to help this man she had to gain his confidence and quickly. She wasn't *that* familiar with the road so had to concentrate. Miraculously a tractor pulled out of a field and ambled along in front of them. She changed down a gear or two, sighed and softened her voice. 'I saw the red star. I know what it means.'

'No, you do not!'

His clipped tone surprised her. Had she sounded condescending? She thought not, but took advantage of their slow speed to glance at his face. Anger still furrowed his brow. Well she wasn't stupid and she'd most certainly let him know that.

'Yes, I do know the red star means he's a member of the communist party. But it hardly matters—'

He cut in. 'Did you know that Truman and Churchill handed Poland on a plate to Stalin after the war? Did you know that some of those who had worked for the resistance and then taken jobs with the US or British army were coached off back to Poland whether they wanted to go or not?'

'Well, I didn't really . . .' Charlotte found herself blustering. She hated pleading ignorance, but couldn't help defending her own country. 'But that was yesterday, and tomorrow is—'

'They never got home!'

'Don't bloody shout at me!'

His mouth dropped open. She didn't look the sort to shout like a fishwife or use the language of a docker. But Charlotte hated being shouted at. David had done a lot of shouting – as well as physical abuse – when he'd first come back from the war. She'd accepted it back then with fortitude, but she would not accept it now.

'I am very sorry.'

'That's all right.' She didn't want to hear the details about what had happened to Ivan prior to his arrival in Britain. One man with nightmarish memories was plenty enough to cope with.

Silently they drove to the police station, which boasted the Miners' Institute and a village pub as neighbours. The sun was getting stronger and a heat haze shimmered further up the hill. There was a smell of coal tar as the road started to bake and melt into a black goo that streamed into the gutter.

Charlotte patted her cheeks with the backs of her hands. Surprising how cotton gloves retained their coolness despite summer heat. Her brow was warm too. She pushed a little damp hair back onto her head and sighed.

Her nylons crackled with electricity as she got out of the car. The heels of her court shoes tapped sharply on the pavement and the wide swirl of her calf-length skirt hung limp in the heat.

The police station smelt of old fry-ups and well-stewed tea. Charlotte wrinkled her nose as she pulled the glove off her right hand and passed it into her left. A uniformed sergeant peered out at them through a square window, the sort normally seen in countryside railway stations where the employees spend more time tending the flowerbeds than dealing with trains. She almost felt like asking for a return fare to Paddington, but the sergeant didn't look the sort to take a joke. The Alien Registration Cards were to be stamped for the two who had remained at the mine. Before handing them over she noted the details. Ivan was right. These two had only just arrived.

'More Poles?' The police sergeant eyed the cards and turned a critical gaze over Charlotte, then Ivan who had followed her into the station. His tone was surly. 'We'll be overrun by 'em before very long, coming over 'ere, taking our jobs, taking our women.'

The last comment was obviously aimed at her. He looked her up and down as though she were one of those whose blood ran too hot to resist the overtures of Johnny Foreigner.

Charlotte snatched the cards from him and put her glove back on. 'We need them to rebuild this country! Just as we needed them to fight the enemy during the war.'

The sergeant was having none of it. With a loud thump he stamped the documents as if he were crushing a series of flies.

Slam! A wooden shutter came down.

'Well!' Charlotte was not the sort to leave things like that. Fists clothed in white cotton gloves pummelled the closed shutter. 'I shall be back, sergeant. And I shall report you! Indeed I shall, my good man!'

A hand fell on her arm. 'Lady!' Ivan was looking at her with a mix of confusion and surprise. 'He is not a man. He is a uniform. Men change once they put on a uniform.'

Charlotte came to her senses and pressed her palm against her brow. Her skin was damp and hot. 'This is unforgivable.'

'He is not worth forgiving.'

Charlotte shook her head and took very deep breaths. Ivan had misunderstood. It was losing self-control that was unforgivable. 'Wait outside for me, will you?'

He looked as if he was going to protest.

She assumed a more authoritative air. 'Please! Wait outside for me.'

He did as she requested and left her alone there in the shabby waiting room where the sun tried to shine through dusty windows and brighten the brown walls and sludge-coloured linoleum.

Alone there in the gloom she almost wanted to cry. What was she going to do about Ivan? He had to have somewhere to live and he had to get a job.

Colin! He'd said he would help.

Just before leaving the building she studied the work details on Ivan's Alien Registration Card. Perhaps there was something there that might show the way. She studied it carefully. This was by no means his first job. His last one, in fact, had been as a waiter and had ended in June. No reason was given. So what had possessed a waiter, however menial the job, to leave the comfortable surroundings of a hotel or restaurant and go to work in a mine? Surely he was worth something more? Her thoughts returned to her conversation with Colin and Edna on the day they'd gone to see the crown.

'Are you good with your hands?' she asked him once she was back behind the wheel of the car.

He looked at her coldly. She guessed he was still thinking about the man at the mine. 'I was training to be an engineer back in Poland.'

'But you don't want to be a miner.'

'I will do what I have to do.'

'How do you feel about making children's toys?' she asked.

He didn't answer straight away. She felt his eyes looking at her as she started the car and pulled away. 'It's for a friend of mine,' she added in the hope that might sway his decision and get her out of a jam. Heaven knows what she'd do with him otherwise. No landlady would take a guest that didn't have a job.

'What is he like?'

'He's a war veteran.'

Ivan relaxed.

Charlotte explained things precisely so there'd be no question of him not understanding. 'If he agrees to employ you, then I'll find you somewhere else to stay. Pensford is far too great a distance to travel.'

'Why did you leave your last job?' she asked.

'I upset a customer,' he replied.

She glanced at the clear-cut profile of the man sitting beside her. Ivan reminded her of someone else who'd once been far from home. Josef was rebuilding lives now back in Germany, similar to herself. It occurred to her suddenly that she did not risk any discomfort in what she did. Perhaps it was time that changed. The house in Clifton was large and there were two spare bedrooms in the attic. They had plenty of room. Surely David wouldn't mind?

'We'll drive to Brent Cottage right now and return your friends' documentation to Mrs Stanley. I'll explain to her that you're not staying because the mine does not want you. I think I may have a job for you. It's in the city not the countryside.' The rest of the idea she had in her mind gushed out unabated. 'I think I can offer you a room. My house is certainly big enough.'

He looked surprised rather than relieved, but who could blame him? The poor man had been shuffled around from one place to another since arriving here, dealing with armies of officials and well-meaning people imposing their own personal brands of helpfulness.

'Things will all be sorted out,' she said brightly and truly believed it. Soon the hedgerows were left behind and suburban semis replaced roadside cottages, then rows of shops, through the city and up Park Street to Clifton and home.

Ivan crunched over the gravel behind her to the front door of the elegant Georgian house in Royal York Crescent. Judging by the gleam of the brass letterbox and knocker someone was home and had just finished polishing.

The drone of the vacuum cleaner greeted them as they entered the house. Charlotte smiled. Polly was here and her favourite domestic appliance was out of the cupboard and scooting along the landing. Today was Edna's visiting day. She'd be along later. Hopefully Colin would be with her. He did come sometimes if he could get time off from making rocking horses, scooters and wooden trains with bright red paintwork and whistles that really tooted.

Ivan stood quietly, his gaze travelling the dark cream walls, the curving sweep of the staircase. Charlotte almost felt as if she should apologize for living in such luxury compared to the lodgings he'd been used to.

She showed him into the drawing room. 'Make yourself comfortable while I make tea.'

Edna and Colin arrived just as she was crossing the hall.

'I've got something to ask you,' she said to Colin, taking hold of his arm as if he might try to escape.

'Oh yes?' he said with mock wariness, tipping the wink to a grinning Edna. 'What have you got planned for me now?'

Taking the opportunity of a lull in the vacuuming, Charlotte shouted for Polly to come down, then fetched the tea tray and followed Colin and Edna into the drawing room.

Charlotte introduced Ivan. At the same time she gave Colin a conspiratory look. 'You remember when we went to see the Coronation crown?'

Face bright as a button, Colin walked stiffly across the room and held out his hand to Ivan. 'She means do I remember her asking me to give one of you lot a job,' he said with a wink. 'We can but try, can't we, mate? We can but try.'

Charlotte decided that the two men were best left alone together. 'I'll get more tea,' she said. 'And I expect Pamela would like a biscuit. I've got some iced ones in the kitchen.'

Edna followed her out, Pamela in her arms.

The cream kitchen was made more yellow by the bright sunshine of a late afternoon streaming through the sash windows, the top halves of which were open. Smells of warm foliage and baking earth eased through. So did the lazy sound of bees buzzing and children playing in a garden three or four doors down.

Polly dragged herself away from her work and joined them. She put the kettle on, Charlotte got out more crockery and set it on a tray, then slid the biscuit barrel in Edna's direction.

'Sounds like a sensible arrangement,' Polly said once Charlotte had explained things.

Edna sat subdued, her attention apparently fixed on Pamela who was making a mess with a soggy custard cream. Her thoughts were of Janet. Ivan was nice, and although his accent wasn't that strong, it was there and Janet was bound to notice. She had to say something.

'What about Janet?' It sounded so feeble and she couldn't stop her face from burning with sudden embarrassment.

Charlotte did not appear to notice her discomfort. 'This house is much too big for just us. It really needs filling up. Janet, I am sure, will understand that.'

Edna persisted. 'She might feel uncomfortable having a strange man in the house.'

As if to emphasise the potential threat, the strong sunlight disappeared, blanked out by gathering clouds. The kitchen darkened and a rumble of thunder sounded like the first murmurings of a hungry stomach.

Polly tutted in response to Edna's comment. 'Children should be seen and not heard.'

Edna prickled. 'She's not a child!'

Both Polly and Charlotte were taken aback. They eyed her as if they were seeing her in a new light, the strength and possible anger beneath the soft exterior. For one ghastly moment she was almost tempted to tell Charlotte why her good intentions might very well backfire. But she couldn't. She'd made a promise she would not tell. Janet would have to deal with it herself.

Charlotte was pouring dark sweet sherries into crystal glasses when Janet got home. Polly had gone, but Edna and Colin had stayed.

'Darling,' she said, decanter in one hand and Ivan's glass in the other, 'do come and meet our new houseguest. He'll be staying in the attic for the time being until he can get a place of his own.'

'Really?' Completely unsuspecting, Janet stretched out her hand and smiled at the broad-shouldered young man with the fine features who looked smart on first inspection, though on second look his shirt cuffs were frayed and his suit smelt of mothballs. A young doctor in need of assistance, perhaps? His face certainly looked familiar.

'Pleased to meet you. I'm going to presume you're studying medicine. Am I right?'

To her great surprise he bowed slightly and clicked his heels together. 'Miss Janet. No. I am not.' He spoke very precisely, almost to the extent of being overly curt.

She had a strong urge to back away from him, but forced herself to stay. 'Have we met somewhere before?'

His eyes were grey and striking, as if an artist had outlined them with a graphite pencil.

His smile was slow, almost secretive. 'I do believe so, but you would not perhaps remember. My name is Ivan Bronowsky.'

Her smile chilled at the sound of his voice.

'Ivan is from Poland,' her mother explained.

'Really?' Janet felt the blood draining from her face. Her mother, *her own mother*, had brought a foreigner into the house. How could she? How could she?

'I'm sure we'll all get on famously,' said Charlotte, a picture of self-assurance in a soft shade of jade with a rope of pearls at her throat.

Janet controlled the urge to take flight, lock herself behind her bedroom door and not come out until this man was gone. But he wouldn't be going, she reminded herself, and she wasn't at all sure how to deal with it.

The conversation was all about work. Colin held centre stage and Ivan said all the right things in the right places, but in the wrong accent.

When it was time for Edna and Colin to leave, Edna went out to the car ahead of everyone else and asked Janet to help her with the children. Colin dawdled by the door still talking to Ivan.

Once the children were inside the car, Edna drew her to one side. 'I hate leaving you like this. Will you be all right?'

Janet stared at some point beyond Edna's head and swallowed. 'I can't believe it. I've seen him before, and that voice . . . I've heard it before.'

Edna's face was clouded with concern. 'My God! You don't really think it's him, do you?'

Janet covered her face with her hands. They fell away when she shook her head and Edna saw that her eyes were screwed up with despair. 'I don't know! But all I do know is that I'll be sharing a house with him and I don't know how long I can stand it.'

After Edna had gone, Janet made an excuse about having another headache and went to her room. She waited until she heard their lodger climbing the creaking stairs that led to the attic. Once she was sure he was up there, she went downstairs to confront her mother.

Everything was in darkness but, just as she'd expected, a light shone from beneath the study door, which was slightly ajar. Her mother often worked late in there when the rest of the house was sleeping. She pushed it open without knocking. Tonight it appeared that Charlotte had already gone to bed, but forgotten to switch the light off. The room was empty, the green china shade of the brass-stemmed desk lamp had been left on, its light focused on an open file lying on the desk.

Intending merely to turn the light off, her attention was attracted to a name she thought she recognized. Someone called Josef was enquiring of the whereabouts of Edna Burbage. Wasn't that Edna Smith's name before she married?

A sound from the hall made her turn round. Her mother did not look too surprised, merely distracted.

'I came down for some water,' said Janet. 'I noticed you left the light on.'

Charlotte smiled. 'Thank you, dear. I've got work to do in here, but I thought I'd clear the washing up rather than face the wrath of Mrs Grey in the morning. But while you're here, I have to say I would wish you to be a little more friendly to Ivan. You were positively cold tonight. Do you think you could manage that?'

Janet considered her mother was being insensitive, at least towards her. Couldn't she see how difficult this was for her? But she couldn't say so, not without betraying the reason why he made her feel uncomfortable. Instead she asked, 'Is he staying?'

'Of course he is.'

Janet leapt on the only chance she had. 'Daddy might not like it.'

'Well!' That was all Charlotte said, hurling the word into the air like a full stop dropped onto the end of a sentence. It was final.

She sat herself in the swivel armchair behind the desk, her attention already straying to the open file and the letters within. 'I phoned him tonight,' she said briskly. 'He's quite happy about it, in fact he said it would make a nice change to have some male company around. I am really amazed at your attitude, Janet. I've always thought you were like me in many ways. You're not usually so off with people like Ivan.'

'It's just . . .' Janet began. Mentally, she berated herself. Say it! Say it now, tell her why you can't help being hostile, especially about the voice, that voice she still remembered. But she couldn't say it and instead settled for, 'It just takes some getting used to.'

Charlotte sighed and rubbed the tiredness from her forehead as she settled down at her desk. 'Well, there are only two choices. You either get used to it or you don't.'

Dismissed! Dismissed like some schoolgirl in the headmistress's study. But she didn't go, just stood there, waiting for something else to be said.

Her mother seemed to have forgotten she was there. She had shut the file in which the reference to Edna appeared and was fussing with other bits of paper, placing them on top the file, picking up a pen, assuming an instant busyness.

Get out! Get out! Get out!

Janet slammed the door behind her. That night she locked her bedroom door and lay fully clothed on the bed, listening to Ivan moving about in the room immediately above her own. Eventually the tell-tale sound of springs in a tired mattress assured her that he'd got into bed. Soon he'd be sleeping, not prowling the house.

I can't stay here, she decided, her eyes suddenly snapping wide open. 'I *won't* stay here!' She planned what she must do. First, a new job. Then a place of her own.

Down in the study, Charlotte sighed and buried her head in her hands. Too many problems, she thought. There are too many problems in this world without having a daughter who was old enough to know better. Goodness, she thought, I was married at her age.

Now she was alone, it was safe to take the file referring to Edna from beneath the pile of papers she had used to conceal it. She took out the latest letter from Josef stating that the party concerned wanted a response to their enquiry about Edna Burbage. The adoptive parents had been in Germany because the father was a military attaché at the embassy. They'd gone skiing one weekend and got caught in an avalanche. Carlos had been left behind at the chateau they'd been renting. The grandmother was disinclined to have him back in Brazil, hence Josef's involvement.

Good God, she thought, Edna's got enough to contend with; a disabled husband, another child on the way. Would she really want to know about her firstborn?

Brookman's words came back to her. *Best say she's dead . . .*

Yes! Tell them that, then tear the letters into little pieces as if neither they nor Edna had ever existed.

So far she had merely delayed doing anything, had told Josef that she was in the process of trying to trace Edna. She felt guilty about holding things up, but she had to be sure. Give it a little while longer and she would know exactly what to do.

Eleven

At the end of a showery Tuesday, a rainbow spanned the Avon Gorge. Polly spotted it and decided it was a good omen. Today would be the day to tell Billy about her plans for a new life in Australia.

He picked her up from Charlotte's at about four o'clock – nothing unusual about that. But something was different. The van looked too shiny, too new.

Australia suddenly took a back seat. Polly frowned at the gleaming black bodywork. 'Have you polished this van?'

Billy winked. 'It's a new one. Nice, innit?' He said it as though new vans were easily found and easily bought, then saw her look of disbelief. 'Not really new,' he added almost apologetically. 'But newer than the old one.'

Polly frowned at him in a practised way, designed to burn into his brain and force an explanation. 'Are you 'aving me on?'

''Course not, Poll! It's all above board, honest! You know me.'

'That's what I'm afraid of, Billy, and honesty don't come into it!'

'Trust me. It's all paid for. And,' he added, a joyous look on his face, 'it's all mine – well, just for now.'

Polly eyed him warily and shook her head. 'It had better be just for now, Billy Hills, or I'll have them same words done on yer tombstone: Here lies Billy Hills – Just for Now! That's after I've killed ya!'

As they drove across Durdham Down Billy said, 'Gotta

pop up the Gloucester Road a minute. Bit of business to attend to.'

Polly didn't argue. There was no rush and she quite liked driving past the queues standing four deep and fourteen long at the bus stops. In fact, it made her feel like a queen and she was almost tempted to give a royal wave, all slow and serene as though she were saving her energy for better things. Meg would get Carol's tea when she got home from school and it was a Tuesday. Polly didn't work at the pictures on a Tuesday.

Billy cut down from Clifton onto Gloucester Road and towards Ashley Down where people lived who had money, but weren't quite as refined as those in Clifton. They eventually stopped outside a house that had high walls and iron gates.

Polly's eyes opened wide with surprise. 'Bloody hell! Who do we know who lives 'ere?'

'Great mate of mine,' said Billy tipping his trilby back on his head as he gave her a quick peck on the cheek. 'Won't be long.'

Billy went through the gates, the gravel grinding underfoot as he bounced over the drive and up to the front door. At first sight his thin frame and the imposing façade seemed to have little in common. Then it occurred to her that he'd taken it in his head to rob it. No. Of course not. Silly cow! Did burglars walk up bold as brass to the front door? Not unless they were stupid. Well . . . possibly.

She leaned forward so she could see the house better. It wasn't too old, which was just as well because she wasn't too fond of old places, but this particular place did have a certain grandeur. She liked the 'Odeon' style, the sleek white façades and black, metal-framed windows. She'd seen them before from the top of a number thirty-six bus out at Brislington near the Bath Road. There was a whole rank of them there just past the White Hart. This place was posher and bigger. Polly was very impressed. White steps led up to square pillars supporting a curved canopy above a flush-fitted front door. Curving windows from either side of the door swept off round the corner of the house.

It was not yet dusk so there were no lights on in the shiny white house. Shame, thought Polly, squinting severely in an effort to see inside. She liked looking inside people's houses, admiring their dining suites and envying their carpets. That's why she always went upstairs on the bus – besides having a smoke, that is. Being nosy was fun.

Fifteen minutes later Billy came out beaming and bouncing his way back to the van. Except for the fact that his clothes weren't as good as they used to be, no one would ever guess that he didn't own much and kept his wealth in a tea caddy rather than in a bank.

'All done!' he said as he slid back onto the warm leather of the driver's seat.

Polly eyed him warily. 'What's all done? Who lives there? What have you been up to?'

'Now don't you worry yerself.'

'I do worry, Billy Hills! And I want to know *now* what you've been up to. I'm getting out of here and I'm not getting back in—'

Billy reached for the door handle and pulled it shut. 'Calm down! Not here!' The cocky exuberance was gone from his voice. He sounded anxious. 'Not here,' he said and nodded towards the house. Two men had come out. They were broad-shouldered, wore double-breasted suits and felt hats. They stood either side of the door eyeing the van like a pair of hungry wolves.

Polly caught the fear in his voice and felt her stomach sink to her knees. It wasn't the first time Billy had erred slightly off the straight and narrow. He was no saint and she was not usually a worrier, but there was always a first time and this was it.

'What have you been up to?' she asked as they drove off.

'I'll tell you when we get home.'

She let it be, but continued to worry. As he drove Billy licked the sweat off his top lip. It hung in beads on his forehead too. Polly eyed him with an air of misgiving. She'd loved the house he'd taken her to. Judging by the outside she'd love the inside even more. But Billy and his 'business' exploits were a continual concern. Her marriage had not been made in heaven – for a start they'd never have let Billy in.

Meg put egg and chips on the table when they got home and the smell of the suet they'd been fried in necessitated the opening of the living room window.

Carol was full of chatter about what she'd done at school and rattled a tin under their nose. 'We're collecting for the Peskylot Children's Villages,' she said proudly. 'It's for all the little children with no mummies and daddies and no house to live in.'

Billy looked to Polly for an explanation. 'Who the 'ell are they?'

'I think she's got the name wrong. It's foreign,' explained Polly. 'Her ladyship – 'er up Clifton – has got a hand in it, among other things.'

Polly made no apology for speaking about Charlotte in such a disparaging tone. Even though her jealousy for Charlotte had lessened over the years she couldn't get out of the habit of treating her with less than respect.

Billy obligingly put half a crown in Carol's collecting tin. Polly raised her eyes to heaven. 'Generous bugger! Charity begins at 'ome. Ain't you 'eard that?'

Billy laughed like a ten-year-old as he grabbed the tin from Carol, shook it maraca style over his head and danced around the room with Carol in hot pursuit.

'It's not really called Peskylot,' Polly explained to Billy after they'd eaten and she was drying the dishes while Meg did the washing. The collecting tin for the Pestalozzi Children's Homes was on the sideboard. Carol was out in the street with other kids swinging on a rope that had been strung over a lamppost.

'I knew that! I ain't daft, am I?'

Polly grimaced, the grinding of her teeth almost painful to her jaw. 'I do wonder at times, Billy Hills. And don't duck down behind that paper. I ain't daft either and I still want to know what you've been up to!'

'Later, love,' he said, his head disappearing behind the *Evening Post* which Meg's friend, Bridget, had brought round for him. No one had got round to telling the old Dutch that Billy couldn't read much beyond his own name. At the moment he was looking at a cartoon strip, the sort that didn't have any words.

'Billy! I want a talk with you.' Polly gave Meg a meaningful look.

Meg immediately put down the plate she was washing and wiped her hands.

Polly slammed her hand down on the newspaper. Billy looked up at her nervously, hoping Meg would stay if only long enough to build up his courage.

But Meg was having none of it. 'I'm off to see Bridget,' she said and left the kitchen.

Billy sank lower in his chair as if that would make him less noticeable and not worth having a go at. But there was no getting away with it. They were alone and Polly had her arms folded, was stretched to a full five feet hardly anything, and her jaw was as square as Desperate Dan's. Billy was trapped. It crossed his mind to sugar the pill a little. His face brightened. His hand dived into the inside pocket of his jacket.

'Here,' he said bringing out a roll of grubby ten shilling and pound notes. 'Have a couple of pounds. Get yerself something nice.'

Polly stared at the money. A smart little black dress she'd seen in Rollos Modes, an expensive dress shop in North Street, Bedminster, danced like Cyd Charisse into her mind.

Billy's face brightened. It looked as though he was off the hook.

Polly's moment of weakness passed. Cyd Charisse danced

out of her mind, replaced by a mean, scrawny little guy with a cheeky patter. 'Bloody hell, Billy. You're a soddin' crook. Do you know that? I don't know what the bloody 'ell I'm goin' to do with you!'

Billy got to his feet and tried smiles and a few soft words. 'Now come on. You don't really believe that sweet'art. You know I do it all for you.'

He attempted an embrace. Polly brushed him away. 'Do all what for me, Billy?'

She glared at him in the same way she did at Carol about torn school clothes or a cauliflower ear appearing on Bully Bradford from next door.

Billy tried one more time. 'Darlin'—'

Polly stood firm. 'Go on. Tell me all about it.'

Slowly it came out. He was running bets for the man who lived in the house at Ashley Down. He was one of many, but he reckoned he had the best pitch – up near the Rovers Football Ground on a Saturday afternoon, which meant he also got a lot of punters for the dog track on the night.

'Which means I make more than anyone, far more than the geezer expects.'

The moment he said that, Polly knew what he was doing. 'You're creaming off! You're keeping some of the money!'

'Yeah, but—' Billy began, his broad grin still intact, his head held to one side, a thing he always did when he was about to make feeble excuses.

'But nothing! I saw they blokes that came out of that house. They make James Cagney look like Pinocchio! You've got to stop.'

Polly was angry. Then Billy turned on the boyish charm and she found herself weakening. The toe-rag still had the cheeky grin that had warmed her heart when she'd first met him. That grin had helped her forget the glamour of the Americans and Canadians she'd known. Sometimes she wished it hadn't.

'It'll be OK,' he said with a disarming smile. 'I can't lose.'

Polly felt as if her blood was turning to steam. 'Lose! Are you mad? Of course you can lose. Lose the money and lose your freedom if the police catch you. Lose yer arms if this geezer finds out you're creamin'. You know I hate you getting involved with blokes like that.'

He had done it before. On those occasions his pitch hadn't been so good and the money earned hadn't been enough to compensate for having to leg it once the cops turned up. This time he told her, it was different.

'Different? Of course it's different! He's a crook! He'll break your legs if he finds out you're keeping some of the money and only passing on a few of the bets.'

'He won't. He's getting a very good cut. He's satisfied. Believe me.'

Polly poked her hair back behind her ears as she thought things through. She could see it all now, Billy bruised and battered by the two thugs she'd seen at the house in Ashley Down. It was almost preferable to see him nabbed by the law and banged up in clink.

Billy's face went all soft and boyish. 'Polly.' He reached out for her.

She avoided him, her features hard-edged. This was not what she wanted. This was not the sort of life she'd envisaged having with him. Security and some sort of status would have been nice, not this worry, not *this* kind of excitement. She turned her back on him and stared out of the kitchen window at the ragged grass and rambling weeds of the back garden. A privet hedge ran round the garden on all sides and there was an apple tree in one corner. It was basic and the rent was paid, but she badly wanted something better.

Billy came up behind her, wrapped his arms around her and gave her breasts an affectionate squeeze. 'I'm doing it all for you, darling – for you and Carol. You always wanted a better life and, so far, you ain't had it the way you wanted it. And it's all my fault.'

Interpreting her silence as compliance, he kissed her ear. 'I want to take you away from all this. Believe me, sweet'art, I want something better too.'

Without him knowing, Billy had given her the cue for mentioning Australia. Polly turned and looked at him. There was anger in the stiffness of her body, but a soft smile pricked at her mouth. 'Cocky swine!'

He grinned, presuming that it was all over, he was forgiven and everything would go on as before.

'Well, I've got me own plans, Billy Hills,' she said as she thought about what she had to say. She smiled and stroked a limp lock of hair back from his forehead. Grey strands were sprinkled among the brown. A few more lines creased his face, but he still looked impish even though he was fast approaching middle age.

Billy acted adamant. 'I'm gonna give you the life you really deserve, Poll, honest I am.'

'Do you really mean that?'

He placed his hands on her hips and drew her closer. ''Course I do.'

All the old hopes resurfaced. 'I know just the place.'

'Good,' he said, his breath warm and unsuspecting against her ear.

She nuzzled his cheek, then his ear and said, 'Australia!'

The word hit Billy like a sledgehammer. 'What?' He immediately held her at arm's length, shock splashed all over his face.

'Australia,' Polly repeated, rushing her words before he had time to leg it. 'Ten pounds each. That's all it costs for a brand new life, opportunities in a land where the sun always shines.' She didn't give him the chance to backtrack. 'Sunshine. Wide open spaces. Big houses with their own swimming pool. Think of it, Billy. Brighter weather and better job prospects.' Eyes and voice shone with enthusiasm.

If Polly hadn't been besotted with the vision in her mind, she would have seen Billy's terrified expression. 'That'll cost money.'

'Ten pounds each.'

He was nervous. 'But we need to talk about it a bit, look into things and that.'

Polly disregarded the hesitation in his voice and the panic in his eyes. Suddenly her fears about him being beaten to a pulp or ending up in jail were forgotten as the visions and hopes of a new land whizzed around inside her head. 'On second thoughts I'd better take that,' she said and grabbed the bundle of banknotes from his weakened grasp. 'We'll need it in Australia and if we time it right it don't matter if you get found out. We'll be too far away for them to do anything about it. I'll write tomorrow. OK?'

Billy felt as though a southpaw had laced one into his midriff. His jaw slackened and his grin hung limp on his lips.

Polly pushed his jaw closed. 'Australia won't let in blokes who look like a bloody goldfish.'

He gulped. 'What about Carol?'

Polly brushed imaginary flecks from his collar then gently slapped at his cheeks, her own face bright with joy. 'She'll love it.'

'What about Meg?'

Polly paused. This was something she hadn't quite figured out yet. Bluffing would do for now. 'She'll come.' She tried to persuade herself that she would though she knew it wasn't likely.

Billy knew too. He shook his head. His expression was uncharacteristically serious. 'She's too old, Poll. I don't think they let in anyone over forty.'

Polly bit her lip. 'I'll find out.'

It seemed ungrateful to regard Aunty Meg as an encumbrance. After all she'd been so good to her over the years. But she wasn't going to let this chance pass her by. Like an unwelcome stranger she turned her back on the problem. Somehow she'd think of something. In the meantime . . .

'We won't tell Meg just yet.'

Realizing he was cornered, Billy looked distinctly pale. Opening his mouth, thinking he could voice important reasons why they shouldn't go, turned out to be a waste of time. Nothing came out.

Polly, her eyes bright with excitement, picked up a tea towel, then a plate and proceeded to rub away at it nervously though it had long dried of its own accord. 'Wait until we've got a sailing date. Meg will probably be pleased to have the house all to herself. The council won't mind.'

If asked just a few moments later she would not have been able truthfully to state just how Billy felt about emigrating because she didn't want to hear any objections or obstacles to going. At present she didn't want to face Aunty Meg's comments on the subject or face the stirrings of guilt that could very well prevent her from achieving her dream. Meg had taken care of her since her parents had died. She had also taken care of Carol while Polly had enjoyed herself or gone to work. The truth about how she might respond lurked deep in her heart, too deep to be confronted.

Edna covered herself quickly after the doctor had finished his investigation. The indignity of an internal examination was something she hated. The upside to a visit to the pre-natal clinic was that she was given free supplies of orange juice and cod liver oil, which came in square shouldered bottles. The juice was thick, sharp and had an odd aftertaste. Adding a tablespoonful of sugar made it taste better. Cod liver oil could not be improved and stank of fish. The nose had to be pinched firmly before it could be swallowed. The bottles were placed in a brown paper carrier bag once she'd explained that her car was in the garage and she'd be getting the bus home. The nurse pursed her lips and one or two of the other women there eyed her enviously. Not too many women could drive a car. Those that hadn't walked there had caught a bus.

Outside the clinic she took a deep breath. Peter and Susan

were at school and stayed in to dinner so she didn't have to rush back. She was halfway to Nutgrove Avenue. Reluctantly dutiful, she decided to make the extra effort to visit her parents.

You don't have to, said a warning voice within. 'I do have to,' she said out loud, then turned to Pamela and said. 'Let's go and see Granny and Granfer. Pamela gave a quizzical glance then went back to the challenge of undoing the button on her ankle-strap shoe.

She took a bus to the centre, then changed to another one that took her to St John's Lane where the bus conductor helped her get off, holding the carrier bag of cod liver oil and orange juice and assisting with the unfolding of Pamela's pushchair, even holding up the bus until the child was safely reinstalled.

A bell signalling lunch sounded as she passed Victoria Park School. Droves of children poured out of the doors and scampered like mice towards the group of mothers waiting patiently by the gate. Steam from the school kitchen rose into the air along with the smell of overcooked potatoes and sliceable custard. Edna remembered her own mother waiting there, determined she'd eat lunch at home rather than muck in with the riff-raff who stayed in for dinner.

'Sixpence does not feed a growing child,' she used to say. 'Not properly anyway.'

Nutgrove Avenue was almost deserted when Edna got there, the only movement from houses on the sunny side of the road where blinds of striped deckchair material hung over front doors. The sun was warm, even for September and shadows fell like black pools across the road.

As she got closer to the house in which she'd grown up, a shiver of apprehension ran through her. Since the deterioration of her mother's mental health, the duty had become an ordeal.

How would she be? Edna asked herself, pausing before jerking the pushchair through the narrow entrance and over the small area of red and black tiles that lay before the front of the house.

The outside door was open. The inside one was closed but unlocked. Dragging the pushchair behind her, she reached for the handle, her fingers stopping just short of it as her stomach churned. No one had seen her arrive. If she turned now and dashed for the bus, no one would be the wiser and she'd save herself the ordeal of seeing her mother as she was, and her father trying to cope.

In a sudden rush of bravery, she told herself not to be a coward, grabbed the handle, turned it decisively and pushed the door open.

The hall seemed dimmer and smaller than usual. A profusion of coats hung from the hallstand, too many for it to handle.

'Don't like!' Pamela wailed.

Edna tried to quieten her, but couldn't help wrinkling her nose at the smell of half-done housework, stewed food and unclean underwear.

Again she contemplated leaving before being discovered, but a door creaked open at the back of the house and her father's figure lumbered into the passageway. His tired expression evaporated the moment he saw her.

'It's our Edna! I didn't know you were coming. Well, there's a surprise!'

'I thought I'd call in,' Edna began, searching for the right words at the same time as noting the grubbiness of her father's clothes and the fact that his shirtsleeves were rolled above his elbows and that soap suds were running down his arms.

'She's in there,' he said and pointed timidly towards the door of the front parlour.

'In there?' Edna raised her eyebrows.

Her father shrugged apologetically. In the past the room had only been used at Christmas or for some family celebration. 'She insists,' he said weakly.

Leaving the pushchair out in the passage, Edna pushed at the door. Stale food and leaked urine combined to sting her nostrils. The curtains were drawn. The newly acquired television set flickered like a warning beacon in the corner nearest the window. Plump in flannelette nightwear and buttoned down slippers, her mother stared at the screen, her features made ghostly grey by the monochrome brightness of the test card.

This was not the same Ethel Burbage who had forced her to give up her Sherman, who had sent her away to have the child in secret. The shell, the looks of the woman were unaltered except for the increase in weight, but something was missing. It's as if she's dying bit by bit, thought Edna, a little of her mind, perhaps her soul, leaving for heaven – or hell – every day.

Her mother began muttering to herself. 'Damned sound! If this sound doesn't sort itself out, then back to the shop it goes!' She twiddled the knobs.

'There's no programmes on yet,' her father said, his voice heavy with melancholy. He turned to Edna and shook his head, the flesh of his face slackening to a sad softness that lengthened his jowls and made his eyes look saggy. 'Sometimes I think she sees things in that screen that no one else can.'

Ethel turned suddenly, pouted and rubbed her chin over her shoulder like a spoilt child. 'I'm hungry.'

Edna noticed the plate sat on the floor beside the armchair. Her father leaned closer to her ear and explained. 'She can't remember eating. That's why she's getting so fat.'

'I heard that!' Ethel Burbage looked Edna up and down. 'So's she! Look at her! Like a little fat pig. Eats more than me she does. Always has done!'

Her lips made a smacking sound as she sucked them into her mouth. Edna wanted to be sick. For the first time in her life she was seeing her mother without her teeth and untidier than she could ever remember.

'She's not herself.' Her father groaned and seemed to sink against the wall.

Pamela began to wail again. Her father took his chance. 'I'll take Pamela out in the garden with me.'

Edna went out to the front door and took a breath of air before re-entering the stuffy front room. She forced herself to smile as she approached the bundled figure and bent low so that their faces were level. 'Mother?'

There was a blank look in the eyes where once there had been a determined hardness. Edna explained things very slowly. 'Do you remember me telling you that I'm having another baby, another grandchild for you?'

The vague look in her mother's eyes suddenly cleared. 'Another one? At your age?'

Edna flinched. 'What's my age got to do with it? I am married. You do remember you've got three other grand-children, don't you?'

Her mother sniffed and patted the unkempt hair that straggled over her shoulders. 'You should control yourself! Men can't. Men are animals. Like that Colin . . . even when they haven't got any legs they're animals!'

Edna shot upright. If anything made her see red, it was criticism of her husband. 'Colin is not an animal! He is a kind and loving man and I'm very lucky to have him!'

Her mother raised her head stiffly, the mocking smile of old suddenly reappearing on her face, a brief though un-welcome respite from the condition that was gradually killing her mind. 'Well, that's certainly true. You're soiled goods, my girl. If he ever finds out about your little problem, your little *black* problem—'

This was pure venom. Edna cut her off. 'Colin does know! I told him years ago.'

'Hah! That's what you say!'

Edna got to her feet, her face flushed. She felt angry and

exasperated. It had been hard enough getting through to her mother in the past, now it was almost impossible.

'You're getting worse as you get older, Mother—'

'Mother? Who are you calling Mother? You're not my daughter. Wouldn't want you as a daughter. Look at you! Simpering little mouse. Drop yer drawers for the first man to show an interest because you've got no choice. That's your sort!'

Edna was speechless. Weakness of mind should, in her opinion, have made her mother less abrasive, more approachable perhaps. This was certainly not the case. Despite her senility, despite the growth of her body and the shrinking of her mind, Ethel Burbage still had the power to reduce her daughter to tears.

Chest heaving with subdued sobs Edna rushed from the room, along the passage and out into the back garden where her father grew prize chrysanthemums in a lean-to greenhouse. Pamela was in his arms and he was pointing at the big round flowers and telling her each of their names, not their generic names, but those he himself had given to each flower.

'This brownish-gold one here I call Edna after your mother. When I'm talking to the plant I pretend that it's her—'

'Dad! I'm going!'

She tugged Pamela out of his arms, wincing as her strong little legs kicked in protest.

'No! Don't want! Don't want!'

'We have to get out of here!' Edna's words were strangled by tears.

Face anxious, his fists clenched, her father ran after her. 'Edna? What did she say?'

Tears would flood any explanation. Best to turn her flushed face away and run back inside despite the fact that Pamela pressed heavily on her stomach. Pamela brushed her small hands at her mother's tear-filled eyes.

'Don't cry, Mummy.'

She didn't stop until she was outside the front door, her father still agitated and frowning anxiously into her face. 'What did she say?'

'She disowned me.'

'Edna. You shouldn't take too much notice of what she says any more. She ain't been right lately and she's getting worse.'

Edna fastened Pamela back into her pushchair out by the front door without saying anything. Her father tapped his pipe against the solid stone of the house. His fingers trembled. He tried again. 'You saw what she was like up at your 'ouse on Coronation Day.'

Edna straightened and looked into the craggy face of her father, noted the diminishing hair and the red capillaries amongst the yellow at the edges of his eyes. He looked pathetic, but then he'd always been pathetic. And so had she. Her mother had seen to that.

Edna said exactly what was in her heart. 'I don't care if she is ill. I hate her. I never realized it before. But I've always hated her!'

The words surprised her as much as they did her father.

'Edna! She's your mother!'

'And I'm her daughter and I'm giving her back as much sympathy and understanding as she's ever given me.'

She saw him blanch, his eyes flicker as he attempted to take in words said in a tone alien to his daughter's nature.

Edna left. Tears of anger stung her eyes as she walked quickly away from Nutgrove Avenue and her mother. But walking wasn't fast enough. 'Blasted car!'

Without looking back she left Nutgrove Avenue, cut through the park and made her way along St John's Lane to the bus stop. There was a sick, heavy feeling in her stomach that made her wish she hadn't carried Pamela at all. Just strain, she told herself, you'll be fine once you're sitting on the bus.

Buses along St John's Lane were frequent and the bus conductor was helpful. 'Come on then, love. Leave the push-chair to me.'

By the time she'd changed buses at the Tramway Centre the pain had subsided and her face felt cooler. Just as well; she didn't want Colin to see her like this. He didn't deserve it.

That night she dreamed a woman who looked like her mother was brandishing a spear and stabbing her in the stomach. When she awoke she was sweating and felt a sticky moistness between her legs.

Colin stirred beside her. 'Are you all right?'

'I need to go to the bathroom.' She struggled out of bed, both arms over her stomach, and tried to control her panic. She was only five months.

'Edna?' Colin sat up in bed, his arms braced to hold him upright. His face was creased with worry.

'I'll be fine.' Gasping for breath, Edna staggered to the door and along the landing.

'Edna!' The anxiety in his voice followed her to the bath-room.

'There's nothing you can do,' she shouted back, her tears mixing with the moisture running from her nose and mouth, a disgusting predicament but unavoidable.

The pain was terrible. She wanted to scream, but if she did that the children would wake and Colin was likely to panic and crawl to her aid. She didn't want that. Whatever hap-pened she was by herself. Thousands of women went through this. She wasn't the first. Best grit her teeth and bear it. Her mother's voice was with her. *You brought it all on yourself, my girl.*

It wasn't Pamela she blamed for kicking her stomach, but her mother for spoiling the day.

Spasms of pain seared her stomach and she tasted blood on her lips. She closed her eyes and told herself she could do it.

Although Colin's legs stood in their usual place in the

corner of the bedroom and he could not follow her, Edna felt his presence as the small form slid out of her body and onto the floor.

Twelve

The kitchen was Janet's favourite room at the house in Royal York Crescent. Daylight filtered down from street level and into the basement courtyard at the front. The rear door and windows looked out onto lawns, shrubs and groups of tea roses in circular beds. Pine cupboards with round, white china handles stretched from floor to ceiling. A large grey and white enamel stove sat next to a new and very fat fridge on one side of the room and there was a butler's sink below the window on the other side. Red and black quarry tiles covered the floor on which sat a large pine table, scrubbed to near whiteness by Mrs Grey's constant elbow grease.

Because it nestled below ground, had south facing windows, and had the benefit of Mrs Grey who insisted on baking her own bread, *None of that sliced muck*, the room was warm and always smelled good. This was where Janet had always felt safe and cosseted, like a fledgling bird in a cosy nest, but since Ivan's arrival she'd avoided it entirely because he ate here rather than joining the family for dinner.

This evening she made an exception. Coley rissoles and mashed potato swimming in tomato soup had been the main choice for lunch at work that day. For once her hunger overrode her determination to avoid their Polish lodger, the unwelcome cuckoo in her nest.

Visions of thick slices of homemade bread liberally spread with butter and plum jam lured her across the hall and down the stairs. Smells of something peppery cooking wafted upwards even before she'd opened the door. Not one of Mrs

Grey's usual delicacies, she thought, but perhaps something foreign cooked at Ivan's request.

Hesitating, she considered her options. Should she control her appetite, retreat and wait for dinner, or follow the dictates of her stomach and barge in?

'You're scum! Running scared from the truth!'

Her brother's voice! He was home unexpectedly from Cambridge again.

The door banged against the wall as she flung it open.

What was this? Geoffrey and Ivan, facing each other, hands flat on the table, stiffly menacing like two bulls about to lock horns.

'You do not know what you are talking about!' Ivan growled the words, like a dog just about to sink its teeth into unprotected flesh.

Unmoved, Geoffrey glared at him. 'Workers of the world unite! That is the creed at the centre of the Communist doctrine. Fairness and equality for all, the dispersal of wealth in fair proportion. That,' he said, slamming his fist onto the table so that the cups and saucers rattled, 'is what it is all about!'

With a courage born of necessity, Janet dashed for the stove and turned off the gas beneath the bubbling saucepan. 'Burnt offerings is what it's going to be about shortly.'

A treacherous rumble sounded in her stomach in response to the spicy, just slightly burning smell wafting up at her.

Geoffrey and Ivan did not budge. Ivan said, 'You are an ignorant fool if you really believe that the Soviet Union is not an empire and a greedy giant gobbling up all the small countries around its borders. Thieves, rapists, murderers!'

Janet had never seen such an acrimonious expression on her brother's face. His eyes were bulging with angry hatred and his lips were pulled back in a menacing leer so that he too looked as if he were going to bite. His voice was as surly as his looks. 'I've been warned about your sort – typical of the fascist pigs that fled Poland when—'

Ivan leapt on him. His hands were around Geoffrey's throat as they both crashed to the floor. Ivan was on top, Geoffrey flattened beneath him, his face slowly turning puce.

'No! No! No!' Janet shrieked like a street girl as she rained blows upon Ivan's back.

'Let him go! Let him go, you dirty Pole!'

Ivan loosed his hands, and tried to turn, to get up and escape the rain of angry blows, but couldn't quite make it.

Geoffrey coughed and, as Ivan got to his feet, now gripping Janet's wrists, managed to sit up.

Janet's sudden courage left her. Ivan was too close, too frightening. He was foreign and, although she would never have held that against anyone in the past, she couldn't help doing so now. 'Let go of me!' She struggled and got her wrists out of his grasp. 'Look what you've done,' she shouted as she helped Geoffrey to his feet. Just as she did so, the kitchen door opened. Tall and elegant in a soft wool dress that was blue in a certain light, but green in others, her mother stood there and, for once, Charlotte's expression was less than serene.

Silently but emphatically, she looked at each of them in turn. 'Is anyone going to explain?'

Janet couldn't stop herself. 'It was his fault!' she pointed her finger at Ivan. 'He almost strangled my brother.'

Charlotte raised her eyebrows in mock surprise. 'Your brother? I haven't heard you call him that for years. And as for strangling him . . .' She grinned sardonically. 'There have been times just lately when the idea has occurred to both me and your father.'

With an undeniable sense of purpose, she pulled a chair out from under the table and sat down. 'Right,' she said, her gaze raking over each of them. 'Who is going to explain why Bedlam erupted in my kitchen?'

'I'm sorry,' said Ivan, clicked his heels and bowed his head. Janet presumed he was going to relate exactly what had happened. She couldn't have been more wrong. 'I cannot talk about it. Do excuse me.' He didn't wait for Charlotte's reply, but marched smartly out of the room.

Geoffrey slammed himself down on a chair. 'Bloody rude!' he said as he rubbed at the redness of his neck. 'Typical bloody foreigner!'

Grim-faced, Charlotte got up from the chair, slammed the kitchen door shut and leaned against it looking as if she meant business. 'What is this about?' She directed her question at Geoffrey.

Geoffrey adopted an air of disdainful indifference. 'We were talking politics. We disagreed.'

'Politics!'

Janet jumped. Geoffrey looked surprised. It wasn't often that Charlotte shouted, but when she did she certainly commanded full attention.

'Geoffrey, you may talk all the politics you wish at university. You may argue at great length with those with as much experience of the world at large as you, but you do not argue such matters in this house. It is obvious from Ivan's reaction that you said something to upset him.'

Geoffrey was noticeably indolent. 'I called him a fascist.'

His mother stared at him in disbelief.

'Ivan attacked him,' Janet interjected, for once taking her brother's side, an infrequent occurrence at the best of times.

Charlotte's eyes glittered with anger as she looked from son to daughter then back to Geoffrey. 'I'm not surprised. Do you have any idea of what Ivan and his family suffered during the forties?'

Geoffrey opened his mouth to say something, then, seeing his mother's steely gaze, changed his mind.

Charlotte went on, 'Ivan's family suffered as much under the victors of that war as they did at the hands of the vanquished. But that's beside the point. I will not have a guest in this house – any guest – assailed by ill-conceived arguments offered by persons of minimal experience. Do I make myself clear?'

Janet had never seen her mother looking so fierce, so ready to defend one of her 'projects' against her own family.

Charlotte repeated the question – louder this time. 'Do I make myself clear?'

Geoffrey was jolted into agreeing, begrudgingly.

Janet's stomach chose that moment to rumble. Charlotte turned to her. 'Judging by that noise, I take it you were coming into the kitchen for another reason.'

'Yes. I was hungry.'

'Fine. But *you*, Geoffrey, may leave the kitchen.'

She opened the door wide. Smothered in hurt pride, he got up from the chair, raised his eyebrows briefly in Janet's direction as if to say, *Oh well, better humour the old girl*, then left.

Charlotte, her expression bereft of its usual serenity, then said to Janet, 'Although you were not involved in this shameful display, I have noticed that you are not as friendly towards Ivan as you should be. Is there any particular reason for this?'

A shiver accompanied another stomach rumble as Janet fought to make the right decision. Should she tell her mother about the man who had pounced on her from out of the shadows? Should she tell her about the way he smelled, the way he spoke – and what he did to her?

No. No. She could not. Her mother made a career helping people rebuild their lives. How much more sympathy and assistance would she heap onto a member of her own family? Janet would be swamped with affection and, not necessarily in the way she wanted. The look of knowing would never disappear from her mother's eyes. She couldn't live with it.

'I can't help it,' she blurted.

Her mother eyed her speculatively as though it couldn't possibly be the truth. Then the moment passed. Charlotte sighed. 'Well, do your best, Janet. Ivan has a lot of healing to do. We must help him as much as we can.'

After her mother had gone, Janet stood looking out of the

window on the garden side of the kitchen. The leaves were turning gold and heavy-headed dahlias flopped forward despite the string and bamboo canes meant to keep them in place. Summer was coming to a close and she was glad. The sooner this year was over and a new one started, the happier she would be. It would be like, she thought, turning to the next chapter of a book, starting a fresh, clean page as yet unread and unsullied by events. But then, she thought, the events in preceding chapters always have a bearing on the present one.

Another hungry rumble came from her stomach. Although her initial yearning had been for bread and cheese, the spicy contents of the saucepan drew her close. Steam rose from the meat and vegetables still hot despite the gas having been turned off. She tentatively dipped her finger into the mixture, brought it to her mouth and sucked on it. The taste was alien, but wonderful; a mix of many spices. She fetched a bowl down from the cupboard, a spoon from a drawer and carved a hunk of sweet-smelling bread from a new loaf. The contents of the saucepan made a satisfying sound as they plopped into the bowl. After sitting down, she spread butter onto the bread and eagerly ate the bowl's contents. Goodness, what had possessed Mrs Grey to cook such a delight? she thought.

After using the bread to sop up the last vestiges of the feast, she sat satisfied, her arm curved across her stomach. Full and contented, she contemplated whether to make herself a cup of tea straight away or investigate the possibility of pudding. There was bound to be a custard tart in the larder, perhaps a cold rice pudding, thick enough to slice in squares, or a piece of Dundee cake.

A need for anything vanished as Ivan came back. He was dressed in a clean white shirt and dark trousers. The top buttons of the shirt were undone exposing a few inches of gleaming, hairless chest. His sleeves were rolled up to his elbows and not because they're frayed, she thought. Faint stripes of dubious colour ran through the fabric. She was positive she'd seen it before and eventually remembered where she'd seen it. Ivan, she decided, was wearing one of Colin's cast-offs.

Mindful of her mother's instructions, she resolved to be polite, but not too friendly. Why should she?

'I think Mrs Grey's left you something on the stove,' she said matter of factly. She took her dish and spoon to the sink and avoided looking at him.

'No, she has not! I left *myself* something to eat. I cooked it. *Myself*!'

Two bottles of what looked to be brown ale thudded onto the table.

'You have eaten my food!' Ivan strode to the stove. His presence, like his voice, seemed to fill the room.

One part of Janet wanted to flee. The other half was defiant and would not be intimidated. She would stand her ground. 'I'm sorry. I didn't know it was yours.'

'Never mind.'

He took a large plate from the rack above the gas rings and transferred the remaining contents of the saucepan onto it, cut bread and fetched a spoon – a tablespoon – much too large to eat it with. But eat he did, sitting at the table, shovelling the food into his mouth as quickly and as messily as possible, swigging from the opened bottle between mouthfuls, and all the time his eyes not leaving Janet's face.

Her stomach rumbled in revulsion, partly due to his actions and partly because unknowingly she'd eaten something cooked by a man she couldn't help regarding as an enemy. The urge to comment was too overpowering to ignore.

'You're disgusting!'

Another spoonful of food went into his mouth. His eyes stayed fixed on her face. 'So as well as being a dirty Pole, I am now disgusting? Is this because I am foreign?'

Janet could not control her anger. After all this man had almost strangled her brother a moment ago. The fact that Geoffrey might have deserved it was beside the point.

'Yes! Yes! Yes! Because of all those things,' she hissed through clenched teeth, mindful of not disturbing her mother for a second time that evening. 'Because of all those things! Because of everything!'

He shook his head and smiled. It was like torture. Torture! It was plain torture to have him here. He spooned the last morsel of food into his mouth. 'What is "everything"?'

She wanted to look away, but didn't want to retreat. She stared fixedly into his face. At last she said, 'I don't like upsets in my life.'

Ivan sprang to his feet, rested his hands on the table and leaned forward. His jaw continued to grind at his food. Fine features were just inches from her face, but she did not flinch or turn away.

'Ah!' he said with an air of sudden understanding.

He sat back down. His features softened, but the intensity of his eyes held her, kept her immobile, determined to be brave, determined not to run away.

'Men,' he said with a resolute nod. 'You are afraid of men. One man above all others must have hurt you very much indeed. Yet it could not have been me. I have only met you one time before and I did not hurt you.'

She knew it! They'd met before!

'Where?' she asked, her voice trembling with emotion. 'Where did we meet?'

He smiled and shook his head. 'I leave you to remember. You will, when you are ready.'

There was something about his voice, the fact that he sounded like Charles Boyer with a very excellent foreign accent, the fact that it had softened, did not threaten. And yet she could not stay in the same room with him. He'd admitted they had met before. She too felt they had met before, but whereas he appeared to remember exactly where and when, she did not and that fact in itself frightened her.

There was something decadent about lying in bed with the

sun streaming through the gap down the middle of the curtains. Sounds of a family preparing for the day ahead drifted up the stairs.

Susan sounded as though she'd taken charge of Peter. 'This is your satchel,' Edna could hear her saying. Peter was answering with a series of 'Neighs' as if in receipt of a nose-bag full of oats rather than a tan leather satchel in which resided a plastic pencil case, school books and a collection of last year's conkers.

Things seemed little changed. Was it possible they were managing without her?

Unable to resist finding out, Edna eased herself out of bed and placed her feet on the floor. Gradually she raised herself and took tentative steps to the bedroom door. Gripping the door handle to give herself support, she listened, aching to be part of a normal morning, but mindful that Colin would not approve.

'Now come along, Pammy. Just a mouthful.' The tone of Colin's voice made her smile.

A loud wail soared in protest.

'Now come on . . .'

Colin had oodles of patience, but she sensed by the sound of his voice it was running out.

There was a sudden clattering of crockery and cutlery hitting the floor. Pamela was not good in the mornings.

Edna smiled, turned and made her way back to bed. Things were fine enough for now, but it wouldn't be long before they were missing her very sorely indeed.

Footsteps thundered up the stairs. She'd been expecting them.

Susan came in with the tray on which tea slopped from cup to saucer and a plate of buttered toast, which slid from one side to the other.

'You have to eat it all up,' said Susan as her mother took the tray from her.

'I did the buttering,' said Peter.

'I can see that,' said Edna with an amused smile as she eyed the thickly spread butter. She asked, 'Have you brushed your teeth?'

They replied in unison. 'Yes.'

'Have you washed behind your ears?'

'Yes, of course we have,' said Susan, as though not to do so was too disgusting to contemplate. 'Though *he* wasn't keen,' she added with a backwards glance at her younger brother.

She was sorry to hear the last goodbye and the door closing on her departing family. The day would be long despite the copies of *Woman's Realm* and *Titbits* that were delivered on a weekly basis. Colin was taking Pamela to work with him.

'Is that wise?' she'd asked when he'd first told her.

He'd shaken his head at her as he might an errant child. 'Would it be wise if I left her here and you picked her up or ran down the garden after her?'

He was right. It wasn't easy to keep a two-year-old occupied. Shame, she thought, that the television wasn't on all day. Pamela loved it, especially Muffin the Mule, a gangly puppet whose strings were obvious to adults but, apparently, not to children.

Colin left the back door unlocked. 'Charlotte's popping in lunchtime, so she said.'

'If Charlotte said so, that means she'll be here,' said Edna as she made herself comfortable and flicked at a copy of *Woman's Realm.*

The district nurse came in at ten thirty to take her temperature and check that the bleeding had returned to normal.

Edna asked her a question that had been nagging her for days, one she hadn't mentioned to Colin. 'Will I still be able to have children?'

Sister Monica paused before answering, her attention riveted on her black bag that she was currently clipping shut. 'Possibly, but you have to bear in mind that you're getting older and have had three children already. You may very well get in the family way again, but there are no guarantees that you'll carry to full term. I suggest that you be thankful for what God's already given you.'

They were in exchange for Colin's legs, Edna wanted to say, but that would sound too bitter by far. They had to be grateful for the happiness they had. They couldn't possibly be happy all the time.

When the phone rang she made her way downstairs despite the fact that each step jarred and Colin had warned her to ignore it. Her father was phoning from the local phone box down by the park to check that everything was all right. She apologized for leaving so abruptly, and asked if he would be coming out to see her.

'No,' he began hesitantly, 'what with yer mother how she is . . .'

'Oh Dad!' She felt and sounded exasperated.

Even now her mother was ruining her enforced confinement to bed, not that she knew it. Although completely illogical, it was hard not to feel that the illness was self-inflicted, that her mother had contracted *this* particular illness at *this* particular time, in order to gain attention.

She struggled back up the stairs. She'd got halfway when the phone rang again. Carefully, so as not to slip or jar the fragile balance between pain and ordinary discomfort, she went back down the stairs and picked up the receiver.

'Whore! Leave my husband alone! You slut! You cheap whore!'

Edna sank down onto the lyre-legged piano stool which served as a seat to telephone users. 'Mother,' she groaned, 'why are you doing this?'

There was a sound of struggling on the other end of the line, followed by a click, then silence. Edna closed her eyes and rested her head against the wall. Her mother was just a shell, a crazy, empty shell. 'In fact,' Edna exclaimed with frustration, 'she might just as well be dead!'

Charlotte swept into the bedroom on the stroke of one

wearing a powder blue suit and a matching hat that seemed to consist of half a handful of swansdown. After the customary greeting, the fluffing up of pillows, and the administering of vegetable soup and lightly buttered bread, Charlotte served tea.

She just loves being in charge, thought Edna, and obediently ate and drank everything that was put before her.

'Now remember,' said Charlotte, 'no getting up for at least two weeks.'

'That's ridiculous!'

'Of course it's not. You've been ill.'

'No, I haven't. I've had a miscarriage. It's a perfectly natural part of being in the family way. Anyway, I can't leave Colin to fend for himself. He's tired out already.'

'Oh Edna!' Charlotte sounded totally exasperated.

Edna would not be moved. 'As soon as I can, I'm out of this bed. Colin and the children need me.'

'Don't rush. Janet told me to tell you that she'll call in for Susan and Peter this Saturday. At least that means you and Colin will only have Pamela to deal with. She said something about taking them to Clevedon.'

'What a wonderful daughter you have,' said Edna, sighing with contentment as she lay back against the pillows. 'What with the miscarriage and my mother's condition, I'd almost forgotten Janet and how much she enjoys being with the children. A day with just Colin and Pamela will be blissful – even if he does fuss. I didn't think she would have time. Is she still seeing that young doctor she was sweet on?'

Charlotte looked at her askance.

Edna bit her lip and felt her face flush warm with embarrassment. 'You didn't know?' she asked cautiously.

'I thought there was someone, and Geoffrey hinted at it, but you know Janet, she keeps things to herself and Geoffrey is not always around, not that he'd say much if he was.'

Edna sensed Charlotte's disappointment that Janet had not mentioned having a new boyfriend. I wonder what she'd say, she thought, if she knew that Janet had also trusted me with her darkest secret of all?

'It can't be very serious if she hasn't told me,' said Charlotte.

'No. And you have been very busy lately,' returned Edna, licking her dry lips and avoiding Charlotte's eyes. Best if the conversation was taken in another direction. She avoided asking Charlotte about her Polish refugees. Once her friend got onto that particular path there'd be no stopping her. She'd heard quite enough about Ivan and his compatriots already. She tried another tack. 'Janet was saying something about a letter from Germany,' she said suddenly. 'She seemed to think it was something to do with me and was from a man named Josef.'

Charlotte looked at her blankly and forced a laugh. 'I'm sure I don't know what she means.' She suddenly remembered seeing Janet in the study late one night, the file lying open on the desk. If only Janet had been more discreet, though it didn't sound as though she'd told Edna the contents of the letters. And now was not the right time, she decided.

Edna perceived a stiffening of the flesh, a clenching of the jaw, almost as if Charlotte was trying to hold something back. She remembered the orphanage and the German prisoner of war who worked there. Charlotte had got him that job. She'd seen them in the grounds sometimes watching the playing children while she'd leaned over Sherman's cot and tickled his chin. She remembered the looks that had passed between them. Never had she seen Charlotte look so beautiful, so completely enthralled. 'Was it the man who worked at the orphanage?' she asked.

Charlotte clasped her hands tightly together and looked down at them, running her tongue nervously along her lips. 'Yes. I did have a letter from him.' She looked up and smiled. He asked to be remembered to you.'

For a moment Edna said nothing, then a slow smile spread across her face. 'Just like the song.'

Another blank look.

'Just one of those things,' said Edna and saw she would have to explain further. 'It's the title of a song.'

'Of course it is.'

Charlotte's thoughts were in turmoil as she drove home. She was angry with Janet and angry with herself.

Janet's prying had forced her to lie. Things were getting terribly complicated. If she was ever going to tell Edna about the letter regarding her son, it had to happen shortly before he got put up for adoption or sent back to Brazil to live with some far flung relative he hardly knew. But when was the best time? Certainly not now! The poor woman had just had a miscarriage. Things were difficult. And as for Janet . . .

Spoilt, selfish little . . . A few of Polly's more choice descriptions came to her mind. Just lately Janet's behaviour had become insufferable. She'd been distant, even rude on occasion and went out of her way to avoid their lodger, Ivan, who had done her no harm whatsoever.

They would have to have a talk about this. Things could not go on the way they were.

Thirteen

The Broadway Picture House was a bit like the saloon or bank in *High Noon.* The façade was reasonably attractive, but a peek round the back at the reinforced windows and the cast iron waste pipes spewing from the lavatories punctured if not completely shattered the illusion of entering a picture palace of opulent delight.

Polly got to work early, took off her coat and transferred the Basildon Bond notepad from her handbag to her overall pocket. She was bubbling with excitement. As soon as the opportunity arose she would dash off a letter to the nice people at Australia House. The fact that Billy's face had set like plaster of Paris at the mention of her plans was ignored.

Like everything else at the Broadway Picture House, including the walls and the doors, her uniform was maroon and resembled an overall that was trying to be a dress. Polly would have preferred a uniform of black with white collars and cuffs, but personal choice didn't come into it. She felt for a pen in her hip pocket without success and turned to her shoulder bag, an Aladdin's cave of cheap make-up and old bus tickets – but no pen.

'Damn it!' She gritted her teeth and had another shuffle through. Nothing! 'Damn it,' she muttered again and made for the glass-fronted payment booth, a dead cert to have at least a Biro or a pencil.

She eased herself into her usual chair behind the narrow counter and the arched opening through which she doled out tickets for the one and threepenny seats in the stalls or the half crown half-empties up in the balcony.

Rummaging in the drawers she found a blunt pencil – not suitable at all for asking the Australian High Commission whether they wanted a ready-made family of immigrants with quick tongues, and, in Billy's case, a casual indifference for the Inland Revenue.

She found a biro first then came across a fountain pen of blue tortoiseshell with a bright shiny nib. She frowned at the latter. It wasn't hers. Perhaps it was out of the Lost and Found Box and had got shoved to the back of the drawer and forgotten about. Oh well, it was meant to be used.

Her head dropped over the open notepad. First she wrote her address, then *Dear sir.* What next? Her heart fluttered and, once she'd got the first few words down, her pace quickened. She knew exactly what needed to be said.

'Mrs Hills!'

Polly popped up like a Jack in the Box and came face to face with a shiny face and bushy eyebrows frowning over washed out eyes.

'What are you up to? Explain!'

Mr Griffiths, or Major as he preferred to be called, spoke in clipped tones with his head held high, just as if he were still in the army and his staff were raw recruits all needing to be licked into shape.

Polly slammed the notepad shut and shoved it into her pocket. She found her voice. 'I was looking for a pen.'

'A pen?'

His voice went from low to high in an incredulous manner and his eyebrows went up too.

'Yes, Major.'

His jaw stiffened. 'You don't need a pen. You sell tickets.'

'But I wanted to write something down, and I couldn't find—'

'I want an explanation.' He turned on his heels. 'Come into my office.'

He marched across the foyer like a general on parade, coping well with the sticky sound his feet made on a carpet well past its best.

Polly followed, each step she took accompanied by a barely hissed swear word just right for the occasion.

Major Griffiths stood ramrod straight behind his desk in an office with pea green walls. A fully drawn Airwick sat on top of a green metal filing cabinet. It made little headway against the smell coming from the men's lavatories next door or the rubbish rotting on the waste ground on the other side of the frosted window just behind his head.

'Close it!'

Pursing her lips helped keep the swear words in, but only just. After closing the door she stood chin up and face bright despite her annoyance at being deflected from the task that was now the very centre of her being. Australia! A new life. A new place. If she kept all those lovely thoughts in her head, nothing Griffiths might say could upset her.

'I don't believe you!' His mouth reset into a straight line the moment the words were out.

Polly frowned. 'You don't believe what?'

'A pen! You were not looking for a pen. You were looking for money! That's the ticket!'

Polly's jaw dropped before indignation lifted it again. 'You cheeky bugger! What the bloody hell do you take me for!' Every night the takings were checked by her, then another member of staff, then Griffiths. Everyone signed to say that everything was correct. Not a penny could go astray.

He didn't give her time to explain. 'I know your sort! Knowle West! Typical. Thieves or tarts. Now! Which one are you?'

Polly stared. She couldn't believe she was hearing this. OK, her husband Billy was no saint. But that didn't make *her* a criminal and she didn't consider herself a tart either. OK, she'd enjoyed herself with more than one foreign serviceman during the war, but hell, you couldn't see to do anything else in the blackout.

If things had been a bit more secure at home, she would have let him have the sharp edge of her tongue, but she wasn't that stupid. She loved her job and needed the money. The pictures were also her idea of the perfect career; she met people, saw the same picture all week and could almost repeat the dialogue word for word by the end of the run. What's more, it fitted in nicely with her home life, and doing a bit of cleaning for Charlotte. Meg and sometimes Billy too were there to look after Carol.

Polly pulled herself up to her full height, which, at five foot two, wasn't exactly statuesque especially when coupled with a figure that was greeting the plumpness of the middle thirties. 'So where's the proof?'

'No need! I just know!' His mouth slammed shut like a letterbox.

Polly was small, but she wasn't silly – neither was she a coward. Resting her palms flat on his desk she leaned forward and stared him straight in the eyes. 'You're not in the army now, *Mister* Griffiths. You can't accuse and sentence all in one go. It ain't like that in civvy street. Now you tell me why the bloody 'ell you're pointin' the finger at me!

Although his eyes seemed to be fixed on hers she had the distinct impression that he was taking in every inch of her body – especially her bosom.

He smiled and his glittering eyes looked into hers.

He pointed his finger at her right breast. 'What's that!'

Polly looked down. The tortoiseshell pen that she'd found buried deep at the back of the kiosk drawer stuck up from the breast pocket of her overall. She frowned. 'I've just this minute found it out there in the drawer. So what?'

'It's mine!' He snatched the pen. At the same time he pinched her breast. It was no accident.

'Get yer bleeding hands off me goods! I ain't used to strange hands grabbing at me bosom region.'

Not nowadays anyway, she thought, as memories of her youth flooded back. If she'd had the time she'd have blushed at her thoughts, but not now. She needed to stand up to him and blushing like a virgin didn't come into it.

She stood straight, hands on hips. There was no way she was going to run from his accusations. 'So you've got yer bloody pen. Can I go now?'

'The money, Mrs Hills! The money!'

'What money?'

Ramrod straight, his eyes seeming to meet above the bridge of his aquiline nose, he stepped round from behind his desk. He was smiling and looked like a snake about to swallow its supper.

Polly shook her head in the manner of someone who'd seen it all before and who's now sick to her back teeth of seeing it again. She smiled knowingly. 'Don't say a word! You want me to be nice to you, right?'

'Nice?' His eyebrows rose and when he smiled a gold filling glinted at the side of his mouth. 'Yes! You would call it that . . . A woman like you. Makes it sound respectable. In layman's terms . . .' He paused for effect. 'I want to take your knickers off. Stick it in you!'

Polly was stunned. She'd heard blokes say it coarsely to her before of course, but that was years ago when she was naive and the blokes from the brewery knew what they wanted and didn't have either the education or the finesse to put it any better. But this bloke – Major Griffiths! An officer he might be, but certainly no gentleman!

She folded her arms just beneath her chest and eyed him as though she could see right through to his long johns and knew they had a darn on the knee and a hole in the crotch. 'Why me, Major?'

He smacked his lips and clasped his hands behind his back. 'I do not want to pay for it from some greasy whore who's been giving it to all and sundry. I want personal attention. Officer issue alone!'

Polly couldn't believe her ears. 'I'm married.'

'That's what I mean. There's only one other man involved. He's in no position to object – if he finds out at all that is. And you're in no position to refuse me, unless you want him to do a while in prison.'

Polly had been about to blow. OK, so she wasn't exactly as pure as the driven snow, but Griffiths was using blackmail and Billy to persuade her to give in. What a bloody cheek! With sassy bravado she perched herself on the corner of his desk. Her skirt rode up a bit and Griffiths licked his lips. 'So why would my Billy be dragged off to Bridewell then?'

'He's been bookmaking. I have seen him myself. Please do not deny it. He plies his trade – if trade is the right word, I feel committing his crime might be a better description – around the side here. Street bookmaking is strictly illegal.'

'Nah!' Polly shook her head. Of course Griffiths was speaking the truth. Billy and half the more shady element on the estate did their deals on the piece of wasteland at the side of the Broadway. On a Saturday night you could buy all manner of things there or, if the coppers were hanging about, the trade moved lock, stock and barrel to the area around the Venture Inn down on Melvin Square. Clothes, fags, booze, sugar and anything still on ration were available, even a good sized carpet and the Ewbank sweeper to go with it.

Everyone knew Billy did it, but no one would shop him. There was too much at stake – including their money if they were betting and their supplies if they were buying! But Griffiths wasn't interested in money. He was interested in uncomplicated sex and he wanted Polly to give it to him.

'What if I say no?'

'You're sacked.'

No! She couldn't afford to lose this job – not yet. Every penny that was needed for emigrating to Australia would come from her job. Billy would put a bit by, but the moment a load of chocolate fell off a lorry down at the docks he'd have to lay out money. She had to do her bit, after all, living abroad was her dream rather than Billy's, but could she really give in to Griffiths's suggestion just for the money?

He suddenly squeezed her knee.

'Keep yer 'ands off. I ain't decided yet.' Despite her air of defiance, Polly was worried. 'Can you give me time to think about it?'

'What is there to think about?'

'The pudding club. I have to take precautions.' It was the only excuse she could think of to play for time.

A vein began to throb just above his left eyebrow. She wickedly wondered whether his face might crack, or better still that he'd have a heart attack and drop down dead.

'No need for precautions,' he said, his voice suddenly like treacle. 'The war, you know.'

'Got 'em shot off, did you?'

His face turned the colour of well-boiled beetroots. 'Just take it from me! There is no problem. I realize a woman of your age has to take care of herself, but I agree to allowing you time to think it over.'

Inwardly she breathed a sigh of relief. She had feared he'd demand his dues there and then. Now he had given her time to think about things. Firstly she didn't want to lose her job, but secondly, and this was much more important, she did not want her husband going to jail. All she wanted was for all of them to go to Australia. Somehow she had to hold Griffiths at bay.

September was proving warm and Saturday started misty. Charlotte dropped Janet at the railway station. She would have taken the bus, but Mrs Grey had packed a hamper, a bulky object at the best of times and impossible on a bus.

Colin brought the children down by car. 'It's kind of you to do this,' he said to her.

'It's a pleasure. Besides, Edna could do with a break.'

Colin nodded and smiled as if not quite believing that a

young single woman could be so considerate. But then, he didn't know how kind Edna had been to her.

By the time they'd changed trains at Yatton the mist was lifting and a watery sun was shining through.

'Where did you say we were going?' Peter asked Janet for the fifth or sixth time.

'Clevedon.'

'Can we swim in the sea?' asked Susan.

'Only if the tide is in.'

'Can we build sandcastles? Peter asked.

'No. There isn't any sand at Clevedon – well, not much anyway. It's mostly pebbles and rocks.'

'So what are we going to do?' bleated Susan as the train pulled into Clevedon Station.

'We're going to take off our shoes and socks and catch tiddlers, winkles and crabs in the rock pools.'

Janet didn't really mean that she'd be joining them and had told no one that there was more than one reason for the trip. The truth was that Jonathan had phoned her on Thursday afternoon saying he had to see her at the weekend, preferably on Saturday. She had tried to persuade him to make it that night. He had been adamant that the only time he could see her was during the day on Saturday. She wondered what he wanted to see her about and why it couldn't wait.

'Help me with this.' Janet grasped one handle of the hamper.

Susan obliged while Peter manhandled the bamboo fishing nets and two preserve jars with tin lids and string handles.

The smell of the sea lured them from the station, along the road through the town and across the grassy lawns that bordered the promenade and the sea wall.

Children clambered over the slippery green rocks, peered into pools, searching for the pop, pop, pop of bubbles breaking the surface, a sure sign that a tiddler or a crab was in residence. If they were really lucky they might even find larger prey left by the ebbing tide.

A scattering of adults watched, some sitting on rocks, some reclining against a seawall warmed by the morning sun. Some sat on deckchairs up on the promenade and dozed between making admiring comments each time their children held up a murky jar supposedly holding some fantastic find.

Peter and Susan took in all that was happening down on the rocks. Like all children they were keen to explore new places. It seemed a long time ago since Janet had felt like that in the days when she and Geoffrey had been brought here.

'We'll sit here,' said a decidedly bossy Susan. Her gaze, along with that of Peter, was fixed on the beach.

Janet bit her lip as she made her decision. Jonathan had told her to get deckchairs for both of them in one of the ornate Victorian shelters at the edge of the grass where they could talk in private. He'd assured her there was one very close to some kind of pool and that she'd be able to see the beach and the children from there. Accordingly she went to the shelter he'd described. It was packed to capacity. Women with heavy jowls and pink-skinned old men dozed behind its sun-warmed glass.

Her gaze settled on the swimming pool, which jutted out into the rocks and was full to the brim with dark green seawater that lapped gently against its slime-covered sides. A flight of wide concrete steps swept down into it. If she sat against the wall behind the top step she could see the children down on the beach and could also watch the promenade for Jonathan. He could also see her without too much difficulty. Both the pool and the steps were deserted. They would have the privacy Jonathan said they needed.

'Just here, I think,' Janet let her end of the hamper down and Susan did the same. In no time at all it was open, a blanket spread and weighted down at its edges with discarded shoes, socks, a cardigan and a Fair Isle pullover. The children were ready for action.

'Do you want a sandwich first? A drink perhaps?'

The food was refused. Brightly coloured limeade was swigged swiftly from a shared bottle. Peter began prancing up and down. Trigger was obviously impatient to be going.

Dress tucked into her knickers, fishing net in one hand and jar in the other, Susan rocked backwards and forwards, her face a picture of childish impatience. 'Come on, Aunty Janet.'

'I won't be able to stay with you long. I have to get back here and look after our things. I'll just show you what you have to do.'

After checking no one was watching, Janet slipped off her stockings, rolled them up and tucked them under the blanket.

Luckily the ebbing tide had left a rock pool a little way down the slope among the rocks at the side of the swimming pool.

'It looks like sky,' said Peter looking down into the water, which was never any other colour than slime green or mud brown.

'A reflection,' explained Janet. Her eyes travelled back to the promenade, the shelter and the pier. Where was he?

She showed them how to dip the nets and how to fill the preserve jars with water. They were impatient rather than quick learners. It all looked so easy.

'I've caught something!' shouted Peter and raised his net. Seaweed straggled like ripped rags then slipped with a splash back into the pool.

'Just seaweed. The pools further down would be better,' said Janet looking purposefully seaward.

'We'll go and see, Aunty Janet, but I think it would be best if you go back and look after our things,' said Susan in a motherly fashion.

Janet patted Susan's hair, her hand bouncing off the bow that flapped like a belligerent butterfly on one side of her head. 'What a sensible girl.'

A wave of affection washed over her as the two small

figures picked their way over the pebbles and rocks, their nets waving like flags above their heads.

After drying her feet and putting her stockings back on behind the privacy of a large towel, she settled down, her back braced against the wall. She glanced at her watch. Five minutes to one. He would be here soon. She wondered again at the importance of what he had to say to her. He had stressed the need for privacy, but surely the café where they usually met was private enough or, at least, it had been. Just lately the people there had become friendlier, had started asking them their names, where they worked and where they lived. Janet had told them. Jonathan had not.

The hamper was full of good things, but she couldn't bring herself to eat until he'd arrived. She stretched her neck every so often just to check what the children were doing. They were engrossed in fishing the rock pools, vying with each other to make the best catch of the day. In between checking on them, she looked over her right shoulder along the promenade one way, then looked over her left shoulder to check the other direction.

It was past two. The promenade baked and the smell of fish and chips drifted from the café up by the pier. Shadows began to lengthen. The afternoon grew older.

He's not coming!

No, she mustn't think that. Of course he was coming. It was his idea to meet her here.

What if something much more important had come up – a crisis at the hospital? He wouldn't come then.

Well! If that was the case, so be it! She'd enjoy herself anyway. The children would compensate for her disappointment. It wasn't quite true. She loved the children, but Jonathan made her feel normal again. The fact that he talked so openly to her about medical matters helped compensate for her new job's shortcomings. And she'd never felt frightened of him. Although they'd kissed he'd never tried to take advantage. It wasn't because he didn't fancy her – she was pretty sure of that. Jonathan was not like Dorothea's Henry, the sort who'd pull a car over into any dark spot, try it on in a taxi or a shop doorway. The proper time, she thought, remembering what Jonathan had said when she'd asked him why he didn't go direct to the hospital board with a view to them listening to his ideas and currying favour with an eye on promotion. 'I can't do things that way,' he'd replied. 'I like everything to be in the right place at the right time, like you going to the pictures with your friend Dorothea on a Thursday, attending your fencing class on a Friday, going dancing on a Saturday and making sure you visit your grandparents on a Sunday. A proper timetable so that everyone knows where they are.'

Most of what she'd told him had been a lie, but she'd been determined not to show how much she looked forward to seeing him on Tuesdays and Wednesdays. Telling him she sat at home most nights was too pathetic for words. Lies sufficed.

Tired by so much watching and waiting, she dozed. The sun and the sea breeze took it in turn to warm and cool her face. The coolness lingered. At first she thought the sky had clouded over. When she opened her eyes Jonathan was looking down at her. Before she could move he was down on his hands and knees planting a kiss on her forehead then on her lips.

He was dressed in light flannels, a sleeveless pullover and a long-sleeved shirt. His tie was firmly knotted despite the warmth of the afternoon. A Panama threw a shadow over his eyes.

He slumped down beside her, his money jingling in his trouser pocket and spilling out onto the blanket as he made himself comfortable.

'I didn't think you were coming,' she said and immediately wished she didn't sound so in need of him. Men took advantage of such adoration.

He picked up the coins. 'Now that's a silly thing to say.' He shifted one hip and shoved the coins back into his pocket.

Placing one arm around her shoulders, he drew her close and looked deeply into her eyes. She felt like a film star on a poster advertising the big film. 'I had to come.' He kissed her again. The tips of her breasts brushed against his chest briefly enough to arouse, but not long enough to gain accusing stares from anyone likely to see.

Rakishly, he shoved his hat onto the back of his head. 'What's in the hamper? I'm absolutely starving.'

The opportunity to answer and to ask him what he wanted to see her about was swiftly lost.

Slap, slap, slap! Peter was galloping his ever-present charger across the concrete. He trailed his fishing net behind him, slapping soggily against the ground with each prancing stride.

Seeing they had company, Susan retrieved her dress from her knickers, eyed Jonathan as though she'd half-expected him to be there, and said, 'Hello. Are you a doctor?'

'Yes.'

'How did you know that?' Janet asked.

'I heard my mum tell my dad that you were going out with a doctor. And she told your mother, she said, and your mother was annoyed because you hadn't told her.'

Janet felt her face reddening.

Jonathan intervened. 'We're just good friends.'

She smiled at him. 'That's right,' she said and was surprised to see a relieved look in his eyes, as though agreeing that they were friends rather than lovers had taken a weight off his mind.

'I'm hungry,' Peter howled.

'Starving I should think,' said Janet. 'I notice that Trigger came to a very abrupt halt without making a sound.'

'He's hungry too,' Peter explained.

Jonathan raised his eyebrows. 'Trigger?'

Janet smiled and handed him a sandwich. 'Peter's horse.'

Both children tucked in with more gusto than either she or Jonathan. Once they were full they went back to the beach.

Janet tidied up quickly before reclining against the wall next to him, waiting to hear what he had to say. He made no move. Narrowing her eyes she fixed her gaze on the beach, the gulls, the horizon. The sea was a counterpane of gleaming diamonds dancing in the sunlight over a rippling sea. She felt exasperated, but knew he was teasing her, waiting for her to ask him what he'd wanted to see her about. Two, she decided, could play at that game. There was one subject above all others that would get him talking.

'How's your mother?'

His response was immediate. 'Did I tell you she painted? I think I did.'

He hadn't, but Janet did not contradict.

'A local gallery in Lavenham is putting on an exhibition of local watercolour artists. Three of Mother's paintings have been chosen. She's bucked to bits, even says she's going along on crutches to see it.' There was a smile on his face and a look of pride in his eyes. 'My, but she's a wonderful woman. I'm lucky to have someone like her as my mother.'

It struck Janet as being an odd thing to say, almost as though he'd won her in a raffle. Perhaps it's me, she thought. All this sea air is enough to make anyone light-headed. She flicked residual crumbs from the blanket. 'I'm glad she's well.'

It was a case of now or never. She took a deep breath and took the plunge. 'So what did you want to see me about?'

'Ah!' he said pointedly. 'The big question.' His eyes were closed, his arms folded and his long legs stretched out in front of him.

Janet stopped brushing crumbs from the blanket. Seagulls screamed as they soared overhead, their keen eyes waiting for the crumbs to be scattered at a safe scavenging distance. 'Do I get the big answer?' she said jokingly but as calmly as she could. It wouldn't do to sound too enthused.

'Have you thought more about finding another job?'

Janet sat back on her haunches as Jonathan wagged his feet

in time to the tune coming from the bandstand. They were playing 'It's a Long Way to Tipperary'. At least it wasn't Doris Day, thought Janet. She would always associate anything sung by her with that awful night when she'd walked home alone.

She composed herself. 'I can't stop thinking about it and asking myself what exactly is it I want from a job or from life in general. I remember when I was younger that I told my mother I was not going to strive for a career. All I would do was get a job and get married. Life, I'd decided, was too short and too perilous. We had just come through a war after all. But now I'm not so sure. The job I've got now seems so empty without any patient contact. I'm interested in people, not laundry lists!'

She reached for a pebble, its golden surface shiny and smooth beneath her fingers. 'A job's come up in the main typing pool so Dorothea tells me. It's a downward move, but I was thinking about applying for it until I saw that Miss Argyle would be in charge of the interviews.'

She flung the pebble as far as it would go, telling herself that if it hit the water it meant something wonderful was about to happen. Unfortunately it landed among the rest of its kind, one pebble among many. She hadn't made a provision for that, at least, not a conscious one.

'Professor Pritchard needs a secretary.'

His statement pulled her up short. A belligerent breeze chose that moment to blow a lock of dark hair into her open mouth. She swept it aside. 'What did you say?'

He opened one eye and looked at her sidelong. 'At Saltmead.'

'It's a long way . . .'

'A flat comes with the job. Are you interested?'

He opened his eyes and leaned closer, a considerably unnerving thing to do. She felt the warmth of his body through the sleeve of his shirt.

'I think you'd enjoy the job and would learn so much. And

I would appreciate you being there, I can assure you of that.' He said it so matter of factly, like one professional to another.

Janet thought of the grim office she now shared with piles of boxes and supply demands. 'Will my office have a decent view?'

'Every window in Saltmead has a decent view. We're surrounded by trees and open fields.'

'Didn't it used to be an American Army base?'

'A prisoner of war camp after that. It can't be bad; no one ever tried to escape from there. I won't say that it's the most beautiful place in the world, but we are making improvements all the time.' He grimaced, then grinned ruefully. 'Though it would improve a lot more if I had my way. A lick of paint here and there wouldn't hurt. Illness doesn't mean you have to do without colour or interest in your life – that's what my mother says.'

His mother! What about his father?

For the first time, she was suddenly aware that he rarely mentioned his father to her.

She should have known there and then that his life was not his own, that his career, his matter of fact way of dealing with things and his attitude towards women, were dictated by his relationship with his mother.

It was easy to say 'yes'. In fact, there was no reason for saying anything else. She would see more of Jonathan, less of Dorothea. It also meant she would no longer be under the same roof as the foreigner her mother had moved into her house who she avoided if at all possible.

'Today Clevedon is wonderful – even with the tide out.' She could even forgive the smell of frying fish, which overpowered that of the brine soaked rocks.

'So you're interested?'

She smiled. 'I didn't say that. I said Clevedon was wonderful.'

The town did indeed seem brighter and would have

remained unsullied if the rock pools had yielded more stranded sea creatures, if the children hadn't got bored.

A narrow parapet, slippery with dark green slime ran all around the pool. Unseen by Janet, Peter and Susan were walking carefully around it, arms outstretched and toes digging into the slippery surface. Peter completed the whole circuit. With a whoop of triumph he jumped off at the shallow end. Susan followed, but her balance wasn't so good. She wobbled and the fishing canes tangled in her legs.

Susan's scream brought Janet and Jonathan to their feet just in time to see Susan's legs slip awkwardly from under her. A plume of water shot into the air as she broke the surface and disappeared in the deepest end of the pool.

Janet ran swiftly, the wet slime of the parapet seeping through her stockinged feet.

Jonathan shouted out to her to be careful, but she paid him no heed. She didn't have time to be careful. Could Susan swim? Perhaps she could . . . perhaps she couldn't . . . and then what?

Breathless and scared, she knelt on the parapet trying to peer through the dull green water. Susan was nowhere in sight. People gathered around her, all talking at once, all making suggestions.

The police! The coastguard! A doctor!

Just as she was about to dive in, Susan's head broke the surface, spluttering and spitting water, her arms flailing in an anxious but adequate crawl.

Janet bent low and reached for her. 'Here, Susan! Here!'

A foot slipped from under her and she began to topple.

'Let me!' Jonathan's voice. He pulled her back before she too was struggling in the water.

'Get back.' He took her place at the side of the pool. Susan's fishing net had flown onto the rocks when she had fallen in. Jonathan used it to reach her, holding it out in front of him. Susan grabbed hold of the green mesh with both hands. Hand over hand, Jonathan reeled her in. A boy of about thirteen helped him lift her from the water and over the parapet.

'Best catch of the day!' Jonathan exclaimed as Susan coughed up the water she'd swallowed. 'Come on. Bring it all up.' He patted her on the back and leaned her forward across his lap. Susan obliged. Still breathless and shaking with fear at the thought of what might have been, Janet brought a towel and wrapped her in it.

'Goodness. What would I have said to your mother if I'd gone home without you?'

The sun and the breeze dried Susan's clothes while she sat wrapped in the towel eating sandwiches and shivering. By the time she was dry everything was packed and Jonathan was giving them a lift to the station.

'I would take you all the way home,' he explained, 'but I do have things to do.'

Janet told him she understood. They arrived at the station too quickly and she found herself wishing they'd had long enough to take tea or sit near the bandstand and eat ice cream. Once the children and hamper were unloaded, she dawdled by the car.

He stuck his head out through the open window. 'One last kiss?'

Janet obliged. He tasted like . . . She couldn't think. Chocolates, wine, smoothly spread butter that made you turn your lips inwards then lick them with your tongue.

She told herself not to get too carried away as there was a danger she might give him the wrong impression. But he had offered her a future away from a dark office and a home in which a stranger now resided.

'So?' He said nothing more, just looked at her quizzically but confidently, as though he already knew what she would say to his offer.

It was impossible to look anywhere except into his eyes. Women would die for eyes like his, she thought. Blue – no –

indigo. Were his mother's eyes the same colour? Or his father's? His mother's, she decided, a mirror image of his own, just as he seemed to be a mirror image of the woman herself.

'Are you going to let me down?' he said when she didn't answer.

Despite the dryness in her throat, she managed to find her voice. 'Perhaps Professor Pritchard won't want me as his secretary. Perhaps he's already got someone else in mind.'

Jonathan smiled and shook his head. 'I've already mentioned you. Besides, he knows your father. It's in the bag.'

Watching him drive away brought back a childhood memory, the time when she was about eight years old and had caught scarlet fever. Her throat had been dry and her skin had burned all over – just like now – and all at the prospect of a new job.

The day had ended well, thought Janet as the neat bungalows and sturdy stone villas of Clevedon were left behind. She rested her brain against the headrest in the third-class compartment, which, of course, had no corridor and therefore no lavatory, and prayed fervently that the children could last until Bristol.

Susan falling into the pool was the only blot on the day and a very minor one at that. Everything else had been wonderful. A job at Saltmead! A flat! What a stroke of luck. Giving in her notice once Jonathan had confirmed the position was no problem although Dorothea might get weepy about it, but that wouldn't stop her.

Away from home. Will I miss it? she wondered, then thought of that Polish accent that still haunted her dreams and shivered.

There was time to ponder on the matter as she gazed past her reflection in the dusty glass to the darkening landscape outside. Lights were coming on in scattered cottages, farmhouses and villages, the latter clustered like sheep around an ancient church where tombstones leaned amid ripe grass and fading poppies.

She smiled at her deepening reflection. Saltmead beckoned. It had lots in its favour, including Jonathan's companionship. Despite the fact that they'd kissed and held hands, she still viewed him as little more than a friend. She presumed he saw things that way too.

Fourteen

Meg never let on that Carol had spilled the beans about going to Australia, though Polly should have guessed it. Carol was a talkative child who'd been close to her great-aunty since a baby, when Polly had spent more time in the company of the American Army than Field Marshal Montgomery!

Like anyone else, Meg needed to talk to someone about her worries. Luckily, Bridget Dando, who'd lived four houses away down in their old street, had moved to the opposite side of the road in Camborne Crescent. In the days at York Street they had entered each other's houses without knocking, going straight to the stove and putting the kettle on. Their old habits were readopted. By eleven o'clock Bridget's head had appeared around the open door, her toothless gums chewing remorselessly, her eyes seemingly everywhere. Not that she could help the latter. She was cross-eyed and although it proved disconcerting at first to see one eye looking right to the kitchen and the other left towards the front door, Meg had got used to it. Besides, Bridget was a good listener and not a gossip even though unloading her worries onto someone with such an unfocused gaze was a bit like Catholic confession – she wasn't sure whether anyone was actually listening.

Meg repeated to Bridget what Carol had told her.

Her look was as forthright as it could be. 'You going?'

Meg clamped her mouth shut, looked into her tea and shook her head.

'Oh!'

'They haven't said a word to me. Me! I've done all I bloody well could fer them over all these years! Cast off like some worn out slipper.'

Bridget made no comment. She seemed to sense when Meg wanted to say more and accordingly waited for the right words and moment to come.

'They've replied, them Australians.' Meg swallowed and sniffed back her feelings.

'So when they going'?'

Meg poked at her hair and looked away guiltily. 'They don't know they've replied.'

Bridget poured tea into her saucer and while waiting for further enlightenment took a noisy slurp.

Meg went on, 'Big brown envelope it was, full of forms an' fings.' She tilted her head back and closed her eyes. 'I threw it out.'

'Don't blame you, me girl,' said Bridget in an accent that originated some way west of Sligo. 'This is where they belong. You'd miss 'em, you would.'

'Of course I'd miss 'em, you silly mare! Of course I bloody well would!' Her voice shook with emotion.

Polly accused everyone of not doing their job properly: the people working at Australia House, the Post Office, even the mongrel pup that Billy had got down the Dogs' Home, which had one ear up, one down. In common with Bridget Dando he also had an eye impediment – though not quite so off-putting – one eye being blue and the other brown.

'So are we still going to Australia?' Carol asked.

'Damn right we are. Them bloody Australians didn't reply to my first letter so I've written to them again. The forms and stuff should arrive any day now.' The happiness gushed out and she gave Carol a big hug followed by a wagging finger in front of her face. 'But don't you tell yer Aunty Meg, mind!'

Carol immediately muttered something about trying out

the new rope swing that Norman Partridge, the local bully-boy, had just slung over the nearest lamppost.

As Carol slunk out, Meg came into the room and settled on the leather chaise longue causing a spring to twang in protest. She took up her knitting; one plain, one pearl, the sound of her needles clicking in time with her teeth.

She regarded the empty end of the chaise with a weathered frown. 'Time this old thing was chucked on the bonfire.' She looked up at Polly. 'Why don't you go round to that furniture shop down by the Rex and buy a new one?' The Rex was the name of the picture house in Bedminster, a cut higher than the Broadway.

'What with? Buttons?' Polly sniffed as though the idea stank like rotten fish. Buying a new three piece – utility or not – was the last thing she wanted. She was leaving the country, wasn't she? But she couldn't tell Meg that.

Meg said, 'I've got enough for a deposit. You can 'ave the rest on tick.'

'Yeah,' Polly replied vaguely, cursing herself for not having the guts to tell Meg the truth. But she couldn't tell her yet, could she? Not until she knew they'd definitely been accepted.

Australia House responded to Polly's second letter with equal efficiency to the first. The following day another large brown envelope slapped onto the hallway lino, the sound of its arrival cutting into Meg's heart. Meg fell on it quickly and clutched it to her breast, hating to be deceitful, but determined not to lose the small family that had become her life. For a moment a sense of guilt softened her intentions, but it was touch and go. Her niece wanted a better life in a sunnier clime where opportunities were supposed to be there for the taking. Should she really stand in the way of a better future for her and Carol? After all, neither mother nor daughter had had a good start in life.

But her determination to hold on to what she held very dear was too strong. If Polly left there'd be nothing worth living for.

'God forgive me,' she muttered as she shoved the envelope into the bosom of her apron. Out in the kitchen the galvanized boiler gurgled and sent clouds of steam to cling like fog to the ceiling. She lifted the lid on the dustbin that sat under the kitchen window. It gaped up at her like a dark hole – straight to hell. Taking the package in both hands she paused for one last guilty reflection. 'It's for our own good,' she said, raised her eyes to heaven, then ripped the envelope in half and dropped it in.

The house in Royal York Crescent was surprisingly silent: no clip-clop of Mrs Grey's sensible heels across the parquet floors; no trace of her mother's high, well-rounded vowels as she talked to someone on the telephone about a charity meeting or a social event to raise money for the destitute in some country she'd never heard of.

Silence in the house was not that unusual. Mrs Grey's day off obviously, and her mother was probably in the study reading a stack of official papers in dull fawn files.

Janet began to make her way there when the sound of a door being slammed came tumbling down the stairs. 'Mother?'

Silence.

She climbed the stairs and went straight to her mother's room, a haven of pale cream, violet and seedling green. The sheets on the bed glowed white. Janet paused, stared at the unsullied crispness and remembered a night long ago when she'd seen her mother lying on that bed with . . .

The sound of raised voices followed by a loud thud broke into her thoughts. She shot off along the landing and stopped by the small door that opened on the narrow staircase leading up to Ivan's room. Carefully, so that it wouldn't creak, she opened it a few inches. Breathless sounds of exertion came from the room above. Someone was doing something very physical. Her thoughts returned to the crisp sheets downstairs and the night when her mother's image had become tarnished for ever. For goodness' sake, her mother was older now. Surely she wouldn't? And Ivan was so much younger than her!

Slamming the door behind her, Janet ran up the spiral stairs until her head was level with the attic floor and she could see the bed, her mother and Ivan.

Her mother was bending over the bed. Ivan was lying on it, arms flung above his head, one leg trailing on the dull green lino floor.

'What are you doing with him?'

'Trying to get him into bed.'

A pair of boots were swiftly untied and placed on the floor.

Janet held back. This was not the scenario she had envisaged.

Ivan muttered something about lost countries, lost causes and absent friends.

'Let's just make you comfortable, shall we?' Charlotte began undoing the buttons on Ivan's flies. She pushed aside locks of hair that had fallen over her face. 'Ivan's been drinking.' She indicated an empty decanter on the bedside table. 'It's annoying, but well . . . what can one expect with all that he's been through?'

If only you knew what *I'd* been through, thought Janet, and suddenly felt jealous rather than fearful of the man lying on the bed. 'I need to talk to you.'

'Not now, dear. Do you think you can give me a hand to get his clothes off?'

Had she misheard? Janet looked from Ivan to her mother. 'No! I couldn't.'

Charlotte looked disappointed. 'Janet, whatever is the matter with you? He's hardly in any state to pose a threat.'

Janet pursed her lips, but didn't move – petulance, stubbornness rather than anger.

'Never mind. I'll do it myself.'

Charlotte pulled off Ivan's top clothes, folded the dark green pullover, the striped shirt and put them on a chair, draped his fawn trousers over the back of it. Once he was stripped to his underwear and army grey socks, she covered him with the pink satin eiderdown and reached for the empty decanter.

Janet remembered her mother covering her up like that when she was younger. But Ivan was not a child. Why did her mother have to care so much about people who should be able to take care of themselves? Her own needs were just as pressing. 'I need to talk to you,' she repeated. 'It has to be now.'

'I'm sorry, Janet,' said her mother, looking down into the stairwell at her as her head poked up like a rabbit from its burrow. 'I've got rather a lot of work to do, and this event with Ivan—'

'Damn you, Mother! Will you please listen for a change?'

'How dare you speak to me like that!'

'It's the only way I can make you listen!'

Charlotte's shoulders drooped and she sighed heavily. 'Oh dear! I do get carried away with other things at times. I apologize.'

Other things? She certainly did, thought Janet. The world gets priority, her own family . . . oh, what was the point? She went on with what she had to say. 'I've been offered a new job.'

'Then I can only wish you good luck, my dear.'

'It's at Saltmead Sanatorium.'

There was a sudden change in her mother's expression, perhaps because Ivan was muttering again between bouts of singing some Polish song in a loud, drunken voice.

Janet continued. 'They specialize in treating polio.'

'I know.' Her mother's tone was very soft. Janet wondered whether she'd known someone who'd worked there – or died there, but thought it best not to enquire.

'Don't tell me that polio is contagious. I know it is, but I'm willing to take that risk.'

'Obviously I'm concerned, my dear, but if it's what you feel you must do, then I certainly will not stop you. I was just wondering how you were going to get there. Dropping your father off at his consulting rooms is one thing, but driving all the way out there is another matter entirely and I do have my own work—'

'There's a flat with the job,' Janet blurted, and prepared herself for an adverse reaction.

'Ah! Then may I ask you to consider whether it is the job you're going for, or is it something to do with this doctor Edna told me about? I do think you should have told me about him.'

Janet mumbled an apology, then added, 'It's not serious.'

'Does he have a flat at Saltmead?'

Janet felt her face getting hotter. There was no doubting her mother's inference. 'I don't think so, and even if he did, there is no cause to read anything into it. Jonathan isn't like that. Our relationship isn't like that. We are both interested in medicine, in fact he tells me far more about his job than Daddy ever has.'

'I'm glad for you. But do think this through, darling. Bear in mind you will be away from home and although I'm sure your doctor friend plays the gentleman at present while you enjoy the protection of your parents' roof, it doesn't mean to say he'll be the same when you're living alone.' She looked like a Madonna and sounded almost condescending.

'He recommended me for the position.' Janet was indignant. 'His name's Jonathan Driver.'

Ivan fell suddenly into deep snoring. Both women looked over at him, silence falling as they considered what to say next. It was Charlotte who spoke first.

'Jonathan Driver? I met him and his parents at a charity ball. His mother was in a wheelchair if I remember rightly. A forceful woman. She reminded me of Boadicea – without the knives on the wheels of course.' Charlotte's face clouded and she headed back down the stairs.

Janet was first out onto the landing. 'What was she like?'

Charlotte stepped quickly down the next flight of stairs,

then the next. Intent on hearing more about Mrs Driver, Janet followed.

'I told you. She was in a wheelchair.'

Charlotte Hennessey-White rarely said bad things about people, but you could tell when she was thinking them. Janet had recognized that look back up there in the attic. She knew her mother had formed an opinion of Mrs Driver and it wasn't a good one.

They were in the sitting room now. Charlotte began fussing with a mix of Michaelmas daisies and chrysanthemums arranged in a blue and orange Imari vase that had dragon handles of royal blue and gold.

Janet watched her intently. 'There's something you're not telling me. Is she awful? Terribly ugly?'

Charlotte stopped fussing and frowned at her daughter. 'She was a charming woman. Her hair was dark. So were her eyes. I don't think she wore make-up, though it seemed from the length of her lashes that she did. But there, some people are like that, aren't they? Honoured by nature so to speak.'

'So what didn't you like about her?'

Charlotte shook her head as if she'd made a grave misjudgement. 'I've never seen a woman so totally detached from her husband and absorbed in her son. Stay friends with him, but nothing else.' She left the flowers, settled herself in a chintz-covered chair and pretended to flip through a copy of *Good Housekeeping*.

Janet's shadow fell over the page Charlotte was pretending to read. 'I want to know.'

Charlotte put the paper down and looked at her daughter despairingly. 'He's a womaniser, Janet.'

'I don't believe it.'

Her mother smiled ruefully. 'Dashing, confident and seemingly interested in your career?'

'He is interested!'

'I doubt it from what I hear. He has women all over the

place, but he doesn't commit himself to any one relationship. His mother won't let him.'

If Janet had been in love with Jonathan she would have called her mother a liar. Obviously she was not in love. Jonathan had talked medicine and encouraged her to make more of herself without attempting to seduce her. Having a good bedside manner inspired confidence in the patient. In this context, Janet had been the patient and, without Jonathan knowing, he had made her feel better about herself.

'I know what I'm doing,' she said.

Her mother took hold of her hands. They were cool, long and elegant, the nails polished and neat, not blunt and stubby like Janet's. 'You're old enough to make up your own mind.' She smiled as if remembering something exceptionally sweet. 'I was married at your age. Just be careful.'

'I want to see the flat before I make a decision,' Janet told Jonathan.

'I'll pick you up from work on Tuesday.'

The crisp smell of autumn fought against the exhaust fumes of city traffic when she stepped out from the top entrance of the hospital. Normally she would have used the bottom entrance, but she couldn't face meeting Jonathan among the bins and laundry dollies of the Housekeeping Department.

'Yoohoo!'

She knew the voice even before she turned round.

Dorothea had a sly grin on her face. 'I couldn't resist,' she said with a girlish giggle.

Janet instantly regretted telling her all about it over lunch that day. 'Are you referring to my meeting Jonathan, or the man, correction, men in your life?'

Dorothea giggled some more. 'You know me. I'm just here to help.'

'You didn't need to.' She made an attempt at being dismissive. 'Haven't you got a bus to catch?'

The hint was ignored.

'Darling, you must be like a boy scout – well prepared.' She leaned close. Her hair smelt of Vaseline shampoo and her neck of Evening in Paris. She glanced furtively around her. 'Luckily for you, the barbers up the road sell French letters.'

Janet reddened. 'How do you know?'

'Because I went in there and got some.' After a short rummage in her bag she nudged her folded fist into Janet's arm. 'Here. Take them. I got them for you.'

'No! I can't.' She kept her voice low. A determined Dorothea continued to thud her arm. Janet glanced wildly about her, concerned lest anyone was watching and had seen what they were doing and heard what they were talking about.

Reluctantly she took the proffered packet and slid it among the folds of a blue and white polka dot scarf that almost filled her handbag. Swiftly and carelessly, she snapped the clasp shut then scanned the traffic.

Jonathan drove a grey Humber Hawk, a car big enough to stand out in a whole heap of traffic.

'There he is,' said Janet.

Dorothea bent from the waist as the car pulled into the kerb. 'He's just as good-looking as I remember him,' she said throwing a wink at Jonathan.

'It's the job I'm after,' Janet hissed.

Just as her fingers touched the door handle, Dorothea grabbed her arm, pulled her close and whispered into her ear. 'I still think he wants to give you more than a job, darling. Good luck. I hope the flat suits.'

Dorothea waved them off as if they were a couple going away on honeymoon. Jonathan had a broad grin on his face. Janet felt obliged to apologize.

'Sorry about Dorothea. She's a good friend, but a bit over the top at times.'

'Seems fine to me.'

Thank goodness he hadn't heard their conversation.

'You look amused.'

'Just happy. We're going to get you working at Saltmead, aren't we?'

On the journey out to Pucklechurch, he asked about her day, and then talked non-stop about his. The more he talked what nestled among the folds of her scarf was forgotten.

The flat was in the original house at the end of a driveway, which connected it with the single-storey huts that formed the hospital. The building was Queen Anne in style, crisp and inclined to geometric brick patterns between each gleaming window.

They parked in a cobblestone courtyard that was shiny and slippery with age. Janet tripped awkwardly on getting out of the car and a buckle on her ankle-strap pinged onto the stones. Jonathan retrieved it then took hold of her arm and guided her to the door. 'Despite that little mishap, I'm sure you'll like it,' he said, his voice full of enthusiasm.

The door was large and as green as the ivy that grappled upwards over weatherworn trelliswork. A lion's head, its teeth bared around an iron ring, formed the knocker.

'Won't be a minute.' He brought a six-inch iron key from his pocket. There was a sound reminiscent of old cogs grating in a disused mill. The lock refused to budge.

'Damn!' He pushed at a stray lock of hair that had slid over his brow. 'Why can't they get a bloody new door or a bloody new lock!'

'Perhaps if you didn't try to force it so much . . .'

'Don't worry your pretty little head,' he said breathlessly, then shot her a quick smile as if to say. *This is a job for a strong man. Lucky I was here!* Like one of those men posed in a Charles Atlas advertisement, 'You Too Can Have a Body Like Mine'.

Something dripped onto her head. She stepped back and looked up over the massed foliage to the gutter that squatted close to the red-tiled roof. The house was old but, from the outside, not disappointing. Would she like the interior?

The door banged open. More water dripped from the gutter and onto her head.

'Something else that needs fixing,' said Jonathan.

'As long as it's not leaking inside I don't care.'

He laughed. 'I almost feel I should be carrying you over the threshold.'

Janet laughed too.

An arched window on the quarter landing where the stairs turned upwards offered an aspect of green lawn interspersed with flowerbeds over which deciduous trees were shedding leaves of yellow, orange and burnt umber.

'It's lovely,' she said. She edged away as Jonathan's arm wound around her shoulders.

'Just here,' he said, his confidence undiminished and led her to a broad, four-panelled door with a brass lock and a Bakelite handle.

Unlike the door, the inside was unspoilt. The flat was on the first floor and full of light. The ceilings were high, the walls painted eggshell blue. Three windows looked out over the garden to the grounds of the sanatorium where low buildings strung in rows of mathematical precision hugged the ground. An ornate cornice ran around the room matched by a central arrangement of grapes, vines and sprawling leaves, a masterpiece of plaster relief.

'I feel like a princess,' she whispered. In her mind she had envisaged a squat bedsit with flaking paint and brown walls, windows running with condensation, gaps around windows and threadbare carpets.

There was a kitchenette with a small gas cooker and, in the living room, a gas fire in what must have once been a beautiful open fireplace with a white marble surround. Chairs with gilt frames, cabriole legs and faded brocade upholstery served to give the room a look of genteel shabbiness.

'The bathroom's down the hall,' Jonathan explained.

She started in that direction, but he grabbed her arm.

'But this room is far more impressive.' He guided her to a door in the corner of the room. The door was solid, six-panelled mahogany, yet it eased open softly like the swish of a curtain.

The bedroom was magnificent. Plaster vines, leaves and grapes covered the ceiling. The walls were mint green, the curtains cream brocade. The bed was impossibly outrageous and dominated the room.

Janet's mouth dropped open. 'It's a tester bed!'

'Tester? Oh. I suppose you mean a four-poster.'

She took another step into the room, her eyes racing over the shiny wood and enamelled portraits set into a baroque credenza. An Edwardian wardrobe decorated with art deco tulips around its full-length mirrors sat on the other side of the room. Although it could not match the credenza for pedigree, its quality was unimpeachable along with the Victorian nursing chair, the sweetheart settee, and the lyre-ended, military table.

Janet was awestruck. 'It's a lovely room.'

Jonathan seemed to swell with pride. 'I knew you'd like it.'

'Oh yes.'

The Indian carpet was ragged along one edge. Janet did not notice it until the heel of her loose shoe caught and she staggered forward.

Jonathan stopped her from falling flat on her face. She went down on one knee, like a debutante being presented to Queen Victoria. Flustered, she scrambled to her feet as the contents of her handbag fell onto the floor. The packet of French letters fell on top of everything else.

Inwardly, Janet groaned.

Jonathan picked up her handbag and put back into it everything that had fallen out – except for the French letters.

Damn Dorothea!

Jonathan was smiling, the afternoon sun seeming to make his eyes gleam more than she'd ever noticed. 'Janet. What a wise woman you are. I knew we understood each other.'

'No,' she said shaking her head. 'You've got it wrong.'

He looked puzzled. 'You do know what these are, don't you?'

Her face felt hotter than hell. 'Of course I do!'

He rested his hands on her shoulders and gazed into her eyes like some Hollywood idol from the silver screen. It crossed her mind that he'd rehearsed the part many times before.

'You don't need to be embarrassed. I'm a modern man. You're a modern woman. We both have needs. What's wrong with satisfying them?'

'Everything!' Janet shrugged his hands off her shoulders. Dorothea's conviction that Jonathan was offering her more than a job was ringing true. 'I've changed my mind. I don't want the job. Now take me home.'

He eyed the offending packet. 'But these?'

'My friend Dorothea gave them to me. She misconstrued, just like you.'

'Obviously.' He shrugged and shoved his hands in his pockets. He looked genuinely hurt. 'I feel a bloody fool. I thought you wanted to get out of that hole you're in. I thought you wanted to work more closely with medicine *and* to leave home.'

'I'm sorry.' It was all she could think of to say and she felt an idiot saying it, even being here.

Jonathan took it as an opening for a second chance. He stood between her and the window, stroked her hair and said, 'Imagine how wonderful it could be, working together during the day, and at night . . .'

The gap between them was minuscule. Janet guessed his motive, took a step back and glared at him. She was seeing him differently now. What she'd interpreted as confidence she now knew to be conceit. No doubt his mother had told him time and time again that he was a good doctor, a handsome catch, but first and foremost, an adorable and loyal son.

'What would your mother think if she knew you were trying to seduce me?'

His expression tightened. Janet continued 'My mother met her. Did you know that? Should we let her know that we're becoming more than friends?'

Mention of his mother seemed to change everything about him. He looked haunted, almost as if he were a boy again, dabbling in something that his mother had specifically banned.

His voice turned cold. 'She's not to know about you,' he blurted. 'She's very precious to me. She gets hurt very easily.'

Stunned to silence, he strode to the window, his hands clenched behind his back. His height and breadth seemed to fill the frame blocking out the view. It was probably no more than a few seconds, though it seemed longer, before he recovered his composure, turned and shook his head mournfully. 'What a shame, and I thought we understood each other.'

He was himself again, glowing with confidence and the self-satisfaction of a handsome, professional man, a doting, loving son.

Janet headed for the door. 'I want to go home – now!'

She presumed they would drive back to Bristol in silence. It surprised her at how quickly Jonathan recovered, as if nothing had happened. He talked of medical matters, of the insensitive stupidity that prevented patients receiving visitors, of heated pools, of swimming lessons and, most of all, of the new vaccine being developed in America on which everyone was pinning great hopes.

When they got to Royal York Crescent he said without a trace of bitterness, 'I'll give you a week to reconsider. After that I'll have to tell Professor Pritchard that he'll have to look elsewhere for a new secretary.'

Tight-lipped, Janet left him there. If she'd attempted to tell him exactly how she was feeling, she would end up in tears and she didn't want to appear weak, not in front of him. The new job, complete with a place to live, had seemed like a dream. The dream was over. Reality had settled in.

Later, she pulled her purse and her scarf out of her handbag and lay both on the dressing table. The interior of her handbag looked oddly bereft although her lipstick, powder compact and tortoiseshell comb were still there. 'Those things . . .' she muttered to herself. Just to make sure, she ran her hands around the silk lining in case the condoms had slipped through an undiscovered rip.

They weren't there. Jonathan had picked them up.

'So will you think about it?' Dorothea asked her the next day at lunch. They were in the hospital canteen, which had high ceilings and was brightly lit. They sat at tables draped with gingham oilcloth, on modern chairs formed from free-flowing plywood on thin metal frames.

The tea was only lukewarm. One sip was enough. Janet slammed the cup into the saucer. 'Not unless the sea freezes over and we have pink snow at Christmas.'

Dorothea giggled. 'Fancy dropping those johnnies, darling. What a giggle!'

Janet grimaced at first, but it quickly became a grin. 'As if a woman would ever carry such things around in her handbag.' Her grin vanished when she saw Dorothea looking at her nonplussed. 'Ah,' Janet said. 'I should have known *you'd* carry them around with you.'

Dorothea shrugged. 'Common sense, darling. By the way, have you still got them?'

'No. I left them behind.' She went on to tell Dorothea how Jonathan had sneakily slid them into his pocket.

'So you're not the only fish in the sea, darling.'

'Obviously not.'

'Oh well. I'll have to get some more.'

Janet remembered the night she'd caught her brother in the altogether except for a condom – obviously supplied by Dorothea.

'While we're on the subject of sex, what exactly is the position between you and my brother?'

Dorothea grinned. 'He was suggestive and I was willing. I think those girls at university aren't very forthcoming.'

'And what about Henry? I thought you two were engaged.'

'Ah yes. But that's a long-term thing, you see. Geoffrey is just a diversion. Do you mind?'

'Why should I?'

The ringing of a bell signified the end of lunchtime.

'For whom the bells tolls.'

They got to their feet accompanied by the sound of metal chair legs scraping across the floor.

Janet sighed gloomily. 'The bell tolls for me. A whole afternoon of typing out the uniform mending rota, swiftly followed by another catalogue of laundry lists.'

'Isn't there anything to make you reconsider Jonathan's offer?' Dorothea asked as they pushed through the swing doors and out into the corridor followed by the all-pervading smell of mashed potato and fishcakes.

Janet shook her head. 'It would have to be something pretty earth-shattering to make me change my mind.'

Polly was sitting on a dining chair in Edna's front room having her hair permed, the stink of the lotion permeating the whole house and sending the kids into coughing fits. Colin ushered everyone, including Carol who had come with her mother, out into the garden.

'We had a drop of rain last night, but the grass is almost dry now,' he said as they all piled out of the back door.

'Let's play cowboys and indians!' shouted Peter as he galloped around the lawn slapping his sides and making clip-clopping sounds.

Carol was contemptuous. 'That's silly.'

Susan slumped onto the low wall that ran between the lawn and the house. 'I've got a bad head and my legs ache.'

Colin suggested football. 'Come on, Susan. If yer feet get going that headache might go too. How about it?'

Susan nodded and got up. Colin noticed her flushed cheeks, but seeing her make the effort to join in, told himself she was perfectly all right.

The game turned noisy, mostly on account of Carol and Peter pushing and shoving each other away from the ball, both kicking it at the same time, and breaking every rule including the ones from boxing, more than once did an elbow or a fist venture below the belt.

Fed up of being relegated to goal, Colin did his best to chase and kick the ball, confident that, as an adult, he could keep up with them.

Gait awkward and legs stiff, he staggered across the lawn, forcing himself to go faster even though he waddled dangerously from side to side. Pretending he was young again helped him forget that the bottom halves of his legs were long gone, that the replacements were tin and not at all flexible.

'You look like Noddy!' shouted Peter as Colin trundled around like a wooden soldier, feet slipping on the damp grass.

'Come on then, Big Ears,' shouted Colin as he fought to dribble the ball down the centre of the lawn, 'Tackle me! Come on! Tackle me!'

Both children chased him while Carol tried to tackle him from the front. Peter caught up and aimed a hard kick at Colin's shin. Colin yelped, was about to joke that it hurt, when his leg slid out from under him.

Everything happened too fast to be avoided. He fell backwards, his feet leaving muddy ruts in the grass.

'No!' he shouted as the horror of what was about to happen became all too clear.

Susan screamed as his weight fell on top of her.

Colin's first thought was for his daughter. 'Susan!'

Carol ran for help. By the time Edna and Polly ran into the garden, he had managed to roll onto his side.

'Susan!'

Her eyes were closed. He reached out and felt the heat of her cheek.

Edna knelt between them both, a horrified look on her face. 'What happened?'

'I slipped.'

'Blinking 'eck,' said Polly. 'You almost buried her.'

Normally, he would have screamed in pretend terror at the sight of Polly with her head encased in pink plastic curlers and tissue paper. But his back ached, his legs ached, and most of all, his heart ached for Susan.

Edna got down behind her daughter, took hold of her head and rested it in her lap. Polly ordered Carol to get a glass of water from the kitchen.

Polly and Carol got Colin onto his feet.

'Daddy tackled me for the ball,' said Peter, his lower lip quivering with fear lest guilty glares be turned in his direction.

Colin's face creased with concern and his breathing was laboured. 'It's my fault. I had no business kicking that ball about.'

Polly squeezed his arm. 'Don't be silly.'

Edna eased the glass of water between her daughter's lips. 'Come on, dear. Just a little.'

Susan spluttered, opened her eyes and drank a little more. She nodded weakly when Edna asked her if she was all right.

After Polly had gone and the children were put to bed, Colin went back out into the garden.

'Nearly finished!' Edna shouted to him, presuming the smell of the perming lotion had driven him out to watch the house martins weave and wheel around the houses and towards the disused air raid shelters down towards Conham Vale. The light was fading fast, but a strip of gilt-edged clouds hovered on the horizon.

Colin picked up a stick that Peter used as a riding whip

and began tapping it against his legs. They made a hollow sound, a grim reminder that they were made of metal, not flesh and blood. I sound like a bunch of old corned beef cans, he thought, almost grinned, then recalled Susan's flame-coloured cheeks. Good God, he was no lightweight. He could have killed her.

He didn't often feel sorry for himself, but tonight he wished with all his heart that he still had his legs. Tonight he felt real hatred for those who had caused the blast that had taken them. No more football. No more cricket. No more swimming or gliding around a dance floor to a quickstep or a foxtrot. A waltz was barely manageable.

He brushed the moisture from his eyes.

'Damn! Damn! Damn!'

With each word he beat his right leg with the stick. On the third stroke it broke into two pieces and he threw them away.

Later that evening, Edna finished pinning and cutting out a new dress for Susan without any need to reread the instructions. 'Beautiful,' she said as she folded up the blue silk material and closed her sewing box. 'Just like our Susan.'

Colin didn't answer. He'd hardly said a word all evening but sat staring at the television set even though it wasn't switched on. He reminds me of my mother, thought Edna, but swiftly banished the thought. Her mother and Colin were worlds apart.

Edna fixed her eyes on him as she left her sewing things and went to the back of his chair, slid her hands down over his shoulders and onto his chest. 'Stop worrying,' she murmured and kissed his ear. 'Susan's fine. She's a very tough little girl.'

'I could have killed her,' he said, and his face creased with worry.

Edna squeezed his shoulders then laid one hand on his cheek and turned his face towards hers. When she saw the look in his eyes, her heart skipped a beat. His pain was her pain. 'Oh Colin!' She kissed him then laid her cheek against his. 'She's all right, and look, I've made her a new dress.'

She went back to her sewing and unfolded the blue silk. The pattern was still pinned to it so she only showed him the silky side. 'Isn't it lovely? It's for Christmas. She'll look like a princess.'

He managed a weak smile. 'I just feel such a clumsy clod at times.'

'Never mind. Susan's fine.'

She refolded the dress. 'She's upstairs sound asleep and none the worse for you falling on her like a sack of spuds. She'll be marching off to school as usual in the morning, just like any other day.'

The silence deepened. No sound of cars, children or passers-by came from the street outside. Curtains were drawn against the night and the house was still as Edna resettled into her chair. It was one of those moments when the smallest sound, the slightest variation in movement is easily heard. That was when they heard something from upstairs.

Colin stirred from his chair. 'What was that?' His eyes met hers. Together they listened to something . . . strangulated . . . retching.

'Someone's being sick!'

The blue silk was swiftly pushed aside. Edna dashed out into the hallway and up the stairs, paused and listened. Was it Peter or the girls? That sound again, definitely coming from the room shared by their two daughters.

As she flung the door wide, the nauseating stench of vomit hit her nostrils. Muffin the Mule went flying across the floor as she kicked it away from the side of the bed and the threat of yet more vomit.

Without caring about the mess, she knelt down. 'I'm here, darling.'

Susan's forehead was hot beneath her hand. The child retched again and again. Her eyes were closed. When she'd finished vomiting she fell back onto the pillow without saying anything, without being aware that her mother was there. Edna immediately knew that something was very wrong.

She got up and shouted down the stairs. 'Colin! Call the doctor.'

Colin's face appeared down in the hall. 'What is it?'

Am I overreacting? Edna asked herself. Her instinct told her otherwise. 'It's Susan. Tell him she's been sick and she won't wake up.'

She heard the phone being dialled and thanked God they were well off enough to afford it. Small mercies, she thought and found herself wishing that Colin hadn't been playing football, that he was just a little more accepting of his limitations. Earlier she had tried coaxing him out of his guilt. Now she found herself blaming him for Susan's sickness.

Minutes seemed like hours. Edna stayed upstairs while Colin remained in the hallway, waiting for the doctor to arrive.

He was a dapper man, a Dr Sampson who wore a brocade waistcoat and an off-white Panama.

Edna watched from beside the bed, Colin from the doorway, looking nervous as if he was afraid to step forward and accept the blame that he'd already laid on his own shoulders.

The doctor examined her and shook his head. 'We have to get this dear child into hospital at once. We need an ambulance.'

Edna knew when to fear the worst. 'What's wrong with her?'

The doctor unclipped his stethoscope and returned it to his bag. 'She has poliomyelitis.'

Edna gasped and sunk to her knees at the side of the bed as if in prayer. And praying was exactly what she was doing. 'No! Not that! Please God not that!'

The doctor turned to Colin. 'Call for an ambulance.'

Edna felt as though her knees had turned to stone. It was

impossible to straighten them, unthinkable to leave her child's side.

Cosy in her cot, Pamela slept through it all. Edna glanced at her then at the doctor.

'Just keep an eye on her during the next thirty days or so,' he said as if reading her thoughts.

Outside, the clanging bells of the ambulance echoed between the houses of Kingscott Avenue. Curtains twitched at bedroom windows. A few brave souls stood at garden gates dressed only in nightclothes and slippers, the women with their hair in curlers.

Heavy boots thundered up the stairs. Edna oversaw everything, hovering around them, clucking with worry as they took her darling from her bed. Susan's face was flushed. Her eyes were closed and her breathing seemed laboured.

The ambulance men wore white cotton masks over the lower part of their faces. Susan's face seemed small against the size of the stretcher and the thick blanket that covered her up to her neck.

Until now she'd been almost comatose. Now she began to throw her head from side to side. 'Mum . . . mmmy?'

'I'm coming, darling.' Edna started to get into the ambulance but a hand grabbed her arm and pulled her back.

'You can't go, Mrs Smith.' Dr Sampson's expression was grimly resolute.

'She's my daughter,' cried Edna.

'Edna, love.' Colin placed an arm around her shoulder.

The doctor took a pocket watch out of his waistcoat, checked the time and put it away again before saying anything. He was close to retirement and had hoped never to have to deal with this situation again. Parents were difficult to deal with when infantile paralysis was mentioned. 'Can we go inside?' he said at last.

The ambulance door slammed shut. So final, thought Edna, so much like a . . .

'She's going to be all right.' Colin held her close. She was sure he had just had the same thought as she had, that their daughter might not be coming home, that the sound of the ambulance door slamming was reminiscent of a lid being slammed on a coffin.

They watched the ambulance trundle away. Before it reached the end of Kingscott Avenue, the emergency bell began to clang its furious note and sent shivers through their bodies.

Edna felt Colin's hand patting her arm and heard him say, 'She's a fighter, luv. You see. Let the doctors do their bit, get her over the worse, then we'll visit her at the hospital.'

She was too numb to say anything until they were inside the house. Colin offered the doctor a cup of tea. He declined.

Edna clung to Colin. There was something about the doctor's expression that made her fear the worse.

'Is she going to die?' Her voice was no more than a whisper, yet the question hung in the room like a raw, open wound.

The doctor pursed his lips and looked down at his shoes before answering. 'I don't think so. However, your daughter is seriously ill. As I have already said, she is suffering from poliomyelitis.'

Edna sank into a chair. Colin swayed a little and leaned on the wall for support.

'This doesn't necessarily mean that she will show any signs of paralysis. Most victims merely recover from the illness without suffering any damage to the nerve cells . . .' he paused. Edna stared at him wide-eyed, but said nothing. Colin did the same. What about *their* child? Would she pull through without having irons up her legs, withered arms or hunched shoulders? They'd seen children like that far too often and had thanked God theirs could run and play.

A vision of Susan's face swam before Edna's eyes. She heard again that long wail, her child calling for her.

'When can I . . .' She glanced at Colin, saw his worried face, and corrected herself, 'we see her?'

The doctor got his pocket watch out again and edged towards the door. 'They've taken her to Saltmead. They don't allow visitors. You won't be able to see her until she's ready to come home.'

Edna exchanged a shocked look with Colin. Didn't anyone care about the fear of a sick child in strange surroundings?

Colin shook his head in disbelief. 'Are you telling me we can't even visit her? That's barbaric!'

The old doctor frowned. Negative behaviour. Exactly as he'd feared and what the sanatoriums, quite correctly, guarded against.

'Yes, Mr Smith. Emotional outbursts are not conducive to a patient's well-being.'

He reached for his hat, left beneath the budgie's cage. 'Good day to you both,' he said and departed into a rosy dawn.

Colin found himself hoping that the budgie had done his job – lots of jobs – all over the doctor's hat.

After he'd left, Edna marched out into the hall and picked up the telephone.

Colin followed her. 'What are you doing?'

'I'm phoning Charlotte. She'll know what to do.'

'Are you nuts? It's nearly midnight.'

The dial whirred round noisily under Edna's slim fingers. 'She's my friend. She'll understand.'

It stung to think she needed someone other than himself. Colin stood helpless, his shoulders slumped and a feeling of sickness in his soul. More than that, he felt guilty. If only he hadn't slipped. Falling on Susan might have had something to do with her illness.

Edna concentrated on the telephone as she waited for Charlotte to answer. She couldn't bring herself to look at Colin. She felt incredibly alone. All she could think of was Susan. She would do anything, anything at all to help her pull through this.

David answered, his voice heavy with sleep. She should

have realized it would be him that would pick it up. Doctors get called out at all hours, even those with mainly private patients.

'David. It's Edna. Can I speak to Charlotte? It's urgent.'

She could have told David about Susan, asked him about visiting, but she'd never felt comfortable talking to him. She trusted Charlotte completely. It was her she had to tell.

Once Charlotte was on the other end of the phone, Edna burst into tears. 'I'm sorry about this,' she gulped between explanations. 'But I'm so frightened. This is all so terrible.'

The sound of the telephone ringing had brought Charlotte close to full wakefulness. David's footsteps out on the landing and his knock on her bedroom door had completed the process.

'I'll make some tea,' David had offered while Charlotte got into her dressing gown and made her way to his bedroom and the telephone.

Charlotte sat on the bed in the warm spot left by David. Sensing that Edna had something private to impart, she waited until she was alone to pick up the telephone. 'Think nothing of it,' she said in response to Edna's apologies about waking her up and wondered if Edna knew that she and David had separate bedrooms. Edna's outpourings about Susan had swiftly obliterated such trivia.

Edna explained that Susan had been taken to Saltmead Sanatorium.

'I know the place,' said Charlotte effortlessly, although mention of it sent a jolt through her memory. Oh yes. She knew the place all right. It hadn't always been called that. At one time it had been an American Army base, then a prisoner of war camp. She had known it well in those days, had had little to do with it since, until now. She agreed to find out what she could.

'Edna's daughter has been taken off to the Saltmead

Sanatorium,' she said to David when he came back with the tea.

'Good Lord! Polio,' he groaned as he passed a bone china cup and saucer to his wife. 'The twentieth-century plague.'

Charlotte raised her eyebrows. 'As bad as that?'

David eased himself back into bed, tucked the covers under his chin and reached for his tea. 'Oh yes. Millions dead and millions crippled. A worldwide epidemic that first raised its ugly head at the beginning of this century and likely to be with us somewhere in the world at the beginning of the next.'

'I'll take my tea with me,' she said getting up and heading for the door. 'Goodnight.'

'Goodnight indeed,' David grumbled behind her. 'Why can't your friends and acquaintances phone at more reasonable hours?'

Charlotte eyed the man she'd once loved to distraction. She was still loyal to him, still supportive, and she knew he suffered pain – both mental and physical – that made him moody. Most of the time she was patient with his moods and thoughtless comments. Today she was not.

'Every hour is reasonable if your child is ill!'

The slamming of the bedroom door reverberated along the landing.

In her pink and white bedroom overlooking the Avon Gorge, Janet's eyes flashed open. She stared up at the ceiling, at first assuming that the sound had come from above her.

Rising up onto her elbows, she peered through the semi-gloom to the bedroom door. The bolt was still pulled across it, but waking up so suddenly had made her want to use the bathroom.

After pushing back the bedclothes she swung her legs out of bed, feeling with her toes for the furry lining of her kidskin slippers. The feel of her woollen dressing gown helped lessen the shivers that ran down her spine. Footsteps sounded from out on the landing coming closer to her room. Slowly, softly she slid the bolt back and opened the door just a fraction afraid it might be Ivan, but determined to face him.

A shadowy figure made her jump until she realized who it was.

'Mother!'

'I wasn't sure you were up.'

Janet opened the door. 'What's wrong?'

Charlotte never looked bleary-eyed or puffy-cheeked even first thing in the morning. Rather she looked bright, keen to attack the day with confident efficiency. Tonight she looked and sounded anxious.

'Edna telephoned. Susan's been taken away to Saltmead Sanatorium in an ambulance. She has polio.'

Janet felt her jaw go slack. Sorrow, sympathy, desperation and regret seemed to flood through her body, yet no words came. One thought above all others did occur. She had told Dorothea that pink snow would have to fall before she accepted Jonathan's offer and even then she'd have to think about it very carefully indeed. The snow was pure fantasy, but the pink cheeks and happy smile of a lovely little girl was real and she had to do something.

Dorothea staggered along as best she could on four-inch heels, a ridiculous height for work. She was trying to keep up with Janet, who was marching along at breakneck pace, her arms full of files and her expression serious.

'What did he say when you phoned him?' asked Dorothea, her face bright with interest. 'I bet he said you had to go to bed with him if you take the job.'

'Don't be ridiculous!'

'So he was fine about you taking the job without going to bed with him?'

Damn the French letters, Janet thought to herself. Small as the package had been, they must have appeared like a banner to Jonathan, an obvious advertisement that she was available.

'He didn't mention it.'

Neither had she. If he had mentioned it, she would have stipulated that it was only the job she wanted, not him.

'Did you tell him about Susan?'

'No. I did not.'

Although shocked to the core to think the lovely Susan was suffering from one of the worst diseases of the twentieth century, Janet had kept her head. Jonathan might not have been willing to take her on if he had known that she was taking the job for Susan's sake. Best, she had thought, to allow him to live in hope.

They stopped by the door to the porter's lodge where the files Janet was carrying would be left prior to burning in the furnaces that heated the hospital and were situated deep beneath St Michael's Hill.

Dorothea glanced around, saw the corridor was empty and lit up a cigarette. 'So why the big fuss about Susan? She's not your kid, darling. Are you sure you're not going sweet on the good doctor?'

Janet pushed open the door of the porter's lodge. 'No!'

She didn't want to explain the reasons why she'd changed her mind. The truth was, it was hard admitting even to herself that she shouldered the blame for Susan's illness. If only she hadn't taken her to Clevedon. Swimming pools, Jonathan had told her, were a suspected source of the dreadful disease. If only Susan hadn't fallen into the water.

Back in Royal York Crescent, Charlotte was seated at her desk with the file on Edna's firstborn child open in front of her. She was feeling both sad and exasperated. Susan's tragic predicament had raised a number of questions. One of these was the letter relating to the child born Sherman Burbage and consequently brought up in Brazil and now orphaned in Germany. Charlotte sighed and stared at the ceiling. As if poor Edna didn't have enough to contend with. The poor woman's in no fit state to cope with another problem, she decided. All their efforts must be put into hoping that Susan got better before anything could be done about Edna's eldest son.

'Poor girl,' she said and sighed audibly. Just at that moment the sound of the vacuum echoed along the landing. Polly had arrived. Now there was a woman with a carefree existence if ever there was. Trouble never seemed to call at her door, or if it did, they never heard anything about it.

Fifteen

Typically for late autumn, it was a misty night, the air a mix of chill and soot forewarning a foggy November.

Already peeved that she'd received no response to her second letter to Australia House, Polly was now hot under the collar because she'd sent Carol and her friend Sean up to the coke-house over two hours ago to get a hundred-weight of coal for the fire. They still weren't back and the fire had burned almost to ash. She gave it a jab with a brass-headed poker. Initially it glowed bright, but gradually faded.

'That fire ain't goin' to last much longer. It's goin' to be flippin' freezin' in 'ere!'

Still grasping the poker, she opened the front door, peering beyond the scrappy lawn and privet hedges. Not that she could see much. The mist was turning to fog and Carol was nowhere to be seen.

'It'll be colder still if you don't put the wood back in the bleeding 'ole,' said Meg as she folded sheets and pillowcases into a pile on the dining table. Close by, deceptively hot, sat two old-fashioned flatirons recently heated from the open fire.

Polly slammed the door and grimaced. 'One day I'll get a proper iron.'

'It is proper.'

'One that plugs into the light socket and got a handle that don't burn yer hand.'

Polly re-checked that the pennies she'd saved for the gas

meter were still in her pocket. Her fingers touched the grimy coppers. No holes in this apron, thank God! Once the gas was gone they'd go into the meter, but until then the irons would be heated on the coal until all the ironing was done – as long as Carol got home before the fire went out.

Polly wrapped her cardigan closely around herself and went out into the kitchen to fill the kettle. Never mind the coal or the gas, she wasn't going to deny herself a cup of tea. At least there was plenty of that in the cupboard. If Billy had been home on time she'd have gone down into Bedminster this afternoon and done her weekly shop. But Billy was not a creature of regular habits and she could always shop locally near the Broadway Picture House, but Griffiths might be lurking around and she didn't want to bump into him.

Daydreaming as she waited for the kettle to boil, her gaze fixed on the scrawny sprouts she'd planted just in front of the chicken run. The war was long over, but everyone on the estate still bought fluffy little chicks in the spring to fatten up for Christmas. But Polly wasn't seeing the sprouts, the squawking chickens or the condensation running down the windows, and she wasn't seeing the rain outside. Instead she saw a long, sandy beach, white-capped waves riding a blue ocean and dappled sunlight on a white bungalow with something pink and pretty growing along its veranda.

Just as the kettle screeched and a white plume of steam rose from the spout, Meg called to her from the living room, her voice accompanied by a loud banging on the front door knocker.

'Polly! Polly!' She sounded worried.

Polly dashed into the living room.

'It looks like the police, though what with this mist . . .' Meg murmured. Her tone changed. 'It's not our Carol, is it?'

'We won't know that until we open the bloody door!'

As she turned the catch, the door was pushed open and she was slammed against the wall.

She managed to right herself enough to eye up the ugly brutes who had entered, definitely not police unless they'd taken to wearing loud, checked suits with soft, felt hats. 'Who the bloody hell are you?'

'Business acquaintances of your old man!'

Billy!

Rough hands and hard knuckles manhandled her back into the living room.

'Get over there, you silly tart!'

One grabbed her shoulders and flung her against the dresser. Pastel blue cups rattled on their hooks; two saucers and a plate went crashing to the floor.

Meg was pushed against the table. The piled ironing toppled to the floor and one of the hot irons fell onto its side. The smell of singed cotton mingled with that of cheap cologne and ripe armpits.

Meg looked amazed. 'I thought they were plain clothes policemen.'

The two men burst out laughing. 'Coppers! Bloody 'ell, we don't look that bloody stupid, do we? Bloody silly cow! Bloody silly mare!'

Polly fixed her gaze on the geezer who still held her shoulder so she could describe him to Billy. She didn't know why she felt she should do that; it wasn't as if he'd likely black their eyes or thump their nose. Billy was dishonest not violent. But she memorized him anyway. Sandy moustache, sandy hair, sandy eyebrows and eyes so pale they were only barely blue. Cheap suit, tan mac and dark green trilby. And obviously he thought throwing in a few basic expletives aimed at them made him something of a comedian.

'I thought they were plain clothes,' Meg whined again as if repeating the comment would make everything right again.

'Silly cow.' The scrawny thug who held her looked at 'Ginger' for confirmation that he was doing OK.

Ginger grinned approvingly then hooked his fingers over the low neckline of Polly's dress and pulled her closer to him. 'So where's yer old man?'

Never one to back down easily, Polly grappled with the thick fingers. 'Get yer 'ands off this frock! It's me best one.'

His face was close to hers and his breath smelled of something sour. His face was not his fortune. She noticed his lashes were almost silver. She'd seen them like that on pigs, when they were dead and hung up on hooks.

'Now look 'ere,' he said menacingly, and she held her breath against the mix of smells. 'If you don't tell me what I wants to know, that frock'll be off yer back and so will yer vest. D'you know what I'm saying?'

Polly glared right back at him. 'Do what you like! I've 'ad bigger and better than you, mate – and I ain't referring to yer height or the size of your nose, you ginger toe rag!'

His pale skin turned bright pink. 'Is that so!' He pushed her with one hand and clawed at the neckline with the other.

Rip went her dress.

Polly screamed.

Ginger sneered.

'Piss off!' Up went her knee. Ginger bent almost double as it connected with his crotch, but damn him, he didn't let go.

A nerve ticked beneath one of his glaring eyes. Polly gritted her teeth for what she knew would come.

'You fucking cow!'

This time he was careful. Shoulders forward, pelvic area held well back, he grabbed her wrists so she couldn't move. His smell was overpowering.

Now it was Polly who sneered. 'You'll 'ave to do better than that.' She aimed another kick at his crotch, but caught his shin.

He slapped her and it stung. But she wouldn't be beaten.

Standing as tall as she could until the backs of her knees felt they were splitting, she spat into his face.

'You're gonna regret that.'

Despite her stinging cheek, she laughed in his face. 'Do what you like, you ginger git, but I'll be spittin' and fightin' all the bloody way!'

She could see he believed her. Hopefully he would make the decision to call it a day and clear off. But the decision he made was not the one she wanted.

A nasty smile crept across his mouth like a slimy maggot. Polly's heart leapt to her throat as 'Ginger' turned to his sidekick. 'If that's the way she wants it, Gordy, then that's the way we'll 'ave it. P'raps the old lady there can tell us where Billy is. Give 'er a 'and with that ironing, Gordy. Make sure the iron's nice and hot, mind or it won't do a decent job.'

'She don't know anything!'

Sheer terror registered on Aunty Meg's face and Polly wished she were ten times bigger and stronger.

She winced as Ginger grasped a handful of her hair, tilting her head back so her face was level with his.

'Then you'd better tell me what I wants to know, Blondie, 'adn't you?' he growled.

'I don't know where he is, you stupid spastic!'

'Don't call me names, you poxy cow!'

'Don't call me poxy! And open your bloody ears. I don't know where he is! I don't know, you stupid bleeders! Why won't you listen to me?'

Meg's eyes were round with fear and her bottom lip quivered as the thug held the iron close to her arm.

Polly watched helplessly. 'Let her go, you swine! I don't know where Billy is I tell ya, I don't bloody know!'

A sudden movement beyond the window caught her eye, too quick to ascertain who or what it was. Perhaps the neighbours had heard and were coming to the rescue.

Ginger's nose was near enough to bite and she would if she

could. It was so close, but then the hot iron was close to Meg's arm.

'So where is he?' Ginger asked again, his breath damply unpleasant on her face.

Where could he be? She hadn't a clue, but in the circumstances and bearing in mind that these two were employed for being bullies not brains, it was OK to lie.

'He's out doing a job for a friend of mine in Clifton. A magistrate actually. She's married to a doctor.'

Charlotte had mentioned something about being asked to 'sit on the bench' as she called it, but had turned it down because she didn't have the time. Polly had merely said it to impress.

Ginger frowned. 'It'll be the worse for him – and for you – if he's grassing on us.'

'Just moving some furniture for her,' Polly said quickly, thinking on her feet as she realized she'd made a fatal mistake by mentioning the law.

'So when's he home?'

'Six,' she blurted. 'He should be home by six.' It was a guess, but would have to do.

Ginger studied her expression for any sign that she might be lying – not that he was likely to be that observant judging by his vocabulary. He narrowed his eyes. 'Now I wonder if yer tellin' the truth. Or are you just trying to save the old lady there?'

'It's the truth, you stupid sod!'

Polly's gaze strayed to the door. If only Billy would burst in with a couple of nifty neighbours at his side.

Ginger looked as pleased as a tomcat that's just given the mouse its last try for freedom. He said to Gordy, 'Give the old lady one to remember us by just so Blondie 'ere knows we mean business.'

'No!' Polly twisted against Ginger's grip.

Meg wailed loudly as the iron was raised.

Polly screamed all the very worse expletives she could

think of and prayed like she'd never prayed before – except for the time when she'd given God one last chance. She'd prayed for Gavin, Carol's father to be on the troop train at Temple Meads Station. He'd let her down. This time He didn't.

A flash of navy gymslip flew into the room. Childish arms held high a heavy willow hockey stick and a youthful voice shouted in anger, 'Get out, you bleeding sod!'

Gordy yelled out in anguish as the hooked end of the stick whacked into the backs of his knees. The flat iron went crashing and so did Gordy, as he fell forwards among the folded bedding and neatly ironed underwear.

'Leave my aunty alone, you bleeder!' shouted Carol as she rained a hail of hefty blows onto the head and back of the prostrate Gordy.

Polly took the opportunity to bring her knee up into Ginger's groin with twice the force of the first encounter. Ginger doubled up, his eyes almost bursting out of his head.

Gordy was groaning, flat out on the floor, his head bleeding. Carol turned her attention to the doubled-up Ginger. 'Get away from my mum!'

Ginger's hat flew across the room and Polly winced as wooden stick crunched bony head. Ginger fell to his knees.

Gordy started to rise. Meg eyed him casually, but there was vengeance in her eyes. With one mighty blow she brought the iron down on the nape of his neck.

'Burn me would you, you bloody swine?'

A smell reminiscent of burnt pork filled the room. Gordy yelled like a scalded cat and made for the door. Polly stepped in his way, Carol, snarling and still armed with the hockey stick stood beside her.

'Not so fast, Gordy!' Polly pointed at the supine form lying between the back of the settee and the dinner table. 'Take that ginger git with you. He makes the room look untidy.'

Ginger kept his hands over his crotch as Gordy heaved him

to his feet. Polly opened the door for them and kicked each one up the backside as they negotiated the doorstep.

'And good bloody riddance,' she shouted.

Coming up behind Gordy, a grinning Carol brought the hockey stick up between his legs, which almost made him jump out of his shoes.

'Cut that out!' snapped Polly and aimed a slap in Carol's direction. Luckily it missed. Polly smiled. Carol didn't really deserve punishment. She was the hero of the hour and knew it.

Carol slung her hockey stick over her shoulder. 'I wanted to knock his balls off.'

'Carol!' Meg looked shocked.

Polly grabbed Carol by the shoulders. 'Less of that kind of talk. You'll never be a lady when you grow up.'

Carol looked nonplussed. 'But I don't want to be a lady, Ma. I want to be just like you.'

Polly blinked and tried to decide whether to slap her face and send her to bed for her sauce or give her a ruddy big hug. After all, she was only ten years old.

'Well, now you know what she's been learning at school,' laughed Meg. 'They've taught her to know a lady when she sees one! And you ain't it!'

'My little soldier,' said Polly and gave Carol a hug. 'Wait till I tells Billy what you just done. Now let's get some tea on, shall we? Bread and blackcurrant jam and a bit of Aunty Meg's sultana cake. How would that be, then?'

'Lovely!'

When they were back in the house, Polly looked at the walnut clock that sat on the mantelpiece. She looked at it a few times more that night. Billy was still not home. To be half an hour overdue was normal for a man who didn't steer too closely to the truth. To be nearly two hours late was worrying.

Edna stared at the test card on the television screen. Intermission, that odd time set aside by the BBC to enable families to sit down and have their lunch, their dinner or just some time to do other things. The BBC was very concerned that family life should not be disrupted.

Colin leaned over and turned it off. Edna watched the last dot of bright light diminish to nothing.

'You can't go on like this, Edna love. She's in the best place.'

Edna sat numbly, her eyes still fixed on the screen. 'I want to see her there. It's been two days.'

Colin sighed. 'You know what the doctor said . . .'

'Perhaps we misunderstood,' she said, her voice brittle and her eyes nervously bright. 'It was the middle of the night after all.'

Sad-eyed, Colin tried to reason with her, saying it was a waste of time and that they had heard correctly.

She nodded, her hands trembling as she fixed a pillbox hat on her head with a pair of silver pins. 'We'll see! We'll see!' she said in that same bright voice.

There were about eight other people waiting to see the doctor. The clock on the wall ticked loudly accompanied by the rustling of well-thumbed magazines, wheezing chests, sneezes and sniffles.

When it came to their turn, Dr Sampson, the same doctor who had come out to Susan, looked up, sighed and leaned back in his chair resignedly.

Edna, determined that she would not be put off by his sullen and impatient attitude, sat herself down and asked him again when she could visit her child. Again he told her it was not possible.

He narrowed his eyes and peered at her over the top of his glasses as though hopeful that a fierce look and strong words might dissuade her from asking any more awkward questions. 'You'll just get in the way and the child will get over-emotional.'

Although Colin put a restraining hand on her shoulder,

Edna sprang to her feet. 'She's a child away from her mother for the first time. Of course she'll get emotional. What do you think we are? Fish?'

Her outburst did not go down well. 'No, Mrs Smith, I do not. I am a man with a great many more patients to see. I have told you the situation as it is. Now, goodbye!'

'Come on, love.' Colin coaxed her out. She was simmering inside. Yes, the medical care Susan was receiving was very important, but surely it wasn't a good thing to isolate her from those she loved?

'I don't care. I'm going to see her no matter what they say,' said Edna once they were back in the waiting room.

'Listen . . .' said Colin, his voice as gentle as his expression.

'No! I'm going out there right away.'

'Listen. Leave it for today. We may hear something, and anyway, Charlotte's looking into it. If anyone can get us into that place, she can.'

Colin hugged her close though she still held herself stiff as a board. Those still sitting in the surgery raised their eyes over the tops of the magazines or looked up from studying their shoes. Colin didn't care. 'Are you listening?' he asked.

His arms were warm and comforting. So were his hazel eyes and gradually her tension lessened.

Colin sighed heavily and his body trembled. 'Now, calm down. Let's give things time. First thing tomorrow we'll tell my parents and yours what's happened. It's only right. Agreed?'

They told his parents first and took Pamela and Peter with them. Pamela was too young to know what was happening. Peter knew his sister had been taken ill, but time off school was definitely welcome although it meant he was isolated from his school friends for fear of contamination.

'Oh my!' gasped Colin's mother when they told her. Tears clung to her sandy lashes as she covered her mouth with one hand and beat at her broad breast with the other. 'Poor little mite!'

Colin's father bit hard on the unlit pipe he clenched at the corner of his mouth. His moustache quivered as he patted her shoulder. He said strong words, but there was no mistaking the pain in his eyes.

He swallowed hard and managed to say, 'Have you told . . .' nodding at the wall in the general direction of Edna's parents' house.

Edna took a deep breath, already recalling the smell of the place from her last visit. 'They're next.'

They said kind words and offered to make them tea before they went. Edna declined. She wanted to get it over with. They also offered to take care of Pamela and Peter while she told her parents.

She shook her head. 'No.'

It was hard not to appear surly, but she couldn't help herself. One child had been taken from her. She wasn't letting the other two out of her sight.

Both the solid front door and the inner glass door of the house in Nutgrove Avenue where Edna had spent a restricted childhood and a less than happy adolescence was wide open. Normally only the outer door was left open during the day, but Edna gave it little attention. She had far more pressing things to worry about than her parents' forgetfulness.

Colin entered the dark passage leaving her to unbuckle the pink leather harness that fixed Pamela into her pushchair. Peter followed him, but not galloping and neighing wildly as he usually did. He didn't quite understand the reasons for his sister having been taken away, but he sensed sadness, as children sometimes do.

Just as Edna proceeded to lift Pamela out of her pushchair, Peter came rushing out of the house. 'There's no one in,' he panted.

A stiff thudding sound from within the passage foretold Colin's return. He repeated Peter word for word. 'There's no one in!'

Edna looked around the street, half-expecting her father to

be ushering her mother down the road after taking her to do a little shopping in one of the small shops along St John's Lane.

An old man pruning a rose bush in the front patch – it could hardly be called a garden – of a house three doors along, straightened and looked in their direction. 'He's gone to the park!' he shouted.

Colin thanked him. Edna couldn't bring herself to say anything. How nice! Her parents were in the park and her child was in hospital. It wasn't fair!

'We could leave my parents to tell them,' said Colin. 'You don't have to see them.'

Edna shook her head. Much as it angered her to waste valuable time trying to get through to her mother that her grandchild was ill, it was something that had to be done, a matter of conscience. Besides, there was still her father to consider. Despite having her mother to contend with, he would want to know.

They walked up Nutgrove Avenue. At the top they turned towards the park where bronzed plane leaves sailed from the trees to the grass each time the wind blew. They took the lower path past the park keeper's cottage, a building of red brick and grey slate, its lines softened by a rampant wistaria, its purple flowers hanging heavy and turning brown, and walked along Sycamore Street, a low wall dividing the park from the road. Children were playing on the swings and a couple with a black and tan dog were walking across the grass, their feet scuffing against the thick carpet of leaves.

In the past Edna had loved the park at this time of year. Today she barely noticed the changing leaves, the smell of woodsmoke as the park keeper burnt up leaves, twigs and litter dropped by careless hands. For once she felt no fear about seeing her mother. She wanted to talk to everyone about it, even to those who wouldn't understand. Talking about the basic facts, the night time visit of the ambulance,

Susan being carted off, being told they could not visit, at least, not yet, helped her deal with it.

Colin was the only person she had difficulty talking to about it because he knew the facts as well as she did and was so accepting of anything the medical profession said because of his first-hand experience when he'd lost his legs. She didn't share that experience.

She sensed Colin watching her, felt his frown and the worry behind it and couldn't respond.

'Can we go and look at the trains?' Peter asked suddenly.

'He'd already asked about going on the swings and had run onto the grass, kicking the leaves, picking up a stick and throwing it for a black and white dog who had promptly brought it back again. Edna had ordered him back to her side.

'No!' she couldn't help snapping. To her mind he shouldn't be playing. Susan was ill.

Colin didn't often get angry, especially with her, but he was now. 'He's just a child, Edna. Life goes on.'

'For him it does,' she blurted.

Colin grabbed her arm and turned her round to face him. 'Don't say that! Don't you dare say that!'

At first Edna wanted to shout at him, to vent all the worry and hurt into the open, but Peter was pulling at her skirt and whining for attention.

'Can we go down to the trains, Mum? Please?'

She looked down into the round face, the bright eyes that belonged to her husband glowing from her son's face. Her heart melted. 'Yes.'

As she turned the pushchair towards the sloping path that led to the far end of the park, the main area of swings and roundabouts and the railway line beyond, she spotted a familiar figure running towards them.

Coat open, hair dishevelled and face anxious, her father raced down the path. He was looking from side to side, scanning the gentle slope that led up through the bushes to the bowling green.

He saw them and came rushing over. Unshaven, agitated and careworn, he held out his hands like some desperate beggar.

'I've lost her!' he cried.

Typical, thought Edna. I'm here to tell them about Susan and already my mother's needs have to come first.

Colin grabbed his arms. 'Calm down!'

'I've got a problem!' her father moaned.

'Haven't we all?' Colin exclaimed, his voice bereft of his usual patience.

Edna turned away from the tiredness of his expression, the exasperation of his voice. She looked about the park, half-expecting her mother to come flying through the flowerbeds, recently planted with wallflowers and pansies for spring flowering, and demanding to know why her father had gone out wearing his best overcoat over his gardening clothes.

Peter fidgeted and wailed, 'What about the trains?'

Colin gave him a quick slap around the ear. 'Cut it out!'

'Colin!' Edna was shocked. She'd never known Colin to raise a hand to his children, or to her for that matter. He saw the accusation in her eyes and she saw the shame appear in his.

Edna put her arm around her father's trembling shoulders. 'What happened, Dad?'

'I was doing a bit of gardening. She was hanging out some washing. She ain't done that for days. It made me think she was on the mend.'

'Oh Dad!' Edna wanted to say that her mother never would mend, that her mind was dying bit by bit and would never be resurrected. She guessed he wouldn't want to hear it.

'I only went to the lavatory,' he said, 'and when I came out she was gone!'

'Now, now,' said Colin. 'P'raps she's just gone shopping down East Street.'

Edna shook her head with unfamiliar impatience. 'It's Sunday, Colin.'

Her father rubbed at his eyes. 'It ain't been easy. Believe me, it ain't been easy. I've got to keep me eyes on her all the time. If she ain't mixing up the porridge with the Persil, she's accusing our nextdoor neighbour of climbing up the drain-pipe at night and stealing her teeth and her glasses.'

Colin looked askance. 'Is there any reason for her to think that?'

If Susan hadn't weighed so heavily on her mind, Edna would have laughed. 'Goodness me, no. Mrs Wiltshire is nearly eighty and hard pushed to get up her front step, let alone shin up a drainpipe.'

A smile flickered around Colin's mouth, then disappeared as quickly as it had come. 'We'll look for her with you,' he said and exchanged a shrug and a helpless look with Edna. What choice did they have? Her father looked older than his sixty-five years. His retirement had not brought the peace and quiet he had hoped for.

'I expect she's down by the trains,' said Peter timidly. He winced as his father rubbed at his head as if expecting another sudden slap.

'Sorry, son,' said Colin and smiled apologetically.

Peter smiled back. All was well again. His hands resumed their customary slapping of his sides.

They took the middle path that sloped down towards the swings, slide and roundabout of the children's playground, which was situated next to the main line into Temple Meads Station. They could not have made a better choice.

Colin pointed. 'There she is.'

A lone figure sat on the roundabout near the railings.

Edna's father broke into a lumbering jog, but Peter got to her first. She grinned toothlessly and said hello.

'Shall I push, Gran?'

'My name's Ethel,' she said to him. 'What's yours?'

'Peter Colin Smith.' He made a clopping sound then a loud neigh. 'And this is Trigger.'

The roundabout went round and Edna watched, thinking how unfair it was that her mother was enjoying a child's ride. It should be Susan sitting there.

Her father scuffed to her side. He was still wearing his slippers. 'Thank God we've found her!'

Edna sank onto a park seat, unable to bear the pain she felt inside. It was as if her stomach was filled with lead, too heavy for either her heart or her legs to cope with.

'Will you tell him?' Colin asked as they watched her father give Peter a hand with pushing the roundabout.

'I . . .' Her mouth was dry. If only she'd accepted the tea Colin's mother had offered.

With a relieved though tired expression, her father made his way back and sat beside her on the bench. Colin remained standing, his gaze fixed on a plume of steam gushing like a great white feather from the funnel of an engine pulling trucks out of the station.

'Dad!' said Edna. She turned to him and took one of his hands in both of hers. 'Susan's in hospital. She's got polio.'

The loose cheeks, the lapsed jowls seemed to grow longer as her father took in the news. At a loss for words, he blinked and shook his head.

The silence lingered and the wind turned cold. Each absorbed in their own thoughts, they watched Peter and his grandmother on the roundabout. We're all searching for the right thing to say, thought Edna. But there is no right thing.

The impulse to talk about things to her mother had disappeared. Weary from lack of sleep and too much worry, she left the possibility – for that was all her mother's understanding could ever be – of telling her to her father.

She saw her father's jaw move as though about to say something. His eyes stayed fixed on her mother. 'I'll tell her. Just as well she won't understand. Unfair though, innit?'

Edna understood, but said nothing. Her mother had lived a full life and now had the mind of a child. Susan *was* a child and deserved to live and play on the roundabout with her brother.

Sixteen

Charlotte understood, but appeared sceptical when Janet told her about Susan falling into the pool, and her decision to move out, and take the job and the accommodation at Saltmead Sanatorium.

'You don't have to do this.'

Janet hung her head over the packing of a suitcase, her hands slowing as she gathered a pile of white underwear. 'Oh yes I do.'

Charlotte took hold of her shoulders. 'I know you're doing this for Susan's sake. It wasn't your fault, Janet.'

It was too easy to say it wasn't her fault. Janet couldn't stop thinking that it was.

'I can't help feeling responsible. Everyone knows that swimming pools are a breeding ground for the disease. I should have known better.' She shook her head. 'I can't stop seeing Susan's cheery little face and the way she could run and play. I have to do something. I have to be near her.'

Dorothea had bawled like a three-year-old when she'd left the hospital, hanging onto her arm, dripping tears over her shoulder. Eventually Janet had promised to go to the pictures with her at least once a month.

Dorothea had dried her tears. 'As long as I'm not seeing Henry that night,' she said, then added coyly, 'or anyone else.'

'Of course.'

'Or Geoffrey.'

How Dorothea had the nerve to be engaged to one man

and dallying with another, Janet didn't know. If the present situation with Susan hadn't been so dire, she would have found it amusing. As it was, she merely considered it sad, even a little sleazy.

Dorothea dabbed at her eyes and slipped her arm through that of Janet. 'So tell me all about your new boss. Is he good-looking too?'

Janet shook her head. 'No.'

Professor Pritchard was a very precise man of around the same age as her father, but without the piercing eyes and the dark, swept back hair. In fact he had little hair, his pate being freckled like a large, rather pink egg. His nose was his most prominent feature because of its colour, a by-product of his predilection for port, if the rumours she'd heard from the medical staff were anything to go by.

He was also a stickler for discipline. If she'd expected to wander the wards as she had at the Royal Infirmary, she was very much mistaken. It was put to her in no uncertain terms that such antics were out of the question.

'Polio is a very contagious disease,' he told her. 'Any infringement of Saltmead rules will be dealt with very seriously. Visitors, including parents, are not allowed. These rules are based on accepted medical thinking that emotional upsets are not conducive to patient recovery, *not* because the staff are nasty, insensitive people. Is this clear to you?'

Yes, it was. Any attempts to see Susan would have to be done in secret.

Her office was little more than a cupboard stuffed with filing cabinets, an oak desk on which sat her typewriter, a large stapler and a tier of wire filing trays. A battered tea trolley filled the gap between her chair and the window. On it were a gas ring, a kettle and the usual accoutrements for making tea, along with a biscuit tin and a bag of sugar cubes. Professor Pritchard's office, which she only entered when summoned by him, was the next one along. The Professor kept his door firmly shut. He was obsessive about his work and did not appreciate interruptions.

The chance to find her way around and to get some idea of where Susan was came a lot quicker than she'd anticipated.

Jonathan, who had been pressurising her into going for a drink with him to the village pub, came along to her office with a pile of old files.

'Could you drop these down to records? They're dead files – patients who are no longer patients, for one reason or another.'

He looked pleased with himself. His eyes were bright and his clothes seemed crisp, as though they were new and had not yet been washed and ironed. She should have wondered about his demeanour and questioned whether the slick presentation was for her benefit. Instead she eyed the files and wondered how long it would be before Susan's notes were on their way to the archives, hopefully because she was cured and had gone home.

Jonathan rested his hands palms down on her desk and leaned forward. Janet was only vaguely aware that his nose was almost in her hair.

'You smell wonderful.'

Janet didn't register what he'd said. Her mind was occupied. 'How many die?'

She didn't see Jonathan's wavering smile or the disappointment in his eyes. He straightened and said, 'Not too many.'

'How many are crippled?'

He frowned as though all his thoughts were concentrated on the question. 'More than we'd like. It depends on whether the nerves of the limbs and the motor area of the brain have been affected. Cells die. Some recover and, as I've already told you, the physiotherapists do a wonderful job.'

Janet continued to stare silently at the files. Please, she prayed, let Susan pull through. Crippled if she has to be, but not dead. Please, not dead.

'Is something wrong?'

When it came to bedside manner, Jonathan had to be one of the best. He was looking at her as if waiting to be told where it was hurting. First as last, Jonathan loved his job and cared for his patients. She had to trust him.

'Susan's here,' she blurted and waited for his reaction.

First there was puzzlement as he tried to remember where he'd heard that name before.

'Susan. She fell into the pool at Clevedon. Remember?'

He threw his head back and ran his hands through his hair. 'I'm sorry. I must seem a heel.'

She didn't contradict his comment but said, 'That's why I changed my mind.'

He looked embarrassed as if considering himself stupid that he hadn't guessed at the reason, though it would not have been possible.

'But you were so prepared that day at the flat . . .' He paused and shifted from one foot to another.

'The condoms really were Dorothea's idea. She misconstrued – just like you did.'

'Ah!'

'Now you know.'

'Yes.'

Nonplussed was the only way to describe him at present – or was it? How about approachable?

'I want to see her,' she blurted, looking at him intently as if willpower alone could force him into agreement.

'You can't.' He cleared his throat anxiously. 'Look, Jan, I recommended you for this job. Don't drop me into it with the old man. I've got a career to think of.'

'Among other things! So it was all tosh about me getting more interested in medicine. All you really wanted was a little something to warm your bed on certain nights of the week. Who warms it on other nights, Jonathan? A little nurse? Someone from the village? You owe me a favour.'

'Now come on.' His smile irritated. She felt like slapping it from his face. He went on, 'I never promised you a serious relationship. You're a modern woman who—'

'You wouldn't want upsetting your relationship with your mother!' Janet snapped. To her great satisfaction, he really did look as if she had slapped him in the face.

'I see you're in no mood to talk sensibly.' Indicating the files he'd left on her desk, he added, 'I want those dealt with immediately.'

'Yes.'

'And you know where it is?'

Janet bundled the files into a tidy heap. 'I think so.'

After he'd left she flung her arms over the typewriter and rested her forehead on the coldness of the metal. This was a crazy situation. Deep down she knew she was placing Jonathan in a very difficult situation, but it couldn't be helped. Susan needed her. She was sure of it and whether Jonathan assisted or not, she would succeed in seeing her. Something would turn up.

Tucking the files under one arm, she left the office, turned right outside the door and followed the direction painted on the wall that said 'Archives'. Flimsy partitioning between offices and wards, relieved at intervals by panes of thickly frosted glass, formed a seemingly endless corridor, loose in its frames and rattling every time a door opened and caused a cross draught.

Recalling the verbal information given to her on arrival, the archives were situated in a less frequented part of the sanatorium. Voices, footsteps and the sucking grind of rubber wheels against polished lino echoed in the emptiness against the cold, brittle glass.

The painted signs carried on, but she came to an abrupt halt at a place where a hospital trolley had been pulled across the corridor. Two men stood with a ladder, looking up at the overhead pipes which ran the length of the corridor. One of them spotted her.

'You can't go this way, luv. There's been a water leak.'

She stopped. 'Can I get there another way?'

The man stroked his chin, early beard growth rasping beneath callused fingers. He pointed. 'Down there, first left, through the tunnel, take a right, then another left past the wards . . .'

'Thank you.'

She headed the way he'd stipulated, then turned a corner out of their sight. Determination and downright curiosity made her follow a sign saying 'Medical Staff Only'. *Dear me, I'm lost.* The words were on the tip of her tongue, just in case someone caught her.

Around another corner, a wider corridor, then a dead end. Her foot knocked against something and sent it scuttling across the floor. A pair of spectacles nestled against the wall. She picked them up and looked around her. There wasn't a soul to ask if they'd dropped their spectacles, or for them to ask her awkward questions, so she put them in her pocket.

Immediately ahead of her was a pair of double doors. She swept forward, not really looking, unaware of her surroundings until she was standing in the middle of a ward.

Grey and ill-lit, the ward was sombre, like the inside of a tomb, except that a tomb is silent. In this place the air was filled with the sound of the heaviest breathing she'd ever heard, each breath evenly spaced from one to the next, devilishly loud and metallic. Yet these were no monsters of the imagination. The source of the sounds was there before her. Three on one side, three on the other, these huge, grey-green cylinders looked as if they should be holding fuel, but were in fact holding something much more precious. Out of the end of each one poked a human head and above that were a bank of mirrors.

'Hello,' said a small, thin voice.

Janet couldn't tell who had spoken, though she was sure it wasn't Susan. There was no moving of head, no interested gaze turned in her direction. So how could they see her?

The mirrors!

A rectangular world seen at second hand and back to front. What the mirror reflected was all they had.

These cylinders, these great breathing beasts were iron lungs, alternately providing air then a vacuum, aiding a damaged respiratory system to breathe. Without them, these children would probably die.

If she'd been less shocked she would have stood her ground, said hello back and perhaps held more of a conversation, but she couldn't. One arm round the files, she reached behind her and pushed the door back with the other. Step by step she backed out, glad to get out of there, glad to regain a corridor that echoed to the sound of her footsteps where the air was still and not traversed by the sound of devilish breathing.

Once outside the doors swung back into place. Janet stood and stared at them. The round windows set at eye level swam like twin moons before her eyes. Until this moment she had never really visualized the full implications of the reports and letters she typed, the files she kept in meticulous order, or the phone calls she fielded for Professor Pritchard or Dr Driver from orthopaedic specialists, neurologists and the doggedly determined physiotherapists.

She had entered one of the wards – yet not any ward – not one where the physiotherapists forcibly exercised withered limbs, but the ward from hell itself where children's lungs were pressurized into working by the relentless persistence of machines resembling metal coffins. The experience left her nerves on edge and ill-prepared for what happened next.

'What are you doing here, Miss Hennessey-White?'

Janet jumped and spun round so fast that she almost fell against Professor Pritchard.

'I'm on my way to the archives,' Janet blurted, the files clasped tightly against her bosom. 'The other way was closed. A burst pipe apparently.'

'I hope you did not go into that ward, my dear. As I told you, polio is a highly infectious disease.'

'No!' she lied. 'Of course not.'

Professor Pritchard knotted his copious brows and studied her face as if she were less than human. Now she knew what a microbe felt like when subjected to microscopic scrutiny. 'Carry on, woman. You're not paid to hang around the corridors.' He turned away.

Shaken, Janet stood as if frozen. Later, she'd be glad that she had. He opened a single door set in an alcove to one side. For a moment she glimpsed gowns, caps with flowing cotton ties and facemasks, clothes that offered some protection against the disease and made the wearer almost unrecognizable.

Unrecognizable!

As she followed the corridors towards her office her fingers curled more tightly around the spectacles that she'd found.

She pictured the door the professor had opened. Had it had a key? She couldn't visualize one in her mind though that didn't mean he hadn't used a key, merely that she hadn't noticed he had. Butterflies took flight in her stomach. This could be it! This could be her way of seeing Susan. The professor's warning about contagion came back to her. Surely she couldn't contract the disease just by entering the ward?

Mrs Prendergast, the hospital almoner, passed her in the corridor close to her office and beamed broadly as if she knew Janet's greatest secret. 'There's always someone in your office, Janet my dear. Aren't you the lucky one?'

Mrs Prenderdgast winked wickedly and Janet almost blushed. Jonathan again! Well, if he had it in mind to offer her help in exchange for a night out at the village pub, he was out of luck.

Adopting a wide smile, she flung the door wide and breezed in, then stopped in her tracks.

'Hello, darling.'

Smartly attired in a rust-coloured suit trimmed at the neck with a thin strip of rabbit fur, her mother rose from a chair.

'Mother!' Janet hugged the files to her chest then groaned. The files! She stared at them in disbelief. 'Oh no!' She'd been so absorbed in her plans that the archives and the files meant to be deposited there were completely forgotten.

Charlotte looked taken aback. 'I'm sorry. Perhaps I should have telephoned to let you know I was coming.'

Janet placed the offending files on the desk and decided her mother deserved an explanation. 'I was meant to take these files to the archives, but I saw . . .' She couldn't go on. The vision of the children entombed in metal cases was too recent and too raw to put into words without getting hysterical. She made a big effort to collect herself then asked, 'Can I get you some tea?'

There was a smile on her mother's mouth as she shook her head. The look in her eyes was not easily readable.

Janet dutifully kissed her mother's cheek and breathed in the familiar smell of expensive perfume and quality face powder. She'd certainly dressed for the occasion, you had to give her that. But what occasion? Initial delight was tempered by instant suspicion.

'I had tea with Professor Pritchard.'

Janet glowered, picked the files up from her desk and, in a fit of temper, slammed them down again. 'Don't tell me! You've been worrying about me catching polio and asked him to accept my resignation! Well I'm *not* giving up my job, Mother, and I am *not* coming home and I thank you *not* to interfere with my private life.'

Charlotte got to her feet, turned her back on Janet and looked out of the window. Her shoulders heaved as though she'd taken a deep breath prior to diving into an even deeper pool. 'Your father got me an interview with the Professor. I was quite sure I could persuade him to let Edna and Colin see Susan once the contagious period was over. He refused and lectured me as if I were merely a child. Visitors are not considered beneficial to patient recovery.' She spun round suddenly, her grey eyes blazing with anger. 'They're children, for God's sake! Mere children! What's the matter with these people out here? Have they no souls?'

Contrite, Janet asked, 'Did the Professor say whether she'd be all right?' She remembered Susan running out from the Arcade that day she'd gone to the police station and got caught in the rain, the feel of her hand, warm and plump within her own. She remembered her at Clevedon, her dress tucked into her knickers, not at all ladylike, but very practical.

Charlotte wiped her forehead with the back of her hand. Suddenly she looked tired, and very much older. Janet's heart went out to her, but she couldn't *physically* reach out to her. It still sometimes felt as though her mother did not quite belong to her.

Charlotte continued. 'The Professor said that she had been unfortunate to pick it up this late in the year, that the incubation period can be up to thirty-five days. Apart from that she could be in here three months, perhaps six or even more. It depends on the severity of the attack, but no matter how long she is here, visitors will not be allowed.'

Janet sucked in her breath and sank into her iron-framed typist chair. 'Poor Susan. Poor Edna.' Their misfortune had touched all of them.

Janet clasped her hands together on the desk in front of her and closed her eyes. She chose not to mention her plans for seeing Susan, at least, not yet. 'Are you home at the weekend, Mother?'

'Yes. All alone. Your father's gone to Devon with Geoffrey. They're going to do some fishing and other things that boys like to do.' She laughed, then stopped abruptly and looked pained, as if it was slightly distasteful to laugh at a time like this, in a place where sick people hoped to be made whole again.

'I'd like to come home this weekend. I'd like to see Edna.'

'Of course.' Her mother showed no sign of being surprised.

'And I think you should know that I'm not living with Jonathan. That's not the way it is.'

'I believe you.'

Janet studied her mother for any sign of what she was really thinking. The serenity of her expression was unchanged. Always smart, always saying the right things.

Her mother glanced at the floor as if she needed to think carefully about what she would say next. She looked back to Janet, her gaze unblinking. 'Ivan is still with us.'

Janet swallowed and tapped her fingernails against the pile of files. 'Is he?'

'He's been through a lot, Janet. Honestly, if you knew . . .'

'So have I!'

'I don't think there can be any comparison,' she said, her voice soft, similar to how it had been when Janet had been a child and had woken in the dead of night from a bad dream.

Janet took a deep breath. 'No! Perhaps not.' She was not going to divulge details about the foreign man, the rape, the darkness of the night – or her hatred of any song by Doris Day.

'I'd better be going.'

After a light brush of lips against cheeks, Charlotte reached for the door, her movements languorously graceful, perfect in her poise and her appearance. Ah, thought Janet, in a sudden moment of reflection and remembrance, but you're not perfect and I know that you're not.

'I'll look forward to seeing you at the weekend,' said Charlotte lightly, then more seriously. 'You're still my daughter, Janet. I don't expect you to be a saint.'

Janet's response was curt. 'None of us are saints, Mother. Not even you.'

For the briefest of moments, her mother's expression stiffened and her smile was short and nervous.

After she'd gone Janet leaned against the door, closed her eyes and cast her mind back over the years to when she had run away from school, come home in the middle of the night, and seen her mother in bed with a man who was not her father.

The Professor gave her plenty of work for the rest of that day, but did not comment on her mother's visit. Saltmead Sanatorium was his world, an empire in which his word was law and the world outside an imposition that he could well do without. All he related to Janet was dictation and instructions regarding the preparation of reports.

Reports were exactly what she wanted to see, and one above all others, that of Susan Smith. Among the pile of buff files for discharged patients and blue for current, was one with a yellow memo attached. She burrowed down to it, saw the name and, trembling with trepidation, opened the file. A preliminary appraisal of her condition had been carried out. One leg. One arm. Janet's hand went to her chest in an effort to ease the sudden stab of pain. Please, she prayed, closing her eyes and focusing all her energies on whatever and whoever might be listening, please make her better.

When she blinked her eyes open, the words Hannah More leapt up to her from the head of the medical report. Besides it being the name of a famous Bristolian philanthropist, it was also the name of a ward close to the one full of iron lungs – and the roomful of protective clothing.

Thoughtfully she opened the top drawer of her desk and took out the pair of spectacles she'd found. Holding them carefully over her wastepaper bin, she pushed each lens out of its socket. Silently they dropped among the bits of screwed-up paper and other debris. They were a little large and slid down her nose, but with enough sticky tape wound around the leaves, they'd serve her well. Until they were needed, they would live at the rear of the top drawer of her desk hidden behind notepads, pencils, and a packet of carbon paper.

After she'd left Janet, Charlotte sat in her car, the engine idling as she eyed the green and cream sign fixed to the fencing beside the main gate. It held great significance for her. Back in the forties it had said something entirely different. Nowadays the inmates were very ill; back then they had been enemies.

Josef, who had sent her the letter regarding Edna's first child Sherman, had been a prisoner here. Even now, she could see his face, impatience with a world gone mad reflected in his eyes. She'd also seen fear. It was only after Josef had returned home and felt safe that he'd reported how a prison guard had died because he was different. He'd also named the man responsible, though she had no idea whether the man was ever brought to justice.

And here she was again, only now it was Susan somewhere behind that high fence, lying in a bed within one of these long, low buildings.

She gripped the steering wheel tightly, closed her eyes then stabbed her foot on the accelerator. Uncaring of speed, she hurtled across Warmley Common at over forty miles an hour towards St George and Kingscott Avenue where Edna and Colin Smith were waiting for news.

When she got there, Edna hung out of an upstairs window, her face almost as white as the net curtains bunched around her head. Charlotte smiled and waved. The curtain fell back into place. Halfway up the garden path the front door flew open. Edna looked apprehensive.

'When can we see her?' Hope shone in Edna's eyes. Dark circles hung like bruises beneath them.

Charlotte wrapped her arm around Edna's shoulders. 'Shall we go in?'

The front room smelt of bleach, polish and Windolene. Edna had always kept a tidy house, thought Charlotte, but I can't ever remember it smelling like this.

'You've been busy,' she said as she pulled off her gloves and thought about how best to report on her efforts with Professor Pritchard – not that there was anything positive to report.

Edna was so eager to hear something good that she had not offered tea as she normally did, but Charlotte adopted a warm smile. 'Where's Pamela? I haven't seen her for ages.'

'In the back room,' said Edna. 'I didn't want her getting this one dirty. It has to be just right for when Susan gets home.'

A warning bell sounded in Charlotte's head. Children made rooms untidy; it would be normal to say that. But dirty?

'And where's Colin?'

'At work. I told him to go. He was getting on my nerves.'

Charlotte was adept at keeping her expression under control. She rarely showed her true feelings, but she did now. Colin was not the type to get on anyone's nerves, even those of the woman he'd married. He was gregarious, funny, the life and soul of any party, but also the shoulder to cry on.

Charlotte sat down in an armchair, her gloves and handbag nestling in her lap. This wasn't going to be easy and the right words were slow in coming.

'Edna, I am afraid they will not allow visitors . . .'

'No!' It wasn't like Edna to speak so sharply.

Charlotte kept calm. 'There's nothing I can do. Nothing,' she said shaking her head and slumping back against the stiff covering of the squarely constructed armchair. Confidence gained from the experience of helping others, mostly complete strangers, melted away. She had failed a friend, the worst failure of all.

'I'm sorry,' she said again.

'My child's alone in that place.'

Charlotte looked at her gloves as she twisted them out of shape with tense, nervous fingers. 'We can only pray.'

'Hah! What for? A miracle? I'm not even asking if my daughter will ever walk again, all I am asking is that I can see her!'

Edna paced up and down the room, threw her head back,

cried, prayed and blamed herself for not keeping the house as clean as she should.

Charlotte hung her head, her lovely kid gloves no more than a screwed-up ball between her clammy palms. Words were not enough. A balm was needed, some kind of salve to ease her friend's pain, something to make her think of something or someone else besides Susan. There was only one course of action to follow.

'Edna. I have to tell you something. You remember Janet talking about a letter?'

Edna was unresponsive. Poor woman! Was it any wonder that she'd forgotten all mention of it in the circumstances?

Charlotte continued. 'I've received correspondence regarding your son, Sherman.'

The crying and praying stopped, just as she hoped it would. She went on to tell Edna about the letters and what she was being asked to do.

The haunted look left Edna's eyes.

Charlotte congratulated herself. Hopefully she'd done this right. She kept her fingers crossed under cover of her crumpled gloves. 'Of course you need to talk it over with Colin, but I think it would . . .'

At the mention of Colin, Edna's new calmness dissolved. 'I don't want him! I want Susan.' But Charlotte had seen the change in her eyes.

Edna's anger stayed in Charlotte's mind as she drove home. Never had she felt so helpless as she did now, so low in spirit. Edna really did need a miracle and so far, she had failed to supply one. So try again, she said to herself. She's your friend. You have to.

At home she wrote a swift reply to Josef, then packaged all the letters into an envelope addressed to Edna.

Edna's reaction had surprised Charlotte. The timing had seemed right and yet . . . Failing was not something she was used to.

That evening, in an effort to restore her dented self-esteem, she wrapped up well and went out into the greenhouse to pot spring bulbs and sow a few sweetpeas for flowering next summer.

When the phone rang she presumed it was Colin with some news about Susan. Dropping the seed boxes, she tore off her gloves and rushed into the house.

Geoffrey was on the other end. 'It's Dad. He's not well. The ambulance is here.'

Charlotte kept her head. 'Is it fatigue? I told him not to work so hard—'

'Mum! He's had a stroke.'

Suddenly it was hard to breathe, let alone speak, but she found the words. 'I'll be right there.'

The train timetable was in the desk in the study, right next to a letter from Josef that she had not included with the rest. When she pulled out the timetable, the letter fell out with it.

In the present circumstances, it only warranted a brief, guilty look. She couldn't possibly deal with it now. Neither could she do any more for Edna. David was ill and needed her. She shoved the letter back into the desk, took the timetable and rushed upstairs to pack a small suitcase.

Before leaving, she grabbed the two envelopes from her desk and left them on the hall table for Mrs Grey to take to the Post Office.

That night Janet dreamed she was at Clevedon again. Jonathan was sitting on a blanket and she was hanging on his every word as he told her of how he was going to be the best doctor ever because that was what his mother wanted. The children were far out at sea, walking on water and waving at her with their fishing nets, but she wasn't really seeing them. Susan screamed and a tidal wave rushed over the beach and Edna ran out of the shelter up on the promenade, waving her arms and screaming with rage, 'It's all your fault! You've killed her!'

'No, it isn't!' shouted Janet and sat bolt upright, soaked in sweat. 'It's not my fault,' she said in a smaller voice, covering her face with her hands, then threw herself into the pillow and burst into tears.

Seventeen

Janet called in on Polly to ask her to help Mrs Grey tidy up at Royal York Crescent prior to her father coming home from hospital.

'Mother's gone to fetch him.'

Polly nodded silently. She was sitting on the very edge of a dining chair, almost as if she would spring up and shoot off at any moment.

'I'd do it myself,' she blurted, suddenly defensive in case Polly thought she was being priggish, 'but things are happening at the sanatorium. I need to keep an eye on Susan.'

Meg bustled in at that point with tea served from a big brown pot. She was all interest. 'And how's Edna taking things?'

Janet shrugged and shook her head. 'Not good, what with Susan *and* her mother not being well.'

'Well, it's difficult enough having elderly relatives. Worse still when their minds are gone wandering,' said Meg and sipped at her tea.

'I'll let you know how things go,' Janet said. Her teacup rang like a bell as she put it back into its saucer. 'Very nice,' she said, admiring the pink roses and gold rim with a brief brush of her finger. 'Bone china, is it?'

'From Woolworths,' Polly lied as Janet got to her feet. Billy had got it from a man who knew a man who had a warehouse. The rest of its origin was suitably vague. 'I'll see you to the door.'

Meg followed them, her slippers slapping like flippers with each step.

Janet paused at the garden gate and pulled on her gloves. 'I'm sorry to have missed Billy. I haven't seen him for quite a while. Is he working today?'

Polly was taken off guard, but rallied swiftly. 'He's working.'

'How wonderful! Has he a proper job now, or is he still freelance?'

Polly crossed her arms and ignored Meg's sidelong glance. 'Freelance! He's gone to see some new business associates up in Ashley Down. They're on about making 'im a partner.'

'Is that what they call it,' muttered Meg.

Janet did not appear to notice Meg's comment.

'I'm glad she didn't hear what you said,' Polly said to Aunty Meg as they waved Janet off down the road.

'Just as well! Business associates indeed! Crooks, more like!'

'I could hardly tell her that he's in the nick, could I?'

Meg sniffed and shook her head. 'You mark my words, if Billy don't sort 'imself out, he's going to come to a very sticky end.'

'Yeah,' muttered Polly. 'And I know bloody well where I'm going to tell him to stick the toffee!'

Billy had not come home on the night the thugs called, but two coppers from the local nick had come calling and told Polly that the van was stolen. That was the first shock. The next was Billy being remanded in custody as the bloke responsible for pinching it. After Janet had gone she visited him in the cells. Dressed in her ordinary clothes, the things she kept for daily wear, and carrying a battered brown shopping bag that Meg had bought at a jumble sale for twopence, she caught the bus to Bedminster. Anyone seeing her would think she'd just gone shopping. After walking the length of East Street, which took her past the main haunts where her neighbours shopped, she re-boarded the same number bus she'd just got off and travelled to the centre. From there she walked to Bridewell where he would stay until sentencing.

'I didn't do it, Poll, honest I didn't!'

Billy's features reminded her of Carol when she pleaded for half a crown after demolishing her pocket money in a single visit to the sweetshop.

'Billy, you were driving it.'

'A friend borrowed me it!'

'He *lent* it to you,' Polly corrected.

The common way he said things usually made her laugh, but not now. It irritated. Far from giving her the security she'd always wanted, Billy had let her down. Like all the other men she'd ever known. She was going to be left all alone.

Billy puffed on his Woodbine, then turned to the fresh-faced constable standing by the door. 'How about a cup of char for me and the missus?'

Once the coast was clear, the truth, such as it was, came out. 'Remember that place I took you to up in Ashley Down?' He leaned as close to her as the table between them allowed.

'Go on.'

'The coppers want me to shop them about their betting rackets. I know 'ow it's organized, you see, and where everything and everybody is. The van's just something they're weighing me with to make me blab, but I won't. I daren't. They'll chop me bloody legs off if I do.'

'Bollocks!'

'Polly!'

Normally her bad language didn't go much further than 'bloody', 'sod' and 'swine'. But these were extenuating circumstances.

Billy grabbed her hands. 'Please, Poll. Say nothing. They're a nasty lot. They means business.'

Up until then she would have shopped anybody if it had freed Billy. Now she wasn't so sure. Never had she seen Billy so pasty-faced and so . . . still. Usually his face, his head and his limbs were a whirr of movement, a flow of continuous scheming animating his whole body. Telling him about the visit from the two bruisers was out of the question. Billy looked frightened. And if devil-may-care Billy was frightened, it stood to reason she should be frightened too.

When she got home, she explained it to Meg as though it were nothing to do with Ginger and his pal visiting them. She talked of it as though it were another matter entirely and that Billy had had his fair share in it. However, Polly's disappointment in him was genuine.

'Men just aren't worth it,' she complained and flounced out into the backyard where she threw corn at the fowls.

Meg felt obliged to tell her friend Bridget all about it. Bridget sat still and listened quietly though you couldn't tell from her disparate eyes whether she was concentrating on what was being said or not.

'Not going to Australia then,' she said when Meg had finished.

Meg sipped at her tea. 'Well, not for a while anyway. Never mind. P'raps they might have changed their minds by then.'

Bridget pursed her lips, drained her saucer and set it down on the table. 'Not ever. Not if you've got a criminal conviction. My cousin Aemon Fitzpatrick got refused because of that. Mind you, he was a safecracker.'

Meg's spirits hit the ceiling. 'Is that right – about them not letting him in I mean?'

For a moment Meg could have kissed her – until she heard a smacking of slack lips as Bridget rolled them over her gums. Bridget's teeth sat in her empty teacup whilst she slurped the rest of her tea from the saucer.

'Well that's it,' said Meg, her spirits higher than they'd been for a long time. 'Everyfink's back to normal.'

Bridget put down her saucer and wiped her lips. 'Trouble is, you can't tell 'er. If you do then she'll want to know how you know. Can't tell 'er you bin dumping the post in the bin, can you?'

Meg fell silent. Bridget was right. She couldn't say a thing.

She had to let Polly live in hope and find out the truth for herself.

'Oh well,' she said after thinking things through, 'at least I know the truth. There's nothing for me to worry about.'

Meg was almost walking on air going back to the house, which suddenly seemed warmer and cosier than she'd ever realised. Polly's coat hung from a hook in the hall. Meg breezed into the living room.

'Well!' she exclaimed. 'I'd better be getting some tea on.'

Polly sat at the draw leaf table, which was positioned in the middle of the room between the fireplace on one side and the fitted dresser on the other. Her head rested on her hands and she hardly looked up when Meg patted her on the shoulder.

'No use crying over spilt milk Poll.'

'I'm not crying, but I bloody well should be.'

'Now come on. Every cloud's got a silver lining.'

'Well the one over my bloody 'ead is peeing on me.'

'Polly! No need for that language.'

'There's every need! He's innocent! Honest he is!'

'How can you be so sure that Billy didn't pinch it? I mean, much as I love the little sod, he's about as pure as the driven slush!'

Polly wanted to tell Meg about Billy's predicament, but had promised to say nothing. She thought of the thugs' visit and shivered at what might have been. 'I didn't tell him anything about our visitors,' she said casually. 'I didn't want him to worry about us.'

'No use crying over spilt milk,' Meg repeated brightly.

The happy face didn't seem right in the circumstances. Polly decided that the enormity of the situation had not sunk in, so she tried to explain. 'I don't know why you're looking so happy, Aunty Meg. We're going to be living on my wages and your bit of pension. It's not going to be enough and you know it ain't.'

''Course I ain't happy.' Meg started dusting with a pair of old knickers in an effort to hide the way she truly felt. 'I'm as worried as you are, but there ain't nothin' we can do about it. Now how about a bit of liver and onions for yer tea? I'll guarantee the gravy's so thick you can cut it with a knife – just as you like it.'

Rolling her sleeves up past her elbows as though she was about to knock spots off Joe Louis, she breezed off to the kitchen, her flowered apron – the crossover sort that was almost a dress – a flash of muddled colour.

'Everything will work out right,' she shouted from the other side of the door. 'You see. He'll be out in no time. We can manage.'

'Depending whether you're you or me,' Polly murmured.

What Meg didn't know was that Major Griffiths had heard through the Knowle West grapevine that Polly was in a more vulnerable position than she had been before. So far she'd avoided his overtures, but that night he called her into the office.

He stood at the window, looking out at the field of red-brick council houses, square blocks of pre-war vintage sitting behind small gardens framed by privet hedges.

'I hear your husband is no longer with you.'

She could almost hear him gloating.

'What's it to you?'

He turned, straightened his blotter and slid his fingers up and down a spike on which some receipts were currently impaled as though he were polishing it. 'Well, I'm sure we can manage a little bonus – *if* you are willing to take on extra duties that is.'

Polly was nervous, but loath to show it. She held her head extra high so that she was looking at him down the end of her nose. This job was all she had for her and Carol to live on. She needed it more than she ever had before, but she had to bluff it out. She folded her arms. 'I thought you were going to report me to the police, money missing and all that.'

He smiled that slow, greasy smile of his. 'I hardly think we need to resort to such subterfuge, my dear, especially now. Circumstances have changed somewhat. I have needs that you can deal with, and you certainly have needs, if not now, you will certainly have them very shortly. Shortage of essentials – food, clothes, rent – is a wonderful impetus to dropping one's inhibitions. After all, you have a daughter to think of.'

'Droppin' me inhibitions? Droppin' me knickers more like,' Polly muttered.

'You said something?'

'No.'

She had been going to say that unless her elastic was slack, her knickers were staying exactly where they were. But her job was so important.

He came out from behind his desk and circled her like a bird of prey, his eyes settling on her plump breasts, her rounded bottom. For the first time she wished her waist was getting as thick as the rest of her. Somehow its circumference hadn't quite kept up with her age. It was still narrow enough to emphasize the bits he was most interested in.

She stood still as his breath moistened the nape of her neck and he ran his fingers down her arm. 'I won't rush things,' he murmured against her ear. 'I will enjoy things more if I wait until you are ready. Yes. I like that. I will wait for you to come to me.'

'Don't hold yer breath.' Polly turned to leave.

His arm barred her from going out of the door. His fingers trailed down her spine. 'Let me know when you are ready, my dear. And you will be. When the money's short and the rent man is banging at the door.'

Before going back on duty, she grabbed her cigarettes from her bag and headed for the ladies' cloakroom.

Muriel, the peroxide blonde with the bright pink lips and the voice of a foghorn, was in there spitting into a block of mascara, a Woodbine hanging from the corner of her mouth. She looked up and sneered when she saw who it was.

'Heard about Billy. That's men for you. Make you a bag of nerves, don't they?'

'Piss off!'

Muriel feigned surprise. 'Oow! Charmed I'm sure.'

Locking herself in a cubicle Polly lit up and took a deep drawl on her cigarette. In a moment her heart would stop pounding, but her despair would take longer to disperse. She was trapped. Bad news travels fast. Well, that was bloody true and Griffiths was bloody right! Employers preferred taking on single women rather than those who were married. Having a husband in prison would make things impossible if she had to look for another job. Griffiths knew that. The decision was hers.

In the break between the afternoon and evening matinées, Polly went along to Griffiths's office and told him her decision.

Carol, Polly's daughter, tucked the hem of her pink gingham dress under her legs and wished for the day when she'd outgrow it altogether and it could go in the ragbag. The hem had been let down and the exposed material was less faded than the rest of the dress and ran all around the bottom like a strip of peppermint rock.

She was sitting with Sean Casey, a boy close to her own age who didn't appear to notice that her clothes were mostly from jumble sales or hand-me-downs from someone else's daughter. Most of her best hand-me-downs came from Geraldine Harvey whose mother bought clothes on tick from a club book so that even if her daughter couldn't walk properly she was always dressed nicely.

'I hate havin' Geraldine Harvey's old clothes,' moaned Carol.

'Her dad was black,' Sean explained.

'How do you know that?' Carol asked as she concentrated on picking the cotton from around the hem of her dress.

'You can see fer yerself. She looks like a cup of cocoa made with a lot of milk.'

'Ain't noticed 'er skin, just them irons and that hippity-hoppity way she walks.'

Sean asked her another question that he'd asked her many times before and gazed at her intently, impatient for an answer. Carol stared into the distance and tried to ignore the bland brick housing, the dead leaves and discarded sweet papers clustered in the gutter. When she was grown up she'd live in a place with green fields and trees all around where she could paint and draw and make model animals from blobs of clay.

'Well?' he said, eyes shining with hope.

'No,' she said emphatically. 'You can never be my lover. You never wash your neck and your nose is always running.'

Sean sniffed loudly, then wiped the snot from his nose on the back of his sleeve. His brows beetled in concentration as he searched for a way to endear himself to her. Suddenly his face brightened. 'I've got a brand new marble, a real number niner. Do'ya want to see it? I bought it with me pocket money.'

Carol grimaced. 'You'd have been better buying a new handkerchief instead of wiping yer snot on yer sleeve.'

Sean shrugged. He was bright enough when it came to making dandies – carts made from pram wheels and orange boxes. But girls were a mystery to him. He liked them a lot, but they seemed to want him to make too many personal changes in his clothes and his habits. He wasn't sure he was prepared to do that.

'How about marrying me?' he asked suddenly. Wasn't that what every girl wanted to be asked?

But Carol wasn't listening. She was on her feet running towards her mother. 'Where you goin', Ma?'

Polly would have hurried on if Carol hadn't seen her. 'Pictures!' she said and her walk turned into a trot.

Carol ran along beside her. Sean held back watching the mother and daughter, and wondering if the younger would end up looking like her mother. He wouldn't mind that. Polly was a little plump, but she was blonde, pretty enough – for an old woman who was at least thirty-five! And she was friendly.

Polly stared straight ahead, a smile on her face and a sick feeling in her stomach. Her stride remained purposeful.

'You ain't got your work clothes on,' Carol commented, running her eyes over the black and white flowered dress her mother was wearing beneath a black, three-quarter swagger coat. 'That's yer best one!'

'Well, just for a change I'm going to *watch* a picture.' She paused and almost choked on the next words. 'With a friend.'

'What, up the bug house?'

The words Carol used to describe the Broadway brought a smile to Polly's face. Griffiths would have a fit if he heard it.

'No. The Odeon.'

She didn't stipulate whether it was in Bedminster or Broadmead because the fact of the matter was she wasn't going to either. Griffiths had summoned her and there was rent to pay and pennies needed for the gas and electric meters and there was coal to buy. Then there was this dress. If only she hadn't run up a debt with Mrs Harvey's club book.

Carol frowned suddenly. 'You're not going to meet a chap, are you?'

Polly sighed. 'Oh for God's sake!' Then she stopped and opened her handbag and got out her purse. 'Look! Why don't you take this thr'penny bit and go and get yerself some chips down at Hamblins.'

Carol took the money, and then said brightly, 'I could wait with you till the bus comes.'

'I'm going to Melvin Square. You go and get yer chips.'

Carol glanced over her shoulder to where Sean was bent over the gutter chasing one of his prized marbles with another. 'Sean's with me. Do I have to share the chips with him?'

Polly stopped again. Griffiths would kill her if she missed the bus and kept him waiting.

Carol eyed her mother and weighed up the possibilities of using her desire to get away to her own advantage. 'What about some scrumpy?'

'What? You cheeky little mare! You're too young!'

Carol pouted and tried again. 'Lemonade?'

'Here,' Polly said after digging out two pennies and two ha'pennies. 'Give these to Sean.'

Then she tucked her bag under her arm and strode swiftly on. 'I'll see you later. All right?'

She didn't look back. She preferred to imagine Carol running to join Sean and the pair of them racing off to the chip shop together. Imagining what they were doing was easier than risking the condemnation on her daughter's face.

Griffiths lived with his mother in a three-storey Victorian house in Britannia Road, which was just behind the London Inn, a principal stopping place for the buses running from the suburbs to the city centre.

Polly trod lightly, her heart in her mouth and a sickness in her stomach. Britannia Road was not attractive. The tall houses looked grim, the whole road smothered in their solid shadow.

The house where Major Griffiths resided had a green front door with a big black knocker and the brass step was dull and bent at one corner. Polly shivered and thought about running away, but the vision of her, Aunty Meg and Carol out on the pavement surrounded by their belongings forced her to stay.

A net curtain quivered at the window to her right before the door opened. Griffiths stepped to one side and waved his arm in a parody of a pantomime prince. He said nothing, but had a satisfied smile on his face.

She stood absolutely still while he closed the door, then followed him over the creaking boards of a long passage, through a door and down bare stone steps into a dank basement. This lower level was not obvious from the front of the house, but at the back the room had windows and a door that looked out onto a garden where striped towels hung lifeless and dripping wet on a washing line that ran from the house to the back wall.

An old *chaise-longue*, a piece of furniture that a lot of people still had, stood against one wall, its springs apparent against its pale pink upholstery that might once have been bright red. There was a desk against another wall, a bookcase against another, two deckchairs hanging from nails and a bamboo table complete with a withered aspidistra. A small fire hissed from a cast iron range that was grey with ash and rusty from neglect. Its warmth did little to dispel either the cold or her nervousness.

'Is your mother home?' Polly asked nervously, wishing to God that the old girl would come limping down the steps and, hopefully, throw her out into the street.

A smug smile appeared on Griffiths's face. 'Of course she is.'

'Won't she hear us? Won't she come down here?' She sounded genuinely worried though there'd been times back in the blackout when making love in the blackness had been made more exciting by the close proximity of other bodies doing exactly the same thing.

Griffiths leaned against the lime-washed wall at the bottom of the stairs, folded his arms across his chest and grinned. 'My mother is deaf and not too good on her legs. That is why I chose this to be my private office. She *can't* get down here.'

Damn! No chance of wriggling out of it even by moaning too loud. She had to get this over with. From somewhere – goodness knows where – she summoned up as much courage as she possibly could.

'So,' she said putting her handbag down on the desk and trying to look as though she really meant business. 'I suppose that thing,' she jerked her chin in the direction of the *chaise-*

longue, 'is going to have to make do. Do you want me to take my clothes off now so we can get it over with?'

Griffiths smile widened. 'Certainly not.' His gold tooth glinted as he shook his head and laughed. 'I want you to seduce me.'

'Seduce you?' Polly stared at him open-mouthed. Having someone take whatever virtue she had left was one thing. It helped assuage the guilt. Having to give it was something else entirely.

He loosened his tie. Black hairs grew on the backs of his fingers. She'd never noticed them before; now she fixed her gaze on them because she didn't know what else to say, what else to do.

Griffiths was saying, 'If I had wanted a quick knee trembler up against the wall, I'd have done it during your shift. You may recall I said I wanted you to come to me. I didn't mean for you to come just because you were short of money. I want you to do it with feeling, as if you really care for me.'

This was hard! This was incredibly hard! OK, she hadn't been a saint in the war years. There were few that had, though you'd never get them to admit to it, but this was different. She was older now and married. All she could do was pray for a miracle.

'Come along,' he said, 'I want to feel as though I am in heaven.'

'Pity I don't know any angels,' Polly murmured as she turned away from him and peeled off her gloves and took off her coat, shivering as she carefully folded both onto the shabby *chaise-longue.*

'What did you say?'

'I said I was just a fallen angel.' She grimaced and said in a quieter voice, 'But even fallen angels pray.'

'Get on with it!'

Slowly she walked towards him, her stomach tightening. Sweat glistened on his face and ran through his moustache. She felt sick. *It would taste of salt.* She saw the vest beneath the shirt, the clutch of hair sprouting above the neckline. She felt sicker. *It would feel prickly, perhaps greasy.* How could she do this? She closed her eyes, tilted her head back, then opened her eyes again and stared at the ceiling. Was anyone up there listening?

Arms heavy as lead, she ran her hands up over his chest, placed her fingers on his jaw and brought his lips down to meet hers. He did taste of salt.

Behind closed lids she concentrated on pretending it wasn't him but a man that she had fancied, exotic but refined; the gentleman that Griffiths could never be, one man in particular, dark and caring. Thinking of him, that man who had played the piano, made her want to cry. He was too good to be used as a substitute fantasy in lieu of this man. Perhaps Al or Gavin or . . . The list was long. Yes, she had had a good war but at least she had been willing and she hadn't done it for money. Perhaps she should have. Perhaps she wouldn't be in this situation now if she had turned professional back then. Sex was something she'd always enjoyed, not a commodity to be sold like bread or porridge.

The feel of his teeth behind his lips bruised her mouth. At the same time his hands ran down her back and squeezed her buttocks. A draught of air blowing through the ill fitting windows and door touched her thighs as he lifted her skirt fold upon fold.

'Undo your buttons,' he said nodding at the shiny black buttons that ran from her neck to the belt that helped hold her stomach in.

As his hands slid beneath the waistband of her knickers she did as he said and undid the buttons of her dress.

'Pull it open.'

Feeling her face flush with shame, she did as ordered. Her breasts ballooned over the top of an ill fitting brassière that she'd had for some years.

He lowered his head and kissed one of her breasts. She looked up at the ceiling wishing she could stick herself against it like the trapped flies she could see buzzing in a forest of spiders' webs. She closed her eyes. She didn't want to see this happening to her. Suddenly it was preferable to be homeless and penniless. This, she decided, would be the first and last time and she wished she could stop it now, but for once in her life she was too afraid to say 'no'. Instinct told her that Griffiths could turn violent.

He was murmuring against her breast, saying things in a foreign accent that she couldn't quite understand.

She asked him what he'd said.

'I was pretending to be Lugosi,' he murmured. 'Pretending to be a vampire. Haven't you ever seen him as a vampire?'

'No.'

'Vampires like to bite their victims. Would you like me to bite you?'

An expectant silence followed. Polly's heart thudded against her rib cage.

The feel of his hands pulling her knickers down over her thighs spurred her to do something.

'No!' She tried to push him away.

'Too late, my dear, too late!'

'I'll scream! Your mother will hear me.'

'No! Do not scream! Do not scream!'

He tried to clamp his hand across her mouth, but she ducked away. He grabbed her shoulders. She twisted, struggled and rained blows onto his chest. Her fists pounded against his ribs. She was sure she was hurting him. She could hear her blows thudding against his body, then realized it couldn't be because the sound was getting louder and not coming from within the dreary basement, but tumbling down the cold concrete steps. Someone was hammering at the front door.

He caught hold of her wrists. 'Ignore it. We haven't finished yet.'

Claw-like, his fingers ripped at her clothes, tearing her bodice away from her brassière, her brassière cup away from her breast. There was fire in his eyes, wetness around his mouth. He was going to have what he wanted whether she was willing or not. No one and nothing would stop him – with one exception.

A voice cawed like a territorial crow from somewhere upstairs. 'Reginald! Reginald! Where are you? Do I have to answer the front door myself? Me? A poor old woman in my state of health?'

'Oh Jesus!' Griffiths let her go and swiftly tightened his tie. He glared at Polly as if she were dirt. 'Tidy yourself up!'

She pulled up her knickers, buttoned her dress, grabbed her bag, smacked him round the ear with it, then pushed past him to get to the front door before he could stop her.

'Well, that's your job gone!' Griffiths called after her.

'Stick your job up yer arse!' Polly shouted back.

The door lock was stiff, but what with her pulling and whoever was on the other side pushing, it jerked open.

Two figures fell forward. A head crashed against her bosom. The other figure fell onto grimy knees that looked as if they hadn't seen soap since the day it was invented.

'Carol!'

Polly looked down into her daughter's face.

'I didn't want the chips, Ma. I wanted to be with you. Don't be mad.'

'I won't be!' Polly grabbed Sean's arm, dragged him to his feet. 'Come on! Let's get the hell out of here!'

Like rabbits bolting from a burrow, the three of them ran down Britannia Road towards the London Inn.

Once Polly was sure there was no chance of pursuit, their headlong run slowed to a march before they stopped at the kerb to cross the road.

'Nice of you to come with our Carol,' Polly remarked to Sean once she'd caught her breath. Hardly a Prince Charming with his socks round his ankles, holes in his pullover and his shabby shirt done up askew, but she really meant what she said.

Sean sniffed and said, 'I wanted to.'

Carol stood on tiptoe and whispered against her mother's ear, 'I think he loves me.'

'That's nice,' said Polly. 'But just keep yer hand on yer ha'penny.'

Carol frowned. 'I ain't got a ha'penny. I've got twopence. So's Sean.'

'Good,' said Polly. 'That's just enough for the three of us to get the bus on 'ome.'

Edna and Colin argued that night. Colin was sitting down at the dinner table, his meal unfinished, head in his hands.

'Sweetheart, if I could do more, I would. Perhaps the doctors are right and Susan should be left to get well without us interfering.'

Edna slammed the teapot down onto the cast iron stand. 'That's ridiculous!'

Colin sighed and tried again. 'Edna, can't you be content that Janet's finding out how she is? She might even get to visit her. We can only sit tight and—'

'I will do no such thing!'

Edna's eyes, usually as soft as brown velvet, had dulled with tiredness and worry since Susan's departure. Now they blazed with anger.

'I've decided to go there and demand to see her.'

Up until now, Pamela and Peter had been watching their parents, wide-eyed, listening to them arguing and getting more worried by the minute. The loud voices were just too much to bear. Pamela began to cry. Peter did too. Edna appeared not to notice.

'Well, I'm not going!' Colin eased Pamela onto his lap and put his arm around Peter.

'Then I'll go alone!' Edna stormed out of the room and thundered up the stairs.

Hanging from an upstairs window, she gazed at the city lights twinkling in the distance. She didn't want to go to the sanatorium alone. Hospitals of any sort frightened her. They brought back painful memories from years ago of being unmarried and giving birth. She needed someone to go with her, someone who cared. Her father might, even though her mother was a drag on him. But Susan was his granddaughter.

'I'm going to ask Dad to go with me,' she muttered. 'I can't wait around for Janet.'

Skeletal weeds, their leaves fallen and their stalks brown, dripped with rain. Blocks of light fell in a series of squares and oblongs, like building bricks hastily adopted to keep the darkness at bay. Late afternoon was swiftly turning to evening and November was giving way to December.

Janet eased open her desk drawer, retrieved the spectacle frames, unbuttoned the top three buttons of her cardigan, then swiftly stuffed the frames down the front of her blouse. The afternoon could get even darker as far as she was concerned, the darker the better.

Professor Pritchard had gone home early complaining of indigestion. Jonathan was having a day off to visit his parents. Even Mrs Prendergast, the almoner, was out inspecting someone's home prior to a patient being discharged.

It was best, Janet decided, if she didn't wear a cardigan. She shivered as she draped it over the back of her chair. The small, cast iron radiator, which she depended on to heat her office, gurgled in warning. As usual it was barely lukewarm.

The corridors were colder than her office. Rain crisscrossed the windows and flurries of dried leaves blew beneath gaps in the doors.

She was in luck. It had been raining for about a week and what with the draughts and the wetness, quite a few members of staff were sick with colds and flu.

By the time she got to the changing room where she'd spotted the uniforms, the sky outside had darkened further. On top of that, a few lights in the corridor had gone out.

Anyone watching from a distance would not recognize her, especially once she'd set the glasses on her nose.

After quietly closing the door behind her, she switched on the light. Protective clothing hung from hangers. Some sat in neatly folded heaps on eye level shelves above labels stating what they were. The hangers had names on them.

PROFESSOR PRITCHARD.

DR JONATHAN DRIVER.

Reluctant to wear someone else's clothes, she automatically went over to the neatly folded piles. She had everything she wanted in her hands and was about to put them on over her own clothes, when a thought came to her. What if someone should see that there were more sets of cover-ups used than needed?

It would be best, she decided, to wear a set of those already hanging up. Someone might notice if there were three used outfits when she came to put them back. She decided on Jonathan's and was glad when she detected no residual male aroma.

Once kitted out in a gown that almost swept the floor, a cap that completely covered her hair, a mask hiding the lower half of her face, and the spectacle frames disguising the top half, she eased her head out of the door like a nervous turtle and looked up and down the corridor.

No one!

Thank goodness.

She caught a glimpse of her reflection in the window that lined the corridor from end to end. If anyone did come along, they'd probably burst out laughing at her appearance. She looked more like a bundle of laundry than a doctor.

It was only a matter of half a dozen footsteps from the changing room to the ward, yet it felt like a mile. Her feet felt and sounded as if she were wearing diver's boots, the big lead-weighted ones that keep a man in a metal helmet stapled to the seabed while air was pumped down to him through endless lengths of rubber.

The door let out a long, lingering squeak as she slowly pushed it open. She gritted her teeth as it squealed closed and sighed with relief before studying her surroundings.

There was a small office to the left and a sluice room to her right. She stopped, listened. A tap dripped. A few seconds passed. It dripped again. No one had attempted to close it off more tightly. From that she deduced the sluice room was empty.

Keeping close to the partition that divided the office from the vestibule, she crept towards the door. At the same time, she swiftly rehearsed in her head what she would say if challenged. She would introduce herself as a duty nurse; she would have to bear in mind the clothes she was wearing.

Professor Pritchard is not feeling too good. I'm just filling in.

Everyone knew he had frequent bouts of indigestion. Most of the sanatorium staff would already know that he'd gone home with yet another attack.

The office light was on, and although the desk had been left neat and tidy, someone had not long arisen from that chair. Pens were laid in a straight line next to a specimen vase in which sat a single rose, a late, lingering bloom from a summer long over.

Despite her nervousness, Janet smiled. Conscientious as they were, a few hard-worked members of staff had probably grabbed the opportunity for an extended tea break. All would be fine – as long as Matron didn't catch them.

Unsure what to expect, she headed into the main body of the ward. To her relief there were no iron lungs; neither was there the more general arrangement of beds lining the walls as she'd expected.

There were only six beds and each was separated from its neighbours by solid partitions that gave way at about four and a half feet to glass. Fraternizing among patients was curtailed in the interest of contagion control. They looked like fish tanks, the big oblong ones used by those who bred tropical fish. Only each of these held a small and very sick human being. Adults, who formed the minority of polio patients, were in another ward.

Janet walked slowly, scanning each face before she realized that the patient's name was held in a card holder on the outside of each individual cubicle. They reminded her of the hymn boards into which hymn numbers were slotted before a service. Beneath each name were a number of hooks holding various medical charts, each set held together by the stout teeth of a metal bulldog clip.

Expectant faces watched her walk slowly down the ward, each hoping, perhaps, that she would stop and come to them, even if only to give them medicine. Human contact was more important than she could possibly have imagined – especially to children.

A brief scan of the name board, and Janet opened the door to the very last cubicle. Susan was sleeping. Her cheeks had a rosy glow, which made her appear very healthy. The truth was very different. Susan was still very ill and had a long way to go before leaving this place.

Susan's eyelids flickered as Janet bent closer and whispered her name before slowly – very slowly – opening and looking up at her.

Janet smiled behind her facemask. 'Hello, Susan.'

Instead of receiving the welcome smile she had somehow expected, Susan's bottom lip began to quiver. 'I don't think I want to get better.'

Regardless of the threat of contagion, Janet took hold of her hand. 'Don't be silly. Of course you want to get better. You want to see your mummy and daddy again, don't you? And what about Pamela and Peter? You want to see them too, I expect.'

Susan's nod was barely perceptible and her lip still quivered as though she were about to burst into tears. 'Yes,' she said weakly.

'Well then . . .' Janet gripped her hand tightly. 'So you have to get better.'

Tears misted Susan's eyes. 'I don't like it here. They hurt me.'

'Oh darling, they don't mean to,' Janet said and cuddled her close. It had been her intention to throw off her disguise once she'd found Susan. But I can't, she thought. If I do she'll break down, beg for me to take her out of here, perhaps scream and convince someone that I have visited her. And then, she thought, I shall lose my job and no one will be here to keep an eye on her.

Behind the facemask, she bit her lip resolutely and closed her eyes. Never had she had to make such a hard decision. But there was no doubt she had to do it. Susan's well-being was in her hands and the responsibility lay heavy on her heart. If these clandestine visits were to continue, she must not let Susan know who she was.

'Would you like me to tell you a story?' she asked, blinking back the tears as she looked intently into Susan's face.

'Yes please. A Christmas story.'

The idea was a good one. December was not far away. Janet racked her brains and swiftly condensed Dickens's *A Christmas Carol* so that it revolved around the Cratchit family and left Scrooge and the ghosts out in the cold.

'Right!' said Janet adopting a cheery voice though she felt like a traitor, 'Tiny Tim was the youngest of the Cratchit family and couldn't walk very well . . .'

Later she felt positively ill that she'd chosen that particular story and had so obviously focused the main story on Tiny Tim and his affliction.

Was it wrong to prepare Susan for the great tragedy that was about to befall her? Back in her flat surrounded by a genteel shabbiness from ages past, she sat in front of her dressing table mirror peeking through her fingers. Were those lines of worry she could see on her forehead or newly acquired maturity? She decided on the latter. Things were going well for her. She enjoyed her work, still enjoyed Jonathan telling her in great detail about *his* work, and adored relaxing on her days off in a room where ladies might once have played the spinet or worked on their needlework while admiring the view from the window.

She rested her face in her hands. So much had changed in her life. Here she was, a marriageable girl with no boyfriend and no career sneaking about a hospital for the sake of a sick child. If she wasn't careful she could get into the same kind of trouble she'd got into at the Infirmary. Strangely enough, she didn't care.

Just before getting into the snug spaciousness of the four-poster bed, she went to the windows, drew back the curtains and looked out across a moon-kissed landscape. Frost covered the ground and spangled on the roofs of the single-storey buildings of the wards and medical facilities. Like rows of rabbit hutches, she thought, housing a host of bunnies all waiting to escape.

She consoled herself that her visit to Susan would put Edna's mind at rest. The fact that someone had visited was better than no one at all. In effect she would be Susan's guardian angel. She was sure Edna would see it that way and would cease to worry.

After receiving Janet's telephone call, Charlotte checked that David was asleep before leaving for Edna's.

His faculties were almost back to normal, though a nerve beneath his eye did pulsate on occasion when he was tired or exasperated. Charlotte put his improvement down to being back in his own bed, his own home. Devon was lovely, but home was best.

'I have to go out,' she explained to Mrs Grey. 'Can you stay a while until Mr Bronowsky comes home?'

Mrs Grey was wiping down the kitchen table having just made a steak and kidney pudding for dinner. 'Is he going to be playing around in my kitchen?' she asked.

Charlotte knew that Ivan enjoyed cooking and had made some very enticing meals for them since they'd got back from

Devon. But, whatever happened, she mustn't hurt Mrs Grey's feelings.

'I expect he'll be too tired,' she said.

'Oh I don't expect so. He's very good,' said Mrs Grey and beamed broadly.

Charlotte smiled as she made for the door. Ivan had won another female heart. Another? She smiled at herself in the rear-view mirror of her Morris Minor. If only she was twenty years younger . . .

The roads were busy. It was gone five thirty and clerks, typists, bank tellers and secretaries were pouring out of offices, all aiming to get home as quickly as possible.

Tightly packed buses pressed against her as she drove through the city centre. Traffic lights changed from red to amber to green and back again. Progress was slow and, for once in her life, Charlotte was impatient. She couldn't wait to tell them that Janet had seen Susan.

Bicycles, mopeds, motorbikes and cars weaved in and out of the traffic barely missing other vehicles and home-bound pedestrians running, willing to chance being knocked down if it meant they caught their bus on time.

The traffic persisted all the way up through Old Market, Lawrence Hill and Church Road only petering out at the St George Fountain where the bulk took the left-hand fork to Kingswood. Charlotte took the Hanham fork.

Kingscott Avenue had a welcoming look about it. Darkness had fallen. Lights in downstairs and upstairs windows blinked on, winked out or were muted by the pulling of living room curtains.

Her ringing of the doorbell resulted in running footsteps, then scuffles from inside. She could see no figure reflected in the upper portion of the door, which was made of coloured glass set into a lead-paned framework. She understood the reason why when Peter opened the door.

'Are Mummy and Daddy at home?'

Peter nodded shyly.

The sound of arguing came from somewhere inside.

She made for the kitchen. 'Edna! Colin!' She swept in with arms outstretched. 'I've got wonderful news!'

Colin was sitting at the table, knife and fork poised over what looked like cottage pie and vegetables. Edna was on all fours, a bucketful of soapy water at her side and a scrubbing brush in her hand. Taking hold of the corner of the table for support, she dragged herself to her feet.

Charlotte pulled at the fingers of her gloves. 'Janet's seen Susan. She read her a story last night. Isn't that wonderful?'

Colin's face cracked into a grin. 'Did that old goat she work for give her permission after all?'

'No,' said Charlotte, stifling a girlish giggle as she pulled out a chair and sat herself down.

Edna, she noticed, had also sat down, but couldn't seem to keep still. The scrubbing brush went back and forth along the edge of the table.

Never before had Charlotte known Colin and Edna to be so hostile to each other as she sensed they were now. It saddened her and she wanted to help. Perhaps explaining how Janet had disguised herself in order to speak to Susan would lighten their mood. She told them everything and watched their faces for any spark of amusement or relief that might show. None did.

'She won't die?' asked Edna.

'No,' said Charlotte, restraining a sob. 'In fact, if you don't get her home for Christmas, you might have her home for Easter, though she might have to go back in for treatment.'

So far they hadn't asked whether Susan would be crippled. She prayed God they wouldn't.

Colin beamed at Edna. 'Well, that takes a lot off our mind, eh Edna? At least we've got some idea how she is.' He threw Edna a crooked half-grin. It was as if he wasn't quite sure of her reactions. He turned back to Charlotte. 'Thank her for us, won't you? At least she's seeing someone she knows.'

Charlotte did not say that Janet had not told Susan who

she was. Not telling them that Susan was likely to be crippled was bad enough. To inform them that she was still, to all intents and purposes, all alone, would be too much.

After Colin had seen Charlotte off, he came marching back in rubbing his hands together and smiling happily. It dissolved when he saw that Edna was again down on her knees scrubbing like mad at the floor. He was sure she'd only scrubbed it that morning, but he wasn't going to mention it.

'What a turn up!' he said to Edna's back, forcing himself to sound happy as the frills of her polka dot apron flopped like damp wings over her back. 'It makes this no visiting business a bit easier to bear.'

Edna stopped scrubbing and looked up sharply. 'Are you saying you won't go with me?'

Colin's spirits dropped as he recognized the stubborn look in her eyes and the uncharacteristic sharpness in her voice. 'You know they won't let us in, love. What would be the point?'

Never had he seen such hardness in Edna's eyes. 'If you won't go with me, then I'll find someone who will. And if no one will go with me, then I will go by my bloody self!'

Edna lay awake until the clock struck one. Sleep wouldn't come. The pillows seemed full of lead shot rather than feathers and her mind was fixed on Susan. She desperately wanted to see Susan, or at least *try* to see her.

She kept to her side of the bed that night, clinging with rigid fingers to the edge of the mattress. Tonight she could not bear to roll close to Colin. He had let her down and she couldn't quite forgive him, but if she did roll close and felt the heat of his body, him stirring at the feel of her body, she would be bound to respond. It mustn't happen. There was too much to think about, to plan.

The following morning she set out for her parents' house in Nutgrove Avenue with Pamela in the pushchair.

Her father was giving her mother a bath when Edna got

there. Her intention had been to ask him whether he'd come with her to the sanatorium to see Susan.

The room was full of steam. His poor red face ran with sweat and his rolled-up shirtsleeves clung damply to his upper arms. He told her, 'She'll be all right. We've got everything 'ere we could ever want. Good job we got this bathroom put in, weren't it?'

Edna leaned against the bathroom door, which was propped open with the laundry bin. Her mother was in the bath, her shrivelled curls clamped wetly to her head by the steam. She frowned and looked around her as if trying to get her bearings.

She doesn't know where she is, thought Edna, and suddenly felt sorry for her. She was a pitiful sight, but not tragic enough for Edna to forget Susan and her reason for coming here.

'Will you come to Saltmead with me?' she asked her father.

His mouth hung open while he thought about it. 'Your mother will have to come with us.'

'Don't be ridiculous!' She couldn't help snapping at him.

He looked hurt. 'But who else will take care of her while we're out there?' he asked.

Edna did not have an answer. With mixed feelings, she watched her mother who, in turn, watched the water trickle through her raised hands.

She suddenly had second thoughts. What was the point of telling her anything? Then a sense of duty overrode her sense of hopelessness. This is my mother, she reminded herself. Susan is her granddaughter. It's only right that she knows what's going on.

Resting both hands on the side of the bath, she bent down, looked into her mother's face and tried to explain. Ethel Burbage sat very still, her face placid and her eyes vacant, though fixed on her daughter's face. Suddenly she said, 'What are you doing out?'

Edna explained about visiting the sanatorium.

Her mother ignored the comment. 'You should be locked in at home. That's what they used to do in my day. The house was locked up with the family inside it and a notice was pasted on the door.'

Anger replaced pity. Edna got to her feet. 'If she's going to start, I'm going.'

'She's right,' said her father quietly. 'That's what they used to do just after the Great War when folks had polio, cholera or scarlet fever. Lock the house up and paste a poster outside. The doctor would call – if they could afford one. And food was delivered. But until it was all over, that's what they did.'

Edna turned cold. Good God, this was the twentieth century. What her parents had just described was medieval.

Her mother's mood changed. 'I want some . . . thing,' said Ethel Burbage slowly holding her hands at shoulder level. One of them held a face flannel.

Edna watched with mixed feelings as her father leaned towards the bath tidy that was only inches in front of her mother's mean looking breasts.

'You need this, love,' he said gently and handed her the soap. 'Do you want me to wash your back for you?

'Of course I don't! What are you doing in here? Dirty old man! That's what you are! Bluebeard! *Bluebeard*!

Edna backed out of the door and out of her father's path. A missile, possibly a pumice stone, narrowly missed his ear.

'And close the door!'

They stood there on the landing, both breathless and leaning against the wall. Edna eyed her father sidelong, noticing the hole in his pullover, the hint of shadow over his chin. He looked faded and thin inside clothes that had once strained over his broad chest and bulging waistline. The pullover was dark green and the horizontal pattern at chest level was a muddled mix of Fair Isle diamonds and squares. She felt she should offer to do something for him, but the weight of her own problems was far too heavy.

'Dad. What are you going to do?'

'Wait for her to finish, then let the bath water out, and make sure she gets herself dressed properly.'

'That's not what I meant.'

His look was fiercely protective. 'Till death us do part. In sickness and in health. That's what I promised and that's what she'll get. I could do with some help though.'

'Well, don't look at me, Dad. I've got Susan to consider, Colin too for that matter. *And* two other children.'

Pamela chose that moment to start crying.

A raucous, low-pitched shout came from the bathroom. 'Get that brawling brat out of here!'

Edna straightened and headed for the stairs, her mouth set in a grim line. Her father followed. His shirtsleeves had come loose and were flapping around his wrists.

'I'm sorry, Edna love. This is all too much . . . too much.'

He sounded as if he was about to cry and Edna almost felt like joining him.

'I'll do what I can,' she said after handing Pamela her teddy bear. She turned and kissed him on the cheek. 'We'll have to get someone in to help with the cleaning, the laundry and some light nursing duties. Not a nurse as such – just someone to help.'

He shook his head. 'My pension don't run to paying any help.'

Edna fastened the top button on Pamela's bright red coat, which had a corduroy collar with matching trim on the pockets. Her mittens were beige with Fair Isle bands of red and orange running through them. 'Don't worry about that. Colin will deal with it.'

She was telling the truth. The toy factory was doing well. They'd never had so much money in their lives. Colin was already talking about moving to a detached house with a bigger garden. Edna had argued that children should feel settled in their younger years and that they should wait until later on.

Her father rubbed at his bristled chin and eyed her

nervously. 'It won't be easy to find someone strong enough to cope with yer mother. You know what she's like. She'll play up something rotten.'

Never in her life could she remember him looking so dishevelled. Her mother had always been difficult to live with. She'd now become a nightmare.

Edna sighed. 'I wish there was more I could do.'

Her father shook his tired head. His eyes were red-rimmed. His skin had a greyish, greasy look, as if he hadn't washed, let alone shaved. 'Now, now. Don't you go feeling guilty about it. You've got enough on yer plate.'

Edna looped her arm through his, tugged it close and said, 'I'll see what we can do.'

'I'm sorry I can't come to see young Susan with you,' her father said as they stood at the front door. 'Won't Colin?'

'No!' she snapped. Colin's attitude had surprised her. She could not accept that her child was best left in the hands of the medical profession. Colin could.

'You have to trust them,' he'd said to her. 'I had to.'

She'd seen regret flash momentarily in his eyes. 'You were grown up. She's just a child.'

The remark was almost cruel and she regretted it, her mood swinging back again later when she reasoned it wasn't really her fault. Polio had touched all their lives.

Her father shook his head sorrowfully as he said, 'Them nurses and doctors . . . if they're that determined . . .'

'So am I.'

He patted her shoulder, then squeezed it in an effort to reassure her. 'I hate the thought of you going alone . . .'

'I won't be alone.'

A cold wind plucked leaves from the gutter and sent them scurrying down over Nutgrove Avenue. Edna pulled on her gloves. Determination, she decided, would not be enough. Someone with courage, nerve and vitality was needed who would stand up to stiff upper lips and starched uniforms. One name above all others sprang to mind.

*

Polly's job at the Broadway was over. Griffiths kept to his office when she called in to collect wages owing and her cards. Muriel, the peroxide blonde with big earrings and bright pink lipstick, did the honours. Polly could tell from her attitude that she was glad to see her go. Muriel would supplement her wage by earning a few bob extra with Griffiths down in the grim cellar where colonies of spiders spun webs in dark corners and a *chaise-longue* with worn springs served as a love nest.

'Got a job yet?' Muriel asked, a sneer painted more heavily on her mouth than her lipstick.

'None of your business.'

'Oow. Sorry I spoke! Not going to be easy though, is it, what with your ol' man in clink. You'll miss the money. Have to make do and mend and buy all the scrag ends of mutton to make a pie fer Sunday.'

Polly reared up, her finger stabbing close to Muriel's nose. 'Cheap meat I'll buy at the butcher's, but I don't want to stay 'ere and end up as "cheap meat" for 'im in there! But then, you always was more scrag end than prime steak, wasn't you, Muriel?'

'Well!' Muriel looked fit to burst. Her plastic earrings rattled, reminding Polly of milk bottle tops strung on string and laid out over seedbeds to keep the birds away.

Polly snatched her money and her cards and walked out, her head high, glad that she'd put on her best black and white checked suit for the occasion.

Billy had been sentenced at the magistrates' court and transferred to Horfield Prison. Although it wasn't that great a distance, Polly had to fit visiting in with making a living and the dictates of the prison authorities. She'd made up her mind to go there straight after collecting her cards.

Smokes were on ration in prison and weren't too easy to get hold of outside given the price they were now – one shilling and sixpence for ten Woodbines. But Betty Knight, a neighbour, worked in W.D. & H.O. Wills where they made the things so she got free issue. It was just a question of passing them to Billy.

On the last occasion she'd visited there'd been a grille between her and him. He'd looked down in the mouth since he'd just gone down for nine months. Strange how little things become important, she thought, as she got the bus that would take her up Gloucester Road to the prison. A guard named Jock McGregor had told her that the visiting facilities were being altered, 'To make more room for the amount of crooks we've got in this city. Must be an army of lonely women out there without their men.' He'd looked at her suggestively. 'I don't mind keeping a lady company if she's got a need for a man in her life.'

For a moment Polly had had half a mind to blow a bubble with the pink gum she had been chewing right into his stupid face. But what he'd said next had changed her mind.

'You'll be just across a table from him next time. It's a temporary measure. And I'll be watching you,' he added. 'Never fear! I'll be watching you.'

She remembered that fact now. 'I need the lav first,' she said and grinned up at him. 'Must be all the excitement.'

'Don't think you can get too friendly across them tables,' repeated Jock. 'Remember I'll be watching you.'

'With a bit of luck you won't be watching close enough,' Polly murmured to herself once she was behind the thickly varnished wood of a lavatory door. Taking care not to squash it flat she slid the packet of cigarettes beneath her stocking suspender.

She'd told Meg what she intended doing before she'd left that morning.

'What if you get caught?' said Meg.

'I'll get a telling off and be banned for a while.' She smirked at Meg's worried face and added. 'Don't worry. I won't end up in there with 'im sharing 'is bunk.' She paused once she realized what she'd said and smiled cheekily. 'Though I could definitely do with it.'

Meg tutted, but not very seriously.

Polly was glad she took the cigarettes. Billy's appearance was not good. He looked thinner, there were dark hollows beneath his eyes and his skin was almost as grey as the prison issue clothes he was wearing. He coughed as he sat down opposite her. A guard reminded them that they were not allowed to touch. They didn't – not above the table. Beneath it Polly passed the packet of cigarettes to Billy.

'It's still warm,' he whispered.

'Came from a warm place,' she winked, then frowned as a series of coughs caused him to bend over the table. 'Billy! Are you OK?'

He nodded, but still coughed, his face as red as a turkey cock's gizzard.

Without her asking, a prison guard brought over a glass of water. 'Wanna stop that smoking,' the guard said. 'It ain't no good for you.'

'Thanks,' Billy croaked as he took the glass.

Polly put both hands on the table and leaned forward. A frown crumpled the bright expression she'd adopted especially for the visit. What with Susan and David, there was enough illness about without him getting sick too.

'Billy?'

His shoulders shuddered with each cough. He'd never had good lungs, but had continued to smoke, continued to rush around chasing the next easy fiver. None of it could be doing him any good.

Once the coughing subsided he managed to smile. 'That guard's probably right. I should give up the fags, not these though, not now I know where they come from.'

He brightened and lit up a cigarette and Polly brightened too.

'Never mind,' she said. 'Just you wait till we get you out of here. Soon feed you up and get you fit again. And then, once yer on yer feet again we can be off to Australia. That sunshine over there'll do you the world of good.'

Billy looked at her pensively from behind a plume of swirling smoke. 'We can't go there. Not now.' He looked away, seemingly preferring to look at the dull walls, the hatchet-faced warders or the smoke curling up from a dozen other lit fags – anywhere rather than at her.

Polly's smile froze, but didn't disappear entirely. Her expression and her voice were resolute. 'We made the decision, Billy and we're sticking to it. There's no going back.'

Billy looked down at the smouldering cigarette that he held between his yellow-stained fingers. She could see his mouth twitching as he sought to get the words out. From experience she knew he was about to say something she didn't want to hear.

'We can't go, Polly, or at least I can't. I was talking about it to some bloke in 'ere. If you've got a prison record they don't let you in.'

Polly's mouth dropped like a slate from the roof. This couldn't be true – could it? Suddenly she felt like a stupid brainless hen she'd read about in one of her daughter's storybooks. Only in her case it was for real. The world had fallen on her head.

She was still numb on the bus going home and stared out of the rain-spattered windows, hardly registering the Victorian villas, the shops lining each side of Gloucester Road. Even when the bus got to the Horsefair, so named because of a fair held in medieval times, she did not really see the white concrete façades of Jones's and Lewis's, two huge department stores that had risen on the ashes of the Blitz. She did recall tales of bodies being found there when they were building; plague victims, they said, from hundreds of years ago.

Thoughts of past deaths and her prison visit combined to make her feel bad. Billy didn't look well. Prison was not good for him, but she couldn't help feeling resentful. If he hadn't got into trouble with the law they'd be off to Australia now for the princely sum of ten pounds each. By breaking the law he had sentenced them to a life in this country and this one alone.

With hindsight she wished she had given in to Griffiths, not because she wanted to, but purely out of revenge on Billy. *He wouldn't know.* But I would, she thought, with a bitter sense of satisfaction. I would.

She got off the bus at the Centre and went to the bus stop that would take her back up to Camborne Crescent. Waiting gave her plenty of time to think about things, mostly about getting another job. It wouldn't be easy. In fact, she thought to herself, having a husband in prison would make it bloody damn difficult!

Lazily, she eyed the traffic going by, uncaring of the spray thrown up by their wheels. What a variety! Buses, bikes, even the odd horse-drawn dray, just like the ones that used to pull up over the Batch from the brewery when they'd lived in York Street down in the Dings.

'Happy days,' she muttered darkly and scowled.

If only she had married a bloke like one of these driving these cars. She eyed the driver of each vehicle as it went by, smiling at some, winking at others.

'Toffee-nosed git,' she muttered at those that looked away. She was alone on the bus stop. Couldn't one of them stop and give her a lift?

Just as the thought finished crossing her mind, a car pulled into the kerb. She stooped down in order to see the driver better and judge whether to be cheeky or charming as the case might be. Instead she came face to face with Edna, who offered to give her a lift home.

'Bit out of your way, innit?'

'I want to ask you something.'

Polly settled herself on the navy blue leather upholstery. 'Been somewhere nice?'

Edna shook her head and kept her eyes fixed on the road. 'I've been to my mother's. I was on my way home, then I saw you.'

Polly frowned. 'Oh yeah,' she said apprehensively, and prayed that Edna wasn't going to prattle on about Susan. In fact, she'd prefer it if she didn't mention it at all. Sickness frightened her, though she didn't dare admit it. And was it catching? Could Edna have caught it from Susan, and could she get it from Edna and then, heaven forbid, pass it on to Carol? The permutations were terrifying, but Polly composed herself and asked how things were.

'I hear you're out of work,' stated Edna.

Straight to the point, thought Polly. Well, that's refreshing I must say.

'Yep! Out on the streets – or I will be if I don't get a job pretty sharpish.'

'My father needs some help with my mother – a bit of general care rather than nursing. Would you be interested?'

Polly hesitated. Looking after Edna's mother? Could she do that?

'I ain't got no medical training at all, though I did work for David of course, but not kind of . . .' She swallowed hard. Edna had seen her with David once. It had almost been the death of her – or at least the death of her friendship with Charlotte. 'Why not!' she said suddenly. 'I could do with the money.'

They had passed through Queens Square and were pulling up over Redcliffe Hill when Edna said, 'That wasn't all I wanted to ask you. I'm going to demand to see Susan. But I don't want to go alone. Will you come with me?'

Sickness and hospitals were places Polly had avoided all her life and didn't particularly want to have anything to do with now.

'You're braver than me,' Edna added suddenly.

From then on it was a matter of self-esteem. Polly had always cultivated the hard-baked exterior of the good-hearted, good-time girl. Edna was calling her bluff and Polly found herself unable to refuse.

'I'll go with you. We'll show 'em they can't keep a mother from 'er kid!'

When they finally got to Camborne Crescent, Edna got out of the car, her eyes brimming with tears. She walked with Polly to the garden gate, hugged her and poured a profusion of thanks in her ear.

'Don't mention it,' Polly said, blushing with pleasure. For once in her life she felt like a saint.

Eighteen

Janet heard about Edna's behaviour from her mother and felt instantly guilty. She promised to visit Susan as much as she could. 'I owe it to all of them,' she said.

Charlotte did not try and dissuade her. 'Just be careful,' she warned and Janet promised her she would be. 'I like this job,' she added. 'I feel I'm really involved in something useful.'

Between eight and nine o'clock, Saltmead Sanatorium fell into a quiet period between the day and nightshifts. Patients had been fed and food trollies returned to the kitchens. Daytime nurses were tying up the loose ends, tidying desks and medicine cupboards before the night nurses came on duty so there would be no cause for complaint. Time was also taken up with gossip as well as patient progress.

Janet timed things carefully. Through trial and error, she knew whom she was likely to see where and at which time.

Tiny Tim had been abandoned in favour of Ali Baba and his magic carpet. *One Hundred and One Arabian Nights* had never been one of Janet's favourites – and it showed. The stories got muddled, not helped by her fear of being caught.

Susan looked forward to her visits, recognizing her storyteller by the large glasses and an outfit too voluminous for her slim figure.

'I like you best,' she said at the end of yet another muddled story where a fictional bird had somehow changed into a magic carpet.

'Because you like my stories?' Janet asked her.

Susan shook her head. 'No. Because you don't put hot things on my leg.'

'Hot things? What hot things?'

Between tears, Susan tried to explain. The child was clearly upset and left Janet questioning whether she'd heard things right. The following morning she asked Jonathan about it, though she couched it in such terms that Susan wasn't mentioned.

Although their relationship had cooled on the personal front, their professional interaction had not altered. Obsessed with his work and, perhaps with a need to prove himself, he went out of his way to explain things to her.

'Hot cloths are applied to the limbs affected by the disease. Current medical thinking is that heat generates cellular regeneration, in other words, gets the nervous system working again.'

On Thursday evening she went to see Susan again and dared to lift the sheet that covered her leg. Susan began to snivel.

'No more!' Her voice wavered.

Janet felt as though her jaw would break as she surveyed the large pieces of lint covering Susan's right leg. Letting the sheet down gently, she made a huge effort to compose herself.

'What story shall we have tonight?'

'Peter Pan. The bit where he flies away with Wendy.'

Telling the story was harder than it had ever been; that thin little leg encased in white lint was not easily forgotten.

Once outside the ward, she pulled the protective hat from her head and tugged the rough cloth of her garment away from her neck. Still wearing the glassless spectacles, she leaned her head against the wall and took a deep breath. It was dangerous to linger half-disguised. If someone saw her, questions would be asked. But it couldn't be helped. Seeing Susan suffer was just too upsetting – and she was the only one seeing this. Not Edna, not Colin, not anyone.

A warning voice inside told her to pull herself together, get her disguise off and get out of here before her secret was discovered. Susan's welfare was all that counted.

Normally she would have stayed in the warmth and comfortable surroundings of her flat for the rest of the evening, but tonight she craved fresh air and escape, so went for a walk to the village.

The air was cold and a light mist dived and eddied in the beam of the torch she took with her. The torch was a necessity as there were no streetlights between the elegant building she lived in and the huddle of cottages that made up the village. The village itself was far from well lit, dependent for the most part on light falling from cottage windows or from lead-paned saints if an evening service was in progress at St Michael's. Pavements were variable and in places non-existent, the old flagstones giving way to areas that were grass in summer, but mud at this time of year.

Squares of light also spilled from the windows of the White Lion, a place of thick smoke, young farm labourers playing darts, and old men playing bagatelle or dominoes. Then the door to the lounge bar swung open and two people came out. By the light that flooded in with them she saw Jonathan and a plain little nurse who sometimes worked on Susan's ward. Somehow hurt and most definitely surprised, she flicked the button on her torch and kept to the shadows. Seeing them together, she suddenly remembered the rose on the desk in the empty office.

She'd always thought the girl plain, but not tonight. Jonathan had changed her, but what had attracted him to her in the first place?

They climbed into Jonathan's big, grey Humber. As the smutty grey smoke belched from the exhaust, it came to her that Jonathan had chosen this particular nurse *because* she was plain, which in turn made her vulnerable. Just like me, she decided. He saw my vulnerability too. The awful memory of her rape seemed to explode inside her. She wanted to go home at once, to tell someone what had happened to her. But her mother had taken her father to Portishead for the weekend, reasoning that the sea air would do him good. Just as well, she thought. Was it fair to burden them at a time like this? Nevertheless, the urge to go home was too strong to ignore.

On Friday night she went along at her usual time to see Susan and explain that she was going home and wouldn't be seeing her until Monday evening. Just as she'd expected, her news was not well received.

'What about my story?'

Janet took hold of her hand and hoped that Susan could see she was smiling even though her mouth was hidden behind a mask. 'I promise I'll have a new story for you on Monday.'

She thought about telling her that she'd be reporting to her parents, but dared not chance it. If Susan should repeat it to anyone on the ward, her job, and Susan's one and only visitor, would be gone.

Before leaving Saltmead, she phoned Dorothea, but was told she'd gone away for the weekend. She was disappointed. A night out with Dorothea might have taken her mind off things. But the alternative, a bath, a cocoa, a good book, and an early night, would serve her just as well.

Luckily she was offered a lift by the almoner who lived just over the other side of the Clifton Suspension Bridge in Leigh Woods. Getting home took only an hour and a half rather than three hours on the bus.

After unlocking the front door at Royal York Crescent, she reached for the light switch that was just inside to her left. With a tired sigh, she let her bag and her mackintosh fall to the floor and breathed in the lingering aroma of the beeswax polish so beloved of Mrs Grey. Chinese vases, dark red rugs and a gilt-framed mirror gleamed in the light thrown from a cut glass chandelier. Despite the good quality furnishings, the house felt cold, almost menacing.

A bath was first priority. The bottom stair creaked beneath

her foot and she would have bounded to the top, but what sounded like laughter came from the direction of the stairs that led down to the kitchen. She paused as a second voice floated up to her. Both voices were loud. Her hand slid back down the banister as she turned towards it and tried to guess who it was. Surely not Geoffrey? He was back at Oxford. Parents were away. There was only Ivan . . .

Outrage replaced weariness. Could it be that their Polish lodger had company? The cheek of the man! Well, she'd soon fix that! How dare he take advantage of her family's absence!

Chin firm and shoulders squared for battle, she skipped down the stairs and with a determined flourish, pushed the door so it swung wide, bouncing against its surround.

The scene was not quite as expected. Two figures sat on either side of the table on which sat a decanter and two glasses. The decanter was almost empty. So were the glasses.

Looking surprised, Ivan sprang to his feet, knocking his chair over in the process. 'Good evening!'

Janet rewarded him with a scowl. Her gaze transferred to Colin. Face wet with tears, he sat immobile as if he couldn't care less whether she chastised him or threw him out. Seeing his look of utter devastation, she realized her mistake. It wasn't laughter she had heard, but a cry of anguish.

Her own anger drained away. So did any fears about the lodger who stood watching her somewhat sheepishly.

She put her arm around Colin's shoulders and hugged his head against hers. At the same time she threw an accusing glare in Ivan's direction. 'Come on, Colin. Let's get you home. Edna will be worried.'

He shook his head despairingly and sank lower over the desk. 'No, she won't. It's Susan this and Susan that. She's forgotten me, forgotten our Peter and our Pamela.'

His voice was slurred. Janet threw an accusing look at Ivan who seemed almost sober. He gazed right back, arms folded, mouth grim set as if ready to respond to any accusation she cared to throw at him.

She looked away. For now she would say nothing, not until she had dealt with Colin.

'Oh Colin! What a mess you're in.' She patted his shoulder. 'Come on, I'll get you in a reasonable state to go home, then I'll get you a taxi and tomorrow I'll come over to tell you how Susan's getting on.'

Ivan headed for the door.

Janet angrily assumed he was retreating in the face of her mounting anger. 'Typical! You get a good man drunk, then sneak off to bed!'

He paused by the door, seeming to dominate the room. His look appeared to say *That's what you think.* But he said nothing, merely left, slamming the door behind him.

Ivan is not important, she told herself. Colin is.

'Coffee first, I think,' she said as Colin's head sank slowly onto his arms. 'Lots of coffee,' she muttered as his head hit the table with a dull thud.

She lit the gas, put the kettle on and got out a cup. No need for a saucer; Colin was in no fit state for social niceties. A search in the larder found *three* bottles of Camp coffee, *one* pound of tea and *six* packs of granulated sugar. Mrs Grey, she mused, had suffered the rationing of the forties and couldn't quite get out of the habit of keeping a large supply of basic necessities – just in case.

While waiting for the kettle to boil, she bent down at Colin's side, adopted a bright look and a cheery voice as she looked up into his face. 'I've seen Susan every day, Colin. Did Mother tell you that?'

Sandy brows frowned over bleary, uncomprehending eyes. 'Susan?'

'I've seen her and I'm going to see her again. But I have to be careful,' she added. That too was true. Determined as she was to give some comfort to the little girl, she was breaking sanatorium rules. If she got caught Susan would have no familiar face to help her through this and Janet would have no first-hand information to pass on.

She stroked Colin's hair back from his temples. 'Susan is being taken care of. The fever's dying. She's one of the lucky ones. She won't be in there for too much longer.'

She bit her lip because she'd sounded as if she were talking about weeks when in fact it was likely to be months. Oh well, she thought, rather a hope-filled lie than a daunting truth.

Susan's tears, red cheeks and cracked, dry lips were not mentioned. Neither did she say that, although the nerve damage to Susan's arm was likely to be minimal, the damage to her leg was more serious. Wait until things get better, she told herself. Colin was in no fit state to take it in. Besides, it was best to paint as bright a picture as possible. Above all else, they had to have hope.

Ivan came back just as she was holding the hot coffee to Colin's lips, shoved his hands into his pockets, leaned against the door surround and said, 'The taxi will be here in about ten minutes.'

Surprised and thinking perhaps she'd misjudged him, she mumbled her thanks.

Colin spluttered and his face reddened.

'It's gone the wrong way,' Janet groaned.

Ivan moved behind the chair and gently cupped Colin's head in his hands. Janet placed the cup between his lips. Colin sipped slowly, his eyes rolling in his head.

There were inches between Ivan's body and her own, and yet she felt his warmth, saw the gentle strength in his hands as he held Colin's head.

Ivan's features were set in grim lines, his eyelids heavy and lowered as he concentrated on Colin. He didn't look drunk himself, didn't sound it either. As always, his voice was steady, moderated. Again it reminded her of Charles Boyer, not the man who had attacked her from the shadows.

'That's the best I can do,' she said after trying to get him to drink a third cup. 'Poor Edna. As if she hasn't got enough to contend with, now she's got a drunken husband as well.'

Gently Ivan lowered Colin's head onto his arms. 'A man is not supposed to cry when he is sober, so he must cry when he is drunk.'

Janet snatched the cup from the table, took it to the sink and struggled to turn on the tap. 'So you helped him drink.' She couldn't help the anger.

'No. I helped him cry.'

'What kind of excuse is that?'

'A good one. Some of us care very deeply, but cannot always give way to our emotions, especially you British. It is being human I think.'

'How would you know? You're Polish!

'Do you mean I am not human or that I am not British?'

'Take it which way you like!'

He stood too close for comfort and his breath was warm on the nape of her neck. The blasted tap still refused to budge and she was in no mood for giving up or for looking round at him and backing down.

'I hope you have a very good reason for saying that,' he said, his voice as coldly precise as if he might use it to stab at her back. 'But what else can I expect from a spoilt young woman who has lived a carefree life and knows nothing, *nothing at all*, about suffering?'

A brawny arm took her by surprise as it slipped to one side of her and he turned the tap easily. The thickness of his upper arm seemed to hem her in. Feeling uncomfortable with his closeness, she sidestepped, half-afraid he would grab her by the neck and shake her vigorously for the awful thing she'd said to him.

There was a moment when the tension between them was so great that anything could have happened, but was diffused by the sound of a car horn. The taxi had arrived.

Ivan looped his arm beneath Colin and heaved him to his feet. 'Come on, my friend.'

'Let me . . .' Janet began, meaning to take Colin's weight on the other side.

'No need,' he said abruptly, his body wedged between hers and Colin's.

He took Colin's full weight so that his tin legs were left dangling. She followed and watched as he gently pushed Colin into the far corner at the back of the car then laid his metal legs along the seat.

Satisfied that Colin was comfortable, he turned to Janet. 'I am going with him. Someone has to see him home.'

She couldn't think of a single thing to say. She felt useless, foolish and angry with Ivan, the world, her attacker and herself. The cab doors slammed shut.

The mist that had prevailed all week formed haloes around the rear lights of the taxicab. Exhaust fumes left a ragged grey trail to the end of the crescent then was gone. Even after the street was empty except for stray cats squabbling in the dark, she stood there, silently, looking at nothing in particular, her mind a mix of different worries, different thoughts.

Ivan's comment about Colin needing to cry stayed with her like a jagged wound in her heart because he was right. Everyone needed to cry – including her – most definitely including her. The wind's cold, she told herself, as she swiped the back of one hand across her eyes, and headed indoors.

The kitchen was warm, the coffee and sugar were still on the table and the kettle tucked under the tap when she had second thoughts about drinking coffee. The whisky was still on the table. Blow the coffee! She needed – no – she deserved something stronger.

After slamming the kettle back onto the stove, she got out a clean glass, sat at the table and eyed the bottle of Highland malt. Sherry or Port would have been preferable, but tonight she would diversify because tonight she felt sorry for herself. No one else is, she thought bitterly. All the anguish of the past few months bubbled to the surface. What did men know about crying? What did men know about anything?

As for that *other* bloody Pole . . . Ivan! How dare he call her spoilt! How dare he accuse her of leading a carefree life while others suffered! He knew nothing, nothing at all, and she would tell him so once she'd built up the courage.

Doggedly determined to confront him when he got back, she poured whisky – a lot of whisky – into the clean tumbler.

'Just you wait, Ivan whatever your name is!'

She held up the tumbler, eyed the whisky determinedly and made a snapshot decision. 'Down the hatch!'

It burnt! The back of her throat tingled and she had to force herself to swallow it, to get it past her taste buds and down her gullet. Closing her eyes and clamping her lips tight together seemed to help. One gulp and the burning sensation passed as the effect of the alcohol drifted into her head. If I have two or three more, she thought, I will become even braver, more ready to deal with him when he gets back.

Planned speeches on what she would say to Ivan lost their initial clarity as each rendering of words was accompanied by yet another tumbler full of whisky. And she blamed Ivan for getting Colin drunk simply because she'd seen him drunk. He was bound to be guilty.

Whisky upon whisky steadily clouded the issue. What he was guilty of became less clear and Janet began to cry. She cuddled herself, her chin dropping as tears squeezed from her eyes. In her mind she wasn't seeing Susan, Colin or anyone else. Ivan and his comments had triggered her deeply buried secret, the one that only Edna knew about. Anguish and anger were ready to bear fruit. The time was ripe and there was whisky in the bottle, which seemed now to be sitting in its own highland mist.

By the time Ivan got back, her head was rested on her arms and the sleeves of her favourite pink sweater were wet with tears.

Bleary-eyed, she raised her head and looked at him from beneath the fall of fringe that flopped over one eye. Her mouth felt loose, but she still managed to say, 'Get out of my house. You've got no business being here. Go home! Go back to your own country.'

He slammed his hands palms down on the table. 'You stupid woman. Look at you. As drunk as two *pfennig* Freda and without half the cause to be!'

She frowned and tried to focus on him. 'Who is she – this woman – this Freda?'

He leaned closer. 'A whore! She got drunk a lot.'

'How dare you!' Her voice sounded slurred and her legs wobbled as she got to her feet, but she lashed out at him anyway, missed and toppled. He caught her, but not before she'd hit her head on the corner of the table.

Before the room had been spinning slightly. Now it whirled with all the energy of a fairground carousel.

'My head,' she groaned as he settled her back into the chair. 'My head!' The tears flooded down her face. He had called her a whore! Her thoughts automatically went back to that terrible night just before the Coronation. There'd been such jubilation in those weeks before Queen Elizabeth II had ascended the throne. Everyone was sure that the world was about to change. Well, it certainly had for her.

Ivan was gentle but brusque. 'Let me look at it.'

Feeling sorrier for herself than she could ever remember, Janet sobbed through her words, 'Get a-a-away f-f-from me.'

She heard the sound of running water, then something cold was pressed against her head.

He asked her if it felt better.

She groaned something unintelligible in reply. After some time she heard the kettle boil.

'Drink this.'

He pressed a cup to her lips. She smelt the sweetness of coffee beans and chicory. Her head ached and she couldn't stop the tears. Please make the coffee stop all this, she prayed as she swallowed it down.

'You called me a whore,' she wailed, her face creased like a baby without its bottle.

'I didn't say that.'

She tried to focus on him, to read the expression in his

eyes. In her drunken daze it seemed as if there was a sneer on his lips and a look of contempt in his eyes.

Janet's gaze never left his, even when he raised a second cup of coffee to her lips.

She hit it from his hands. 'I'm not a whore! It wasn't my fault! It wasn't my fault!'

A mix of tears and slobber poured down her chin, but she didn't care. 'It was dark,' she went on, unable now to stop herself. 'He was there in the darkness. I didn't even see his face.' Face upturned, she looked into Ivan's eyes. 'Imagine. I never saw the face of the man who took my virginity. Is that silly, or is it sad?'

Despite her misted eyes, she saw his expression change. Sympathy for her knocking her head had seemed begrudgingly given, but not now. His expression was gentle. 'You were raped,' he said matter of factly.

Janet's head sank closer to the table as she nodded. Her neck seemed too weak to hold it. Her voice was full of despair. 'I didn't see him. I heard his voice. He was Polish, at least, I think he was.'

Ivan knelt down at her side and put his arm around her shoulders. 'So I reminded you of him?'

She nodded again. If she'd been sober, she would have pulled away and told him in no uncertain terms that he was taking liberties. But tonight she was drunk, very vulnerable and needful of someone to care.

'I understand,' he said softly.

'It's stupid,' she said as her head flopped upon his shoulder. 'I thought I'd seen you somewhere before. I thought you were him.'

'But you said you didn't see him.'

Janet sniffed as her sobs subsided. 'I didn't see him.'

'But you did see me somewhere before. It was on Coronation Night. I ran after you with the money, which you had given me for your drink and I had no change.'

'Oh!' Janet's voice was small. Speaking loudly would only

send shock waves through her head. A vision of a waiter running after her and waving a pound note popped into her head.

'Do you want to go to bed now?' Ivan asked.

What did he mean? She eyed him warily, but couldn't see any reason to worry. She shook her head and wished she hadn't. It felt as though her brain had come loose from its moorings, like a seaside yacht in a violent storm.

He made cup after cup of coffee and she drank it. Every so often he put the wet cloth under the cold water tap, then put it back on her head. He did not press her further about the rape and she did not offer any further information.

He talked about Colin, his voice full of genuine concern. 'I am worried. He is worried about his children and his wife. I listen to what he says, but do not say anything. For now all he needs is for someone to listen to him. And I do this.'

'Funny. I confided in Edna. She's the only person who knows besides . . .' She looked directly into his eyes, wishing suddenly that she could turn the clock back and had chosen to drink coffee rather than whisky. Alcohol had a lot to answer for.

Ivan caught the sudden alarm in her expression. 'I will tell no one.'

She smiled. 'Thank you.'

He smiled back. 'That is the first time you have smiled at me. I like it.'

'Just tell me I'm not like two *pfennig* Freda any more.'

His smile drifted away. A thoughtful look came to his eyes. 'There was no shame in what she did. Freda did what she had to do to survive.'

Janet rested her chin on her hand and threw him a questioning look. 'I thought you said she was a whore.'

He nodded. 'Yes. She was. She lived in Hamburg. She had no job, no husband and three children to support. The hotel she used to own with her husband had been bombed. The family lived in the cellars. It was all that remained. And they were hungry, like a lot of people at that time. She had sold everything she could including her husband's medals and uniform. She sold the furniture, clothes . . . she even foraged in the bins at the back of a block of apartments where the Allied military were billeted. Anything she found – vegetable peelings, bones, rotten fruit – was boiled up in one big saucepan. Old tea leaves were reused.' He paused and looked down at his hands. Janet rubbed at her forehead, unsure whether she was really hearing this or whether it was just the whisky distorting what he was saying.

'Eventually, there was only her body left to sell. But there were many hungry women with or without children. The younger ones got the higher prices. Women of Freda's age were many. They did not get a very high price.'

She wanted to ask him how he knew all this. Had he been one of Freda's customers?

'No,' he said abruptly as if reading her thoughts. 'I was not one of her customers, but I was a friend. All who have suffered need friends to listen, to help, to do what they can.'

A silence pervaded the kitchen as they finished off the last of the coffee. Janet felt strangely at ease. In an odd, inexplicable way, it felt as though she had met him for the very first time. She felt she owed him an apology, but was not quite sure how to offer it.

She attempted to focus on the kitchen clock. 'It's late,' she said and staggered a little as she gathered the cups and whisky tumblers. She looked down into the washing up bowl as if searching for the right words, the ones Ivan truly deserved. Perhaps it was the whisky that prevented them coming. What she did say was founded on what he'd said about Coronation Night and sounded second best.

'Don't worry about giving me the money back.'

'Ah!' He groped in his pocket. 'It is yours. You must have it.'

'No. Please. I was rude to you, both on Coronation Night and . . .' She paused, blinked her bleary eyes and swallowed her pride, 'many times.'

He caught her hand in his and pressed the money into her palm. 'I like things to be right. It is my way.'

He smiled and she smiled back, the words he spoke and the way he said them flowing into her mind like warm treacle.

Too much whisky, too much coffee and the bump on the head meant that she woke up with a headache the next morning.

Staggering from her bed, she drew back the bedroom curtains, wincing as the light stabbed at her eyes.

'Never again,' she muttered and covered her face with her fingers.

Determined to beat the throbbing headache and take stock of the world, she slowly lowered her fingers and focused on the Avon Gorge.

Last night was like a series of one-act plays: Colin drunk; clashing with Ivan; Ivan taking Colin home; Ivan coming back and talking to her like a . . . good friend.

She groaned into her hands and closed her eyes. 'Oh no!' She'd told him about *that night.* She'd told him why she had been hostile to his presence and he'd told her where they'd first met. Throwing herself onto the bed, she burrowed her head between the pillows, welcoming the darkness and vowing that she could not possibly face him this morning.

But the pillows gathered around her head did nothing to hide the sound of Ivan banging on the bedroom door later.

No! She couldn't face him!

'Janet! You have to come. Your mother is on the telephone.'

She got up, meaning to open the door straight away. But the thought of what she had told him made her hesitate.

'Go down. Tell her I'll be right there.'

At the sound of his receding footsteps she reached for her dressing gown, hastily put on her slippers and went to take the call.

He was still by the telephone when she rushed down the stairs and passed the phone to her.

Janet threw him a tight smile then swiftly looked away. A man who was almost a stranger knew what had happened to her on that fateful night in June, which was certainly more than her mother did.

She held her hand over the telephone until he had headed down the stairs to the kitchen where Mrs Grey would probably stuff him with eggs, bacon and thickly buttered toast.

Her mother was shouting down the telephone, as if being loud would compensate for the crackling from which long-distance calls habitually suffered.

'Janet. I know we are only at Portishead, darling, but this is not a good line. Can you hear me?'

Janet made a determined effort not to shout in return. 'It's not too bad. How are things down there?'

'Your father's a bit better. We'll be home by midday tomorrow.'

Sunday morning. 'That's good.'

'How's Susan? Has there been any progress?'

'Nothing's changed.'

'Are you still wearing your disguise to see her?' She sounded amused.

Janet lay the back of her hand against her aching forehead. 'Yes, though I feel like Philip Marlowe with a touch of the Seven Dwarfs. Can you imagine what I look like in clothes made for a man six inches taller than me?'

Her mother giggled. Janet thought how young she sounded.

'Never mind, Janet. I would have done the same myself. Have you told Edna and Colin about all this?'

'Not really.' Janet crossed one arm over her waist where the cord of her dressing gown was starting to unravel. There was no point in telling her mother that she had tried telling Colin, but he had been sprawled in a drunken stupor over the kitchen table at the time. Instead she said, 'I don't think they can take much more.'

Her mother sighed. 'I agree.' It sounded as though there were layers of problems that Janet knew nothing of.

Suddenly Janet felt an overwhelming sense of isolation, similar to how she'd felt at boarding school. 'I miss you,' she said.

Her mother didn't hesitate. 'I miss you too.' For once there were no other people, no other problems except their own, but it didn't last. 'Oh, by the way, dear, I did post some letters to Edna. Do you know if she's received them yet?'

Janet remembered the file and the letters she'd seen on her mother's desk. She vaguely remembered the contents. At the time they hadn't really sunk in, but now, remembering Edna at the zoo telling her about her secret child, it all fitted into place.

'I'll ask her,' she said softly. 'And Mother?'

'Yes.'

'I think you've done the right thing.'

There was another pause before her mother said, 'I hope so, dear. I sincerely hope so.'

On the following day, Charlotte and David came home at midday to a Sunday roast prepared by Janet and cooked by Ivan. Luckily for them there was no Mrs Grey to interfere and the clatter of pans and preparations were like the warming up of an orchestra, fine-tuning itself for the main event.

Her father specifically asked to eat in the kitchen. 'I feel warmer here,' he said. His face was pale and looked clammy as if a fine spray had been applied.

Charlotte had been going to give Janet a lift back to Saltmead, but David's appearance gave cause for concern. 'I can't drive you, darling. I'm needed here. But if Ivan could drive you out there.' A worried frown creased her brow. 'It's your father, you see,' she said after closing the drawing room door where he was presently dozing in his favourite chair, 'I can't possibly leave him.'

The prospect of being driven by Ivan would have sent butterflies fluttering in her stomach previous to last night. Today it didn't happen.

'Say nothing about the letters,' Charlotte added. 'I doubt whether she's told Colin about them.'

The car journey back to Saltmead was surprisingly pleasant. There was no tension between them, no long awkward silences. Colin and Edna were an easy topic of conversation and en route they stopped off at Kingscott Avenue.

When she knocked at the door, Edna answered. At first she smiled then her face dropped. 'Stay there,' she ordered, holding out a warning hand, and shouted over her shoulder, 'Colin! Shut the children into the dining room.'

Janet exchanged a quick look with Ivan who had approached the house with her.

Following the slamming of a door, a troubled looking Colin appeared in the passageway, then disappeared as Pamela and Peter began crying.

Edna was like a sentry filling the doorway and blocking their way. 'Keep your distance. I don't want the other two getting sick.'

She looked tired and agitated. Perhaps a little good news might help. 'I've seen Susan, Edna.'

Edna nodded, her eyes seeming like saucers in her pinched, pale face. 'I know. Will you give her my love?'

Janet hesitated in replying. How could she possibly explain to a distraught woman how careful she had to be? She nodded anyway. 'Yes. Of course I will.'

'I'm sorry.' Edna started to close the door.

'Wait!' Janet grabbed the door and dropped her voice. 'Have you received the letters my mother sent?'

Edna glanced nervously over her shoulder then nodded. 'But you haven't . . .' She'd been about to ask whether she'd told Colin, but he chose that moment to appear at the window. He waved and looked as if he were about to open it.

Seeing him there made Edna agitated. 'You'd better go.'

'All right.'

There was no need to ask whether Colin knew anything about the letters. It was obvious he did not.

Nineteen

As Edna turned right at the top of Wedmore Vale, she blessed the day back in 1945 when she'd met Polly and Charlotte on Temple Meads Station. They'd been there when she needed them, just as now.

She arrived at Polly's house in Camborne Crescent at around nine thirty. Although both Janet and her mother had stressed that visiting was not allowed at Saltmead, Edna refused to believe it.

'I'm sure they wouldn't refuse a worried mother,' she said when Janet had told her of how she read stories to Susan almost every night.

'They won't let you in,' Janet had stressed again. 'Please understand that.'

Edna had pretended that she accepted what Janet said as fact, but her determination to see her child was too great to be denied. Polly had agreed to go with her to the sanatorium. No one else, not even Colin, had been told she was going.

Impatient to get going, she blew the horn so Polly would know she was there. 'Hurry up,' she whispered, taking care not to meet the gaze of a group of gossiping women with meaty arms across wide stomachs. Probably wondering who I am, she thought, perhaps surprised to see a woman rather than a man calling for Polly in a car. Polly had always had a bit of a reputation and was almost boastful about it.

Not bothering to turn the engine off, she tapped the steering wheel as she waited, taking a glance at her watch, then at the street, anything to make time pass more quickly.

Camborne Crescent was not a place she would choose to live in and today it seemed drearier than ever. A grey sky hung over the red-brick houses, and sweet wrappers whirled across the pavement in a cold wind, finally seeking shelter beneath the straggly privets. The remains of Coronation bunting hung ragged and dripping with recent rain from between the streetlights. No one had bothered to take them down. They'd probably be there next year, she thought ruefully, or even longer.

Polly came dashing out of the house, made up to the nines and flouncing down the path in a full-skirted dress with penny-sized black spots scattered on a white background matched with a black bolero jacket. As if she were off to a party, thought Edna, and smiled. Even after all these years, Polly was still a bundle of energy.

Her black patent sling-backs clattered like gunfire down the garden path. 'Do you like it?' she asked with a beaming smile as she twirled on the spot.

'Lovely,' said Edna. The truth was she really thought the full skirt and the neat little bolero would look wonderful on someone taller and smaller-busted than Polly. Something else she couldn't say, but she didn't want to waste time. Getting to the sanatorium was all she could think of.

Beaming as though Christian Dior himself had sung her praises, Polly started for the car door then stopped. 'What are they doing here?'

Pamela and Peter looked at her soulfully from the back seat.

'They're coming with us.'

'They can't!'

'They have to.'

'Why couldn't Colin have them?'

Edna coloured up, but stayed forthright. 'I haven't told him I'm going there. To tell you the truth, I thought that your Aunty Meg might have them.'

'Crafty cow!'

Without hesitation, Polly opened the back door of the car. 'Come on, kids. Out you come. Yer Aunty Meg will 'ave you fer the day. She's making cakes. You could give her a hand.'

They left the children licking cake mixture from a large china bowl and a wooden spoon. Meg promised them a piece of the finished cake that was presently in the oven, its aroma of mixed fruit, cinnamon and butter making their mouths water.

Edna's stomach rumbled. She'd been too nervous for breakfast.

'You look nice, dear,' said Meg to Edna and offered them both a cup of tea before they set off.

Edna thanked her for the compliment, but declined the tea. 'We have to go.'

'You do look nice,' said Polly, lighting a cigarette as they pulled away from the kerb.

Edna wore her best green suit, which had a straight skirt and a box jacket. She'd styled her hair differently, tying it back and teasing some bits forward into a fringe. Occupying herself with trivialities helped to hide the pain of Susan's illness following on so soon after the miscarriage.

'Don't think much of yer perfume though,' Polly added after Edna had thanked her.

'I'm not wearing perfume.'

'Thank God fer that,' Polly laughed. 'Smells like bleedin' bleach.'

'I've been doing a lot of cleaning,' Edna explained as they took a left onto St John's Lane. 'I have to keep everything very clean and germ free for when Susan comes home. If I'd kept things cleaner in the first place, Susan would never have got polio.'

'You silly cow,' Polly chided. 'She could 'ave caught it from anywhere. I thought the swimming baths were the best bet for picking up summat like that, or the pictures, anywhere there's a load of kids.'

'Anywhere,' said Edna. 'No one knows for sure.'

'Well, there's a girl in our street—'

Edna interrupted. 'When are you going to Australia?'

Polly recognized the fact that Edna did not want the conversation to continue, but wished she'd chosen a different subject.

'Never.'

'You've changed your mind?'

'No, Billy's buggered it up. They might 'ave took convicts years ago, but they sure as 'ell don't want 'em now!'

'He's in prison?' Edna looked shocked. 'What did he do?'

'Supposed to have nicked a van – but he didn't.'

Polly sounded convinced. Edna was shocked. 'What are you going to do?'

'The best I can.'

Polly's mouth shut tight as a clam. Absorbed in her own thoughts, she stared out of the window for the rest of the journey. Every so often Edna glanced at her, wondering what she was planning, but she wouldn't ask. Her own thoughts were occupied with Susan. All the same, she couldn't help thinking that Polly was up to something and the imprisoned Billy Hills just might have a problem.

Polly *was* thinking about Billy and not being able to emigrate. But she was also thinking about Edna and all that scrubbing and the stink of bleach and boiled laundry. Edna was one of the most spick and span people she knew. What a silly thing to think that Susan catching the polio was her fault. Another thought came to her. Should she have allowed the children to stay with Meg? Would Carol be all right?

Arriving at Saltmead Sanatorium broke the silence that had persisted throughout most of the journey.

'I know this place,' said Polly, screwing her eyes up tight at the sight of the high fence, the concrete drive and the single storey prefabricated buildings. 'It used to be a prisoner of war camp. Charlotte used to come here to 'elp German prisoners go 'ome – something like that anyway.'

Edna barely acknowledged her, but eyed the wire fence and

the low huts, the concrete paths and the uncut grass beaten flat by the pouring rain. Susan was somewhere in this dreary place, so close yet so far.

'I came here once,' said Polly, then immediately got out of the car.

The rain was lashing down, creating puddles in the cracked concrete and gurgling down drainpipes. They huddled under one umbrella and made their way through the puddles. By the time they'd found the entrance, raindrops drizzled from Edna's fringe and Polly's flared skirt hung heavy with water and clung to her seamed stockings.

The waiting room was square with cream walls and a brown floor. There were no chairs to sit on and no pictures or posters on the wall except for a notice pinned next to a hatch which said, 'Please Knock'.

Edna raised her gloved hand and tapped politely.

'That's not enough to get some attention. I've got a tougher fist,' said Polly and gave the closed hatch a few hefty blows.

The nurse who answered had a round face, pink cheeks and merry eyes. Like a chocolate coated Brazil nut, her exterior hid a hard centre. Edna explained why they were there.

The nurse pursed her lips. 'I'm sorry. Visiting is not allowed.'

'Can you at least tell me how she is?' asked Edna.

The nurse was adamant. 'It is not my responsibility to report on a patient's progress. Only a doctor can do that.'

Polly pushed forward. 'So can we see a doctor?'

The nurse raised her eyebrows questioningly. 'Are you a relative?'

'No, I'm not, but—'

'Then you cannot possibly see a doctor.'

Edna pressed forward. 'I'm the mother of Susan Smith. Can I see a doctor?'

The nurse looked at her as if she had no importance

whatsoever. 'I very much doubt it. Professor Pritchard won't see you and will not allow any other doctor to see you until the patient is recovered and able to leave our care.'

Edna immediately interpreted this to mean that Susan had not recovered and might, in fact, never recover. She panicked. 'Will my child live? Is she going to live?'

Polly recognized that Edna was losing control and grabbed her arms.

'Really, this kind of behaviour will do no good,' bleated the nurse.

'Edna! Edna! Calm down!'

But it was no use. Edna burst into hysterics and there was nothing Polly could do about it except get very mad.

She spun like a dervish towards the open shutter. 'Look, you bloody old cow!'

'There is no need for that!'

The shutter came down with a loud bang.

Polly put her arms around Edna and eased her onto her feet. Her usual bubbly brightness had disappeared. This was a very serious situation and she felt genuine sorrow for her friend.

'Come on, Edna love. Let's go home. We ain't doing no good here.'

She tried to head her towards the door. After just two steps, she stopped dead.

'I know! Let's ask for Janet.' Before Polly could stop her, she was hammering on the closed shutter. 'Janet! Let me see Janet!'

The shutter went up and the stern face of the ward sister returned. 'You have been told to leave,' she said sternly.

Edna gripped the cream painted shelf on which the shutter usually sat. 'Janet Hennessey-White. She knows my daughter. She's seen her!'

The pale lips of the woman in the stiff veil and starched uniform seemed to turn to blue then back to mauve.

Polly cringed and instinctively apologized, something she

didn't make a habit of doing. 'She's upset,' she explained. 'It's not true what she's saying – not really!'

Edna would not be calmed. 'Janet Hennessey-White works for the Professor. She's seen Susan,' she shouted, 'she's seen my daughter! She told me so, and if she can see her, so can I. I'm her mother!'

'Come on,' Polly hissed as she guided Edna towards the door.

'But Susan . . . and Janet . . . !'

Polly pushed Edna out of the door and glanced back just once and then only briefly. It was enough time to see that the woman behind the hatch had acquired a face like thunder.

'Bloody hell! That's torn it,' Polly muttered on as she sat Edna back behind the wheel of the car.

'I only wanted to see Susan,' Edna whined childishly. 'Is that very wrong?'

'No,' said Polly and a wealth of sympathy immediately swept over her, and not just for Edna and Susan. Janet was about to land in some hellish hot water.

Susan opened her eyes. The world had always been good to her, but it didn't seem that way any more. The hospital was a horrid place, but the lady who came to tell her stories had made it a bit better.

She hadn't been for two nights now and she missed her. She missed her mother too and her father. She even missed her little brother and sister.

Her lips were dry. She licked them, then wondered if her mother had left her some water on the bedside cabinet. Then she reminded herself it would be a nurse who might have left her water, not her mother. She tried to lift her arm to reach it, but it wouldn't move so she began to cry.

A voice sounded somewhere in the darkness beyond the glass partition. 'Susan! You're awake. Now come along. No need to cry. If you're a very good girl you'll soon be better.'

She looked up to see if the eyes that looked back at her

were those of the lady who told her stories. 'Are you going to read me a story?' she asked.

Two chill blue eyes peered over a crisp white mask. 'No. I told you. You're here to get better. And if you're a good girl, you will get better.'

The words frightened her. Did they mean that if she were a bad girl she wouldn't?

Another face appeared wearing the same white mask as the first, but this person had a lot of wrinkles around her eyes.

'Take no notice,' said the older woman. 'Children that cry incessantly for their mothers tend to be unstable. Leave her alone and turn off the light.'

The world was plunged into darkness.

Susan felt her lips quivering, but willed herself not to whimper.

My brave little girl. That's how her father usually referred to her. But why had he left her here in this terrible place? And where was her mother?

If only the lady who told her stories would come. She wouldn't feel frightened then.

She suddenly needed to use the toilet. Frightened, immobile and confused, she lay silently, afraid to make a sound. There was a pain in her groin because she wanted to pee, but was afraid to call out. She held it in for as long as she could, then burst into tears as the warm wetness seeped out of her body. Desperately she tried to cry softly so that she wouldn't see those two women again, at least, not until she had to.

Twenty

Doing a bit of housework for Charlotte and for Edna's parents was all well and good, but it wasn't really keeping the wolf from the door. Polly didn't want to leave Mr Burbage in the lurch, not the way things were with Edna at the moment, but she had to do something.

'You're on yer own,' she muttered to herself as she considered a large hole in Carol's shoe and a severe lack of elastic in some of her own knickers. 'You're skint. Now what are you going to do about it?'

Thirty-four and her quality of life had dived nose down into a pile of poo. What she wouldn't give to roll back the clock to the time when she was young – well – younger than she was now. Jitterbugs, Glenn Miller, good-looking guys with a few quid. What wouldn't she give for a bit of fun and a few more pounds in her pocket.

'Damn and blast you, Billy Hills,' she hissed as she rolled herself a badly needed cigarette from a couple of stumps that she'd saved from yesterday. 'Look what I've bloody come to.'

It occurred to her that although Billy was not entirely blameless for ending up in prison, the people he'd been working for had a lot to answer for. What's more, he'd been so bloody loyal to them. And what about me? she thought, aiming a kick at the dog who had just chewed up her best shoes. He can't have been thinking about me. Luckily, the kick missed, her slipper flew off and the dog caught it and ran out into the garden. Oh well, she thought wryly, what the hell! They were old anyway and she had more important things on her mind.

Billy would carry the can and keep his mouth shut and, because she didn't want to worry him, she'd still said nothing about the visit from O'Hara's henchmen. No husband, no money, a right mess. What a load of aggro she was getting, though it was nothing compared to the aggro Carol had given that ginger git who'd come calling. Hope he's got a bump the size of a potato, she thought with a wicked smile.

Her thoughts went back to Billy. Keeping his mouth shut was what the visit had been all about. They'd known he was about to get nicked and didn't want him squealing. The police had badgered him to tell them more about the illegal operations of the bloke he'd been working for. So far he'd said nothing. There was a price on keeping quiet, thought Polly, as she poked at the last lumps of coal in the grate, and I'm the one paying it. That had to be worth money. It definitely had to be worth money!

She sat back in the chair as the unfairness of it all gave birth to an idea. Those blokes owed them for Billy's silence.

'And now,' she said, getting to her feet and throwing the fag stumps into the fire, 'it's time to collect a down payment!'

'I'm off to Ashley Down,' she told Aunty Meg and explained why.

A smart black jacket teamed with a matching skirt in dog's tooth check seemed just the thing to wear. It looked smart and businesslike, and that was the way she wanted to look.

Mouth full of hairgrips, she stood in front of the mirror that hung over the fireplace. As she fixed a featherlight hat to her head, she glanced at the boy and girl skating in Dutch national dress painted onto the mirror.

'Look at them,' she said to Aunty Meg and indicated the two figures with a nod of her head. 'That's what I'm doing – ice skating – only I'm more likely to fall flat on me arse than they are.'

Meg sat herself on the broad arm of the armchair, a

nervous frown hanging over her eyes. 'Are you sure about this? I mean, he might be a bit angry.'

'Angry? How about me? I'm bloody angry! Lost me job 'cos the bloody manager wanted me to take more down than the posters at the end of a two-week matinée. Cheeky sod! Well I told 'im where to get off!' She didn't mention that they'd been living off money meant to finance their emigration to Australia. She'd only get upset.

'Are you sure you don't want me to go with you?' Meg asked.

Polly shook her head and clipped on a pair of black plastic earrings that Carol had bought her for her birthday in Woolworths.

'Twopence for the bus is all I need, thank you very much.'

Meg leaned over the front gate and watched her niece totter off on three-inch black suede court shoes, her rear end rolling provocatively beneath a slim-fitting skirt that reached to her calves.

Polly was no longer the bubbly young woman who'd discovered love and lust under the anonymity of the blackout. She was older now, a wife and a mother. But she was still attractive. Meg could understand why her boss up at the Broadway had tried it on. But she couldn't help but harbour the suspicion that Polly might very well have given in to his advances if it hadn't been for Carol, not that she could blame her. Responsibility for their bed and board had fallen pretty heavily onto her niece's shoulders. Lucky for them all that Carol had intervened and had also told Meg all about it, not that she'd let on she knew. Besides, Carol had sworn her to secrecy.

Polly took a deep breath and tugged the hem of her jacket down over her hips before pushing open the gate of the house in Ashley Place. The glass at the windows seemed as inky black as on the first occasion she'd seen them. Billy had been with her then and she wished with all her might that he were with her now. But it was on his account that she was here. If only he'd never met these people in the first place . . .

'Forget it,' she said aloud, aware that her heart was beating like a hammer against her rib cage, the sound of it filling her head and drowning out the scrunching of gravel beneath her feet.

There were three chilly white steps leading up to the front door. Just as her foot landed on the first one the door sprang open. At first she didn't recognize the man in the loud check suit who sprinted down the steps and grabbed her arm. Once she got a whiff of him, and saw his eyes, his hair and the ginger moustache, she knew immediately who he was.

'Let go of me you ginger-haired stinker!'

He shook her like a terrier shakes a rat. 'Get the hell out of here!'

'I want to see the boss.' Short as she was, she managed to stand her ground and glare levelly into his face.

'I am the boss.'

'No you ain't! I want to talk to the organ grinder, not 'is bleeding monkey!'

His face came close to hers. 'As far as you're concerned I *am* the boss.'

A shout came from the open door at the top of the steps.

'Cassidy!'

Ginger, who was obviously Cassidy, didn't look round, but glared at her menacingly. Polly would have laughed into his face and reminded him that he'd almost been beaten senseless by a schoolgirl armed with a hockey stick, but her attention was drawn to the man who had shouted from the top of the steps. He looked powerful, not because he was built like a bull, more because he had an aura of someone used to giving commands and having them obeyed. Military, she thought. He reminded her of Griffiths though better-looking.

After Cassidy (Ginger) let her go, she brushed at her sleeve with as much gusto as she would in banishing a large spider and spat the word 'Pig!' Cassidy merely stepped aside and folded his arms, a sardonic grin lifting one side of his mouth.

The other man came down the steps.

'Billy Hills's missus,' explained Cassidy. 'Mouthy cow! Want me to chuck 'er out?'

The man looked at her questioningly. 'Is that right?'

Polly swallowed her nervousness. 'Yes. And before you chuck me out, think carefully. You got my old man put inside. But the police are asking questions. And things being the way they are . . .'

He ran his eyes over the blonde waves, the checked suit with the nipped-in waistline, the skirt that was just a little too tight for her ample figure. It shouldn't have happened but, for the first time in a long while, she felt sexy. The look in his eyes said he liked what he saw. Her mission was halfway accomplished.

Her surmise proved correct when at last he placed his hand on her shoulder. 'Come inside.'

Cassidy brought up the rear. At the top of the steps the man beside her turned to Cassidy. 'My car needs cleaning. See to it, will you.'

It was not a request. Polly felt her knees buckle. The man beside her sounded Irish, but for a moment she had almost believed it to be something else. Well, it wouldn't hurt to mention it.

'You almost sound American,' she said and wondered if it was possible she'd had a date with him once. She couldn't be sure. She'd had so many.

'Irish. Michael O'Hara. You can call me Mickey.'

'Mickey.'

Too old really for a name like that, but who cares, she'd call him 'sir' if he wanted. He was the best-looking bloke for his age that she'd seen for a while and his lilting accent was reminiscent of the handsome servicemen she'd known with their strong arms, square chins and the best chat-up lines ever. He's Irish, Polly reminded herself. Besides, remember you're a married woman and you're here for Billy. You can't be swayed by a sexy accent.

Polly shrugged her coat more squarely on her shoulders and followed the smart, suited figure into the cool interior of the white house.

Once inside she stopped in her tracks. 'Wow!'

It was love at first sight. The floor tiles were black and white – her favourite colours. Wall lights fashioned from plastic to resemble black-stemmed tulips with white petals gleamed from alcoves on either side of a white marble fireplace through which black veins ran like broken blood vessels. Aims to get even or Billy a decent deal paled into insignificance. This was the house of her dreams.

The sound of their footsteps echoed against the gleaming white walls, the black leather furniture, the chromium and glass doors. He took her into a smaller room off the main entrance hall and indicated that she be seated.

As he nipped the end off a Cuban cigar she fancied she saw him admiring her legs through a haze of rising smoke. Polly coughed, shifted in her chair, and tried to look as if she didn't like the way his eyes settled on her bosom and her belly before returning to her face. He was interested and she liked his interest.

Remember Billy, she said to herself, and sat up a bit straighter. The right words found their way to her tongue.

'I'm Billy's wife.'

'I already know that.'

'Oh yes! Of course.'

'So what do you want?'

'Billy didn't say he was working for a Paddy.'

Mickey O'Hara smiled and slid onto the corner of the glass and plastic desk, one foot remaining on the floor, one foot dangling. 'He didn't say that you were a pretty little blonde with a lot to say for herself.'

Polly felt flattered, but uneasy. His look was too bold, his face too handsome in short, the sort of man who could sweep her off her feet without really trying given the right circumstances. *Dangerous thoughts.* Good God, how long had it been since she'd had a man's arms around her? (Billy's that is, not the rat Griffiths'.) Too bloody long! Bloody hell, how would it be after a few months? *Control yourself! Remember you're a married woman.*

'Tell me why you came here. Pity to waste the bus fare when I might be able to give you exactly what you're looking for.'

Damn the bloody man! His gaze settled on her breasts and his meaning was double-edged, but she'd swallow it. Better him being suggestive than showing her the door.

'Blokes in prison cost their family a lot of heartache and a lot of money,' she said stiffly. 'A woman alone trying to bring up a child without her bloke around has a bloody hard time of it.'

O'Hara narrowed his eyes. 'I believe you.'

'I need help!' She said it quickly before she lost her nerve. 'I reckon I'm due some help from you.'

'How do you reckon on that?'

'Billy's taken his punishment like a man. And he ain't said one word to the coppers about you lot, even though they want him to. Not a word.'

His look hardened.

Polly warned herself not to push her luck.

He said, 'So you think it's worth money to keep him and you quiet.'

'If you wants him to stay that way, there has to be something in it for us. Billy deserves it.' Inside she was shaking like a leaf, willing herself not to blink or tremble.

O'Hara chewed on his cigar before answering. 'Well, I am surprised. I truly thought he'd salted a bit away from the wider than average cuts he was taking.'

Christ, Billy you're an idiot! He knows! He bloody well knows!

She kept her nerve. 'OK, so he's not entirely honest. But then, neither are you lot. Is he the first to ever take a bigger cut than he was s'pposed to? Come on. Tell the truth. You allow for the likes of him taking a bit off the top. Takes a thief to know one.'

It sounded good and she congratulated herself on what she had said. Criminals ripped off criminals – a plausible excuse that might work in her favour.

It didn't seem to at first. Mickey O'Hara was attractive, but had a mean look in his eyes and his jaw was set like a slab of concrete.

Suddenly a slow smile crept across his face and became a laugh. 'You've got balls, Mrs Hills, I'll definitely give you that. And you are right, surprisingly enough.' His laugh got louder. His shoulders began to shake. 'What the hell can we expect if we employ criminals, eh?'

Polly laughed too, albeit nervously. 'That's right. That's bloody right!'

Mickey O'Hara's laughter stopped dead and he got to his feet. A harder look came to his eyes. 'I can't promise anything, but I'll be in touch. Are you working at present?'

She swallowed her pride and owned up to the truth. 'Just a bit of cleaning and looking after an old lady – that's what I do. But it ain't enough. Not nearly enough.'

He glanced at a leather-strapped wristwatch. 'I have to go. Can I give you a lift?'

'Yes please. The Tramway Centre if you could. I can get me bus home from there.'

Inwardly she sighed with gratitude. She'd planned to walk at least part of the way home. Every penny she had in her handbag would be needed to go towards this week's Sunday joint: a breast of lamb or a stuffed bullock's heart if they were lucky, a pound of tripe if they weren't.

Before getting into the shiny black car, she stood and stared at the house taking in the details in case she never had cause to see it again: a flat roof and windows that curved at one end and seemed to dive into the wall at the other. She liked the style, kind of 1940s with a hint of Hollywood.

On the way home she asked Mickey O'Hara why he was in England rather than Ireland.

'I enjoy working here. It's basically the same as I did at home, but there's a lot more of it.'

'Of crime?'

His grin was sardonic and swiftly gone. 'I meant construction. That's what I do. What you call a builder I suppose.'

'You've got a nice house. Did you build it?'

'No. I'm not that sort of builder. I just organize things to do with the construction of buildings.'

It seemed reasonable enough and Polly badly wanted to believe him because the house was so perfect, so absolutely what she wanted, that everything to do with it was fine by her. It's been a long time since I 'ad a bit of glamour in me life, she thought.

'I'll take you all the way home,' he said as they drove through the Centre.

'There's no need.'

'Don't argue. I don't like arguments.'

She clamped her mouth shut and every so often looked at him, wanting to touch him, to breathe in his smell, to hear him talking again.

Strange how one look from a bloke could upset your life. He made her want to lose weight, to keep her lipstick moist, to stop biting her nails so she could paint them a rich, flirtatious red. *Flirt!* Her nylons made a whispering noise as she crossed one leg over the other and smiled sidelong at him. *Flirt!* Yes, that was what she was doing, but she just couldn't help it.

'Here it is,' said Polly as they turned into Camborne Road and wanted to cringe low in the seat. The red brick of the council houses glistened in the rain. A brown and white dog glanced over its shoulder as it did its business on the pavement outside number twenty-three. Luckily the privets were pretty high so no one in the house beyond would have seen them pull up.

Pound to a penny that the curtains are twitching over the road, thought Polly. But I'm not going to look. It's none of their bleeding business!

'Not quite Ashley Down,' Polly said.

'I take it you don't like living here.'

'Would you? I'd like prospects, something better. I had the chance to go to America at one time, but . . .' She shrugged, but held her head in a perky pose that Meg said made her look almost girlish.

O'Hara pulled on the hand brake then rested one arm along the back of the seat behind her. The other rested on the steering wheel.

'America isn't all it's cracked up to be.'

'How would you know?'

The way he grinned suddenly made her feel small, inferior and, oddly enough, as though she'd seen him somewhere before.

He said, 'Half of Ireland lives there. I know it well.'

She'd half-expected him to make a pass. It surprised her when all he did was run his finger down her cheek.

'I might have a job for you,' he said. 'I need a hostess in my nightclub.' He restarted the engine and fixed his gaze on somewhere close to the end of the bonnet. 'Up to you. Call me.'

Too stunned to move, she watched the car until it turned at the far corner and disappeared. A job! A nightclub hostess! Meg wouldn't approve, she'd say that sort of job was not much better than being a prostitute, but then, thought Polly, rather that than cleaning someone else's house even if they did have a vacuum cleaner.

'Slut,' she muttered as she got out her key.

She was bright as a button until she saw her daughter sitting on the stairs, her face in her hands and a black look on her face.

'Who's that bloke?'

'Never you mind.' Polly straightened her jacket with one hand and self-consciously fluffed up her hair with the other.

'Not another uncle. Not a new dad, is he?'

Polly almost blushed. 'Of course not! I'm married to Billy. What the bloody 'ell do you take me for?'

'Well,' said Carol, undeterred by her mother's indignation and looking and sounding too much like Aunty Meg for comfort, 'you do like the blokes a bit, don't you?'

Polly aimed a slap at Carol's face, but missed. 'You cheeky little cow! Who told you to say that?'

'No one. I just got me own opinions!'

'Well, *that's* bloody true!' Polly broke into a grin then a chuckle. 'No doubt about it, but yer a right little cow, Carol Hills. You've got too much to say fer yerself. Trouble is, I knows damn well where you got it from!'

Mickey O'Hara didn't usually take chances. If he had any sense he would keep away from Polly Hills before she realized who he really was and threw his life into turmoil. It both surprised and amused him that neither she nor the woman who'd come tramping onto the building site had recognized him. It was all to the good. The first he could easily avoid, the second he would get to know better, have fun with, and chance his luck. If she did remember where they'd met, he would deal with it accordingly.

Twenty-one

The woman looked as though she was wearing a starched tablecloth on her head, and stood with a trolley at the side of the bed. On the verge of a whimper, Susan watched a plume of steam rise from a large enamel bowl. It reminded her of when her mother made a suet pudding wrapped in a bread cloth and boiled for hours. Later it would be served with jam, treacle and a large portion of thick, yellow custard. Pretending this too was food helped her cope with the truth.

'I'm not hungry,' she said weakly.

'Silly girl,' said a voice from behind the white mask.

Be a brave girl. Dad. It was Dad she pretended was here when the lights went out or when she got a smack for wetting the bed. That was why she tried to drink as little as possible. That was why her lips were cracked and dry and her tongue was furred with white stuff that tasted like soggy feathers.

The smell from the stuff in the bowl was horrible. 'I don't want it,' she said and began to cry. Her eyes followed the progress of the bowl from one end of the trolley to the other. Her stomach was already churning in response to the smell, its contents steadily rising up her gullet.

'Now, come along,' said the nurse as she stripped back the bedclothes to expose Susan's sad little limbs.

As the nurse reached for the contents of the bowl, Susan turned to one side and spewed the little she'd eaten onto her pillow.

Janet needed a miracle. Following Edna's outburst, she'd

been hauled into Matron's office and asked to explain herself. Before entering, Janet had told herself to stand firm. She owed it to Edna and Susan to keep her head, and if she kept her head, she'd keep her job. That's what she hoped for anyway.

The office was possibly the warmest room in the building by virtue of two paraffin heaters, one on either side of the room. The smell was impossible, an acrid aroma of unspent fuel that glowed red on one heater and blue on the other.

Matron asked her to explain.

'Mrs Smith wanted to see her daughter. She's missing her desperately.'

Matron's dark bushy eyebrows met like two mating caterpillars above her nose. The hairs on her chin bristled as her lips went inwards. Janet found it hard to stop staring at them. They seemed to have a life of their own. She said, 'Sister Doris insists that she heard Mrs Smith say that *you* have been visiting her daughter. Is that right?'

'And you're going to tell me it's not allowed.' She couldn't help sounding impatient.

'No. It is not allowed. And for very good reason. Normally I would indeed dismiss the comment, but the child Susan keeps asking for the lady who tells her stories. Would that be you, Miss Hennessey-White?'

The image of Susan lying small and helpless made Janet want to shout how unfair everything was. But she couldn't do that, not if she was to continue visiting her. She must keep her head.

'Of course not.' She was not a liar by nature, but in this instance she had no choice.

'I shall have to report this to Professor Pritchard,' Matron went on, her fat chin appearing to move independently of her mouth. 'Fortunately for you he's feeling ill and has gone home early. I will take the matter up with him on Monday morning. Until then, you are dismissed from these premises.'

Janet opened her mouth to protest, then stopped. Best

leave it for now. She had no alternative but to head home for the weekend. It hurt her to do so, but she left without visiting Susan.

If Janet thought she was going to have a quiet weekend, her mother had other ideas.

'I'm going to see Polly. Would you like to come?'

Janet demurred. 'I need to see Edna so I can tell her myself how Susan is getting on.' She had not and would not mention the possibility of losing her job. It wasn't just a case of keeping things to herself, a habit she had got into a long time back when things had been difficult between her parents. She was hoping for a miracle, in which case no explanation would be needed.

'You're in luck. I'm seeing Polly at Edna's parents' house in Nutgrove Avenue.' She didn't explain why. 'Edna should be there too. It's Polly's pay day.'

Janet slid off the sofa where she'd been reading an article in *Picture Post* about problems in Palestine, a million or so people turned off land they'd farmed and lived on for generations.

'I'll get my coat.'

The day was chill. The sun was doing its best to break through a thick mist, but there was no breeze to blow it away and only a watery gleam where the sun was supposed to be.

On a day such as this, Charlotte would normally have put on her fur coat. Today she did not. She wore a blanket-checked coat with patch pockets and big buttons. Janet asked her why.

'Polly's in a bad way at the moment – financially, that is. I don't want to appear too well off.'

'Mother! You are well off.' It was hard not to laugh, but she couldn't stop grinning. Being well off had always been a source of embarrassment to her mother. Granted a change of clothes might make her seem less affluent, but her poise and her accent were unalterable.

'That's not the point,' Charlotte said. 'Anyway, I've got vegetables for her.'

Normally the heavy, wooden front door at Nutgrove Avenue had always been open and only the inner door had been closed, its ruby red and Prussian blue glass throwing light patterns over the floor, walls and ceiling. Today the front door was shut.

'To stop Ethel running off,' said Charlotte as if Janet had asked for an explanation.

The leaden note of the cast iron knocker seemed to swim up and down the street before fading to nothing. The sound of footsteps echoed along the passageway on the other side of the door before it opened and Polly appeared dressed in a white blouse and black skirt with a white apron.

'Goodness. You look like a housemaid,' said an amused Charlotte.

Polly smirked and curtseyed. 'Good day, madam. Her ladyship will see you now.'

Janet laughed.

'Very droll I'm sure,' said Charlotte, her foot on the step, poised to enter.

Polly let go the door and studied her fingernails. 'No, I don't think I was cut out to be a housemaid. I ain't no good at taking orders. What do you think, Jan?'

'I think you're right,' said Janet, smiling at the thought of Polly ever being a maid of any description.

A door beyond Polly's shoulder towards the rear of the house suddenly caught both Charlotte and Janet's attention. Suddenly a figure rushed down the dark passage that led from the front door to the back scullery. It was Edna. Her face was taut and her eyes were wide and anxious.

'You can't come in!'

Charlotte paused. 'It's just us, Edna.'

Edna stopped halfway, glanced at Charlotte, then looked directly at Janet. 'You can't come in, Janet. I've got the children here.'

'Now come along, Edna. There's no need for this,' said Charlotte in her most sensible voice.

Edna looked wildly from mother to daughter and back again. 'Yes, there is. I've just told you. I've got the children here.' Again she looked at Janet. 'They might catch it.'

Edna was talking nonsense. Charlotte knew that. 'Edna, they're in no more danger of catching polio from Janet than they are catching it from you. You went to the sanatorium with Polly. Don't you think they could catch it from either of you?'

Charlotte could tell by the look on Edna's face that it wasn't sinking in.

'That's not the point. Janet's there every day.'

Charlotte was adamant. 'Edna, you can't keep the children in isolation. Surely you've been told how long the incubation period is?'

Edna's eyes were hugely round and her hair swung round her face as she shook her head and said, 'I don't care how long it is. Janet works out there. Perhaps I can let you in – as long as you stay away from the children, but Janet can't come in. They'll catch it.'

Polly began to look unnerved by all this. 'What about my Carol?'

Charlotte sighed. They'd been standing on the doorstep for a few minutes now. The cold was getting to her and it seemed that the handbag she held in her right hand was far heavier than it had been. She swapped it from one gloved hand to the other. 'Look—' she began.

Janet interrupted. 'I don't need to come in. I just wanted to tell you that Susan is now receiving more intensive heat treatment. I've visited her as much as I dare and I've continued to read her bedtime stories. She's missing you all. That's what I wanted to tell you.'

Hands clasped nervously in front of her, Edna came forward. Tension still showed in her face and her eyes looked too big to be real: 'I appreciate you visiting her, Janet, but I can't let you in. It wouldn't be right.'

Although Janet offered to wait outside, Charlotte insisted they left. 'I'll see you shortly,' she said to Polly as she handed over the vegetables.

They were silent as they motored along St John's Lane, up Sheene Road and past the crowded shops of East Street, the lengthy expanse of the tobacco factory, and the stone, castellated solidity of Bedminster Police Station.

As they crossed Bedminster Bridge, Janet said. 'It wasn't really about me being contagious. That wasn't really what Edna was getting at.'

Charlotte responded too quickly for what she said to be sincere. 'Darling, she's just upset and terribly worried about Susan.'

'No, that's not it! It's the fact that I took Susan to Clevedon and I was concentrating on what Jonathan was saying rather than on what Susan was doing. Edna blames me, and she's right.'

'Of course she's not!' Charlotte sounded anxious, almost angry, but it did no good. Janet could not get the idea out of her mind.

When they got home, Charlotte went upstairs to see how David was. He had recovered well from the slight stroke, but was inclined to rest during the afternoon.

Janet offered to make tea and Charlotte accepted with gratitude.

The tea caddy was made of tin and covered with stencilled pictures of Chinese temples and ornate pagodas. Janet flipped open the lid. A mere scoopful sat at the bottom. She went to the larder, a walk-in affair that had once been termed the butler's pantry. As in the past, this was the place where a good stock of basic essentials was kept. It included a cold slab on which sat a pound of smoked haddock for tonight's dinner and the Sunday roast, a rib of beef, its dark meat encompassed in yellow fat. Quarter pound packets of tea were sat next to packets of cubed, granulated and Demerara sugar on the top shelf. If she stretched herself to full height and stood on tiptoe . . .

The worst thing that could happen, happened. Using the tips of her fingers she rolled a packet of tea to the edge of the shelf, tipped it over and tried to grab it. At the same time, her knuckles hit a packet of expensive Demerara that sat close to the edge of the shelf. Both items fell onto the unforgiving stone floor and burst open, tea leaves and brown sugar spilling out over the floor from the broken packaging.

Janet groaned and buried her face in her hands. Today had been bad enough already. Trivial as it was, this small occurrence was the final straw.

'No! No! No!'

She sank to the floor, her desolation complete. Nothing in her life was going right. Even the larder door had closed shut on her and she didn't feel the least bit inclined to open it. She sat head in hands and knees drawn up, sobbing into her fingers.

Ten minutes or so passed before light from the kitchen fell in, followed by the shadow of someone standing in the doorway.

'Janet?'

She knew without looking up that it was Ivan, but didn't want to look at him. Getting drunk, she'd decided, was something she would never do again. Fancy opening her heart to him! She hardly knew the man!

'Are you all right?' he asked.

'No. But it's none of your business.'

'Are you going to stay in here all day?'

'Yes. Go away.'

'You will get very cold.'

Never 'you'll', she thought, always 'you will', 'you are', 'you will not'. That's how foreigners spoke, taking extra care by pronouncing the words in full; no slang, no abbreviations.

'I don't care.'

He paused. She assumed he was going to close the door and leave her there. Instead he came over and squatted down beside her.

'Use this,' he said.

She peered out from between her fingers. He was offering her a man-size handkerchief. It looked freshly laundered. She took it roughly, rubbed at her cheeks, indignant at her tears and at him for finding her like this. Then she blew her nose long and loudly.

'What do you want?' She knew she sounded rude, but she didn't want him to get any ideas after what she'd told him in confidence.

'Tea,' he said and looked pointedly at the mess on the floor. 'You wanted it too?'

She nodded.

He remained squatting, looking at her as if trying to assimilate why she was talking to him like she was. His next words sent a jolt through her system.

He shook his hand at the mix of tea leaves and sugar. 'You are too strong to let this worry you.'

She spoke sharply. 'How would you know?'

He paused as if weighing up what he was about to say and how she might respond to it. Then he settled himself down against the wall beside her, his legs drawn up close to him, his elbows resting on his knees.

'You have told no one, I think, about what happened to you. You only told me because of the whisky.'

'I should not have.'

She could have kicked herself for saying it like that . . . like he said it.

'You needed to. It was a terrible thing that happened to you, something you have to live with. It is not easy.'

This was a man saying this! Her response was immediate.

'What the hell do you know about it?'

His voice dropped. 'A lot.'

A silence followed. She sensed that although his body was here, sitting beside her, his mind was elsewhere.

At last he said, 'My wife was raped.'

'I didn't know you had a wife.'

'I don't, not any more.'

Again, the silence, pregnant with possibilities.

'The Germans released me from prison. There was no point in keeping me there. The Russians were coming. We were all going to be liberated. There was much drinking and dancing. Some soldiers of the Red Army joined in, conscripts taken from the Steppes and put into a uniform, given a little training but not too much, just enough to be brutal.

'Some women hid because they had heard tales about these Russian soldiers. Freedom after so many years of occupation clouded my judgement and that of my wife. What was there to fear? These were our liberators.

'One night they came to my house. They had heard I had been in the Resistance. They did not trust anyone who had been. They called me a capitalist spy and said I had to go for questioning. My wife cried and held onto me. I knew what they were going to do. My wife was raped, then killed in front of my eyes.'

Words didn't come easily. She suddenly felt ashamed, not for what had happened to her, but because he had suffered so much more and she had treated him so badly.

'I'm sorry.'

He appeared not to hear her, but stared at the floor as if he could see his past among the scattered leaves and sugar.

'Then it was my turn,' he said, his voice little more than a whisper.

'They beat you up?'

He swallowed, his eyes still fixed on the floor. At first she thought he was not going to answer, but he did.

'They used me as they had used my wife – but didn't kill me. For a long time after I wished they had.'

‘I didn’t know,’ she whispered, hardly able to believe that such a thing could happen to a man.

‘You were not supposed to,’ he said and got to his feet. He shook his head as if dispelling the memory. ‘Life goes on.’

His expression brightened. He put his hands on his hips and nodded at the mess on the floor. ‘If you make the tea, I will clear this up. Is that a deal?’

She nodded.

He offered his hand so she could get to her feet. Without hesitation she took it and went to put the kettle on.

Monday mornings at the sanatorium were usually no different from any other day of the week, but the moment Janet entered the grimly decorated reception hall, she felt that something momentous had happened.

As usual a char lady was on her hands and knees outside Professor Pritchard’s office door rubbing lavender polish into the cracked brown lino.

Janet greeted her as she always did. ‘Good morning, Mrs Davies.’

‘Oow! Guess what?’ said the cleaner, her steel curlers bobbing out from under her checked turban as she sat back on her haunches. A half-smoked cigarette jiggled at the corner of her mouth causing an inch of ash to scatter over the newly polished floor.

The piece of gossip she’d been about to deliver was strangled in her throat as the door to the Professor’s office sprung open.

‘Janet!’

Jonathan almost fell over Mrs Davies as he rushed out of the door. ‘In here! I want to speak to you.’

Warily Janet eyed the open door. The Professor never allowed anyone to use his office. And Jonathan had called her Janet in front of a member of staff! What was he up to?

She followed him into the office. Mrs Davies gave her a toothless grin and muttered, ‘When the cat’s away . . .’

She closed the door on whatever else was said.

Janet raised her eyebrows at Jonathan, who had gone behind the big mahogany desk from where the Professor had kept the sanatorium in battleship readiness.

'Should you be there?' she asked him.

He smiled, placed his hands on the arms of the Professor's handsome leather chair and slowly lowered himself into it. 'The Professor is no longer with us. A heart attack. Because of the suddenness of his departure, I have been put in temporary charge.'

'You?'

He seemed less lost behind the desk than the Professor, who was a much smaller man, had done. Or perhaps it was that he had grown into his promotion.

'Don't sound so surprised. I deserve promotion.'

'Goodness!'

'Is that all you can say?'

Absolutely astounded, Janet sank into a chair. 'What next?'

'Get your notepad. I've got a lot of dictation to give you. I'm going to introduce new ideas,' Jonathan said. 'I want to let a little light in, tomorrow's methods, not yesterday's.'

Janet thought of Susan and her promise to Edna. 'May I ask you . . .'

At that point the office door swung open and there stood Matron, plump arms folded beneath equally plump breasts. 'Dr Driver. I believe you wanted to see me.' She glanced at Janet and immediately presumed the reason for her summons. 'Ah yes. Unqualified staff visiting my patients. May I suggest that Miss Hennessey-White is released forthwith following her very unprofessional—'

Jonathan interrupted. 'Oh, I can't possibly do that. There's too much paperwork to be done. Whatever grievances you have regarding Miss Hennessey-White's behaviour have to be ignored for now. There are far more important matters to deal with.'

Matron stood speechless, both her size and her status

seeming to diminish as Jonathan opened and shut files and drawers, his eyes swiftly fixing on any of the Professor's papers that interested him. It was as if the office, the whole world and everyone were no longer of any importance to him. He had gained the position he'd coveted from the moment he'd arrived at Saltmead, and he was well and truly rising to the occasion.

Janet got up to leave. 'I'd better—'

'No. Please stay, Janet.' said Jonathan.

His voice is different, thought Janet. It was almost as if it had aged and dropped an octave the moment he'd placed his backside in the Professor's leather chair.

His gaze never left Matron's formidable countenance as he said, 'Perhaps you'd like to sit down, ladies.'

It was obvious from Matron's expression that she did not approve of a mere secretary sitting in on a meeting between two people of a more superior profession. Even when Janet brought two chairs closer to the desk, Matron neither acknowledged nor thanked her.

Jonathan was in his element. 'We are all very sorry to hear of the death of Professor Pritchard, and I will, on behalf of Saltmead Sanatorium, send a letter of sympathy to his family. However, the work of this establishment must continue. People are counting on us. I trust also I can count on the help of both of you.'

As he outlined his plans for running the sanatorium, sunlight shone weakly from behind a gold-edged cloud in the window behind him and made it look as if he were wearing a halo. He couldn't possibly live up to it, thought Janet, smiling to herself. Jonathan was far from being a saint. The swiftness of his transition from sympathy for the Professor's death to the implementation of modern ideas in the running of the sanatorium was amazing. Although she was in favour of those changes, she couldn't help thinking that he was being disrespectful and premature; after all, the Professor hadn't yet been put in his grave. But that was typical of

Jonathan. His career, his crusade against polio, was all that mattered to him.

'Until such time as hospital management decides otherwise, it falls to me as senior physician to see that patients are treated properly both mentally and otherwise.' He sounded zealous and looked it too.

Matron's expression was pure self-satisfaction. 'Everything will go on as before, Doctor. You can count on me and my nurses to ensure that the patients receive exactly the same treatment they always have had.'

He was gushingly charming. 'So pleased I can count on your support, Matron. Obviously I will not be running things in exactly the same way as the Professor, but please be assured that the well-being of the patients is closest of all to my heart.'

'I'm glad to hear it, Doctor.'

'And now with the help of Miss Hennessey-White, I will peruse the medical records and write accordingly to the near relatives of all our patients. I think it only right that they should know that there's a new captain at the wheel!'

Matron nodded a tight-lipped approval.

Jonathan lit a cigarette after she'd gone, sighed and closed his eyes. 'The first hurdle. Now for the rest of them.' He curled his fingers over his cigarette, the smoke escaping from the gaps between them. 'Get me the patients' address list, will you?'

Janet eyed him apprehensively. 'You really are going to write to them about the Professor's death?' She'd assumed it was just a ruse to placate a less than pliant Matron. Patients' relatives cared about their loved ones, not the medical personnel nursing them.

Jonathan stretched and folded his arms behind his head. 'Of course I am. I'm going to tell them that we are implementing visiting hours. Of course it cannot be allowed to affect treatment schedules, but I do believe it is imperative to the patients' well-being.'

Janet had a tremendous urge to burst into a Highland Fling. She'd wanted a miracle and here it was.

She noticed his mood change, a seriousness come over him that was in direct contrast to his initial exuberance. He settled behind the desk and reached for the telephone. 'You can go now.'

'I presume you're ringing your mother.'

He looked at her tight-lipped, obviously remembering her less than polite comments about his relationship with her. 'Of course.'

Although he looked serious, he also looked like a child demanding his parent, the sort seen in shops, petulantly hanging onto their mother's coat with podgy, clenched hands.

This, she decided, was a moment to take advantage of. 'Can I ring Susan's parents and tell them they can visit now?'

He held her gaze and for a moment she thought he was going to refuse. 'Certainly. Give them a ring, but make sure they know that they will have to stay outside the glass partition.'

Twenty-two

When the post came on a rainy Wednesday morning, Charlotte was taking her coat from Mrs Grey. David, who usually got the post first, was still in bed, his health stable, though still a cause for concern. There were the usual bills, plus a letter addressed to her, blue and marked *par avion.*

Charlotte tensed. 'I'll deal with this post before I go,' she said to Mrs Grey.

In the privacy of the study she ripped the envelope open and read the letter inside. She had promised to hand over any further correspondence to Edna for her to answer, but this letter had come direct to the house because Josef wanted her and her alone to read it. Lucky for her that David was ill and didn't always get up too early.

At first sight it seemed the letter was professional enough. If Edna agreed to taking on her son, Josef was coming to England and he hoped to bring the boy over with him. But the last words were meant just for her. '*And I would like to see you again. I hope that you would like to see me too.*'

It seemed that she could hear her heart as she stared at the suggested date. Late April, just after Easter. The letter would have to be handed over to Edna. Hopefully she would interpret the last sentence as being typical of something an old friend might write. Only Charlotte and Josef would truly know the emotion contained in those simple words.

*

It was a Saturday morning and although it was winter, the sun was pleasant.

David had taken to sitting out on the first-floor veranda that overlooked the back garden of the house in Royal York Crescent. Luxuriant grapevines grew over the iron trellis-work, which helped diffuse strong sunlight in summer and brisk winds in winter. From here he could view the apple trees at the end of the garden – bereft of leaves at this time of year – or study the spiders' webs among the ironwork, which, in the morning, spangled like strings of pearls before the sun drank the moisture.

'This is nice,' he said, settling comfortably in his chair as he eyed the garden over a lowered copy of *The Times* that dated from Thursday. He took a little while getting round to reading things nowadays. 'I think I could get used to doing nothing on a regular basis. Perhaps I should retire. We could move to Devon permanently. I like it there.'

Charlotte was sitting at an elegant Georgian bureau just inside the door. She was writing letters to those who had been so helpful when David had been taken ill. His comment had taken her unawares. Devon was lovely. The people were lovely, but would there be enough for her to do? The suggestion worried her, but she assumed a false brightness.

'Full-time retirement? Isn't that a little premature?' she called through the open door.

'I don't think so. There's a time for every season under heaven . . . I like Devon,' he added.

Charlotte joined him out on the veranda and patted his hand. 'We must not make any rash decisions, darling. Let's see first how quickly you get back to your old self. It's early days.'

David took her hand in both of his and there was a pained expression in his eyes. 'My dear Charlotte, it could be later than you think.'

Usually she would have reassured him that he wasn't that old and that he was sure to get better, but Ivan chose that moment to enter the room closely followed by Janet and a man she did not recognize who stared about him in disbelief, overawed by the mix of elegance and warmth of their home.

Ivan addressed Charlotte. 'I am sorry to interrupt, but I need to talk to you.'

'I told him he must,' said Janet.

Ivan introduced the other man as Lech Rostok. He had a creased face and dark circles beneath his eyes.

'You asked me if I knew men with certain problems. Lech has a problem,' Ivan went on.

'Take a seat out here,' said David, his voice surprisingly full of energy for someone who was still not quite one hundred per cent. 'It's crisp but bracing.' He folded his newspaper and set it to one side.

'I'll get some tea and biscuits,' said Janet and left them there.

'Lech is not earning any money,' Ivan began. 'Yet he works very hard.'

Lech, his gnarled hands continuously twisting the cloth cap he held, stepped forward and said in broken English, 'I was told I would be doing engineering . . . good . . . man I work for also have room for me. I share with two others.'

Charlotte repressed the urge to condemn living accommodation that she herself had not inspected.

The man continued. 'He said there was no more work for me there and I might have to leave. He said there was not too much work around for foreigners and I might be sent back.' His eyes were round with terror. 'I cannot go back! They will kill me if I go back!'

Ivan interrupted. 'Lech worked for the Americans just as I did. If he went back to Poland he would be imprisoned as a spy.'

'But I only worked in the army kitchens,' he said, turning to Ivan as if he could in some way make it right with the new Polish regime.

'Go on,' Charlotte said to Lech.

'He said he could find other work for us. He knew someone who needed men. There would be no need to leave our room. But we had to keep quiet about it. No work, no stay in England. If we took this work we could stay.'

'And what about getting your Alien Card stamped?' Charlotte asked.

'He said there was no need to. We were not moving home. But then I say the police have to know when we change jobs. I did not want to upset them. But he said he would have our cards and deal with that.'

Charlotte sank back in her chair. 'So you gave him your card.'

Lech nodded. 'When I asked for it back, he said it was better he should hold onto it.'

'I bet he did!' David exclaimed.

'So what job do you have?' Charlotte asked, although she knew the answer before he said it.

'Building.'

'And how much are you being paid?'

'Ten shillings a week, but I do not have to pay for the room.'

Ten shillings was deplorable, but again Charlotte said nothing. 'What is the name of this man?'

Lech shrugged. 'I can't remember.'

Adopting a determined stiffness to her actions Charlotte took up her pen and tore a piece of paper from her writing pad. 'Where do you live?'

He gave her the address of a large house in Coronation Road, a thoroughfare that ran along the side of the Cut, a dreary stretch of mud-lined waterway that ran from Bedminster Bridge to the greener surroundings of Ashton.

'I'll make enquiries,' she said, feeling more excited than she let on. This was exactly the kind of evidence Brookman had asked her for. 'In the meantime we need to keep in touch, but without rousing suspicion. I have to get to the root of this problem. You and the men you know are, no doubt, only a few of those being exploited. But if these people get to know that I'm onto them they'll just scatter and everyone will be told to keep their mouths shut. We have to be able to communicate, perhaps at some kind of social gathering like a football match, some kind of weekend occupation that can take you away from where you are living.'

Charlotte straightened and gazed out of the window, but saw nothing except a list of possibilities running through her mind like a shopping list. 'Perhaps I could arrange some sort of project for the displaced, some kind of community work.' Though goodness knows what, she thought to herself. 'It will take me a few days to find something suitable, but I'm sure it can be done.' She shivered as she placed her hands on David's shoulders. 'Come along inside, darling. It's getting a little chilly out here.'

It was a partial truth. The day was chilly, but her reason for shivering had been more to do with the thought of beating those who were exploiting foreign labour. Lech Rostok had opened an avenue of investigation. It excited her almost as much as receiving Josef's letter.

As everyone settled in the drawing room and Charlotte closed the veranda door, Janet appeared with the tea. She was wearing tartan trews and a polo-necked sweater. Charlotte thought how attractive she was, brighter than she'd looked for a long time. She also seemed much more friendly towards Ivan, almost as though they had some shared secret that no one else was privy to.

Janet put down the tray and Ivan poured tea, offered milk, held the tongs and delicately dropped cubes of sugar into cups.

'So what will you do, Mother?' Janet asked.

Charlotte explained about setting up some kind of weekend project. She was full of ideas and expressed them quickly, though sketchily. 'Firstly we address practicalities. It would be very beneficial if such a project also paid money, no matter how little. These men need some extra money. If we could find some part-time project that will provide extra cash for now and, perhaps, better pay and accommodation in the long run—'

Janet interrupted. 'We need men to paint the sanatorium. In fact, we could be needing employees there before very long, depending on how swiftly the old employees adjust to the new regime.'

'Wonderful!' Charlotte clapped her hands.

Things are looking up, she thought. Edna and Colin can visit Susan, and Janet has overcome whatever was colouring her attitude towards Ivan. They were, she thought, observing the closeness of their heads as they talked about painting the sanatorium, very good friends now, perhaps a little more than that.

Her only real worry was David. He only did two days at his consulting rooms in Park Row, and even then he came home with a face shiny with sweat and tiredness too intense to be believed.

'I'm all right,' he snapped when she fussed with the cushions of his favourite chair or asked for the umpteenth time whether he wanted coffee, tea or something a bit stronger.

But he wasn't all right. She knew it. He knew it. But neither talked about it.

'Susan?' Edna tapped her fingers against the cold, clear glass that divided her and Colin from their daughter.

Colin waved a big meaty hand above Edna's head. His smile was as wide as the river and the lines of worry that had creased his face for the last few months were like feathers in his face rather than furrows.

Susan waved back, her face tiny above the piled bedclothes and the snow-white sheet.

Colin squeezed Edna's arm. 'Won't be long, love, and she'll be home with us.'

Edna's eyes stayed fixed on Susan.

The trundling of a trolley approaching made Colin turn his head. Edna hardly seemed to notice it.

'This child has to have her treatment now. You'll have to go,' said the nurse brusquely, but not rudely. She busied herself with the bits and pieces she had on the trolley, a steaming enamel bowl, shiny steel implements and a pile of crisp, white gauze.

Edna stood her ground. 'I'm not going.'

The nurse's eyes softened over the top of her white gauze mask. 'You'll find it upsetting.'

'I don't care.'

Starched headdress fluttering like a white bat, the nurse turned away and bustled about her trolley, dipping the gauze into the steaming bowl.

The steam rising from the bowl was hypnotic. Colin's hand stole onto Edna's hand. It felt cold and remained immobile.

'It's for her leg, isn't it?' Edna said softly.

Colin's hand dropped away. Feeling incredibly helpless and frozen out, he stared at the floor. Edna was already obsessed with Susan as it was. What would it be like, he wondered, when she finally came home? What would her leg be like then? They'd been given hope, but he feared the worst.

After every last piece of gauze had been immersed in the bowl, the nurse came out from behind the glass and said quietly, 'If you want to put on some protective clothing, you can come in, but only one of you, mind, there's no room for more than that.'

Edna's voice rang out. 'Yes!'

'Come with me.'

Colin watched as Edna followed the nurse out to somewhere just beyond the door to the ward. She came back wearing a gown, a mask and a cap under which she'd tucked every vestige of hair.

'Quickly,' said the nurse gripping the trolley, 'or the gauze won't be hot enough and that would never do.' She turned suddenly stopping Edna in her tracks. 'Now just remember that what I am about to do is for your child's own good, so please do not be too emotional. It will only upset her.'

Shoulders tense, Edna followed the nurse into the room. She stifled a little sob and, although it was hard, she resisted the urge to throw herself over Susan and hug her to bits.

Alone with his thoughts, Colin watched as the two women bent over the bed. He smiled to hide the clenching of his jaw. He'd rather lose his arms as well as his legs than lose his child – or his wife.

Smiling brightly, Susan reached out for her mother.

'Hold my hand, darling,' Edna said, gripping the weak little hand tightly as if her own willpower might somehow travel down her arm and into her daughter.

The nurse pulled back the bedclothes exposing Susan's legs. Both limbs were pale and looked lifeless and seemed to have lost some of their form as though the muscular structure had been eaten away. The affected leg was thinner, weaker and whiter than the healthy one.

Unsure of his role in all this, Colin watched on the other side of the glass, his eyes moist and his heart breaking.

Beyond the glass partitioning, mother and daughter's eyes stayed fixed on each other.

'Tell me a story,' Susan said, her bottom lip trembling.

Edna couldn't think of a single one. As the hot gauze was lifted from the bowl, she said, 'Hold on tightly and pretend you're paddling in the sea and it's very cold, very salty and the fish are swimming around your knees.'

Her heart fluttered. She could have screamed herself so wouldn't have blamed the child for doing so. Susan's fingers tightened on her hand. She squeezed her eyes shut and clenched her jaw tightly.

'Hold on,' Edna urged as the hot dressing was heaped around her leg. 'Hold on!'

Tears squeezed from the corners of Susan's eyes. It must have taken a monumental effort, but Susan did not scream and Edna felt humbled.

Like any caring mother, she wanted to take on her child's suffering, to feel her pain, to keep her from harm. But Susan had got through it by herself though tears were bound to come.

'I want to go home,' she grizzled.

'You will soon, sweetheart,' said Edna.

'With Peter and Pamela and everyone?'

'Everyone,' said Edna, and for some unaccountable reason she thought of Sherman, the letters and what she should do about it. Late at night, when the children had gone to bed and Colin had fallen asleep in the chair, she had retrieved the letters from their hiding place in the tea caddy. The standard lamp in the sitting room had a shade with a tasselled trim and hand-painted flowers. The dark parchment it was made of cast an amber glow and seemed to transport her to a warmer country as she secretly read and reread each letter until she almost knew the words off by heart. The letters had come with a piece of advice. *You have to tell Colin!*

Charlotte's voice rang in her ears. Of course she should tell him, but the moment never seemed right. Like now, she thought, there's just too much to think about.

Gradually, as the heat of the thermal dressings lessened, Edna felt Susan's grip lessening.

'Is that it?' she asked the nurse.

'For now.'

Obviously she's got other patients to torture, thought Edna, as she watched her make her way out from the glass partitioning that surrounded Susan and into the next cubicle where an initial whimpering gradually grew into a loud cry and then a scream.

Moist-eyed, Edna smiled down at Susan. 'You were very brave.'

Susan swallowed as if she'd just been about to cry. 'Will I be like my daddy?'

Edna couldn't speak. Neither could she look at Colin who was standing on the other side of the glass. 'What do you mean, dear?'

'Will I have tin legs just like the ones he's got?'

Edna gulped back what might be sobs, or could just as easily have been a cry of anguish. 'Of course not.'

Outside the glass that enclosed two of the people he loved most in the world, Colin controlled his emotions. He stood stiffly, but dignified. No one looking at him could guess just how helpless he was feeling and how much he was dreading the time when Susan finally came home.

'She looked over the moon to see you,' Colin said brightly as they left Pucklechurch and headed back to the city.

The way the pale flesh had turned pink as the hot gauze was laid on it was still in Edna's mind. 'Sorry Colin. I wasn't listening.'

Colin repeated what he'd just said.

'I'm sorry you couldn't come in,' said Edna.

A kind of half-smile skewed Colin's mouth to one side. 'Never mind. When a kid's ill it's Mum that they want. No one else. Not the best and kindest doctors, nor the prettiest nurses. Just their mum. It's always been that way. Always will.'

Colin could not possibly imagine what he'd just said. It struck such a deep chord that Edna immediately twisted her face away from him just in case he could read what was in her eyes.

Who, she wondered, would be there when Sherman was

ill? His adoptive parents were gone. There was no one, no one at all.

The Post Office in St George was a place of dark wood, heavy glass and high counters. When Edna went in there to buy stamps, she asked the woman behind the counter whether the paper from the notepad she'd bought in Woolworths would be suitable for airmail.

'Oh no, my dear. You don't need to bother with that,' said the woman. A chain that kept her spectacles from getting lost, tinkled like tiny bells as she shook her head and slapped her hand down on the stamp ledger. 'You need one of these. See? It's already stamped. You buy the whole thing.' Proudly she held up a crispy piece of oddly shaped paper. 'These are for airmail,' she said excitedly. 'You just write your letter then gum it down all around the sides. See?'

Peter came in from school for lunch when she got home. 'I'm starving,' he proclaimed and promptly took a bite out of the fish paste soldier that Pamela was presently nibbling.

'It's ready,' said Edna. 'Wash your hands and sit up at the table.'

Bubble and squeak, a mix of leftover vegetables from Sunday, was frying in the pan and getting crisp around the edges. Topped with a fried egg, a plateful duly found its way to Peter who sat at the table, knife and fork held upright, ready for the attack.

After making Pamela another plate of fish paste soldiers, Edna sat herself down at the table. When she had left the Post Office, she had gone into Woolworths and bought a notepad, just as she had been going to do in the first place. The airmail envelope was still in her bag.

She fancied Peter was eyeing her quizzically.

'What are you writing?' he asked.

'Don't speak with your mouth full,' Edna replied.

Not to be put off so easily, he asked, 'Is it a story?'

'Just a shopping list,' she lied.

The airmail letter she'd bought was too precious to waste. She had to get the words down properly. This was her son she was writing about, a child that needed her as much as Susan did, a child who might be ill one day and want his mother to be there.

Peter was still curious. 'Do you want some of my bubble and squeak, Mum?'

'I'm not hungry.'

Despite Peter, she managed to get down the basics of what she wanted to write.

Once he'd gone back to school and Pamela had fallen asleep on the settee beneath a patchwork counterpane, she retrieved the precious airmail letter from her bag and carefully wrote that yes, she was his mother and, yes, she wanted her son.

After folding it carefully she gummed the edges where indicated. If she changed her mind about sending it off, it would tear very easily and she could throw it away. But, thanks to the vision of Susan lying small and alone in a hospital bed, she didn't think she would.

'Your father called from a phone box today,' Colin said that evening after greeting both children with a kiss on the cheek. 'He says you haven't been over this week.'

Edna groaned, braced both hands on the sink, closed her eyes and threw back her head. 'I'm tired! Doesn't anyone around here realize that?'

Colin had been about to give her a kiss on the cheek too, but changed his mind. He recognized a bad mood when he saw one. Edna had quite a few of them nowadays and he knew all the signs. Tentatively, he rested his hands on her shoulders, felt her stiffen, so dropped them down to his side. He'd tried being gentle with her, but he was tired and his patience was wearing thin. 'Well, she is your bloody mother!'

'Don't remind me!'

His tone gentled. 'I know how you feel about her, Edna, but if anything happened to her and you hadn't seen her for a while, you might feel bad about it.'

She sighed. He closed his eyes and thanked God as the stiffness left her shoulders and she shifted her weight from one hip to the other.

'I suppose so. It's just that I am so tired of driving out to Saltmead and back again . . .' She turned and ran her hand through her hair.

She was still slim, as girlish as the day they'd married, and Colin still loved her, still wanted to do his best for her. 'Tell you what, love,' he said, cautiously resting his hands on her hips, ready to retreat should she reject him. 'It's Saturday tomorrow and I've got to go into the factory so I can't drive you there, but what if I ring Janet and ask her to take you over your mother's? You can give Polly her wages while you're about it.'

Edna looked awkward. 'If Janet forgives me. I feel terrible about how I treated her.'

Colin grinned. He knew she was still embarrassed about not allowing Janet near the children – Janet who had almost lost her job to see Susan.

'I'll ring,' he said and went straight for the telephone. She looked over her shoulder as he left the kitchen and wanted to cry. He's so good, she thought to herself, and I'm being a cow. But she was tired, terribly tired and full of guilt, remorse and downright confusion.

'Ivan's coming with her,' he said when he came back from making the phone call.

'Right.'

'What's for dinner?' asked Colin, as he sat himself down at the table.

'Bubble and squeak,' said Edna.

'With an egg,' added Peter.

On Saturday, Ivan and Janet arrived as scheduled. Edna

started to apologize about how she'd behaved about the children and how she should have been in touch sooner.

'It doesn't matter,' said Janet, hoping her newly found contentment would filter through in her smile and make Edna happy again. 'All that matters is that Susan gets well.'

A lot of the houses in Nutgrove Avenue had Christmas trees or fairy lights at the windows. On the journey over the children had been enthralled by the sudden sprouting of Christmas decorations, their little faces pressed tight against the car windows. There was no tree or decoration of any sort in the window of number nine and both doors were wide open. Edna looked at it bleakly, her actions stilted as she got out of the car and pulled the front seat forward so Pamela could scramble out too.

'You want this?' Ivan held out a brown wages envelope with Polly's name on it.

Edna looked at him appealingly. 'Will you bring it in?'

The smell of old urine mixed with soapy steam rolled up the passageway from out back. Edna hesitated. How embarrassing! What would Ivan think?

'We'll go in here,' she said and opened the door of the front room in which a big bay window looked out over the road. It was little used, but she couldn't possibly take a stranger out back where her mother's bloomers were being boiled free of stain and smell.

The front room was too tidy to be welcoming and she shivered as she entered. She always had. Perhaps it was something to do with the pristine plainness of it, the cold green lino, the beige and brown mat in front of the grate, the sharp brightness of the chrome-plated companion set and ashtray. It might have been none of those things, but purely the fact that the room was little used. But not today.

A figure huddled close to the dull darkness of an empty fire grate.

'Hello, Dad.'

Her father held his head in his hands, his half crescent of hair standing proud of his head, unwashed and stiff with old Brylcreem.

'Dad?'

Slowly his fingers parted like the folds of a fan and his face appeared. Beaming now, he got up from his chair. 'It's lovely to see you, pet.'

The sound of Pamela's running footsteps echoed down the passageway behind them as the little girl ran off to the garden.

'This is Ivan,' Edna said, suddenly remembering the handsome man who stood at her side. 'I've got Polly's money.' She took the brown envelope from Ivan's hand. 'Where is she?'

'She's not here.'

Her father's recumbent expression altered. His eyes stared, his mouth hung open and the jowls hung like bags of blancmange.

'Dad? What is it?'

'She's gone again. Polly's gone after her.'

Edna wanted to shake him for sounding so pathetic, but who was she to talk? How often had she been weak, soft and easily manipulated?

He wrung his hands then ran one through what remained of his hair leaving it standing out each side of his head like a sticky white halo. 'It's getting difficult.'

She was reminded of some poor halfwit that used to live further down the road. The children used to bait him, shout names and follow him to the shops just to force him to share his sweets with them, a sad way of buying friendship. But her father was not a halfwit. He was just tired, confused and afraid.

Edna turned to Ivan and Janet. 'We have to find her.'

Ivan immediately made for the door. Janet followed him. 'I'm coming too.'

Ivan placed his hands on her shoulders. 'No. You stay here.' He jerked his head at Edna's father. 'He needs someone to look after him.' Then he turned to Edna. 'Where shall I look?'

Her father, his voice heavy with weariness, said, 'The park. She likes the flowers, and the bowling green.'

Edna gave Ivan a brief description. 'She's thin with sharp features.' She had another thought. 'Look for Polly. She's pretty, blonde and dressed in black and white.'

'I know her,' he said. 'She comes to visit at my house.'

My house, thought Edna, and briefly felt a sense of things passing, never to be the same.

As she chased around Victoria Park looking for Ethel, Polly muttered, 'Silly cow! Time she was put out to Barrel.' Barrel was the nickname for Barrow Gurney, the site of a psychiatric hospital to the south of the city.

Polly wasn't too sure of her bearings around Victoria Park. It was a case of marching on and keeping her eyes open. The smell of leaf mould and wet grass drenched the air and small children – too young for school – ran along the low walls next to the road. At one time they'd had railings on top of them, but along with a pile of old saucepans, they'd gone years ago to make Spitfires, or so they'd been told. She kept to the level path, presuming the old girl's legs wouldn't cope with the one that led up to the Bowling Green. Eventually she came to a concreted area where swings, a slide and a roundabout were skirted by cast iron seats and close cut grass.

'Have you seen an old lady go past here?'

The young woman she asked was sitting on one of the seats, a Pedigree coach built pram in front of her, a baby in her arms. She started at Polly's question. Polly apologized for frightening her.

The young woman nodded her acceptance of the apology and asked, 'What did she look like?'

Polly eyed the fat baby that sucked at the woman's breast. No wonder she'd started. Fancy getting her bosom out in the middle of the park!

'Thin. Sharp features. Wearing a pale green candlewick dressing gown.'

The woman's eyebrows rose in sharp surprise. 'Bit mental, is she?'

'No! She's just ill,' snapped Polly.

'Well, I ain't seen her.' The woman pulled the child off her teat and covered her flaccid bosom with a less than clean cardigan and shouted, 'Clifford! Come on. Time we was off.'

The command was directed at a small child whose legs were dangling from one of the swings. His knees were the colour of cracked mud.

Polly turned away in disgust. She might come from the Dings and live in Knowle West, but for Christ's sake, she'd always kept her Carol clean and she'd never breastfed in public. Disgusting!

A train rattling by drowned Clifford's wails and his mother's shouts as Polly made her way up the steep path that led back through the park towards the Bowling Green. All the way up she looked around her for any sign of Edna's mother – and not necessarily wearing a dressing gown! The truth of the matter was she had an awful feeling that Mrs Burbage might be dressed in a lot less than that. She'd just been about to give her a bath and had got her half-stripped when the faint smell of burning had come up from the kitchen. The potatoes for tonight's shepherd's pie had boiled dry and Mr Burbage was out in the garden tending his runner beans so she couldn't depend on him to do the obvious.

Three old gents in bowling whites were playing on the green when she got there. A very stout man was bending, about to take his shot, moving forward with uncommon grace, almost like a ballet dancer. She watched for a moment while she got her breath and willed the old chap to hit the jack. Hope I do too, she thought, and giggled to herself. Mickey O'Hara was getting himself a new employee to work in his nightclub and she was happy about it. Aunty Meg was not. She'd tried telling her that she'd be working as a receptionist, but it didn't wash.

She'd decided to pack in looking after Ethel Burbage. She hoped Edna's father wouldn't be too upset. She'd tell Edna about it as soon as they'd found the old girl.

Although apprehensive at what he might say, Polly had plucked up the courage to tell Billy about the job Mickey had offered her. He'd looked a bit concerned – probably jealous. But she'd pretended not to notice. Damn the bloke, he'd got 'imself into that bloody position and they were all having to put up with it.

There was a loud crack as the ball hit the jack and sent it racing across the lawn. It shook Polly from her thoughts and spurred her on to find Mrs Burbage – the old cow!

I'll murder the old witch, she thought, shivering as she pulled her coat around herself and headed further up the hill to where a mass of laurel hedge and dense fir trees surrounded the park keeper's house. A man wearing trousers with string tied just below his knees – obviously a gardener – came from that direction pushing a wheelbarrow full of garden tools.

Polly rushed up to him. 'Have you seen—'

He pointed at the park keeper's house. 'A woman in pink corsets with 'er stockings round 'er ankles?' His cheeks were apple red and he was grinning from ear to ear. Well, if he expected her to blush he was in for a disappointment – even if she was mortified!

She gave him a fierce poke in the chest. 'And how would you know a pair of corsets from a liberty bodice unless you wears 'em yerself? I've heard about blokes like you hanging around in parks!'

He went redder – just as she'd wanted him to. But his smile remained and he looked at her as if he was in with a chance. Bloody cheek!

'Are you—?' he began.

'Married!' she snapped and swept past him up the path heading in the direction of the park keeper's house.

These bushes smell dusty, she thought, as she turned between the clusters of bottle green laurel. She was keen to get this over with and would have marched on regardless if she hadn't heard someone calling her. Darting back out from the bushes, she narrowed her eyes better to see the figure running up the path towards her. Nice looking, athletic and long-legged. Who the bloody hell did she know like that?

Ivan! Now if she were going to take in lodgers, she'd stipulate that they'd all have to look like him – especially if she wasn't married.

'What the hell are you doing here?' She folded her arms beneath the warmth of her bosom as if good-looking blokes trying to get her attention never had impressed her.

'I came to help you find Edna's mother.'

'Get yer coat off.' She nodded at the khaki trench mac he was wearing, turned and started for the front door of the park keeper's house.

Ivan followed her, his mac already off his shoulders and halfway down his arms.

The door of the park keeper's house opened onto a small hallway with panelled walls and a wood-block floor. Mrs Burbage was sitting on the stairs of the house staring into the distance and humming distractedly. The park keeper was standing over her stroking the sort of moustache and side whiskers that had gone out of fashion around the time the 'talkies' came in.

'Sorry about this,' said Polly. 'She's not well.'

Eyes still fixed on Mrs Burbage, the man nodded thoughtfully. 'I knew 'er when she was eighteen,' he said.

'You're kidding!'

'No, I'm not.' He looked pleased with himself.

Polly grinned as a sudden vision of a more youthful Mrs Burbage sprang into being. It was always hard to think of older people having been young at one time, singing, dancing, falling in love – locking limbs with the opposite sex.

Polly bent low and touched the old woman's shoulder. 'Come on, Ethel. Time to go home before we find out all about yer lovelife.'

Edna's mother raised her arm, but continued to stare into the distance. 'There it is! The eleven o'clock to Weston! Will the tide be in, Mother? Can I paddle? Can I build sandcastles?' Her voice was high like a small child's.

You're a grown woman! Of course not. Pull yourself together.

The words and the impatience were checked. Words were useless. Ethel wouldn't understand and Polly didn't want to say them.

'Come on,' she said, placing her arm around the old woman's shoulders and gently raising her to her feet. 'You'd better wrap up. There's a bit of a draught when the train comes in. And when we get to Weston there's bound to be a cold breeze coming off the sea.'

'I don't mind,' cried a smiling Ethel Burbage, her eyes round and shining with the joy of a six-year-old child on her first trip to the seaside. 'Can I ride on the donkeys?'

'Only if you've got a threepenny bit.'

It didn't really sink in. That was the way it was. Nothing really sunk in and when you thought it had it was swiftly forgotten. She turned away from Polly and raised her smiling face upwards to Ivan. 'Are you going to build a sandcastle with me, Daddy?'

Touchingly, Ivan smiled back and at the same time placed his mac around her bare shoulders. 'Of course I am,' he said gently and together he and Polly took Edna's mother back to Nutgrove Avenue.

'No matter how bad she was in the past, it's sad to see her like that,' said Janet to Ivan after they'd dropped Edna and the children off. 'I'm glad my mother's not like that, though I sometimes wish she was more involved with her family and less with the flotsam and jetsam of the world.'

He was driving and kept his eyes fixed on the road ahead. He looked thoughtful.

'A penny for them,' she said softly.

Ivan raised his eyebrows. 'A penny for what?'

'Oh, for tomorrow, yesterday, the day before if you like, but mostly for your thoughts. What are you thinking about?'

'Tomorrow,' he said grimly.

'Oh?'

'I am taking your mother to help the flotsam and jetsam.'

Twenty-three

Unwashed men, dirty bed linen and drying laundry hanging from lengths of string tied across the room, bare windows, bare boards and six camp beds, the sort they'd used in the air raid shelters during the war. This was where a man named Lech Rostok and five other refugees were living. Charlotte resisted the urge to wrinkle her nose.

'I apologize,' Lech Rostok mumbled nervously and looked ashamed. 'It is difficult,' he said apologetically.

'It's disgusting,' Charlotte snapped, 'and no fault of yours! Did you remember the name of the man who put you here?'

'Mr O'Hara it was. He arranged everything.'

'Did he now!' She made no attempt to hide her outrage. It was not for any private individual to arrange accommodation or work for these men. That task fell to her department.

'He said it would be cheaper and we would be closer to the building site,' said Lech.

Her jaw ached with anger. These men were living in squalor and someone had to answer for it. At least they were willing to tell the tale.

'And where will I find this Mr O'Hara?'

Lech shook his head. 'I don't know. He comes to us.'

'When do you expect him?'

'At eight o'clock. He pays us tonight. He pays us every Friday.'

I bet he does, thought Charlotte. After collecting the wages from the site foreman he takes his cut and gives them the rest. She clenched her jaw tight enough to hurt, then snapped, 'Right!'

Leaving the smell and the squalor behind she went from there to see Brookman in his office. It was five thirty and she found him putting on his bowler and picking up his brief-case. Mr Brookman kept very regular hours. He did not join the more menial staff who came in on Saturday mornings. He looked from her to the clock that clanked away the minutes by virtue of a brass pendulum hanging like a rigid tail from its case.

'I hope this is important.'

Charlotte slammed her handbag down on his desk. 'It's about these men being exploited by this building company.'

Brookman concentrated on rolling up his paper and tucking it under his arm. 'Have you any proof?'

'I've seen where they're living. It's disgusting. Six men to one room, no decent washing facilities . . .'

'I thought we were talking about the illegal employment of displaced persons not the overcrowding of tenements. Decent accommodation is scarce enough for our own people.' Brookman made for the door.

Charlotte kept pace with his longer stride despite her high heels and the slimline skirt of her pale green costume, which was silk-lined and had a daringly high kick-pleat at the back. 'Someone's exploiting both their accommodation *and* their employment.'

'So see the landlord.' He reached for the door, his gaze fixed straight ahead of him.

'I suppose I could. I'd love to give him a piece of my mind . . .'

Brookman laid his hand firmly on her arm. 'Do bear in mind, Mrs Hennessey-White, that this country is desperate for workers and equally desperate for houses. A lot of our own people are also living in very bad conditions. Is it so much to expect that a bunch of foreigners are also living in dire conditions? Be patient, my dear lady.'

He smiled at her smugly, tapped his bowler and marched off. Charlotte stared after him completely lost for words. He had a point. She knew that. A lot of people were still living in less than perfect accommodation. But there was still no need to turn a blind eye. Standards had to be maintained and if the likes of Brookman weren't going to do anything, then she'd do something herself.

She made her way to her car and drove back to the house where some very tired, very disillusioned men were sleeping six to a room. Tonight was the high spot of their week. It was payday and Mr O'Hara would be calling.

Lech Rostok opened the door of their lodgings. 'I won't come in,' she said as the smell of decay and many men living without women to look after them seeped from the grimness within. 'I'll be back tonight. I want you to give me some sort of signal when O'Hara arrives, just so that we're absolutely sure.'

'Signal?'

'Hang something out of the window the moment he leaves the building so I can have my car started and ready to follow him.'

'Yes.'

'I'll be back around eight thirty.'

For the first time since she'd met them, Lech and the others who had gathered round him looked hopeful.

'Thank you for helping us,' said Lech. 'Ivan and you. Thank you from all of us.'

Charlotte smiled nervously. 'Something will be done. I promise.'

As she drove home she regretted making a promise. How easy it would be just to stay at home with David, listen to the radio or read a book. Tackling O'Hara could be dangerous. But it was too late. She had given her word and she had to stick to it.

Company was needed if she were going to be successful and,

more to the point, unscathed from her dealings with Mr O'Hara. To that end Janet and Ivan went with her and parked outside the grim Edwardian building where a peeling sign said 'Hartsbourne Hotel'.

Janet looked it over. 'Is this it?'

'Yes. Hardly hotel accommodation,' said Charlotte disdainfully. 'Six men to a room. And one bathroom between four rooms.' She automatically wrinkled her nose. Smells, she noticed, stayed with her longer than the look or feel of a place.

'Do we go in?' Janet asked.

Charlotte shook her head. 'We wait. I want to follow this man. Lech will give us a signal when he leaves and we can have the engine started and ready to go.'

Headlights shone brightly then were shut off as a sleek black car pulled into the kerb. One man got out. The driver stayed behind the steering wheel.

'The man,' said Ivan.

'The man,' Charlotte echoed, her gaze fixed on the strong figure making for the solid but scruffy door of the Hartsbourne Hotel.

O'Hara – if this was he – chose that moment to pull the brim of his trilby down over his eyes.

Charlotte sighed. 'Blast! I wanted to see his face.'

Ivan leaned forward. 'Wait for the signal, then get ready to look at him more carefully when he comes back out.'

'I will,' said Charlotte and found herself counting the minutes from the time he went in. She flattened herself against the steering wheel and looked up the building to the fourth floor. Ten minutes, she reckoned, and O'Hara would be ready to leave the smelly room. Sure enough someone waved a less than white vest out of the window.

Still with the brim of his hat pulled low over his face, O'Hara came out, crossed the pavement in two strides and got into the car.

Charlotte started the engine. 'Let's go.'

They drove along Coronation Road keeping up with the car, but not getting too close. Charlotte thanked all those gangster films David had taken her along to see before the war. Janet, however, had not seen them.

'Can't you go faster, Mother?'

'No. Edward didn't. I'm doing it like he did.'

'Who's Edward, for goodness' sake?'

'I know this,' said Ivan excitedly. 'Edward G. Robinson. He was playing a G man and was following some gangster – James Cagney, I think. If you don't want to be seen, you keep well back and try not to have your tyres squeal as you take a corner.'

Janet eyed Ivan Bronowsky in a new light. 'Oh!'

Charlotte resisted a smug comment, but sighed with satisfaction. Thanks to Edward G. rules for following suspected criminals were very specific. And that was how she regarded these men. They were criminals, exploiting government money and unfortunate people.

There was little traffic – a few bicycles, a horse-drawn baker's van returning late to the depot.

Charlotte kept the car and its occupants in sight, but left about twenty-five yards or more between them.

Their brake lights came on and an orange indicator shot out of the side of the car between the doors. They were turning right at a sharp incline on City Road where it joined Gloucester Road.

Janet sucked in her breath. 'Slow down. They'll see you.'

Charlotte pressed her foot lightly on the brake as a thought suddenly crossed her mind. If they could see her then she could see them and she badly wanted to see them, especially the man who had shielded his face with his hat brim.

There was only one thing for it. With a determined jab, she transferred her foot to the accelerator pedal, gripped the steering wheel tightly and shot forward.

'Mother!'

There was no stopping Charlotte once she'd made a decision, and that smell was still with her. The thought of those men having to live as they were made her more determined than ever.

'Brace yourselves!' she shouted.

Metal crunched against metal as the chrome bumper on the front of the Rover met the rear bumper of the car they'd been following.

'Mother! You've hit him!'

'Oh dear,' said Charlotte with obvious satisfaction. 'Stay put,' she ordered. 'Let me handle this.'

Janet and Ivan exchanged shocked looks. What was she up to?

A draught of cold air entered the car as she got out and headed for the occupants of the other vehicle who had got out of their car with a huge flourish of flapping coats and big arms.

They heard her say, 'I can't apologize enough.'

Ivan shook his head thoughtfully. 'Are you sure your mother was never a general?'

Janet didn't answer. Her eyes were narrowed and she leaned forward, peering through the windscreen. 'There's someone in the back seat of that car,' she said. 'Can you see?'

'Ah! They do not want to be seen,' he said as whoever was in the back ducked down out of sight.

'Goodness, but that man looks angry,' said Janet switching her attention back to her mother and the two men from the car in front. Things looked bad. The driver, a sallow-looking man with a ginger moustache and pale blue eyes rushed forward, grabbed Charlotte's shoulder and tipped his hat back from his face.

'You stupid cow! Why the bloody hell don't you look where you're going?'

Ivan stepped out of the car, but kept the open door between them and him.

Janet tried to push the door open. Ivan stood firmly against it. 'Let me out,' she hissed.

'No. Be quiet. I will take care of things if they get angry.'

Charlotte threw Ivan a warning look and he understood immediately. *Don't speak.* If he said much more his accent would become more noticeable which could very likely betray their mission.

'Leave the lady alone.' At O'Hara's insistence, the man with the ginger moustache let her go.

Charlotte wondered at his accent. He spoke with authority, but in a smooth voice graced with the lazy intonations of somewhere west of Kerry – or was it further west? Could it be America? That was how he sounded to Charlotte's ears.

'Thank you,' she said, beaming as she looked straight into his face and recognizing him as the man in the double-breasted suit who had watched from the shadows on the building site as two men fought upon the pavement.

His smile was wide and did not diminish when he spoke, but stayed fixed as though slapped on with a brush. 'No problem at all, ma'am. Glad to help out so I am.'

Phoney, she thought. That accent is phoney, like something picked up from a Hollywood film.

'I'm so terribly sorry for hitting you.' She adopted a top-drawer voice, the sort she'd heard women at social gatherings use when they were trying to make an impression. 'I have so much on my mind at the moment . . .'

O'Hara came close and stood over her, big teeth showing through his smile, his pale blue eyes reminding her of the sort of jellyfish that looked innocent but packed a nasty sting.

To avoid any deep questions, she had to come up with a very good excuse for running into him. With this in mind she glanced at Janet's tense face behind the windscreen. She looked pale and slightly sickly beneath the orange glow of a sodium streetlight. An idea occurred to her.

'My daughter's in labour,' she blurted. 'And this is my son-in-law.' She indicated Ivan. 'We have to get her to the hospital . . . unless . . .' She looked quickly from one man to the other. 'Unless one of you gentlemen happens to be a doctor! If you could help . . .'

Like all men faced with the prospect of dealing with an impending birth, they made their excuses and reached for the car doors.

'But what about exchanging names and addresses?' she cried out with a hint of hysteria. 'I am quite willing to pay for the damage.'

'We'll take care of the damage ourselves,' said O'Hara, pulling his hat down over his eyes as he reached for the car door.

'If you're sure . . .' Charlotte smiled to herself as they drove off. With a smug expression she got back behind the wheel of her car and Ivan returned to the back seat.

Janet was red-faced. 'Well, that was quite a performance!'

Charlotte slipped the car into gear. 'Did you get the registration number?'

'Yes. I did!'

Charlotte eyed her daughter with amusement. 'You're blushing.'

'Is that surprising? I'm pregnant according to you. What would have happened if I'd got out of the car and they'd seen that I wasn't?'

'You didn't get out – and you didn't need to.'

Ivan made no comment.

Charlotte drove slowly along the Gloucester Road keeping a distance she regarded as safe between her and the car they'd just smashed into. Height, weight, dress and facial details of the two men in the car were safely stored in her mind. Whoever was in the back had kept a low profile, but what she did have might just be enough. Tomorrow she would get the particulars typed out and on Brookman's desk. She would also get the registration number of the car checked by the Chief Superintendent himself. She and David had met him socially. Armed with these details they could at least keep an eye on the situation in the short term and hopefully, eventually, apprehend the people responsible.

An arm came out of the driver's window of O'Hara's car to indicate they were turning right. She assumed the indicator had jammed.

Charlotte eased to the left and stopped at a traffic light. There was time to scrutinize, but not by me, thought Charlotte. They've seen my face too much already. 'Tell me what they're doing,' she said.

'They're turning into a house. It looks like something from *International Architecture*,' said Janet.

The house was in Ashley Place and had big gates and a gravel drive. Janet twisted round in her seat as they drove slowly past. Ivan did the same. Someone stalled in front of them bringing them to a standstill long enough to see O'Hara's car come to a halt in front of the house. The driver got out and held the car door open for O'Hara who in turn held the rear door open for the unseen passenger to get out.

Janet sucked in her breath. 'Well, would you believe it?'

As Charlotte pulled away Janet almost spun in her seat, then slumped back looking absolutely amazed.

Charlotte frowned with impatience. 'Would I believe what?'

'I don't believe it,' Janet said, her gaze fixed on the bus that had pulled out in front of them.

Charlotte tried to turn round. 'For goodness' sake tell me. What is it? What did they do?'

'I will tell you,' said Ivan. 'The two men got out of the car, then *Polly*, your vacuum lady. She was dressed very nicely, as if they were going or had been somewhere very special.'

Janet maintained her silence. Charlotte frowned and took her eyes off the road long enough to see her daughter's shocked expression.

'Janet? Is this true?'

'Am I right in saying that Polly gave up her job with Edna?'

'Are you telling me . . .'

'Polly has a benefactor who has a very nice house and a car with a dented bumper.'

Polly gritted her teeth. It was no coincidence that Charlotte's car had hit Mickey's up the backside. A little gang of nosey parkers were following her, taking an interest in her business. Bloody cheek! Typical! Mrs Charlotte Hennessey-White – Protector of Public Morals. Well she wasn't having any of it. As if she didn't have enough trouble convincing Billy about her relationship with Mickey, she didn't want any unnecessary tales getting back to him.

She visited Billy the following day and had to make it appear as if everything was the same. She adopted her most alluring voice, all sweet and sugary like Marilyn Monroe, who'd now replaced Jean Harlow as her role model.

He seemed concerned about her new career. Adopting her breeziest voice, she did her best to soothe his fears. 'It's a proper job, Billy. Help pay the bills, won't it?'

Polly waited for Billy's reaction, aware that the prison officers surrounding them were watching him almost as closely as she was. He looked unsure.

'I'm going to be working as a receptionist.' She made it sound as convincing as possible. Just because Meg didn't believe her didn't mean that Billy wouldn't. It entered her head to compare it with the time when she'd worked for Charlotte's husband, but thought better of it. Now was not a good time to remind Billy that she'd been less than pure when they'd met. She had egged David on because of a perceived wrong on Charlotte's part and although she'd never admitted to feeling guilty, she certainly felt it at times.

'Christmas is coming, Billy. Imagine our Carol with no presents, poor kid. Right down in the dumps she'd be. I don't get that much with the cleaning and stuff.' She sat poker straight and adopted an officious expression that she'd often seen on Charlotte's face, and everyone believed Charlotte, didn't they? She didn't tell him that she'd already given up helping out with Edna's mother. She still did a bit for Charlotte of course, but that was a social event more than anything else. After a quick whiz round with the vacuum, it was tea and biscuits around the kitchen table.

Billy rested his chin on his fists and looked glum. 'I can tell you Father Christmas won't be visiting this joint, that's for sure. S'pose I could make a few decorations, but the only paper I got for paper chains is 'anging over the crapper.' Although he grinned, there was a melancholy look in his eyes.

Keep him cheerful, thought Polly, and she laughed although she didn't think it was that funny.

Determinedly, she went on, sticking to the details although they were far from the truth. 'I'll be working in his office handling the paperwork and the phone calls. He's got a lot of business deals going so he reckons.'

'Course 'e 'ave.' Billy smiled as though he really trusted Mickey O'Hara, the man he refused to squeal on. Polly sensed he didn't entirely believe her, but preferred to play innocent.

'But if you don't want me to work for 'im . . .'

'Don't be silly. You do what you 'ave to.'

Thank God for that! She smiled brightly. Prison visiting was not a pleasant event, but things hadn't gone too badly. Most of her success she put down to the fact that she had made the effort to plaster on the lipstick and look good for her husband. The black suit she was wearing had a white trim around the collar and cuffs. The outfit had originally been plain and she'd added the trim herself after seeing a picture of one in a magazine – Chanel it had said, which she pronounced 'Channel'.

'Well,' she said, her breasts rising as she sighed heavily, 'that's it. Either O'Hara takes care of me and Carol or you takes care of 'im – if you know what I mean.' She spoke in a low voice – no sense in letting the blokes in blue know anything.

Billy seemed OK about things although it occurred to Polly that he didn't really have much choice being in clink. But she countered the discomfort easily enough. He should have kept working with Colin. Or he should have got a proper job. Or kept his nose clean so they could have emigrated to Australia. Billy had let her down and she was having trouble forgiving him. The list of things he should have done and hadn't seemed to get longer with the passing of the years.

That night Meg was taking Carol and her friend Sean to the early matinée at the Broadway and had promised them a fish and chip supper on the way home. Polly, back from her prison visit, still with her make-up intact, but her costume hanging up behind the bedroom door, had changed into a black skirt and white jumper, which Meg had bought for her from a jumble sale at the Ruskin Hall in Brislington the Saturday before. She was curled up in an armchair with a tattered copy of *Woman's Realm* and two more magazines lay against the old brass fender that had come with them from York Street. Meg's friend, Bridget, had purloined the magazines on separate visits to the doctor's surgery; she was a regular there now it was free. Eyes were next on the list. Both Meg and Polly pitied the optician who had to deal with her. She always pretended to be deaf if they tried to give her more information or asked her for money.

'So how was Billy?' asked Meg.

'Fine.'

'Is that all?'

'Well, he ain't out dancing and prancing, that's for sure!'

Meg pursed her lips and fixed her fists on her hips. 'Sarcasm is the lowest form of wit.'

Polly raised her eyes from the magazine. 'Where did you get that from – a Christmas cracker?'

Meg tugged her coat onto her shoulders and changed the subject. 'So when's Edna's kid coming home?'

Polly turned her eyes back to the magazine. All she'd been

thinking about up until now was Mickey O'Hara. Mention of Susan brought her down to earth with a bump. Let's put it this way, I'm glad it's not our Carol.'

'Poor little bugger. Sure you won't come?' Meg asked as she tied a green paisley headscarf beneath her chin. Two metal curlers bundled with hair dangled on her forehead like tired sausages.

Polly didn't look up. 'No thanks. I might pop out later with Muriel Haskins for a quick drink down the Engineer's Arms though.'

'I didn't think you liked 'er.'

Polly shrugged, but did not surface from behind the magazine just in case Meg looked into her eyes and saw she was lying.

'I'll see you later then.'

Just minutes after Meg and the kids had left, Polly was upstairs and changing back into the suit she had worn to visit Billy. Hopefully there wouldn't be too many of the neighbours on the bus stop or hanging over their garden gates aching to ask her where she was going.

She grimaced as the rusted iron of the front gate clanged like a trap behind her. The kids playing marbles in the gutter did not look up. Brian Casey over the road was playing with the throttle on his motorbike. For once she was thankful of his damned tinkering. The noise masked the sound of her heels click-clacking up the road to the bus stop.

So far so good. Nosy parkers were indoors digesting their evening meals, listening to the radio or taking the washing in off the line before it froze solid. Alone at the bus stop she glanced at her watch. A couple of minutes and the bus should be there – providing it was on time. Ten minutes late was not unusual and the conductor wouldn't care if you did complain. A man wearing a trench coat and smoking a cigarette came and stood beside her. He smelt of strong tobacco and stale beer. She stepped away from him although she lit up herself.

A few other people straggled to the bus stop, eyed her speculatively, then looked away. Most, she guessed, were going to the Engineer's or perhaps as far as the London Inn. But she was going further than that and her stomach churned with a mix of nervousness and excitement at the thought of it.

It took two buses to get to Ashley Place. Mickey had told her to be there by eight thirty, but both buses had been late. Sodium streetlights, orange suns against the darkness, flashed past at regular intervals. She counted them . . . one . . . two . . . three . . . Seconds turned into minutes, until one, then two hours had gone by.

It was closer to nine o'clock when she got to Ashley Place. One or two buses trundled along past her, but there were few cars, their headlights seeming to flicker and distort as rain began to fall. Every so often she glanced over her shoulder. There was no sign of Charlotte! Polly grimaced. Next Tuesday she'd be up at Charlotte's, but not to take tea and tittle-tattle. Oh no, next week she'd be giving her a piece of her mind.

'I can't stay long,' she said as she entered the house. But I wish I could, she thought. I wish this was mine and I could live here for ever. This was her ideal home, its austere black and white decor unblemished by the autumnal shades of current fashion.

'Hardly worth you coming!' Mickey's tone was cutting and surprised her.

'The buses were late.'

'You should have let me collect you.'

She gripped her handbag more tightly. She so wanted to please him, to have him like her. 'Oh no! I wouldn't want to put you to any trouble.'

It sounded weak, but how could she say that he couldn't collect her all the time? The neighbours would be looking and they'd report her being picked up by a bloke in a flash car. The news would go round the street like a forest fire. 'And where there's smoke . . .' they'd all be saying.

Yeah, she thought, and the flippin' flame would go all the way into Horfield Prison and Billy's cell.

Mickey cupped her elbow in his hand and guided her to a white leather sofa. She sank into its marshmallow opulence, feeling the same pleasure as she did when she sank into a hot bath.

'Bloody 'ell! I feel like Joan Crawford!'

He smiled engagingly. 'More like Jean Harlow, I think.' He looked happier.

Polly felt her face getting warm. She wanted to say she was doing her best nowadays to look like Marilyn Monroe, but he might think her cheap. After all, hadn't Marilyn appeared on a calendar in the altogether? And she didn't want him to think her cheap. She wanted him to think well of her, even desire her. Yes! That was it. The way young men in uniform had desired her back in the forties, their lust shining like fire in their eyes. That's how she wanted Mickey to regard her. Just like they used to do.

His look started at her head and journeyed downwards – almost as though he were stripping her clothes from her body and leaving them in a pile on the floor. By rights she should go. But her legs had turned to lead. Her heart was beating twenty to the dozen and an old familiar tingling was getting her going in all the right places.

He reached for a cigar from a heavy silver box, its gleam reflected in the black tiles of the coffee table it sat on. 'As I promised, I am going to show you the club tonight. After that I can drive you home – save you having to wait on a bus stop. My boys will be back with the car shortly.'

He turned and opened the door of a circular object that turned out to be a cocktail cabinet. Glasses clinked against bottles. Without asking her what she wanted, he poured two drinks.

'Nice piece of furniture,' she said with a smile.

'I got it made specially. Drinks in this bit . . .' He demonstrated how the top pulled down exposing bottles and glasses against a mirror-lined interior. 'And this,' he said, tapping what looked like a drawer beneath it, which opened at his touch. 'For personal paperwork.'

'That's clever.'

Polly was under no illusion that this man was in control of the situation. But she couldn't let it stay that way. She had to say something. She cleared her throat, determined that she would not sound at all nervous. 'So! How long have you had the club?'

She didn't really want to know. It was just that she had to say something to stop herself from shivering like a frightened little fool.

'Long enough! Port and lemon?' He handed her a glass of dark red liquid.

Polly looked at it and blinked. 'A tart's drink!'

His eyebrows rose in surprise.

She glared at it and got to her feet. 'That's what my aunty calls it. And if you think that's what I bloody am, you can go and . . .'

'I've got the same,' he said, raising his glass as if in a toast. 'I like it and I presumed you did too. I apologize. I can get you something else if you'd prefer . . .'

Slowly and as gracefully as the situation allowed, she sat down again. 'No! That's all right.'

He didn't think she was free and easy. Well, that was something. She took a big gulp, then another, before putting the glass back on the table.

'Well, I 'ave to say, I needed that!'

His smile seemed sarcastic. Was he amused at her discomfort? She attempted to study his expression, but he'd turned away.

'They're back.' He was looking beyond her to the well-raked gravel drive and the sleek black car that had just pulled in.

He helped Polly to her feet, put his arm around her, and

guided her towards the front door. 'Well, Cinderella! Shall we depart for the ball?'

Polly beamed up at him as though she'd won first prize in a raffle. She looped her arm through his and said in a Mae West accent, 'Better than going to a ball, honey! Let's you and me have a ball!'

Suddenly she wanted very much to let her hair down. What the hell! Why shouldn't she have a good time? With a sashay to rival Diana Dors, Polly sallied to the front door, a wide smile on her bright red lips. She hadn't felt this happy for a long time.

But you're married!

Why was it that the voice of conscience sounded so much like Aunty Meg?

Yeah, but Billy ain't perfect, is he?

And when was the last time Billy had made her feel like a film star? When was the last time he'd taken her dancing?

The journey from the room with the white sofas to the car in the drive was like walking on air. The car, the garden, the buildings and the road beyond were no more than a multicoloured blur. She felt young again and a handsome man with a warm accent was taking her out.

Edna was clearing dishes. Colin was hanging around in the doorway watching her, wanting to say so much, but not daring to. What could he say that would grab her attention and not cause an argument?

He decided on: 'Old Tom Rayburn's offered me a goose for Christmas. How do you feel about that?'

The bustling figure in green sweater and tartan skirt stopped rubbing at dishes, paused and turned slowly round to face him. Her face was very white, which made her brown eyes seem as big as saucers. 'Do you think Susan will like the Christmas tree?'

This was not the response Colin had been hoping for. His

face dropped. 'Look, love, I don't think our Susan's likely to be home for Christmas. The doctors said . . .'

Forgetting that a cup was enfolded in the tea towel, Edna flung it onto the table, which sent the cup crashing into pieces on the floor. 'I *want* Susan here for Christmas.'

Colin spread his hands in a helpless gesture, opened his mouth to say something, but the words seemed too difficult to utter. It was not possible for Susan to be home for Christmas; that's what he wanted to say, but all he ended up saying was, 'Please, Edna. Please!'

Edna kicked at the pieces of broken cup. It was part of a set that she'd bought cheaply from Billy Hills. 'Look what you made me do!'

'I did?' shouted Colin, unable to control his emotions any longer. 'You did it, because *you* will not listen to a bloody thing I say, or the doctors, or anybody. Susan is *not*, I repeat, *not* coming home for Christmas!'

Noises came out from the sitting room where Peter and Pamela were watching Muffin the Mule or some other children's programme. Peter had taken something from Pamela and the little girl was wailing piteously.

'I'll go,' muttered Colin and pushed himself up from his chair and poked his head around the door of the living room. 'I told you kids to behave yourselves. And you shouldn't sit so close to that television. It's bad for your eyes.'

'You shouldn't say that,' Edna snapped, slamming a cupboard door behind her, having got out a dustpan and brush.

Colin's face was bright red. 'I thought you agreed with me about them sitting too close to it?'

'I meant "kids". It's not an English word.'

'No! American, dear. Another black mark against the Yanks.'

Edna winced, then dropped to her knees and proceeded to brush the broken bits of china into the dustpan.

Exasperated, Colin sighed, fell onto a kitchen stool, and buried his head in his hands.

Pamela's crying gradually ceased. Peter poked his head out of the door. He made a face as though he'd well and truly judged his parents' mood, then ducked back in again.

Colin felt and sounded tired. 'Have you quite finished?'

Edna didn't answer.

'What's happening to us, Edna?'

'Nothing!' she shrugged. Although she was desperate to tell him everything that was in her heart, she couldn't do it. She'd posted the crisp blue letter on the way home from her mother's – *after* Polly had told her that she had a new job. Telling him about it was incredibly difficult. It was as though she'd dug a moat around herself and she couldn't for the life of her bring herself to lower the drawbridge. She found herself wishing she'd left the job of telling Colin to Charlotte. She was so much stronger, so sure of what to do and when to do it.

The sound of the phone pierced the deadly silence that had fallen between them, but did nothing to lessen the animosity and pettiness.

Are you going to get that?' Edna snapped.

Colin's head remained buried in his hands.

After slamming the dustpan and brush down onto the clean wooden draining board, Edna stalked off.

Colin heard her pick up the telephone and say, 'Yes, Dad. It's me. What is it now?'

Never had she sounded so terse. He shook his head as she continued. 'Dad, I cannot come right now. You'll have to deal with it yourself.'

A silence followed. He guessed that Edna's father was repeating a request for her to come over and deal with something.

Edna answered impatiently. 'No. I will not. She's bound to turn up sooner or later. I expect she's in the park again. If it gets that late and she still hasn't come home, call the police.'

No matter how bad her mother had been, Edna had always

had time for her father. What had happened to her? What was happening to them?

Colin eyed her accusingly as she came back out into the kitchen. She saw his look, stopped, and said, 'I've got other things to think about. She'll turn up.'

'It's getting dark outside,' he said.

In confirmation of his statement, the wind began to throw the falling rain against the window. It sounded like hailstones.

'She'll turn up,' muttered Edna as she picked up the dustpan and made for the back door. 'She's like a bad penny. She always turns up.'

The last bus from Melvin Square to Old Market was running late and the rain was coming down in sheets.

'Can't see we'll be stopping to pick anyone up in this weather,' said the driver to the conductor. The latter only nodded. He was yawning and yearning for his bed.

There were no passengers on the bus and it looked like a swift run back to the depot. By the time the bus had rounded Kenmare Road and started the steep descent down Donegal Road, it looked like being a fast run and downhill as far as the chip shop at the bottom of Glyn Vale.

Lurgan Walk on one side and Cavan Walk on the other dissected the hill at its halfway point. By the time they got to the bus stop at the top of Glyn Vale the rain had got heavier and likewise the driver's eyelids.

Like dry sticks the windscreen wipers swiped over the windows, dissecting the water into two separate halves, dismissing it for a moment before it was instantly reformed.

The driver blinked himself awake and glanced behind him. The conductor was sprawled across a seat, mouth open and eyes shut. Lucky sod!

It was no more than a moment, no more than a glance. A figure, blurred by rain and drowsy eyes, danced into the road. The driver shouted and stood on the brakes. There was a bump, a screeching of tyres as the bus crossed the road and crashed into the front garden of a house.

Later, he sat with his head in his hands and cried.

'It happened so fast,' he wailed once the ambulance had arrived, the crowd had gathered, and the police were asking questions.

The conductor said nothing because he'd seen nothing. 'It was raining and dark,' he said, but did not mention the fact that he'd fallen asleep.

'We went into a skid,' the driver went on, resigned to the fact that there were no witnesses, no one to corroborate that he had, for the most part, kept his eyes on the road.

The police asked him if he knew he'd hit someone.

He hung his head, sighed and nodded sadly. 'She was dancing,' he said. 'Or at least that was the way it seemed.'

Ethel Burbage was buried at eleven o'clock in the morning on a bitterly cold day in mid December at Arnos Vale Cemetery, a windswept slope falling from the steep Victorian streets of Totterdown to the Bath Road. Sweeping from Bath Road to Barton Hill were streets of grim back-to-backs and jumbled warehouses, the slag heaps of Barton Hill and the mean streets of Redfield. Beyond that were the green slopes of Purdown, where the great gun, 'Purdown Percy' had thundered away at enemy fighters in the dark days of the Blitz.

The flat, lower end of the cemetery, adjacent to the Bath Road, was crowded with the more magnificent edifices of Victorian gentry including one of an Indian prince, with elephants at each corner supporting a domed temple between them.

Ethel Burbage's last resting place was high on the hill. Once the coffin had been lowered into the ground, the mourners hugged coat collars to chilled cheeks, and shoved hands, already gloved in kid or wool, into pockets. Mufflers were tightened and hats pulled firmly down onto heads as they walked gingerly down the cinder path that wound between lopsided tombstones of once remembered people, their epitaphs eaten away by time, weather and luxuriant plant life.

Edna's father lingered at the grave, the hem of his overcoat tugged to one side by the icy wind. Edna watched him, not quite believing that he could truly have loved her mother. She hadn't been lovable.

Janet clasped Edna's hand as she passed and offered her commiserations.

Edna sighed. 'Trust my mother to die at this time of year when everyone's looking forward to having fun. Isn't that just typical?'

Janet squeezed her arm. 'Never mind. Where would you be without her? And where would I be without my mother?'

Edna looked at her askance.

Janet saw the look and went on. 'You might not have married Colin if she hadn't pushed you. And you might not have had three lovely children.'

Edna's attention returned to her father. 'Do you know, I think he actually loved her. Isn't that amazing?'

Now it was Janet's turn to look askance. She tried to read Edna's expression, fancied it was hard, but the wind chose that moment to blow Edna's hair across her face. By the time she had tucked it firmly behind her ear, the bitterness Janet thought she had seen was gone.

Wiping his eyes, then blowing his nose, Cyril Burbage left the graveside. Edna offered him her arm. He needed her support more than she needed his.

There was space to be thoughtful. Perhaps it was the weather, or perhaps it was because there was little to be said about Ethel Burbage – without talking ill of the dead – but silence reigned as they wound their way back to the arched gateway and beyond to the main road and the funeral cars.

Edna looked small, like a puny adolescent rather than a grown woman with three children. She also looked tired. And so would I, thought Janet, and wondered how the devil she would have coped with a disabled man, a difficult mother and, now, a very sick child. Tragedy, like a lot of things, went in threes.

Charlotte eased along beside her and said, 'At least it's one less burden for Edna to cope with. We can at least be thankful for that.'

Edna joined Colin and his parents. Polly joined Janet and Charlotte.

'I was saying that Ethel's death is a blessing in disguise bearing in mind Edna's other problems,' said Janet.

Polly looked at her accusingly. 'Edna ain't been coping with 'er. I 'ave! And I'll tell you somefin' now, if Edna don't sort herself out she's going to drive poor Colin to suicide! Or at least to drink!'

Janet felt no compulsion to tell anyone about Colin getting drunk and crying. The world might not understand, she thought, as she eyed the cold sky and the straggly trees as if they were the most beautiful things in her world.

A figure appeared by the cemetery gate. Polly immediately lost interest in either Janet or the funeral. 'I'll see you later,' she said breathlessly, then ran off to where a broad-set man in a dark overcoat and trilby stood smoking a large cigar.

Charlotte leaned towards Janet. 'That's him! The man involved with the refugees!'

But with others around, Janet sensed that her mother would change the subject.

Charlotte buried her face in the fox fur that was draped around the shoulders of her smart black coat. 'It would be nice if Susan was home for Christmas.'

Janet shook her head. 'That won't be possible, Mother. Easter perhaps, but certainly not Christmas.'

Her father, who looked pinched, cold and too slight for the size of his best black overcoat, nodded. 'You're probably right, and you are the one there on the ground so to speak. You should know.'

Janet stared at him. Suddenly she felt warm and eminently

self-satisfied. An idea was beginning to form in her mind. Up to now it had been lingering, like an actor waiting on the sidelines for the right part to present itself. Her father's comment was the prompt she'd been waiting for.

Ivan was standing at the cemetery gates. It had been his choice to stay slightly apart from family and friends. She smiled at him and he smiled back, though kept his distance.

'You look like the cat who's got the cream,' said Dorothea who had chosen to wear grey rather than black to the funeral.

'You could say that,' said Janet.

Presuming Janet was referring to Ivan, Dorothea giggled before sloping off with Geoffrey. Henry had disappeared completely from the scene, rumoured to have run away with a woman twice his age.

It would not have been prudent to explain her plan to Dorothea; that would be like broadcasting it worldwide on *Family Favourites* and she didn't want anyone to know until she had laid the foundations. But she needed to tell someone she could trust, though not Edna. She had quite enough to contend with at present. That left Ivan. Strange, she thought, that at one time she would not speak to him, and now he was the only person worth telling until her plan became reality.

Twenty-four

Snow fell early that year. Like thick icing it sat on the corrugated roofs of the single-storey hospital buildings. Flakes beat gently against the glass windowed corridors that ran between each prefabricated unit, drifted into corners and draped like ragged nets across ward windows.

Janet's office was not the warmest of places. Rubbing her arms helped keep the circulation going and wearing two sweaters and a cardigan kept the draughts out. The radiator, a cast iron monster that sounded as though it suffered from chronic indigestion, still rarely rose above warm. Hot drinks helped and, as the wind rattled the windows, now was as good a time as any for another brew, she decided.

She picked up the kettle, a small, squat thing with a bent spout, and gave it a shake. No water. She went to the small kitchen just along the corridor. On her return she saw Edna and Colin coming out of Jonathan's office. They looked down. An apologetic Jonathan stood in the doorway.

'I'm sorry,' he said, 'but Christmas is out of the question.'

Scrooge in *A Christmas Carol* immediately sprang to mind, but Jonathan wasn't really being mean.

'Edna! Colin! Care for a cup of tea?' She held up the kettle.

'Ah! Janet!' Jonathan looked relieved. He spread his arms seeming to usher them towards her.

Edna looked hesitant. Colin looked morose at first, then seemed to brighten. 'Why not? Come on, love,' he said, his arm curving around her, dropping away as she shrugged him off.

Janet took them into her office, lit the Primus, then found them chairs.

Edna carefully folded her coat over her knees, then settled her handbag onto her lap. Colin gripped the back of the chair as he lowered himself onto it, his legs stuck out stiffly in front of him. There was little enough room in the office. Their presence, especially Colin's legs, made it seem smaller.

Their disappointment was obvious. She felt obliged to lift their spirits. 'So you've been having a chat with Jonathan?'

Edna's gaze was fixed on the floor. Colin was trying to look jolly, glancing at Janet as he spoke, but glanced nervously back at Edna as if looking for confirmation.

She sensed the tension between them. Married people did not always get on – heavens, her own parents were proof of that! But Edna and Colin? She wouldn't have believed it. They'd always seemed so happy together.

'It appears our Susan won't be home for Christmas,' said Colin in too blithe a manner to believe. 'But never mind. We'll get over it, won't we, love?' He patted Edna's hand.

Edna was like a statue, unblinking and silent. Janet felt so sorry for Colin, but managed to maintain her cheerfulness.

'I heard Easter mentioned,' she said as she poured the hot water into the pot. In her heart of hearts she knew what the problem was. Addressing it would be the hardest thing of all.

Colin nodded. 'Yes. We'll see if we can get her an Easter egg. There ain't that much chocolate around yet, but no matter the price, we'll get her one, won't we, love?'

Listening to the pain in his voice, it was hard to concentrate on pouring milk and spooning sugar into a cup.

She passed the first cup to him, then took the second cup to Edna and dropped to her knees in front of her. If Colin couldn't put into words what Jonathan had so obviously just told them, then it was left to her.

Best, she decided, to be direct.

'Doctor Driver's told you that she'll have to wear a calliper on her right leg, hasn't he?'

Colin seemed to melt into his chair.

Edna raised her gaze from the floor and looked into Janet's face. There were dark circles beneath her eyes. Janet guessed she hadn't slept properly for months.

She nodded. 'Yes.' Her voice was small and soft, like that of a child before falling asleep.

Colin chose that moment to get to his feet. 'I need the um . . .'

Janet gave him directions to the gents' lavatories, wondered whether that was really what he wanted or whether he wanted to cry again. Funny, she thought, a man can cry in front of another man, but not in front of a woman. Perhaps he felt he needed to be strong for Edna.

As the door closed behind him, Edna let out a great, long sigh, almost of relief. 'It's not easy to accept,' she said, her brown eyes flickering as though she'd just awoken. Her shoulders seemed less tense, her whole demeanour less introspective than when Colin had been in the room.

'She might not need to wear it for ever. Physiotherapy is being used a lot more now than it used to be,' Janet offered.

Edna's brow furrowed deeply. 'I know.' She gripped the cup tightly and clamped her mouth shut, almost as if she were trying to keep something in. 'I can't help feeling the way I do. I can't help it that Colin annoys me nowadays. It's just that . . .' She paused and Janet saw the moistness in her eyes as she struggled for the right words. 'I sometimes think that God must be dead. If little children are so important to him, why do they have to suffer? Why do they have to be alone, especially at this time of year? Children should be with their mothers at Christmas.'

Janet felt a tightening in her chest. She could imagine how Edna was feeling, a mix of despair and anger that just had to come out. 'Susan won't be alone – I promise you.' She noticed that Edna had said mothers, had not mentioned fathers, or parents.

What Edna said next surprised her. 'You've got a good bedside manner, Janet. You should have been a doctor.'

Janet smiled wryly. 'Now there's a thought. Doctor Janet. Tell me all your woes and I'll see if I've got the magic pill that will put them right.' She said it laughingly, not meaning for it to be taken seriously, at least, not yet.

'Do you remember me telling you about Sherman?' said Edna. Her look was very intense.

Janet nodded. 'Yes.'

Edna unclipped the crossover clasp of her pigskin handbag. 'I've received a letter.'

The paper was of poor quality, the sort processed from every bit of cardboard a post-war Europe could salvage.

Edna unfolded it as though it were the most precious piece of material ever to cross her palm. 'It's from my son,' she said. Her voice caught on the words as she said it, like stifled sobs.

She passed it to Janet, who vaguely noted an address in Germany. The writing, though well formed, had a certain immaturity about it.

Dear Mrs Smith,

Mr Schumann has told me all about you. I understand that you are my mother but regret that I cannot come to you yet. You see, my grandmother in Brazil is dying. I feel I must remain part of her family until she is gone so I cannot come to you until then. I have spoken to Mr Schumann about it and he says I can stay here at the village as long as I want. You cannot be my mother yet. Mr Schumann said I should tell you about this.

Love,

Carlos Di Mambro.

Did she read it twice or was it three times? She couldn't tell. The letter was so moving. At last Edna took it from her hand.

'Mr Schumann says he is a very serious child,' said Edna.

'He sounds it.'

Edna folded the letter up and put it back in her bag.

'I take it he's coming to live with you,' said Janet.

Edna nodded. 'I've offered.'

Janet had a suspicion about the answer to her next question, but she asked it anyway. 'How does Colin feel about it?'

Edna bent her head so that her hair, which was still brown with only a few stray grey strands, fell forward and hid her face. 'He doesn't know. I haven't told him.'

'Oh!' said Janet and sank back onto her haunches.

'This ain't right.'

Meg stood with her arms braced across her ample chest.

Polly pouted and the reflection in the mirror did the same. 'I'm only filling in at the club until something else comes along. It's not goin' to be a regular thing.'

To her ears the explanation sounded genuine, but Meg wasn't fooled.

'Pull the other one!'

Polly swept Deep Crimson over her lips, folded the top one against the bottom one so that the coverage would be even, then pouted. 'I need the job; we need the money.' She made it sound as though she were really putting herself out.

'And you know 'ow you'll earn it in that type of place, my girl, drinking, dancing, and showing everything you got.'

She saw that Meg wasn't fooled. There was no point in pretending. 'So what's wrong with dancing and drinking? I want some fun. I deserve some fun!'

'What about your husband? What about your daughter?'

Mouth petulant and movements quick, Polly shoved her lipstick into her black suede clutch bag, then snapped it shut. 'It's my life!'

Meg wagged her finger. 'No. That's where you're wrong. You've got to consider other people. And you're not. You're only thinking about yourself.'

Meg's sharp words struck a chord, but the fun loving side of Polly didn't want to hear it.

She turned sharply, her blonde curls flopping over one eye like Veronica Lake.

'All I ever wanted was a nice bloke who'd look after me and mine. I thought I 'ad one – and what does 'e bloody go and do? Gets locked up in clink! That's bloody what! And 'ere I am, stuck on the outside, 'aving to get work where I can or otherwise we're up so and so creek without a bloody boat let alone a paddle!'

She stomped past Meg and grabbed a black three-quarter-length coat from where she'd left it on the back of the settee. The coat had been full-length and old-fashioned when Meg had bought it at a jumble sale. Trimmed to a more fashionable length it looked a million dollars. With the material cut off she'd made a pillbox hat that perched jauntily on Polly's head – a glamorous outfit at a giveaway price. The coat swung seductively over a black skirt, matching black shoes and nylons with pronounced seams snaking up the backs of her legs. Swallowing the guilt she told herself she deserved to live a little, and anyway, Meg wouldn't tell Billy, would she?

Christmas was a quiet affair, everyone seeming to keep to their own houses and private worlds. Geoffrey was home for Christmas and although he glowered over the dinner table at Ivan, the latter did not rise to the bait. Christmas dinner was about the only time Geoffrey spent at home. The rest of the time he was out with Dorothea. Janet spent time with Ivan. They went out for New Year, saw Polly with the thuggish looking type they'd seen her with before. There was no sign of Edna or Colin.

Charlotte worried about David. He'd hardly been into his consulting rooms and she was sure the stroke had taken far more out of him than his colleagues in the profession were letting on. Pink capillaries erupted in the grey pallor of his face with amazing frequency, his hands shook slightly, and he seemed continually weary.

Tonight he was sitting in his favourite armchair in front of the french windows. A strong breeze hurled a shower of sleet and rain against the glass.

Charlotte drew the curtains against the worsening weather. They settled in their respective chairs with a tray of tea and crumpets on the small table between them. She lay her head back, closed her eyes and sighed, 'Oh bliss.'

This was one of those peaceful moments when partners of long standing can either talk or sit quietly and merely enjoy each other's presence.

Their talk was sporadic. David mentioned how much he admired Colin for coping without legs and running a business and taking care of a family. 'Limbs are very precious,' he said thoughtfully, 'but not so precious as time. You get to learn that as you get older.'

Recognizing his need to talk deeply and truly, Charlotte got up and sat herself on the chair arm beside him. She kissed him on the head and ruffled his hair. 'Philosophy? At this time of night?'

David squeezed her waist. 'Not really. I was just reminiscing. We've had our problems, darling, but what are they compared to his? We're lucky. Very lucky.'

The silence between them was immensely sweet. Communication between two people married as long as they had been did not need to be vocal. Each knew the thoughts of the other and was in tune with them.

'Has Mrs Grey gone home?' David asked.

'Yes.'

'So we've got the place to ourselves.'

She knew exactly what he was suggesting and was not sure that she should agree to it. She started to voice her concern. 'David, you know what the doctors said . . .'

He laughed. 'Doctors? You don't want to take notice of all they say, darling.'

'If you're sure, Doctor David?'

'Very.' He squeezed her hand.

She got up and his arm slipped from her waist. 'I'll go on up.'

'I'm right behind you.'

Unwilling to leave him, she waited and watched as he got up from the chair, reached out and tottered slightly. 'David?' She tried to control the concern in her voice.

He smiled mischievously and for a moment she saw again the young doctor she'd fallen in love with.

'Time waits for no man,' he murmured. It was the most poignant thing he could possibly have said.

No longer driven by the procreative passion of youth, their lovemaking was slow, soft and gentle. It was like playing a well-loved tune; the melody was easily remembered and languorously performed.

After making love, he kissed her and said goodnight.

She lay awhile in the darkness remembering other times when they'd made love. In their youth it had been frequent and fiercely passionate. After the war it had turned from passion to violent lust on his part and a kind of resigned acceptance on hers. That's where Josef had come in. Did I love him? she asked herself. David stirred beside her.

'Are you going to your own bed?' he asked.

'No.' She turned and put her arm around him. 'No. I'm staying with you.'

In the morning, when she woke up, she was still in his bed and wasn't sure of the time. A small chink of daylight showed through the curtains. She blinked away her sleepiness, got up onto one elbow and reached for the brass monster sitting on the bedside cabinet. Eight o'clock, but the minute hand was not moving. She checked her watch. Nine forty-five!

She threw back the covers and swung her legs over the edge of the bed. 'David! Quickly! The alarm hasn't gone off.'

David did not respond. Charlotte shook his shoulder. He didn't move.

'David?'

The clock, the room and the world in general seemed to fade from existence as Charlotte realized that David had said goodnight for the very last time.

New Year's Day, 1954, not the best of dates for a funeral, thought Janet. An inconsequential, a midweek, run-of-the-mill date might pass without anyone noticing. She concluded that although her father's death had occurred between Christmas and New Year, it could not possibly be forgotten. It was sandwiched between the two, as a normal working weekday was sandwiched between two weekends.

He was buried in the family grave at Westbury, a pretty little cemetery not far from the village and close to the golf links.

'He would have liked that,' said Charlotte with a tight smile.

Janet looked at her brother, Geoffrey, and twitched her head, motioning him to offer Charlotte his arm. Her final look of complete exasperation, the last before gritting one's teeth and snarling the requirement into words, eventually did the trick.

Janet took her mother's other arm and the three of them made for the waiting limousines.

'Are you all right, Mother?'

Charlotte nodded. 'I suppose so. It's just that I wish it hadn't been now, I wish more things . . .' She paused and sighed. 'He wasn't a bad man, you know. And he was a good doctor.'

One of David's numerous cousins came up at that point and offered Charlotte his condolences. 'He will be greatly missed, my dear.' He took her mother's hand, kissed her on the cheek, then looked from Geoffrey to Janet and back again.

'So when are you going to become a doctor, young man?'

'Never!' said Geoffrey.

'Geoffrey doesn't want to be a doctor,' Charlotte said.

The uncle raised his eyebrows. His eyelids were heavy, like soup spoons falling over his eyes. 'Really? What a shame.'

Janet saw Geoffrey bristle. Her mother dropped her gaze to the floor. Geoffrey's lifestyle and choice of career were still something of a mystery. His personal life was less so. He was still seeing Dorothea, much to Janet's surprise.

Dorothea attended the funeral, but had stayed in the background until it was over. Now that they'd reached the cars, she came bouncing up, a picture in Astrakhan fur and thickly soled boots. She immediately slipped her arm into Geoffrey's and said to Charlotte, 'So terribly sorry, Mrs Hennessey-White. My parents send their condolences.'

Charlotte merely smiled and nodded. 'It's very kind of you to come, Dorothea.'

'My pleasure,' Dorothea answered, hugging Geoffrey's arm close to her own. Suddenly, she gave Geoffrey a quick dig in the side and mouthed, 'Go on.'

Geoffrey shuffled his feet and looked nervous.

Charlotte looked expectant. Something was about to be said. Dorothea's face said it all and she ended up having to say it.

'Geoffrey and I are getting married!'

Janet's jaw dropped.

Charlotte looked a little shaken. 'I see.'

'So you're going to gain a daughter – if that's all right with you,' said Dorothea, beaming broadly.

'Geoffrey is twenty-one in February,' said Charlotte. 'It's entirely up to him what he does.' Some widows would have been angry to be told such a thing on the day of their husband's funeral. Charlotte was surprisingly calm.

Dorothea hugged Geoffrey close, then kissed him on the cheek. 'And you're going to gain a grandchild,' she went on.

Charlotte's face turned white.

Janet was dumbstruck. Dorothea had actually kept a secret. She hadn't said a word to anyone.

'Then of course you must marry.'

'See! I told you it would be all right.' Dorothea slapped a dirty great kiss on Geoffrey's cheek, then dragged him off along the pavement to the last car in the row of hearses that sat outside the cemetery.

Shocked to a standstill, Janet kept her arm linked with that of her mother. She peered at Charlotte's face, trying to see signs that she might have a heart attack or at least fall to the ground in a dead faint.

'Mother? Are you all right?' she whispered and found herself really caring whether anyone had overheard Dorothea's statement.

The creases at the sides of Charlotte's eyes became wrinkles as she smiled and patted Janet's hand. 'Of course I am.'

'Mother, they shouldn't have—'

'Of course they should! Of course they should,' she repeated. 'Life goes on, Janet. No matter what happens, life goes on and we must go along with it. Faith in the future is like keeping a penny for tomorrow just in case you need it.'

Before leaving, Polly flounced up to Charlotte, her jaw clenched and a determined expression on her face. 'I've been wanting to talk to you for a long while, but things have been happening,' she said.

Charlotte invited her to talk whenever she wanted and apologized for not being available. The irony was wasted.

'Well, as soon as things are a bit sorted, I'll be over,' Polly said.

Weeks later, Charlotte was still sorting things out; papers, clothes, pipes that would no longer be smoked, golf clubs used a few times then left to gather dust. Evidence of a man's life. Even his old uniform still hung in the wardrobe. Initially she had planned that this would be the first to be thrown out, possibly given to the same rag and bone man to whom Janet had given her things.

Charlotte sat down on the bed and buried her head in her hands. She'd cried many tears, and in nights past and for nights to come, she would relive that poignant moment when they'd made love and kissed goodbye for the very last time. Yesterday would still be with her tomorrow. But you must get back to normal, she told herself, and decided to make some tea. The tea was not drunk. The house echoed to her footsteps and the music on the Home Service seemed to get lost amongst the emptiness. Even Mrs Grey was having a day off to go along to see her GP to check on her varicose veins.

She had to get out of the house. She didn't know or care where. Anywhere!

Just as she was picking up her gloves and the swansdown hat that matched her grey suit trimmed with white piping, the telephone rang.

She paused. Work for the bureau had been put on hold. O'Hara had indeed proved to be the owner of the car. Things seemed to have reached a dead end.

Shall I or shan't I?

She reached for the front door meaning to ignore it, but paused again. It might be the solicitors, the bank, the garage, the funeral parlour, perhaps a friend, or a relative.

The ringing persisted. She rushed back into the study and picked it up.

Brookman was on the other end. The first thing he did was to commiserate with her on her great loss. After that, excitement resounded in his voice. 'I've some interesting news on our Mr O'Hara.'

Charlotte urged him to continue.

He cleared his throat. 'As you know, the large volume of displaced persons coming out of Europe do pose some definite problems. They have to be controlled, hence the Aliens Register and the documents they have to carry with them at all times.'

Paperwork, paperwork! Charlotte winced. She'd seen men who had fought for the Allies grit their teeth as petty officials told them where they could work and live.

She forced herself to concentrate on what Brookman was saying.

'As long as those documents are kept in order, the Bureau for Displaced Persons cannot be responsible for any anomalies.'

Charlotte's spirits sank. Nothing could be done. But Brookman had more to say.

'On investigation it was found that a local police sergeant has been stamping the documents whenever these employers wanted to move workers to a different construction site. He was being paid very handsomely to falsify records. Your people were being employed very cheaply. As most could not speak English they could not protest.'

Her spirits soared higher than they had for weeks. 'So this policeman's been arrested?'

'He has. But he's not saying much about the people paying him and making the most money. There are others at the top, principally this Michael O'Hara. He's the one we really want. It's almost a tradition that the Irish control illegal hiring on building sites, but we think in this case that things are not quite as they seem. We have reason to believe O'Hara is not who he says he is. Could his accent be anything other than Irish?'

Charlotte frowned as his face and a memory flashed into her mind. 'Yes! American!'

'Ah!'

Brookman's short, sharp exclamation said it all. There was something more to this.

She said what was in her mind and had been since first seeing him. 'I keep thinking I've seen him somewhere before – perhaps in the war. His hair might be a different colour of course . . .'

'Does the name Mickey Noble mean anything to you?'

'Not really.'

'If this man is Noble he's an American ex-serviceman and was questioned about his papers back in nineteen fifty after a pub landlord was certain he was the man who'd attacked a soldier in his pub four years before that. O'Hara, or Noble, was questioned. The investigation went so far then suddenly the landlord withdrew his accusation.'

'Why did he do that?'

'I don't know. But as I have said, an investigation was instituted and it seemed to be heading in a questionable direction. If O'Hara is Noble, it means that he is here on false papers. It also means that this is a man wanted by the United States Army for the suspected killing of a fellow soldier. Fingerprints would be useful plus any relevant documentation to back it up. I'll post you the details.'

Noble. Mickey Noble. What was it about that name and about that man? Where had she seen him before? She sighed, closed her eyes and tried to remember. It was no good. I'm getting old, she thought, and felt suddenly drained of energy. But the question remained. Who was Mickey Noble?

Twenty-five

Mickey O'Hara was trying to seduce her. Polly knew he was and the very thought of it made her feel like a young girl again, not a married woman with an eleven-year-old daughter.

'Have another port and lemon, honey.'

Honey! How long had it been since she'd heard that word. Coupled with his accent it took her back to a time when the world had seemed full of good-looking Americans who spoke like Gary Cooper at best or James Cagney at worst.

He took her out just one night a week – that's all it was. Saturday night at the Lucky Cat Club, which was approached down steps slippery with moss. If it had had windows they would have looked out over the river, but they were boarded over. Originally the basement of a large Georgian house – all that remained of the house nowadays – now a gathering point for those who liked thick smoke with their whisky and the company of women who were called Gertie by day and Gloria once darkness had fallen and the streetlights had come on.

Polly was bright-eyed and bushy-tailed, partly because she was on her third drink and partly because she was attracting looks from blokes in double-breasted suits with gold fillings and big cigars. A lot of women smoked too. One in a dark blue dress was using a cigarette holder like the one Charlotte had used at the birthday party the day before the Coronation.

'I'd look like Jean Harlow if I had one of them,' she said to Mickey.

His eyes followed the girl. 'That's one hell of a hot baby.'

Biting back her jealousy, Polly watched too. The girl was standing behind her boyfriend, her arms wound around him. Her hands looked as though they met somewhere below his waist.

'Hmm,' murmured Polly. 'That's a baby likely to get burned.'

Mickey laughed, put his arm around her and kissed her cheek.

Polly studied his features as though trying to guess what he thought of her, where their relationship might end up. Was she likely to get burned too? She didn't want to think so. He wasn't the best-looking bloke she'd ever gone out with, but he certainly knew how to treat a girl. And that smile! As long as he smiled like that, looked at her like that, she was putty in his hands.

And Mickey knew it. What Polly didn't know was that it amused him to have her in his thrall. Polly looked at him sometimes as if she were trying to remember where she'd seen him before. It pleased him to charm her into forgetfulness. Weakness, obsessive behaviour no matter whether it was with regard to gambling, drinking, drugs or sex, Mickey liked to control. And in this particular case it was doubly delicious. A cruel streak ran through him so he would never tell her where they had originally met. If she remembered of her own accord, then so be it. But in the meantime he would take advantage of her in any way he could. What if she was married? What was it to him?

The people in the nightclub were no more than blurred blobs of colour moving against a background of mellow lights. The scene came back into clearer focus as a head bent towards Mickey's. Ginger! He whispered something into Mickey's ear. Polly pouted. Were they talking about her? Had Ginger ever told Mickey how an eleven-year-old girl had soundly beaten him with a hockey stick? Not likely, she thought.

Ginger was looking towards the girl in blue and the young toffs she was with, who were beginning to make a nuisance of themselves. The girl in blue had undone the buttons on her boyfriend's shirt. Now she was down on her knees, unbuttoning his flies, obviously drunk and egged on by the crowd of young men and the one or two women with them.

Mickey got to his feet and excused himself.

Polly pretended to be a lady and looked the other way, but still heard the shouting and screaming as Mickey and his mates bundled the upper crust crowd out of the club and up to the pavement.

He's very manly, she thought to herself as she eyed the thick red padding of the bar, the glasses and bottles behind it, their gleam reflected and magnified by the mirrors behind them.

All his, she thought. And they all do what he says. She liked that in a man – authority. Hell, it seemed an age since she'd lain in bed with Billy on a Sunday morning, the best time of all for cuddling up together after peeling their nightclothes off beneath the bedclothes.

A warm flush began to creep over her body. It seemed to start from her toes, but she couldn't be sure. All she did know was that she suddenly needed Billy – a man – Mickey – physically.

It was fifteen minutes or more before Mickey came back smoothing the wide lapels of his suit and straightening his tie, enough time for her to get her feelings under control. She patted her cheeks with the back of her right hand.

'Sorry about that, honey.' He kissed her cheek. His fingers caressed the nape of her neck. The tingles it caused spread over her body like a spider's web.

I mustn't, she thought. Let him take you home, but nothing else, mind you. Be a good girl, Polly Hills.

Thinking it was one thing. Telling him to get lost was an option, but one she didn't choose. Like an overripe apple, she was falling from the tree. All she could hope for was a soft landing.

'You're going to let me take you home, aren't you?'

'Yes.'

There it was, the word was out.

He looked into her eyes as he repeated it. 'Yes.'

And they both knew it wasn't just the lift they were talking about.

Just as she'd expected, he took a detour. Protestations about her being a respectable married woman stuck in her throat.

The car was spacious. There were no lights on the narrow roads around Durdham Down and there were places to park beneath the trees where the darkness was thickest and privacy was assured.

It started as soft caresses, his hands gently moving around her neck, cupping her face as he kissed her mouth. Her best black coat was thrown over the front seat. The heat of his hands warmed her breasts, but still she shivered as the touch of his palms resurrected old thrills she thought long past. His fingers moved slowly, teasingly beneath her skirt, over her stockings to where they ended and her bare flesh began. She groaned and almost begged for more.

It was like Chinese torture. He was drip-feeding the pleasure so she couldn't help but want more. And she'd been starved for so long. Would it really be so dreadful to give in, to enjoy it just this once?

The house was in darkness when Polly got home. The streetlights were out. Curtains upstairs were tightly closed. A faint moon shone through a crisp frost. Camborne Road was sound asleep.

Creeping home silently was not new for Polly. It was second nature to slip off her shoes even before putting her key in the door. She lit a match to see the lock better, snuffed it out quickly once the key was in then pushed the door open.

Although little light filtered through the dimpled glass of the council house door, there was enough to see by. She wouldn't need to reach for the light switch. Anyway, council house hallways were hardly spacious. Front door, living room door to the left, coats, jackets and macs hanging on coat hooks to the right, stairs to the bedrooms straight in front of her.

The lino beneath her feet was as cold as the concrete path out in the garden. But she gritted her teeth. Rather cold feet than a ticking off from Aunty Meg. She wouldn't attempt the stairs. They creaked about halfway up and would quickly give the game away. It wouldn't hurt to sleep on the settee for one night even if the springs did play a bit of a tune if you moved too vigorously. If she lay very still there'd be no sound at all. In the darkness of the living room with just the glow of a dying fire for company she could think about things – and there was a lot to think about.

Hanging on to the handle so she could stop the door if it creaked, she pushed it open. Just as she'd envisaged the coal that had been heaped and black when she'd gone out was now no more than a glowing bed of red embers. The glow made the room look as if it too was smouldering slightly. It also illuminated Aunty Meg who was hunched in her favourite armchair pulled close to the fire. Polly's heart fell to her feet.

'So you did it!' Meg's voice was sharp and accusing.

For once Polly was dumbstruck.

Meg continued. 'You're no saint, Poll, but I never expected you to play around once you were married even though yer bloke's got 'imself in clink.'

Polly opened her mouth to protest her innocence, but stopped when Meg looked directly at her. There was no doubting the accusation in her eyes. She rethought things, decided to brazen it out and stepped closer to the fire.

'I work for him. That's all.'

'Don't make me laugh, Poll. I know damn well what work that sort wants you to do!'

Polly feigned indignation. 'I work in his nightclub of course. Like a sort of manageress.'

'Oh, it's a manageress now, is it? I thought it was supposed to be an office job?'

Polly made a great show of tidying her hair while studying her reflection in the mirror above the fireplace. The glow of the fire lit her face from underneath. Shadows accentuated her features and for a split second she almost thought it was Old Nick looking back out at her. Bloody hell, she weren't that wicked!

'There's no money in office work,' she managed to say. 'It's a job for stuck-up cows like Charlotte's Janet or timid little tarts like Edna. It's not for me.'

Meg slapped her meaty hands down on the chair arms so hard it made Polly almost jump out of the black gaberdine suit she was wearing. 'Well, it's all coming about, ain't it? Running around with two-bit scum and running yer friends down. You ought to be ashamed of yourself!'

Polly's defiance turned to anger. 'Mickey's looking after me. He thinks the world of me. See? Look what 'e gave me.' She took the cigarette holder from her bag and showed it to Meg in the palm of her hand. The girl who'd been thrown out of the club had left it behind.

Meg barely glanced at it. 'Billy gave you a ring – gold too.'

Polly felt her face grow hotter and it wasn't because of the fire. She'd been a willing partner in the back of Mickey's car. She'd missed having sex with Billy, but she'd told herself it would be all right. She didn't love Mickey. At least she didn't think she did.

'He's all right,' she blurted at last and set the cigarette holder down on the mantelpiece. She turned to Aunty Meg and did her best to sound as emphatic as possible. 'He's all right. Honest he is.'

Meg pushed her hands down on the arms of the chair and pulled herself to her feet. She faced Polly square on, her accusing expression just inches from Polly's face.

'What have you done, Poll? What have you done? You're just a toy to him. He'll play with you and then throw you aside like some old rag doll with her stuffing coming out. And then you'll be running back to Billy. And what will you say to him, Poll? What will you say?'

Polly stuck her chin out defiantly. 'So who's going to tell him?'

The stairs out in the hall creaked slightly. Blinking away the sleep Carol was settled on a stair and flattened against the wall.

She'd heard the noise and had almost convinced herself that Father Christmas was back with the presents she'd asked for, but had never got at Christmas. But no, of course not. She wasn't a kid. She knew what her mother was like. She'd been out with another man, and from what her Aunty Meg was saying, he was something to do with the nasty pair who'd come in and pushed them around.

'I'm not 'aving it,' shouted Meg. 'It's not right. An' Billy will find out about it – mark my words!'

Carol frowned and muttered. 'Mum, you are a stupid cow!' She shook her head sagely and lay closer to the wall so she could hear better. Her mother didn't always think straight, but Carol did.

Polly was saying, 'He won't find out! Are you going to tell 'im?'

'I didn't say that. But anyone can write a letter addressed to Horfield Prison.'

Carol began to slide her way back up the stairs as a single thought took root in her mind. When she got to her room she took her pencil case out of her satchel along with a sixpenny notebook. Someone had to do something.

Twenty-six

Dorothea and Geoffrey settled for a registry office wedding, partly out of respect for David's death, and partly because Geoffrey didn't hold with capitalist frippery.

The bride wore a bottle green coat with a dark fur collar and a black pillbox hat with a little veil at the front and a feather at the side. Geoffrey was hostile to top hats and tails, but was persuaded to wear a suit and tie.

They were to spend their honeymoon at the Savoy, a gift from Charlotte. Although Geoffrey protested that such opulence was abhorrent to his nature, Dorothea was over the moon about it.

'And it's only for two nights,' she had pleaded.

He didn't have the heart – or the courage – to disappoint her.

Janet asked Dorothea a big favour before she left.

'Three Easter eggs, that's all.'

'All?' Dorothea stared at her goggle-eyed. 'Chocolate has only just come off rationing, you know.'

'I do know,' said Janet as she rummaged in her purse. 'Harrods are bound to have some. Will ten pounds do?'

Two crisp white fivers exchanged hands. 'Good grief,' said Dorothea, 'are they for anyone I know?'

Janet snapped her bag shut. 'Edna's children.'

'Oh yes! Of course.'

Janet had realized long ago that Dorothea had the memory of a sieve. 'Don't forget.'

Geoffrey intervened. 'She won't forget. I won't let her forget.'

'You are so masterful,' said Dorothea, rubbing herself up against him and looking up into his face like some harem slave in a cinema advertisement for Turkish Delight.

'I want big ones,' Janet added.

'I know,' said Dorothea and grinned wickedly. 'So do I. That's why I married your brother.'

In the brief time when Dorothea was upstairs getting her overnight case, Janet took hold of Geoffrey's arms and kissed him on the cheek.

'Good luck, Geoffrey. Have a nice time.'

Geoffrey smiled and shook his head. 'Bad luck really, isn't it? All the blokes she's had and I'm the one to put her in the family way.'

There was nothing she could say in response to that or the look on Geoffrey's face. He'd been forced to accept a job as an anaesthetist, a dire appointment for a man who'd wanted nothing more to do with medicine. The baby had put paid to any thoughts of travelling and getting further involved in politics and it was obvious he wasn't too happy about it. Hopefully he would feel differently when the baby was born, though somehow she doubted it.

Sorting out David's estate and arranging Geoffrey's wedding had delayed Charlotte meeting Polly. She hadn't come in to help Mrs Grey and, on the occasions Charlotte had seen her, she'd seemed to be in a hurry and had been more than a little huffy.

It was a surprise when she turned up at the front door demanding to see her.

'My dear, I am so glad you came. I've got something to tell you,' said Charlotte.

'And I want a word or two with you,' Polly exclaimed. 'I told you I did. It was just finding the time.' There was a determined set to her jaw and she rolled up her coat sleeves as if she were about to scrub clothes or fight someone.

Me, probably, thought Charlotte, but closed the study door behind them anyway.

Charlotte pre-empted her strike. 'I saw you with a man named Mickey O'Hara, and I have to speak to you about him.'

Polly was taken aback. She had been going to give Charlotte a ticking off for spying on her and had presumed she'd deny it, but Charlotte had mentioned him first. Still, she wasn't going to be pushed around.

'So what business is that of yours? What right do you have to go sneaking around following me? What I do – whether it's right or wrong – is between Billy and me. It's none of your bloody business!'

Charlotte folded her arms and a deadly serious expression came to her face, the sort of expression that worried her. 'Oh yes it is, Polly, but I'm not condemning you. I can understand how difficult it must be with Billy still inside.'

'Oh, you do! Well just for the record—'

'Sit down!' Polly had never heard Charlotte shout before and was taken aback. She accordingly sank into a chair.

'Mickey O'Hara, the man you've been having an affair with—'

Polly jerked forward. 'An affair! How dare . . .'

She stopped herself. Charlotte was already looking accusingly at her as though remembering what had happened in those years immediately following the war when Polly had wanted a better life in another country, preferably the United States. First Gavin didn't come back, then she'd blamed Charlotte for getting Aaron, her next lover, sent home to the States. Then she'd started an ill-conceived affair with David, Charlotte's husband, something Charlotte had long ago forgiven her for.

'Remember Aaron?'

Polly nodded slowly as the bitter sweetness of knowing him came back to her. 'I remember.'

'Then we both remember.'

The silence persisted as both ran through their memories. Fellow soldiers had beaten Aaron to death. All Polly had known – or thought she had – was that Charlotte had destroyed her dream. She'd wanted a replacement man who could give her a better life. She'd also wanted revenge on Charlotte. David had been an easy target, but Polly hadn't known just how ill and how dangerous he had been. But David was gone now.

'I'm sorry,' she said suddenly and shrugged her shoulders as she always did at those times when she was feeling helpless to change things.

Charlotte walked the room, arms folded, head aching and telling herself she was getting too old for confrontations of any description. She'd started feeling more like that since David's death, but she managed to continue.

'If you're talking about the past, it's all water under the bridge, Polly. We've been friends since then and there's nothing to stop us being friends in future. But there's something you've got to know, something you've got to help me with.'

'I can't help you with anything.'

'Mickey O'Hara.'

'I work for him. That's all.' She knew she sounded like a liar and wished Charlotte didn't look at her so intently.

'You're close to him.'

'That's typical of you! You're a nosey cow, Charlotte! And like I said, I only work for the bloke. I go in, do me job, and go home again.'

Exasperated, Charlotte sank into a chair. 'I *saw* you, Polly. I saw you at Ashley Road and I saw you in the back of his car. As I said I'm not condemning you. What you do is your own business, but . . .' She paused and for a moment her look hardened and made Polly feel as though she'd done something really dirty, really wrong. 'I have to say that I am very surprised at your choice of lover.'

Polly felt her face turning red. Charlotte's tone was so

scathing, as if her patience with everyone had come to an abrupt end.

Polly decided to bluff it out. 'Like I was saying—'

'Don't lie!' Charlotte's voice rang around the room, bounced off the books, the cabinets, the oil paintings of horses bounding over fences. 'Just answer this very simple question. Do you ever feel as though you've met him before?'

Polly frowned. She'd thought at times that she'd bumped into him before, though only in a very casual manner, like when you keep seeing the same bloke in a pub or passing the same postman in the street. Thinking about it made her feel slightly uncomfortable.

'What do you mean?'

Charlotte knew when she'd struck home. 'Just answer the question. Do you think you might have seen him before? This is very important.'

Polly faltered. 'I've seen a lot of people before. I like going out to pubs and things. I always have done. So what?'

Charlotte sighed, clasped her hands in front of her and told her very clearly who Mickey O'Hara really was – Sergeant Mickey Noble, the man responsible for Aaron's death.

Polly sank down into a chair. Her legs were like rubber, her blood like ice.

Charlotte went on. 'I've received the paperwork about him. He was the sergeant at the POW camp at the time I used to visit. It's the same man Josef Schumann referred to in his letter, the one he sent back in nineteen forty-six. Do you remember that letter and its contents?'

Polly failed to find her voice at first. When she did it was barely above a whisper. 'I remember. Josef said they beat him to death because he was black and had stood up to Noble.' She stared at the floor, but saw nothing – except what could have been if people had been different, if Aaron hadn't been coloured.

Charlotte shook her head. 'That was only part of it. The truth was that they beat him to death because he was better than they were. Josef said Aaron was intelligent. He spoke German and was gifted in music.'

Polly sniffed, dabbed at her nose with the handkerchief Charlotte handed her then held her head high. 'Played the Joanna lovely, 'e did. I remember a wonderful night in the Llandoger when Aaron played 'As Time Goes By'.

The memory made her smile. Romance had blossomed, not just between them but with everyone there. Touched by the music, they had all became Bogart and Bergman and the smoke-filled pub had become a North African bar as the theme from *Casablanca* had filled the air.

Charlotte's voice broke into her thoughts. 'Do you want to help me get this man deported and tried for what he did?'

Polly's eyes blazed. 'I want to kill him!'

'You can't do that and I can't guarantee the United States justice system will do that. What I can guarantee is that if we can prove he really is Mickey Noble then he's got at least a life sentence ahead of him.'

'Hanging would be too good.'

'Fingerprints would be enough, but if you could find any paperwork relating to his passport, including a birth certificate, it would all help. He obviously got a false birth certificate, then applied for a passport and National Insurance, against that.'

'What do you want me to do?'

Charlotte sighed with relief. She knew how volatile Polly could be on occasion. This was obviously not one of those moments. 'You have to be careful.'

'I will be.'

'You mustn't arouse his suspicions.'

Polly didn't answer. She was pursing her bright red lips and looking up at the ceiling. 'We might have to wait a bit.'

'We do?'

'He's away at present. On business, he reckons. And then there's a lot of other things going on and there'll be lots of people about. And then he's having a cocktail party next week.' She looked suddenly wistful. 'I ain't never been to one of them, so if you don't mind, we'll let it bide till the week after. In the meantime I'll let things go on as normal. Don't want to raise his suspicions, do I?'

'No,' said a bemused Charlotte. 'You certainly do not.'

'P'raps I could wangle you an invite to this party,' said Polly, casually studying her pink painted nails.

Charlotte shook her head adamantly. 'Oh no. Besides, Susan's coming home. Edna's having a little party. Are you around?'

Polly screwed up her eyes and chewed her lips as if she were considering it. 'No,' she said at last. 'I think I'll be otherwise engaged.'

Susan was coming home!

Edna whizzed around the house like a banshee, duster in one hand and tin of polish in the other. She had Ivan there to empty the guttering above the front door and to paint Susan's bedroom. She'd chosen yellow.

'Something bright,' she exclaimed. 'This has to be the best party ever, seeing as she's missed Christmas.'

Colin was busy with a full order book for a new line of aeroplanes and boats and instead of his work force putting them together, the necessary components, plus glue and instructions, were supplied in the box for the buyer to assemble. He apologized to Edna. 'I'm sorry about being so busy, but I promise I'll make it up to you when the summer comes. How about us going away for a week in a caravan at Weymouth or somewhere? Can you manage to organize a party by yourself?'

'Janet will help. She can't wait for Susan to come home either,' said Edna.

Colin wondered if there was an underlying barb in what she said, that she was accusing him of not caring enough about his daughter coming home, but he was too busy to dwell on it.

*

On the day of Susan's homecoming, Edna dashed out to the front gate clasping her unbuttoned cardigan tightly across her chest. The ambulance bringing Susan would probably enter from the end where Kingscott Avenue joined the main road. There was no sign of it. Just in case it took an alternative route, she checked the other end too. The mobile shop, a converted baker's van that stocked nothing much more enterprising than Oxo cubes and corned beef, was the only vehicle in sight at that end of the street.

She went out twice more before a vehicle she recognized *did* enter the street. Charlotte pulled into the kerb and waved. Ivan was in the passenger seat and there were packages in the back.

'Hello, darlings!' she cried.

Colin waved from the door. Peter stood at his side and Pamela was in his arms.

'Besides bringing Ivan, I've brought these,' Charlotte said, handing Edna the packages, which were brightly wrapped in pink and pistachio green. 'Chocolate Easter eggs from London. Janet arranged for Dorothea to collect them while on her honeymoon. Isn't that incredible? Sometimes I think it's quite wonderful to have a brand new daughter-in-law.'

Edna did not question what it was like the rest of the time. She didn't know Dorothea very well, but wasn't entirely sure she was quite the right girl for Geoffrey.

'I also brought this,' said Charlotte exuberantly. 'Ivan? If you could just get on the other end . . .'

Ivan exchanged a bemused look with Colin, but did as he was told. Between him and Charlotte, a brightly painted banner unfurled saying 'Welcome Home, Susan'.

'We could tie one end onto that tree,' said Charlotte indicating a particularly spindly rowan that looked lucky to have survived the winter, 'and the end of the canopy above the porch. What do you think?'

She hadn't really wanted an answer from Edna, that much

was obvious in the way she dragged the banner forward, Ivan trailing behind it.

'You can't,' Edna blurted.

Charlotte looked at her. 'Why ever not?'

Edna nodded in the direction of two women, watching from either side of a garden gate two houses along the road. One or two other neighbours eyed what was going on from their gardens while forking the earth around spears of tulip, daffodil and narcissus.

'There's a few more watching from the bedroom windows,' Edna added, lowering her eyes.

Charlotte looked taken aback, but certainly not put off the task in hand. 'Perhaps they want to welcome her home too,' she suggested.

Edna shook her head. 'Oh no, they don't. Peter came in crying last night. They've told their children not to play with him just in case they get something.'

'That's nonsense!' Charlotte said loudly. 'I should know. I'm a doctor's wife!' The watching women fidgeted. 'I'll have a word with them later,' she added. She noted how quiet Edna was, how nervous she looked. Best, she decided, to be as jolly as possible.

Ivan refolded the banner and placed it at the side of the two steps that led up to the front door.

'Is your father here?' Charlotte asked.

'Yes. Is Janet coming?'

'She will be.' Charlotte slipped her arm into Edna's. 'Let's go inside. Ivan will take care of things out here.'

She threw him a certain look, a Charlotte look that said almost as much as words. Ivan grinned to himself once they'd all gone inside. Goodness, but she was a strong woman, more forceful by far than any of these housewifely types that were eyeing both him and the house with distrust.

The house was overheated and Charlotte was forced to shrug off her coat. Nuts of burning coke glowed dull red in the fire grate. Edna's father dozed in a chair at the side of the fire, his head to one side, mouth wide open, his empty teacup sliding slowly from his lap towards his knees. Colin grabbed it. The action was swift and soft, but enough to wake the old man up.

He blinked and straightened up. 'Is she here?'

'Not yet,' said Colin, raising his voice slightly so he could hear better. 'I'll make some more tea. Do you want another cup?'

Edna's father said he did.

Edna was looking out of the front window towards the road, her face white with tension. 'There's another car,' she said and headed for the door.

She did not recognize the man behind the wheel of the big black car as it eased into the kerb, but she did recognize his passenger.

Smile as wide as the Severn, Polly stepped out of the car, her many petticoats swishing and crackling against her nylon stockings as she placed one high-heeled court shoe onto the pavement.

'I brought you this,' she said to Edna as she kissed her cheek and handed her a carrier bag. 'Easter eggs,' she said proudly and threw a swift glance over her shoulder. 'Mickey got them for me.'

'Thank you.' Edna found it hard to say anything else. She'd wanted Susan to be in the car, which was silly really. Susan would be coming home by ambulance. And Polly looked so . . . like Marilyn Monroe, she thought; the hair bleached almost blizzard white; the glossy red lips, the low-cut bodice of her dress, the nipped-in waist, the height of her heels. How could anyone walk in shoes like that?

'Are you and your friend . . .' Edna dipped her head in order to see the driver better, meaning to invite both of them in, but Polly interrupted.

'We have to go.' She nodded and waved at Ivan, who appeared to be doing something along by the hedge.

'Haven't you got an inside privy?' Polly asked, presuming that Ivan was answering the call of nature.

Edna frowned. 'What?'

Polly shook her shiny head and got into the car. 'No matter. Have a nice party. Give Susan my love.'

'Aren't you staying?'

'No.' Polly looked away, her expression as sharp as her reply. 'We have to go.'

There was no time to ask about Carol and why she wasn't here for the party. Polly, the car and her secret male escort were gone.

Edna barely acknowledged Ivan as she went back inside, the string handle of the carrier bag cutting into her fingers.

'More Easter eggs,' she said to Colin as she slammed the bag down on the table. 'But she isn't stopping and she hasn't brought Carol. Yet another one too frightened to come near us.'

'Oh no!' said Charlotte. 'You've got it all wrong.'

She went on to explain what was going on and that it had nothing to do with catching anything – except a criminal. Explaining Polly's relationship with O'Hara was the difficult part and impossible to gloss over. 'I didn't like to tell you.' She glanced guiltily at Colin then looked away. 'Especially seeing as Billy's a friend of yours.'

'The little . . .' Colin began, but suddenly changed tack. 'What am I saying? Billy and Polly are two of a kind. She's no angel, but then neither is he.'

Edna lost interest in the conversation. The fact that Polly might be having an affair was of far less importance than her daughter's welfare. Again she went outside, down the garden path, her cardigan wrapped around her as a shower of rain sprinkled her shoulders before a gusty breeze blew it away. Pavements sparkled under sudden sunlight and trickling water tinkled like fairy bells along gutters and down drainpipes.

Edna shaded her eyes against the brightness. Again she

looked towards the most likely end of the street, then again in the other direction. The avenue seemed so empty. Even the mobile shop had gone.

Disappointed, she turned towards the house. Halfway up the garden path, a voice called, 'Here it comes. Here it comes!'

She turned and was vaguely aware that Ivan was getting out of Charlotte's car. She'd completely forgotten him. He'd obviously taken shelter from the rain.

'Here it is,' he said, smiling and pointing towards the junction of Kingscott Avenue and the main road.

Edna raced back to the gate, the metal cold but unnoticed beneath her clenched hands. Neighbours watched too.

Silvery metallic and gleaming in a sudden splash of sunlight, the ambulance stopped. Edna's father, Colin, Peter, and Charlotte with Pamela in her arms all came tumbling out of the front door.

The doors of the ambulance were opened, and Colin's arm slid around Edna's shoulders. She hardly noticed him. Her heart was drumming in her ears. Susan was home and nothing else mattered.

'Surprise!'

The first person down from the ambulance was Janet. She was wearing a straw hat decorated with artificial fruit and a circlet of small, yellow chickens painted on cardboard.

The ambulance men grinned as co-conspirators. Bursts of giggles came from within the ambulance. Susan was in a wheelchair.

Charlotte's voice rang out and even captured the neighbour's attention. 'Three cheers for Susan!'

'Hip, hip, hooray!'

For the first time in many, many months, Edna's face burst into a mask of joy instead of desperation.

'Well, you're a sight to behold,' said Colin.

Peter was standing open-mouthed. 'Can I have one like that?'

He meant the wheelchair. Besides the fact that Susan's cheeks were coloured a vivid cochineal, she also was wearing an Easter bonnet and a large spotted bow around her neck. Brightly coloured crêpe paper covered the frame of the wheelchair. Mirrors were fixed on each chair arm. Two more were fixed at head height onto the back of the seat. Balloons, no doubt filled with helium from the hospital supply, were tied all over it. On top of that a piece of wood was fastened across the front and, at its centre, was a steering wheel. Edna recognized it as being one of those used on the toy pedal cars Colin made at the factory.

Colin planted a big kiss on Susan's cheek. 'Glad to have you home, love.'

Edna hugged her, but was suddenly aware that Susan was leaning to one side and peering over her shoulder.

'Mummy! You've made a banner just like people put up for the Queen when she got crowned.'

Edna looked over her shoulder and eyed the banner that she'd told Charlotte not to put up. So that was why Ivan was loitering out here! There it was, fastened along the outside of the hedge that faced the road. No matter how many times she'd run out to the front gate, she could not possibly have seen it.

'Forgive me,' said Ivan, but Edna just gazed happily into her daughter's face, and then less happily at the various neighbours who were looking back at her.

They were back in the house before the rain started. More tea was made, cake handed out, and the Easter eggs admired.

Janet had presumed that Edna would put the eggs back for Easter Sunday. She actually put only two of them back, but broke a quarter off the other one, which she handed to Susan.

'And me,' whined Peter holding out his hand.

'No,' said Edna, slapping it away. 'You'll have yours on Sunday. Susan's been ill. She deserves a little treat.'

'That's not fair,' said Colin. 'This is a celebration for everyone.'

Janet sensed the tension between them, took out a chocolate egg from the carrier bag Polly had left and broke it into pieces. 'I'm sure Polly won't mind them having some now,' she said.

Janet half-expected Edna to protest, but she didn't. It wasn't, she decided, that Edna was purposely being cruel to Peter and Pamela. Susan was home and, for now, was the centre of attention. Things would settle down in time.

'I'm going to wash my hands,' said Janet. Pamela had been particularly messy with the chocolate.

Edna's next comment took her by surprise. 'There's no need to. You won't catch anything.'

'I didn't think I would.'

'I keep everything a lot cleaner than I used to. No one will get polio in this house ever again.'

Colin interrupted. 'Now look here, love . . .'

Edna appeared not to notice him. 'Germs are everywhere. We have to be vigilant. I don't think I was vigilant enough.'

Janet almost shivered as the feeling of guilt returned, but forced herself to rise above it. 'Before he died, my father said that polio could be picked up anywhere – including swimming pools.'

'Swimming *baths*,' said Edna.

Susan pressed a piece of chocolate into Janet's hand. 'That's for taking me to Clevedon,' she said, a happy smile on her firm, round features.

Janet looked at her, this child whom she had cosseted as much as she could when no one else could get near her. Susan had just provided the opening for what Janet wanted to say. It came out in a rush. 'Susan fell in the swimming pool on the day we went to Clevedon. Surely I'm more to blame than you are.'

'I know,' said Edna.

'You know?'

Edna smiled. 'Of course. But the pool at Clevedon is a

swimming *pool* full of seawater that goes in and out with the tide. It's not a swimming *bath*, is it? It's a pool!'

Edna's logic sounded reasonable, though Janet wasn't sure how it filled and whether a pool was different to a swimming bath really mattered. But you've done your best, she said to herself. It's all you can do.

Susan asked if the banner welcoming her home could be taken down from the garden hedge and hung from her bedroom wall.

Colin kissed the top of her head. 'I don't think so, my sweet. Lovely as it is I think a picture of Andy Pandy or Muffin the Mule would be more like it, eh?'

Edna pushed between Colin and Susan, and wound her arm around Susan's neck. 'Of course you can, darling. Anything you want you can have. And you're too old for Andy Pandy, aren't you?'

Colin looked put out.

Edna didn't seem to notice. 'Can you get it down for her, Ivan, and put it up in her room? I'd much appreciate it.'

Ivan went out to get it down. Janet followed him out. 'It was a brilliant idea,' she said to him.

'I like making little girls happy,' he said jovially. He flashed her a smile. 'Big girls too.'

She wasn't one for blushing, but her tongue could be pretty sharp if she wanted. However, there was no chance for a tart response.

'Is that child home for good?' asked one of the few neighbours still leaning on a garden gate.

The woman had pork chop cheeks and a small, red mouth. Her hair sat in pinched waves packed tightly against her head.

Janet got to her feet and looked down into the woman's face. 'Of course she is.' If she sounded superior, it couldn't be helped.

The woman clasped her hands before her as if making an

instant decision – probably about standing her ground. 'How do we know it isn't catching?'

'Because the medical profession know better than you do.'

'Oh. And how do you know that?'

For a moment, Janet had a most terrible urge to smack the woman's plump cheeks. Lest she lose control, she folded her arms across her chest and tucked her hands beneath her armpits.

'I can categorically tell you that you have more chance of catching polio from me than you have from that child. I work at Saltmead Sanatorium. I am in contact with much worse cases than her all week. I have not suffered so much as a cold. So far as I am aware, I have not passed this dreadful disease onto anyone I have come into contact with, though of course,' she said, leaning closer to the woman so that her chin was not too far from her nose, 'there is always a first time.'

The woman looked startled.

When it was time to go, she hugged Susan, who was still sitting in her wheelchair, her parents close by, her siblings sat like courtiers at her feet.

'Next time I come I'll expect to see you up and about in your calliper,' Janet said to her.

Susan's smile melted. 'I don't like wearing it. It hurts.'

Janet pinched her cheek. 'It might rub a little, young lady, but if you want to walk again you have to grit your teeth and bear it.'

'Now, now! That's enough. Never you mind, Susan my sweet. You don't have to wear that horrible thing unless you really want to.' Edna draped herself between her daughter and Janet.

Charlotte opened her mouth to say something, but Janet got there first. 'She has to get used to it, Edna. It's for her own good.'

Edna's look said it all. No one was going to tell her daughter what to do. She'd gone through enough. There was a lot of spoiling to be done and Edna was the one about to do it.

'My child will not be forced into doing anything. I won't allow it.'

Janet remained forthright. 'You have to. It's for her own good. She can't be dependent on you for ever.'

'I can see trouble coming,' said Charlotte as they drove back to Clifton. Ivan was sitting beside her.

Janet was in the back seat staring out of the window. Like her mother, she was worried. She shook her head helplessly.

'What can we do? Susan's her child, not ours.'

Edna was up early the next morning. Her first stop was the bathroom where she poured oodles of disinfectant into the bath and the toilet. Hands were washed in water laced with a liberal lashing of Dettol. Nothing would ever infect her children again.

Susan's bed was in the front room downstairs. Edna went down the stairs and gently pushed open the door. Susan was lying on her side, one arm behind her, one in front with fist closed. Her legs were bent, the left more so than the right, like an athlete taking off for the long jump. Only Susan could not possibly jump like that. Her right leg was floppy and lacked muscular form.

Edna couldn't resist tickling her daughter's cheek. She wanted her to open her eyes, just in case . . . in case of what? In case she was dead. It was a fear she'd experienced a hundred times. God might take Susan away because she hadn't paid enough attention to her own mother and she'd given Sherman away without a fight.

Thinking of Sherman, or Carlos as he was now, reminded her of what he had said about his grandmother dying and not being able to join her until she had gone. She still had to tell Colin about him needing a home. I'll get round to it, she told herself, but first I have to make sure Susan is OK.

Susan rubbed at her eyes before opening them.

Edna smiled brightly. 'Hello, darling. Let's get you dressed.'

She brought in a bowl of hot water, a face flannel and a towel. Susan chattered like a magpie.

'I'm not ever going away again. I don't like hospitals. There's no one to talk to. Only Janet. And I didn't see her every day.'

Edna became absorbed in everything Susan said. In between interruptions from Peter asking where his clean shirt was, and Colin asking whether she was going to get Pamela from her bed, and was she going to give her breakfast, and was she going to take Peter to school, and did she know where his clean socks were hiding . . .

Every so often she dashed out to save a situation, but hated to leave Susan.

Uncomplaining, though pushed for time, Colin got the kids their breakfast while Edna fussed over Susan, who was obviously enjoying all the attention. He told himself that it was only temporary, that she'd get over the novelty of having Susan home again and they'd go back to being a family.

As if that wasn't bad enough, Edna's cleaning obsession persisted. The bathroom and kitchen were scrubbed to distraction every day of the week.

A week after Susan's homecoming, she was still the same. Colin was losing patience.

'What about these kids?'

'I'm busy. Susan needs a bath. Hot water's good for her.' She dashed out of the room and up the stairs before he could say anything.

Colin sighed at the sound of running water. Yet another dash of Dettol was being consigned to the drain, no doubt.

It wasn't easy getting Susan up the stairs because one leg was useless and the other was a little weak after being in bed so long. But at least she could make it by hanging onto the banister and dragging herself up stair by stair. He agreed that it was a wonderful achievement. He only wished Edna would stop pampering the child at the expense of her other children.

'Another week,' he muttered to himself. 'I'll give her another week to sort herself out, then that's it!'

Tie half-fastened and braces undone, Colin strapped Pamela into her high chair and placed a bowl of porridge in front of her, liberally laced with treacle, which he stirred in before giving her the spoon.

'Toast is burning!' Peter reached for the grill.

Colin got there first. 'Mind you don't burn yourself.'

Peter sat sullen with his arms folded. 'It's burnt!'

Colin picked up a knife and began to scrape. 'Not for long.'

'Yuck! I hate burnt toast.'

Colin put a plate in front of him.

Peter was unimpressed. 'It isn't burnt. It's scraped.'

'Like it or lump it!'

In between seeing to the kids Colin swigged tea and grimaced when he did. He hated cold drinks, cold meals, anything that should properly be served hot.

Just when he thought he had enough time to make a decent brew, Peter piped up, 'Daddy. I think Pammy wants more porridge.'

'No she doesn't. She's just had—oh no!'

The dish had been upended. Sticky globules dripped down the side of the high chair and onto the floor. Colin closed his eyes, tried counting to ten, but then took it to fifteen. The sound of letters through the letterbox came from the hall just as he was reaching for the dishcloth.

Peter slid out of his chair. 'You stay there and clean up, Daddy. I'll get the post.'

For the first time in a long while, Peter did a graceful canter out to the letterbox, collected the post, cantered back again, and handed it to Colin.

Colin flicked through the mix of brown and white envel-

Twenty-seven

Edna was dashing around the house, attempting to divide her time between Susan and the kitchen where bangers and mash and rice pudding were cooking nicely.

'Dinner's nearly ready,' she said to Colin as he entered the front door. She was on her way to the front room when Colin grabbed her arm.

'I want to talk to you.'

Edna was taken by surprise. Wriggling against his grip, she tried to prise his fingers from around her arm. 'I have to see Susan!'

'I want to talk to you.'

'It can wait.'

'No, it can't!'

In a final act of desperation, she slapped his face.

He stared at her as his cheek reddened. 'You've never done that before, old girl.'

Her voice was spiteful. 'You haven't gripped my arm like that before. Now! Let go! My child needs me.'

'She's not the only one!'

'Peter and Pamela are quite capa—'

'Carlos!' he said. 'What about Carlos?'

She stared at him open-mouthed, then dropped her gaze to the letter that he'd taken from his coat pocket and now dangled in front of her face.

'There's more than one child that needs you. Do you think you can possibly drag yourself away from Susan long enough to make sure his path in life is a little easier?'

Edna stopped struggling and stared at him in amazement.

'It won't be easy,' he went on as if reading her thoughts, 'for him as well as for me. But I think we have to try. Your child should be with us.'

Edna could not take her eyes off him as she tried to say something, something that would convey exactly how she felt about her children, and about him. But healing wasn't easy. It would take time to put her feelings into words. At last she managed to say, 'I'll have to write, to arrange things.' She spoke in a broken fashion, as if she were drawing together all the bits and pieces of information that were needed to bring this about.

Colin shook his head. His voice was gentle. 'You've got Susan to contend with and I've got a business to run. God knows I've neglected it lately. Let's hand the matter over to someone who knows about these things.'

Edna's eyes glistened with tears. 'Thank you, Colin.'

He kissed the top of her head, just as he had done so with Susan a week or so ago. 'Thank *you*, Edna. Thank you for being who you are.'

When he got to the factory, Charlotte was there with her car boot wide open. Ivan was loading it up with toys for the sanatorium.

'I want to talk to you,' he called from beneath the white Perspex canopy supported on a wooden frame above the front door.

Dusty and dull as it was, his office seemed like a palace this morning as Colin told Charlotte of how he had inadvertently opened a letter addressed to Edna.

'And in that regard, I want to ask you to arrange things,' he said. 'It may seem a bit daft, but I think it might cure or, at the very least, help Edna get back to her old self. I've read this letter and want you to handle matters.' Charlotte took the letter, noted the postmark and looked at Colin a little warily.

Colin was amused. 'Blimey, Charlotte. We don't often see you lost for words, do we?'

'What does Edna have to say?'

Still smirking as though he were a small boy, had climbed the tree and picked the best conkers, he said, 'She keeps looking at me as though Cary Grant's just walked in the door and no one told her he was coming.'

Charlotte had known Colin for a long while and had always admired his big-heartedness and his down-to-earth sensibility. Her curiosity was aroused. 'Why are you doing this?'

Folding his hands in front of him, he carefully outlined his reasons. At last he said, 'Susan has become more than the apple of her eye. It's not going to do any good in the long run. Somehow I had to divide or, perhaps, expand Edna's loyalty and love. Sherman – or Carlos as he is now – should do the trick. One child will compensate for the other.' He grinned thoughtfully. 'I'm kind of glad that we let all them Poles into this country. Some of them are real good apples.'

'It all sounds very logical,' said Charlotte, at a loss to say anything else, though logic didn't really figure in his decision. This was about love, and Colin was full of it.

'I'll leave you to arrange the time and the place,' he added. 'I know you've got other things to do.'

'Indeed I have,' said Charlotte ruefully. 'Some of which are connected to very bad apples.'

In a moment of extreme need Polly had given into Mickey O'Hara's sexual advances. Now she baulked at the very thought of it, yet she must not show that his presence now sickened her. All she wanted now was revenge.

Charlotte had told her that fingerprints would be useful, but that it would go some way to assuaging her guilt if she could get into the circular cocktail cabinet that held his personal papers. In the meantime she'd pretend that nothing had changed.

Tonight Ginger was driving and they'd called for her at home.

'If I'm not back by dawn, call Charlotte,' Polly had whispered in Aunty Meg's ear before leaving.

'Can we go to the house?' she asked Mickey.

'Sure.' He grinned. 'I'll give you a guided tour.' He was aware how much she liked the house he lived in, but she fancied his comment had a double meaning.

At present Mickey sat in the back with her using a clipper on his nails. Both the sound of the clipper and the shavings landing on her black pleated skirt disgusted her, but she held her tongue – just in case she bit it off! Tonight was too important to mess up and she did her best not to appear nervous.

As he put the clipper away, he looked at her thoughtfully. 'Are you feeling all right?'

She forced herself to bubble. 'Yeah! Why shouldn't I be?'

'You just seem a bit quiet this evening. I thought someone might have said something to upset you.'

She sensed he was studying her closely, but did not look at him, preferring to stare as if entranced by the cluttered shops that ran the length of Gloucester Road. Most had already closed for the evening though some still closed at midday. Not everyone had changed to all day Saturday opening.

He pulled her closer, the heat of his breath moist upon her neck. Earlier on in their relationship, she had found the smell of the eau de cologne he wore incredibly attractive. In the light of what she now knew it made her feel sick. Charlotte had told her a terrible truth that had opened a door in her mind. *Now* she remembered him. *Now* she recalled the emotions she had felt at that time, Aaron's irresistible charm and the things he had told her about the prisoners, and about the man who had made his life hell.

The creeping of Mickey's hand up her skirt brought her back to reality and she couldn't help almost jumping out of her skin.

'No!' She gripped his hand just as it got to the top of her

stockings. The thought of it going any further made her flesh creep.

He clenched his jaw and she half-expected him to hit her. Mickey O'Hara didn't like rejection and she was treading on thin ice. Deep down she now knew that if something was not freely given he'd take it anyway. There would be no tenderness, no exchange of words meant to soften and excite.

Mickey's voice, all tenderness extracted, brought her back to the present. 'You don't regret what happened the other night, do you, Polly? It would upset me no end if you did.' He was being sarcastic and she heard Ginger snigger. But she mustn't upset him.

She managed to smile, but it felt tight and alien across her mouth. 'Of course not.' Her gaze shifted to Ginger, who had adjusted the rear-view mirror. She could see his grin and the mockery in his eyes.

'Not with him looking.'

'You don't want him looking?' Now it was Mickey who was mocking her. 'I can't say I mind meself, but then, we've all got our own personal tastes, isn't that right, Polly? Some women prefer fair men, some women prefer dark men, some women prefer them the darker the better. Is that not so?'

Polly managed to maintain her smile under the intensity of his stare. The statement was delivered with menace. It seemed Mickey was referring to her relationship with Aaron. Yet she couldn't let him know that she understood, that she remembered him from the time she'd gone to see Aaron at the camp. Mickey Noble – now called O'Hara – had been the sergeant who had told her he'd been shipped home. He was dangerous, deadly.

He pulled her tightly to him. 'And tonight, honey, you've got me.'

'Please don't.' She struggled to untangle herself from him, annoyed that Ginger was chuckling to himself in the front seat.

'Please,' she said again and purposely ran her hand down

his chest, down further to the warmth of his loins. There was a hardening beneath her hand. Suddenly it was easier to smile because that meant she still had some control. Well, that was a turn up for the books! Polly Hills still had the power to arouse and, perhaps, just for a while she would make him forget to be too vigilant and could find something to destroy him.

Aunty Meg was at her friend Bridget's and both were bent over a copy of the local sporting paper, checking their football pools.

Bridget had made herself comfortable. Her teeth sat in a saucer next to another saucer in which she'd poured her tea. Corsets the colour of tinned salmon had been discarded and tossed onto the sideboard. Due to this noticeable lack of support, her stockings nestled around her ankles like circular sausages.

Overcome by the knowledge that, yet again, she'd only thrown good money after bad, Meg sighed and sat back on the decrepit dining chair that must once have belonged to Bridget's grandmother, if the state of the springs and the picture of the large fat lady over the mantelpiece were anything to go by. The chair had been worn down with weight a long time ago.

'I'd have bought a house if I'd won,' said Meg. 'And a van for our Billy, a pony for our Carol, and a bedroom suite for our Polly. What would you buy?'

Bridget looked round her as though assessing what she did have and wondering whether it was worth replacing at all. 'Nothing.'

'Not a new house?'

'What's wrong with this one?'

'It belongs to the council. Wouldn't you like one of yer own?'

Bridget thought about it for a minute, her diverse eyes seeming to focus on two different aspects of the room at the same time. Did she think different thoughts at the same time too, Meg wondered?

'No,' said Bridget at last. 'I'd pay off the rent arrears, then, just for the hell of it, let it all mount up again.'

Bewildered, Meg blinked at her and waited for an explanation.

Bridget grinned. 'Got to 'ave me fun. Every time the rent man knocks on that door . . .'

As if on cue the front door knocker was banged and banged again.

'Blimey, Bridget. Someone's trying to knock yer door in!'

Bridget went back to studying the football pools. 'Let 'em knock.'

Whoever was outside had no intention of waiting. A loud grating sound followed as if someone was lifting the letter-box.

'Aunty Meg!'

Meg lurched to her feet. 'It's our Carol.'

Bridget went to the door and Carol came tumbling into the room. 'He's home!' she shouted excitedly.

Meg's mouth dropped open. She didn't need any explanation about who it was and her face lit up with glee even before she clapped eyes on him.

'Meg! Me old China!' Billy rushed from behind Carol and threw his arms around her ample proportions.

Meg was speechless and blushing like a filly. 'You're home!'

'You're right there!'

'But no one said . . .'

'It was in the pipeline at a rate of knots once I 'ad that letter from our Carol telling me what's been going on. But I wanted to be sure. I figured there were some people outside of prison in need of a surprise so they've gone in the frame and I've flown the coop.'

Meg gulped. The Irishman in the slinky car had picked Polly up earlier that evening. For some reason Polly had insisted that Meg see her off, and although she'd been loath to be party to what she regarded as a betrayal of Billy's trust, she'd felt obliged to do so. But she told Billy that Polly had seemed nervous, had stated that if she wasn't home by the following morning that she was to tell Charlotte and she would know what to do.

'Do you know what her and Charlotte are up to? I reckon it's got something to do with that bloke who sent his apes round 'ere . . . I think they've got it in mind to sort 'im out.'

Billy threw his head back and groaned.

Meg was frightened. 'Will she be all right?'

Billy headed for the door. Meg grabbed his arm. 'Well?' she said, desperate for his answer. 'Will she?'

His grin was tight and there was an earnest look in his eyes. 'Depends on how quick I can get there. Got some pennies for the phone box?'

Meg gave him a handful from the gas money and watched him go, afraid for him and afraid for Polly.

Billy ran like a madman to the red phone box on the corner of Newquay Road, the pennies jingling in his pocket. He phoned Charlotte.

Once she'd got over her surprise that he was out of prison, Charlotte outlined what Polly was up to. In response Billy said, 'I've shopped them, Charlotte. The coppers'll be up there any minute. You have to help me. I have to be there. If O'Hara finds out it was me and the police don't get there in time, then he'll take it out on Poll.'

Charlotte's response was immediate. 'I'll be right there.'

Janet chose that moment to arrive back from Edna's where she'd been outlining the details regarding Carlos. Just as she was about to remove her coat, Charlotte came rushing down the stairs looking as though the hounds of hell were snapping at her heels. 'Is there a war?'

Her mother headed for the door as she answered. 'You could say that.'

Janet held her arm. 'Tell me!'

Grabbing her car keys and handbag, Charlotte explained things as quickly as she could.

'You can't go alone.'

Disturbed by the noise, Ivan appeared from the garden where he'd taken to growing plants in the greenhouse and spending a lot of time out there. He looked questioningly at both women. 'What has happened?'

Janet explained quickly, then added, 'She's off to fight a war – single-handed.'

'Don't try and persuade me not to go,' snapped Charlotte.

Ivan began stripping off David's old gardening gloves. 'I won't. We're going with you!'

Janet snatched Charlotte's car keys. 'I'm driving!'

Janet drove like a maniac. The tyres squealed all the way to Camborne Road where Billy was waiting by the phone box and piled into the back of the car as quickly as he could. Carol tried to get in as well, complete with her hockey stick.

Billy pushed her back and slammed the car door. 'You're too young. You stay here with Aunty Meg.'

Carol swore and flung the hockey stick into the privet hedge.

The tyres continued to squeal around every bend between Camborne Road and Melvin Square.

'Just pray we get there in time,' said Janet.

'Preferably alive,' said Ivan as Janet sped across Melvin Square and took a left into Clonmel Road.

Polly was nervous. She'd expected Mickey to fix drinks from the cabinet in the sitting room then perhaps use the bathroom while she sat innocently sipping at her drink. It wouldn't have given her much time to investigate the cabinet, but perhaps just enough.

Unfortunately, he did not do that.

'Up here,' he said as he pulled her towards the stairs that swept upwards in wrought iron splendour from the open-plan sitting room, and she knew he wasn't going to take her on a guided tour. In that instant, her courage failed her.

'Just a minute. My shoes are killing me.'

She ran back down the stairs meaning to head for the door and get the hell out of there. But Ginger was between her and the door, smirking above his velvet-collared Teddy Boy coat.

As if it had been her original intention, she slipped off her shoes and flung her handbag onto the white leather settee.

By the time she got back up the stairs, Mickey had an impatient scowl on his face.

'You won't be needing anything,' he said, grinning wickedly as his fingers pulled at the buttons of her jacket. 'Nothing at all.'

Polly was frightened. Thoughts of passion were squashed dead. She had to get out of this, wait for the opportunity, but until then, she had to play a part.

She covered his hands with her own and smiled as coquettishly as she knew how. 'Now come on, darlin'. Ain't the best things worth waiting for?'

His scowl deepened. 'No!'

Polly knew when not to protest and when she was in danger. She went along with it, smiling as though she was really looking forward to him stripping her naked and thrusting his equally naked body against hers.

He pulled her jacket and blouse away from her shoulders, down to her elbows so that her arms were pinioned at her sides. 'I'm going to have you here.'

'On the stairs?'

'Why not?'

His mouth bit into the soft flesh between her shoulder and her neck and it hurt. Polly bit her lip and closed her eyes. This was not what she wanted and certainly not what she'd expected. How the hell could she get out of it?

He pushed her back onto the stairs, fell on top of her and used the vilest language possible to describe what he intended doing to her. Polly squeezed her eyes shut and wished and hoped for another guardian angel like the one who'd come crashing into Griffiths's place armed only with a hockey stick and the bus fare home.

Mickey's hands were under her skirt, tearing at her underwear, pushing her legs apart.

'It hurts,' she shouted referring to the stair riser that was digging into her back.

'Not so much as . . .'

Everything stopped as a heavy banging echoed through the house. Someone sounded determined to get in.

Ginger's self-satisfied smirk had been replaced with confusion. He looked up at Mickey for guidance.

'Answer it.'

Mickey's weight pinned her down. Like him she watched Ginger make his way to the front door and prayed that the police were on the other side of it.

Ginger sounded surprised. 'What the hell do you want?'

'My wife!'

Billy came charging towards the staircase, his thin face creased with anger and his fists clenched as big as he could get them.

Polly struggled. Mickey laughed and pressed her tighter against the stairs.

'Let him see you. Let him see what a tart you are!'

Polly screamed as Ginger landed a blow on Billy that sent him flat onto his back. Billy might be streetwise, but he was certainly no fighter and she could tell from Ginger's grin that he knew it too.

The grin was wiped off his face as thick arms pulled his behind his back, spun him round and with one powerful punch sent him flying across the room, crashing into the circular drinks cabinet which toppled and fell forward spilling glass, drinks and paperwork all over him.

'Ivan!'

Mickey glared, then raised a fist. 'Stupid broad! I should have known better!'

The Irish accent had disappeared. In that split instant before the fist fell on her she saw the man he truly was, the US sergeant who had treated her with callous contempt because she'd been involved with a coloured GI.

Ivan did not get there in time to stop the first blow, but he did stop any more from falling. Mickey had spent his war years as a prison guard, or in stores, transport or catering. Never had he braved battlefields, lived in wild places and built up the muscles of a hunted man. Ivan was stronger and more agile than him and held him in a stranglehold until the men in blue arrived to clean things up.

'Is she all right?' Ivan asked Janet when everything was over and Polly was lying side by side with her husband.

'Oh yes.'

'Polly's too tough for the likes of Mickey Noble to damage,' said Charlotte as she applied a cold compress to Polly's jaw.

When Polly was at home recovering, the police came round to say that they'd got all the information they needed to send Mickey Noble back to America to face justice, thanks to Billy. Janet and Ivan arrived just after they'd left. Things were busy at the factory and Ivan had been delegated the task of offering Billy a job.

'He's out at the moment,' said Polly, who was draped over the settee eating chocolate misshapes from a brown paper bag. Magazines trailed from her lap, along the back of the settee and onto the floor. Some of them looked like Christmas issues, most seemed out of date. 'Nice of you to take a day off work to come and see me,' she said to Janet.

'I've left the job at the sanatorium. I don't want to be a secretary any more.'

Polly raised her eyebrows. 'Don't it pay well?'

'Not too bad,' said Janet, 'but I think I've found my vocation in life.'

Polly grinned and looked meaningfully at Ivan. 'Oh yeah?'

Janet and Ivan exchanged looks of mutual understanding.

'Alas,' said Ivan and shrugged sadly, but all the time he smiled.

Janet laughed. 'You're a wonderful man, Ivan Bronowsky.' She took his hand and squeezed it tight. 'But that isn't exactly what I meant.' Her expression turned serious. 'I've decided to look into becoming a doctor. If I can't do that I will do something similar to what my mother's been doing all these years, something more worthwhile than taking down notes and typing out reports. I will be helping Mother for a while. She doesn't show it, but she's not really got over Father's death.'

When Ivan excused himself to use the bathroom, Polly leaned closer to Janet and softly asked, 'Billy didn't see me and Mickey – you know – doing anything, did he?' All the cockiness was gone. She looked really concerned.

'Billy was out cold and my mother explained that she'd asked you to gain his confidence and get evidence against him. So in fact you're something of a heroine.'

Polly looked embarrassed. 'More like a bloody fool.'

Janet sighed. 'We've all been that in our time.' It occurred to her then just how much she had in common with her mother's generation. 'I wonder why we fear to be less than perfect?'

Polly slapped her on the shoulder. 'Cos it's the truth. We're all human!'

It was easy to grin, to be pleased that Polly was again the buxom blonde with a winning smile, a playful look in her eyes and a tart remark on her lips.

Blustering into the house like a whirlwind, Carol kicked the carpet aside and scattered piles of newspapers from off the arm of the chair. She was waving a piece of paper in her hand. 'Sean's sent me a love letter,' she shouted, then flung her arms around her mother's neck so that the piece of paper, which looked like the rough stuff the butcher used to wrap sausages, fluttered under her mother's nose.

Polly laughed, a loud raucous sound that only a mature

woman of her particular character could get away with. She patted Carol's hand. 'You'll get plenty more of them in yer time, my girl.' She glanced at the paper and wrinkled her nose. 'It smells of fish.'

Ah, thought Janet wryly. I was wrong. It wasn't the butcher.

'I'm going to write him one back,' said Carol, her head cocked to one side, a cheeky look that she'd inherited from her mother. 'I'm good at writing letters.'

'So I hear,' said Polly wryly, turned to Janet and said, 'Do you know what she wrote to Billy?'

'Only if you want to tell me.'

Polly dug her elbow into Carol's side. 'Go on then. Tell her.'

Carol tossed her blonde plaits and their tired white bows back from her shoulders. 'I said that mum was like a lonely princess and a lot of wicked wizards were out to get her.'

Janet nodded approvingly. 'You have a wonderful imagination.'

Carol went on. 'And then I told him about them men I belted with my hockey stick.'

Janet raised her eyebrows and looked to Polly for an explanation and was almost disappointed that Ivan chose that exact moment to return.

Polly grinned and hugged Carol close. 'She told Billy what I was afraid to tell him.' She explained a little further. 'If he'd known that the heavy mob had been round, he'd have shopped them sooner, but I was annoyed with 'im. We couldn't go to Australia, you see, not with 'is record.' She smiled ruefully. 'Bloody sod! He'd let me down. I thought he deserved to stay there a while.'

When Billy finally came in, Ivan put it to him about the job. Billy began shaking his head, though his eyes were locked with those of his wife.

'It all depends,' he began and shifted nervously from one foot to another.

Sensing that an explanation was in order, everyone looked at everyone else. After pinching a chocolate from the brown paper bag, it was Carol who burst the bubble.

'We're going to Canada!'

Polly beamed from ear to ear. 'It's true. They don't mind a bit of form and Aunty Meg can come too, especially since she had that win on the pools. It ain't much, but enough to keep her over there.' She threw Billy an accusing look. 'And he can take that job with Colin while we're waiting for things to 'appen. It'll keep him out of mischief.'

Thinking of Polly, her lifestyle and her attitude in general made Janet burst out laughing as she dropped the car into first gear to get to the top of Park Street. 'Polly is unbelievable. It's pretty obvious that she has been more than a little naughty whilst Billy was in prison, yet still he's going along with her plans. Did you see the way he looked at her? He can't seem to make a move without her. And he must know that she's less than perfect.'

'Like we all are.'

The quiet implication in Ivan's statement was not lost on her. Earlier she had spoken to Polly along those very same lines. You didn't love people because they were perfect; you loved them despite their imperfections.

Ivan confirmed it. 'He loves her.'

Meg and Bridget were out the back, supposedly taking in washing, but now gossiping over the garden fence. Billy was in the lavatory reading an excerpt from the *Evening Post* that was hung on a string from the cistern – or at least trying to. An official prison visitor, a parson in fact, had helped him with his reading and writing and he'd been practising the skill in private. He wanted to surprise Polly, to show her he could be something better than he was. There was a bit of mending to do between them, but nothing that couldn't be got over. Going to Canada wasn't really to his liking. Neither was working for Colin, but he'd go along with anything for now so they could continue as a family. Their less than perfect relationship, in a less than perfect world, must not fall apart.

The window was open and as he stumbled his way through the words, breaking them down into smaller, more manageable syllables, he could hear Meg speaking quite plainly.

'So there you are, Bridget. They can't go to Australia now, thank God.'

Bridget started to laugh, though cackle might be a better description. 'You're a wicked one. Chucking their post in the bin.'

'I don't care. I couldn't let them go, not without me.'

'Did your Polly suspect anything?'

'Yeah! That them Australian people 'ad forgot to post the stuff to her. She wrote to them about three times, and she never looked in the ashbin. If she had she would have seen 'em there.'

'And now yer goin' to Canada.'

'Yeah!' said Meg and sounded supremely satisfied. 'They don't mind dependants, especially if they've got a little nest egg. That little win on the pools made all the difference. And then Billy's bit of form got squashed – or almost. Anyway, it's not enough for them to worry about. He ain't going to rob a bank, is he?'

He heard a throaty sound, then Bridget said, ' 'Ere you are. A new penny. I've spat on it for luck.'

He winced at the sound of the gummy old woman spitting. If Meg hadn't had the win, he'd have got out of going to Canada just by telling Meg about it and making Polly feel guilty. He'd been worrying about finding a way out of it for ages. Now it looked as though one had been presented to him.

Still sitting on the lavatory, Billy was no longer trying to work out the words on the piece of newspaper. After hearing Meg's confession, his mind was working overtime. If he took the job with Colin he'd be up before everyone else, just after the postman came. The paperwork would come in an envelope marked Canada House and he would be there waiting for it, but he'd have to be able to recognize it.

House was a word he knew. Soundlessly he formed the syllables CAN.A.DA.

Twenty-eight

Charlotte paced the upstairs drawing room. The doors to the veranda were open wide to let in the unique air of the third week in May. Was it Milton who had said something about the third week in May being as close to the Garden of Eden or Paradise as you were likely to get on earth? She shook her head. She couldn't remember.

She walked out onto the veranda, leaned on the ornate ironwork, sighed at the garden and walked back in again.

Janet sat in a chintz easy chair with a magazine she wasn't reading. Her mother's nervous pacing was too distracting. 'Mother, those shoes are going to the cobbler's very shortly.'

Charlotte stopped and looked down at her shoes. 'Surely not. There's nothing wrong with them.'

'There will be if you keep pacing backwards and forwards. You'll wear holes in them and you're making me dizzy.'

Charlotte sighed and looked at her watch. 'I can't help it. It's been such a long time. I don't know how Edna's going to take it. Colin's prepared her, but I don't know how she'll be. I don't know how I'll be.'

Janet watched as her mother's gaze drifted back to the garden. It took on such a panoramic vista when viewed from the first floor. Down on the ground floor the surrounding heights of other terraced crescents seemed to crowd it.

Janet got up from the chair and stood beside her. 'How's Colin taking it?'

'It was entirely his idea, you know. I just think he's a man in a million. Apparently it was something Ivan said to him, after he'd inadvertently opened the letter from Josef.'

'So you said.'

Her mother had told her the same thing a number of times during the past few weeks. She sensed her unease. Had she done the right thing? 'Whatever was said, it must have been pretty awesome.'

'Or heartfelt.'

They fell to silence before Janet said, 'Now listen. You don't have to come in. I can handle everything. I know I can. As long as you're sure that you don't want to see him – Josef I mean. But I do know he means a lot to you.'

Charlotte looked surprised and started to stammer.

Janet reached out and laid her hands upon her mother's arms. 'I saw you with him, Mother. I ran away from school one more time. I ran back again when I saw the two of you . . .' She paused. 'But I don't blame you, not the way things were between you and Daddy.'

Charlotte looked down at her feet, looked away to the left, trying not to blush like a schoolgirl. All she could say was, 'I don't think I should see him. It wouldn't be right – not yet. Not just yet. Your father isn't long gone . . .'

'As you told Geoffrey and Dorothea . . . life must go on.'

Charlotte nodded. 'Do you think you can cope with things by yourself?'

Janet smiled. 'Am I not my mother's daughter?' She looked at her watch and said, 'I think it's time. Are you ready?'

Colin had arranged everything. It was a Saturday and Polly was going to look after the children for the day. She knew what was going on, but would not bring it up unless someone mentioned it to her.

Polly got the children to sit around the table with colouring books and crayons that Billy had got hold of for her. She didn't ask where he'd got them. She made a point of showering Susan with attention. Even so she saw the way the little girl checked to see where her mother was.

'Bloody hospital,' said Polly under her breath. What sort of place was it that separated children from their parents?

'Now, come on. Who wants to do colouring and who wants me to make them some cut-out dolls?'

Peter wanted to colour in a picture of a cowboy on a rearing horse that he'd found. Pamela continued to scribble absent-mindedly, her gaze flitting between bright red scribble and the task Polly and Susan were bent over. Polly had always been good at drawing. A bit of white card, a pencil and some crayons, and a cut-out doll would be on the table.

As she buttoned her coat, Edna nervously approached the table. 'Are you sure you'll be all right?'

Polly was adamant. 'Of course we will. Won't we, Susan?'

Susan nodded. Edna was surprised. She'd assumed that Susan would kick up a fuss at her going out without her and without an explanation. But she couldn't put today's events into words. There was too much emotion involved.

'You smell nice,' Polly said almost as an afterthought.

Edna knew what she meant. Of course she'd put on a touch of Evening in Paris, but that wasn't really what Polly was referring to. The tang of bleach was less noticeable now, even around the house. Today deserved perfume.

Charlotte sat in the driving seat of her car outside Temple Meads Railway Station. Janet had leaned against the driver's door studying her mother's tense expression.

'I need a cigarette,' said Charlotte.

'You don't smoke.'

Charlotte swallowed her nervousness. 'Until now.'

Janet squeezed her arm. 'Don't worry. I can manage.'

Charlotte looked down at her lap and sighed deeply. 'Yes. I know you can.'

Janet glanced up at the station clock as she made her way up the incline to the entrance. Twelve forty-five. The train from London Paddington was due in at one o'clock, though it wasn't likely to be on time. For her mother's sake she hoped it was. Charlotte was not the type usually given to nervousness and neither, for that matter, was Janet. But this was an exceptional occasion for everyone, more specifically for Edna and Colin.

Moderately audible loudspeaker announcements gave out information regarding departures, arrivals and likely platform numbers. Children clutching tin buckets and wooden-handled spades fidgeted as they waited for the seaside excursions to Clevedon, Severn Beach and Weston-super-Mare.

Heat shimmered beyond the station canopy where the rails gleamed gold in the sunlight. The weather promised a warm Whitsun. Out in the car Charlotte felt cold and strangely excited. *Like a woman in love.* But I'm not in love. I wasn't in love. *Was I?* Surely it wasn't wise to go back? No one could. That's why she was sitting here in the car, waiting for Janet to see things through.

Closing her eyes and blowing out a cloud of blue smoke, she cast her mind back and tried to remember what he looked like, what he had said, and what he had felt like, especially the latter.

He'd been kind. She remembered that most of all. He'd been a U-boat commander, a man who had sank much Allied shipping, but had still remained human. No doubt he had his own ghosts and guilt, just like the rest of them. And now? What did he look like? What would he think of her? What could she say to him about her life and everything in it? There was so much to think about, so much they could talk about.

Suddenly, she could stand it no longer. She got out of the car, ran up the incline, and weaved through the crowds to where Janet was standing trying to hear what the station announcer was saying.

Janet turned and saw her. She did not register any surprise. 'You changed your mind?'

'Perhaps.'

An inaudible announcement came over the flaring trumpets of the loudspeaker system that gave Charlotte an excuse to change tack. 'Was that for the London train? What platform did he say?'

'I'll find out.' Janet marched up to a porter who was loading racing pigeons onto a parcel dray that had a heavy metal drag bar at one end. He pointed her in the right direction for the incoming train. Mother followed daughter down the steps to the subway.

'Tea?' asked Janet once they'd reached the right platform. 'And if you feel you don't want to be involved . . .' Her voice trailed off as she waited for her mother to make up her mind.

Charlotte looked to where Janet was pointing. Was it her imagination or was the clock turning back? She wasn't seeing the cafeteria as it was now, crowded with happy families off for a day at the seaside. She was seeing as it had been when she'd first met Edna and Polly in December 1945. Faded Christmas decorations had hung limply between the bluish glare of aged bulbs. She recalled Edna's apprehension. At first she'd thought it was to do with Colin's injuries. Later she had found out about Sherman and Edna's uncertainty as to whether she should tell Colin before marrying him. And Polly, who had set her sights on achieving another world and had simply ended up with another man.

'Mother? I asked if you wanted some tea while we're waiting.'

Charlotte's thoughts returned to the present. 'Yes,' she said, and wished her stomach would stop churning.

Edna wore a navy dress with a very full skirt and a wide, white collar that covered her shoulders.

'You look wonderful,' Colin said.

She could see from his eyes that he meant it, but it did nothing to lessen the knot of nerves that was strangling her from the inside out. It suddenly got the better of her.

'I can't go in! We should go home. Susan might be crying for me.'

Colin shook his head and paid the taxi driver. Neither he nor Edna was in a fit state for driving, besides, he'd guessed she'd try to call the whole thing off and leave the formalities to Charlotte or Janet. But he didn't think that was right. This was her son, her responsibility.

'Susan will be fine. Polly's a born entertainer.'

Edna stopped at the entrance to the station looking as though she were about to be devoured by an open mouthed monster. 'I . . . I . . .'

Colin gently put his arm around her. 'It's for the best, for all of us. We agreed.'

She looked at him wide-eyed as if searching for the strength to go on. 'Colin. I haven't hurt you terribly, have I? I never meant to, it's just that I'm not so brave as you and—'

'This was my decision, Edna.' He looked lovingly into her face, the same face he'd looked at in a photograph that he'd taken halfway round the world in his navy days. And he told himself he was doing the right thing. This was right for him, right for their children, and most certainly right for Edna.

'I don't know what to say to him.'

'You'll know what to say when you see him.'

With a hissing of steam and a screaming of brakes against metal wheels, the train pulled into the station just as Colin and Edna came up the steps and onto the platform.

At the exact moment that they arrived, Janet got up from the table in the cafeteria and looked down at her mother. 'Are you coming?'

Charlotte demurred, her lips moving but not speaking.

'Stay here then,' said Janet and made for the door.

Edna and Colin turned the corner just as Janet came out of the cafeteria.

Noting their nervous expressions, she smiled warmly at them. 'How are you both?'

They muttered minimum greetings. Janet expected nothing else. She was apprehensive enough herself. Goodness knows how they were feeling.

Carriage doors creaked open. Expelled steam squealed onto the platform like a series of strangled sighs.

'I expect they'll be in First Class,' Janet said to Colin.

Edna's eyes scanned the length of the First Class carriages. Her heart beat twenty to the dozen. Her legs turned to jelly. Suddenly, it was all too much. 'I can't do this.'

She'd gone no more than a few yards when Janet grabbed her arm. 'You have to meet him.'

'I can't!'

Janet flinched as Edna's tear-filled brown eyes looked into hers and her voice quivered. 'What would you think if your mother had given you away to strangers?'

Janet paused to collect her thoughts before answering. How often had she condemned her mother? How often had she told herself that her mother didn't care about her, that other people's problems were more important than hers? She now knew the truth and could reply with confidence.

'At first I might not understand, but in time I would appreciate why it was done. And that's all that matters, isn't it? Everything working out all right in the end.'

'A happy ending?'

'Something like that.'

Behind the grimy glass of the cafeteria, Charlotte eyed the two of them – her daughter and her friend. She saw Janet laying her hand on Colin's arm as if sensing his anxiety.

Her decision was sudden. The chair legs squealed as she pushed it behind her.

I have to be there, she decided. I have to be with them.

She pressed a half crown into the waitress's hand and rushed out of the door.

To begin with, she saw only Edna, Colin, Janet. There was no one else – at first. And then there was. Two other figures appeared out of the steam, one adult and one child.

She saw Josef before he saw her, said nothing, but stood immobile and just stared and stared.

Almost as if he sensed she was there, he turned, took off his hat and gazed at her with joy in his eyes. 'Charlotte!'

The years fell away like the pages of a well-thumbed book.

'Josef.' She said it softly, not much more than a whisper.

He came closer and smiled. 'It is good to see you.'

'It is good to see you too.'

There was no time to say much, to reminisce or compliment each other on how well they both looked. There was a job to be done.

Janet's eyes began to water as she watched her mother. The wear and tear of almost fifty years seemed to fall from her face.

Edna and Colin were less interested in her or Josef than they were in the dark-skinned boy standing at Josef's side wearing short trousers, a striped blazer and a navy blue cap.

Each of them waited for the magic words that would set them all free. When they came they were spoken with soft resolution, a slight accent and a hint of wonder.

'Good day, madam. Are you my mother?'

Edna's hand flew to her mouth. Tears threatened, but she held them back. All the same, her eyes were moist. Sherman! She wanted to say Sherman. But he wouldn't know the name she'd given him. It wasn't his any more.

It was hard, very hard, but she swallowed the old name and forced herself to call him by the only name he truly regarded as his own.

'Carlos!'

Her first instinct was to run to his side. Instead she stopped, turned to Colin and took hold of his hand. Stiff-legged, his face beaming and his eyes moist, Colin walked forward with his wife to embrace the child that was hers, but would also become his.